THE
BOOK
OF
LOST
THINGS

Also by John Connolly

The Charlie Parker Stories
Every Dead Thing
Dark Hollow
The Killing Kind
The White Road
The Reflecting Eye (Novella in the Nocturnes Collection)
The Black Angel
The Unquiet
The Reapers
The Lovers
The Whisperers
The Burning Soul
The Wrath of Angels
The Wolf in Winter
A Song of Shadows
A Time of Torment

Other Works
Bad Men
The Book of Lost Things

Short Stories
Nocturnes
Night Music: Nocturnes Volume II

The Samuel Johnson Stories (For Young Adults)
The Gates
Hell's Bells
The Creeps

The Chronicles of the Invaders *(with Jennifer Ridyard)*
Conquest
Empire
Dominion

Non-Fiction (as editor, with Declan Burke)
Books to Die For: The World's Greatest Mystery Writers on the
World's Greatest Mystery Novels

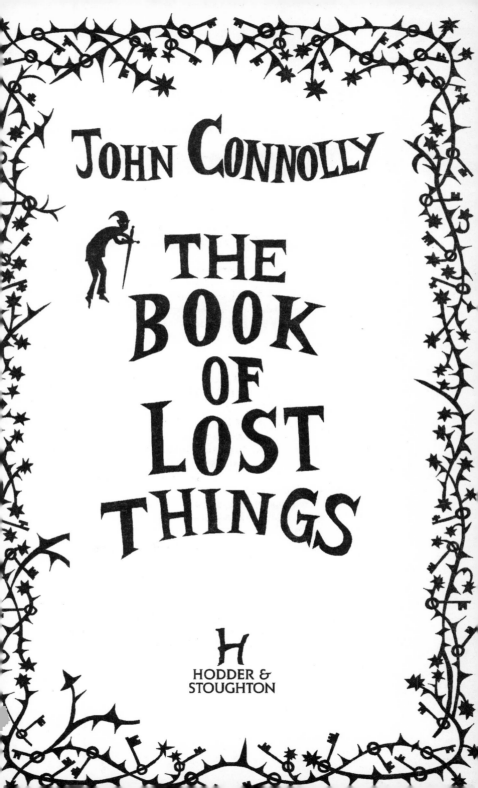

JOHN CONNOLLY

THE BOOK OF LOST THINGS

HODDER &
STOUGHTON

First published in Great Britain in 2006 by Hodder & Stoughton
An Hachette UK company

This tenth anniversary edition published in 2016

1

Illustrations by Anne M. Anderson

A CIP catalogue record for this title is available from the British Library

Hardback ISBN 978 1 47365704 5

Printed and bound by Clays Ltd, St Ives plc

Hodder & Stoughton policy is to use papers that are natural,
renewable and recyclable products and made from wood grown in
sustainable forests. The logging and manufacturing processes are expected to
conform to the environmental regulations of the country of origin.

Hodder & Stoughton Ltd
Carmelite House
50 Victoria Embankment
London EC4Y 0DZ
www.hodder.co.uk

This book is dedicated to an adult, Jennifer Ridyard, and to Cameron and Alistair Ridyard, who will be adults all too soon, for in every adult dwells the child that was, and in every child waits the adult that will be.

Deeper meaning resides in the fairy tales told to me in my childhood than in the truth that is taught by life.

Friedrich Schiller (1759–1805)

Everything you can imagine is real.

Pablo Picasso (1881–1973)

I

Of All That Was Found and All That Was Lost

Once upon a time – for that is how all stories should begin – there was a boy who lost his mother.

He had, in truth, been losing her for a very long time. The disease that was killing her was a creeping, cowardly thing, a sickness eating away at her from the inside, slowly consuming the light within so that her eyes grew a little less bright with each passing day, and her skin a little more pale.

And as she was stolen away from him, piece by piece, the boy became more and more afraid of finally losing her entirely. He wanted her to stay. He had no brothers and no sisters, and while he loved his father it would be true to say that he loved his mother more. He could not bear to think of a life without her.

The boy, whose name was David, did everything that he could to keep his mother alive. He prayed. He tried to be good, so that she would not be punished for his mistakes. He padded around the house as quietly as he was able, and kept his voice down when he was playing war games with his toy soldiers. He created a routine, and he tried to keep to that routine as closely as possible, because he believed in part that his mother's fate was linked to the actions he performed. He would always get out of bed by putting his left foot on the floor first, then his right. He always counted up to twenty when he was brushing his teeth, and he always stopped when the count was completed.

He always touched the taps in the bathroom and the handles of the doors a certain number of times: odd numbers were bad but even numbers were fine, with two, four and eight being particularly favourable, although he didn't care for six because six was twice three and three was the second part of thirteen, and thirteen was very bad indeed.

If he bumped his head against something, he would bump it a second time to keep the numbers even, and sometimes, he would have to do it again and again because his head seemed to bounce against the wall, ruining his count, or his hair glanced against it when he didn't want it to, until his skull ached from the effort and he felt giddy and sick. For an entire year, during the worst of his mother's illness, he carried the same items from his bedroom to the kitchen first thing in the morning, and then back again last thing at night: a small copy of Grimm's selected fairy tales and a dog-eared *Magnet* comic, the book to be placed perfectly in the centre of the comic and both to be laid with their edges lined up against the corner of the rug on his bedroom floor at night or on the seat of his favourite kitchen chair in the morning. In these ways, David made his contribution to his mother's survival.

After school each day, he would sit by her bedside, sometimes talking with her if she was feeling strong enough, but at other times merely watching her sleep, counting every laboured, wheezing breath that emerged, willing her to remain with him. Often he would bring a book with him to read and, if his mother was awake and her head did not hurt too much, she would ask him to read aloud to her. She had books of her own – romances and mysteries and thick, black-garbed novels with tiny letters – but she preferred him to read much older stories to her: myths and legends and fairy tales, stories of castles and quests and dangerous, talking animals. David did not object. Although, at twelve, he was no longer quite a child, he retained an affection for these tales, and the fact that it pleased his mother to hear such stories told by him only added to his love for them.

Before she became ill, David's mother would often tell him that stories were alive. They weren't alive in the way that people were alive, or even dogs or cats. People were alive whether you chose to notice them or not, while dogs tended to make you notice them if they decided that you weren't paying them enough attention. Cats, meanwhile, were very good at pretending people didn't exist at all when it suited them, but that was another matter entirely.

Stories were different, though: they came alive in the telling. Without a human voice to read them aloud, or a pair of wide eyes following them by torchlight beneath a blanket, they had no real existence in our world. They were like seeds in the beak of a bird, waiting to fall to earth, or the notes of a song laid out on a sheet, yearning for an instrument to bring their music into being. They lay dormant, hoping for the chance to emerge. Once someone started to read them, they could begin to change. They could take root in the imagination and transform the reader. Stories *wanted* to be read, David's mother would whisper. They needed it. It was the reason they forced themselves from their world into ours. They wanted us to give them life.

These were the things that his mother told David, before the illness took her. She would have a book in her hand as she spoke, and would run her fingertips lovingly across the cover, just as she would sometimes touch them to David's face when he said or did something that reminded her of how much she cared for him. The sound of his mother's voice was like a song to David, one that was constantly revealing new improvisations or previously unheard subtleties. As he grew older, and music became more important to him (although never quite as important as books) he thought of his mother's voice less as a song and more as a kind of symphony, capable of infinite variations on familiar themes, and melodies that changed according to her moods and whims.

As the years went by, the reading of a book became a more

3

solitary experience for David, until his mother's illness returned them both to his early childhood but with the roles reversed. Nevertheless, before she grew sick he would sometimes step quietly into the room in which his mother was reading, acknowledging her with a smile (always returned) before taking a seat close by and immersing himself in his own book so that, although both were lost in their own individual worlds, they shared the same space and time. And David could tell, by looking at her face as she read, whether or not the story contained in the book was living inside her, and she in it, and he would recall again all that she had told him about stories and tales and the power that they wield over us, and that we in turn wield over them.

David would always remember the day his mother died. He was in school, learning – or not learning – how to scan a poem, his mind filled with dactyls and pentameters, the names like those of strange dinosaurs inhabiting a lost prehistoric landscape. The headmaster opened the classroom door and approached the English master, Mr Benjamin (or Big Ben, as he was known to his pupils, because of his size and his habit of withdrawing his pocket watch from the folds of his waistcoat and announcing, in deep, mournful tones, the slow passage of time to his unruly students). The headmaster whispered something to Mr Benjamin, and Mr Benjamin nodded solemnly. When he turned around to face the class, his eyes found David's, and his voice was softer than usual when he spoke. He called David's name and told him he was excused, and that he should pack his bag and follow the headmaster. David knew then what had happened. He knew before the headmaster brought him to the school nurse's office. He knew before the nurse appeared, a cup of tea in her hand for him to drink. He knew before the headmaster stood over him, still stern in aspect but clearly trying to be gentle with the bereaved boy. He knew before the cup touched his lips and the words were spoken and the tea burned his mouth, reminding him that he was still alive while his mother was now lost to him.

Even the routines, endlessly repeated, had not been enough to keep her safe. He wondered later if he had failed to do one of them properly, if he had somehow miscounted that morning, or if there was an action he could have added to the many that might possibly have changed things. It didn't matter now. She was gone. He should have stayed at home. He had always worried about her when he was in school, because if he was away from her then he had no control over her existence. The routines didn't work in school. They were harder to perform, because the school had its own rules and its own routines. David had tried to use them as a substitute, but they weren't the same. Now his mother had paid the price.

It was only then that David, ashamed at his failure, began to cry.

The days that followed were a blur of neighbours and relatives, of strange, tall men who rubbed his hair and handed him a shilling, and big women in dark dresses who held David against their chests while they wept, and filled his nostrils with the smell of perfume and mothballs. He sat up late into the night, squashed into a corner of the living room while the grown-ups exchanged stories of a mother he had never known, a strange creature with a history entirely separate from his own: a child who would not cry when her older sister died because she refused to believe that someone so precious to her could disappear forever and never come back; a young girl who ran away from home for a day because her father, in a fit of impatience at some minor infraction, told her that he was going to hand her over to the gypsies; a beautiful woman in a bright red dress who was stolen from under the nose of another man by David's father; a vision in white on her wedding day who pricked her thumb on the thorn of a rose and left the spot of blood on her gown for all to see.

And when at last he fell asleep, David dreamed that he was part of these tales, a participant in every stage of his mother's life. He was no longer a child hearing stories of another time. Instead, he was a witness to them all.

David saw his mother for the last time in the undertaker's room before the coffin was closed. She looked different and yet the same. She was more like her old self, the mother who had existed before the illness came. She was wearing make-up, like she did on Sundays for church or when she and David's father were going out to dinner or to the pictures. She was laid out in her favourite blue dress, with her hands clasped across her stomach. A rosary was entwined in her fingers, but her rings had been removed. Her lips were very red. David stood over her and touched his fingers to her hand. She felt cold, and damp.

His father appeared beside him. They were the only ones left in the room. Everyone else had gone outside. A car was waiting to take David and his father to the church. It was big and black. The man who drove it wore a peaked cap and never smiled.

'You can kiss her goodbye, son,' his father said. David looked up at him. His father's eyes were moist, and rimmed with red. His father had cried that first day, when David returned home from school and he held him in his arms and promised him that everything would be all right, but he had not cried again until now. David watched as a big tear welled up and slid slowly, almost embarrassedly, down his father's cheek. He turned back to his mother. He leaned into the casket and kissed her face. She smelled of chemicals and something else, something David didn't want to think about. He could taste it on her lips.

'Goodbye, Mum,' he whispered. His eyes stung. He wanted to do something, but he didn't know what.

His father placed a hand on David's shoulder, then lowered

himself down and kissed David's mother softly on the mouth. He pressed the side of his face to hers and whispered something that David could not hear. Then they left her, and when the coffin appeared again, carried by the undertaker and his assistants, it was closed and the only sign that it held David's mother was the little metal plate on the lid bearing her name and the dates of her birth and death.

They left her alone in the church that night. If he could have, David would have stayed with her. He wondered if she was lonely, if she knew where she was, if she was already in heaven or if that didn't happen until the priest said the final words and the coffin was put in the ground. He didn't like to think of her all by herself in there, sealed up by wood and brass and nails, but he couldn't talk to his father about it. His father wouldn't understand, and it wouldn't change anything anyway. He couldn't stay in the church by himself, so instead he went to his room and tried to imagine what it must be like for her. He drew the curtains on his window and closed the bedroom door so that it was as dark as he could make it inside, then climbed under his bed.

The bed was low, and the space beneath it was very narrow. It occupied one corner of the room, so David squeezed over until he felt his left hand touch the wall, then closed his eyes tightly shut and lay very still. After a while, he tried to lift his head. It bumped hard on the slats that supported his mattress. He pushed against them, but they were nailed in place. He tried to lift the bed by pressing upwards with his hands, but it was too heavy. He smelled dust and his chamber pot. He started to cough. His eyes watered. He decided to get out from under the bed, but it had been easier to shuffle into his current position than it was to pull himself out again. He sneezed and his head banged painfully against the underside of his bed. He started to panic. His bare feet scrambled for some purchase on the wooden floor. He reached up and used the slats to pull himself

7

along until he was close enough to the edge of the bed to slip out again. He climbed to his feet and leaned against the wall, breathing deeply.

That was what death was like: trapped in a small space with a big weight holding you down for all eternity.

His mother was buried on a January morning. The ground was hard, and all of the mourners wore gloves and overcoats. The coffin looked too short when they lowered it into the dirt. His mother had always seemed tall in life. Death had made her small.

In the weeks that followed, David tried to lose himself in books, because his memories of his mother were inextricably interwoven with books and reading. Her books, the ones deemed 'suitable', were passed on to him, and he found himself trying to read novels that he did not understand, and poems that did not quite rhyme. He would ask his father about them sometimes, but David's father seemed to have little interest in books. He had always spent his time at home with his head buried in newspapers, little plumes of pipe smoke rising above the pages like signals sent by Indians. He was obsessed with the comings and goings of the modern world, more so than ever now that Hitler's armies were moving across Europe and the threat of attacks on their own land was growing ever more real. David's mother once said that his father used to read a lot of books, but had fallen out of the habit of finding pleasure in stories. Now he preferred his newspapers with their long columns of print, each letter painstakingly laid out by hand to create something which would lose its relevance almost as soon as it appeared on the stands, the news within already old and dying by the time it was read, quickly overtaken by events in the world beyond.

The stories in books *hate* the stories contained in newspapers, David's mother would say. Newspaper stories were like recently caught fish, worthy of attention only for as long as they remained fresh, which was not very long at all. They were like the street urchins hawking the evening editions, all shouty and insistent, while stories – real stories, proper made-up ones – were like stern but helpful librarians in a well-stocked library. Newspaper stories were as insubstantial as smoke, as long-lived as mayflies. They did not take root but were instead like weeds that crawled along the ground, stealing the sunlight from more deserving tales. David's father's mind was always occupied by shrill, competing voices, each one silenced as soon as he gave it his attention, only for its clamour to be instantly replaced by another. That was what David's mother would whisper to him with a smile, while his father scowled and bit his pipe, aware that they were talking about him but unwilling to give them the pleasure of knowing they were irritating him.

And so it was left to David to safeguard his mother's books, and he added them to those that had been bought with him in mind. They were the tales of knights and soldiers, of dragons and sea beasts, folk tales and fairy tales, because these were the stories that David's mother had loved as a girl and that he in turn had read to her as the illness gradually took hold of her, reducing her voice to a whisper and her breaths to the rasp of old sandpaper on decaying wood, until at last the effort was too much for her and she breathed no more. After her death, he tried to avoid these old tales, for they were linked too closely to his mother to be enjoyed, but the stories would not be so easily denied, and they began to call to David. They seemed to recognise something in him, or so he started to believe, something curious and fertile. He heard them talking: softly at first, then louder and more compellingly.

These stories were very old, as old as people, and they had survived because they were very powerful indeed. These were the tales that echoed in the head long after the books that contained them were cast aside. They were both an escape from reality and an alternative reality themselves. They were so ancient, and so strange, that they had found a kind of existence independent of the pages they occupied. The world of the old tales existed parallel to ours, as David's mother had once told him, but sometimes the wall separating the two became so thin and brittle that the two worlds started to blend into each other.

That was when the trouble started.

That was when the bad things came.

That was when the Crooked Man began to appear to David.

II

Of Rose and Dr Moberley, and the Importance of Details

It was a strange thing, but shortly after his mother died, David remembered experiencing a sense almost of relief. There was no other word for it and it made David feel bad about himself. His mother was gone, and she was never coming back. It didn't matter what the priest said in his sermon: that David's mother was now in a better, happier place, and her pain was at an end. It didn't help when he told David that his mother would always be with him, even if he couldn't see her. An unseen mother couldn't go for long walks with you on summer evenings, drawing the names of trees and flowers from her seemingly infinite knowledge of nature; or help you with your homework, the familiar scent of her in your nostrils as she leaned in to correct a misspelling, or puzzle over the meaning of an unfamiliar poem; or read with you on cold Sunday afternoons when the fire was burning and the rain was beating down upon the windows and the roof and the room was filled with the smell of woodsmoke and crumpets.

But then David recalled that, in those final months, his mother had not been able to do any of those things. The drugs that the doctors gave her made her groggy and ill. She couldn't concentrate, not even on the simplest of tasks, and she certainly couldn't go for long walks. Sometimes, towards the end, David was not even sure that she knew who he was any more. She started to smell funny: not bad, just odd, like old clothes that hadn't been worn in a very long time. During the night she would cry out in pain, and David's father would hold her and try to comfort her. When she was very sick, the doctor would be called. Eventually she was too ill to stay in her own room, and an ambulance came and took her to a hospital that wasn't quite a hospital because nobody ever seemed to get well and nobody ever went home again. Instead, they just got quieter and quieter until at last there was only total silence and empty beds where they used to lie.

The not-quite-hospital was a long way from their house, but David's dad visited every other evening after he returned home from work and he and David had eaten their dinner together. David went with him in their old Ford Eight at least twice each week, even though the journey back and forth left him with very little time for himself once he'd completed his homework and eaten his dinner. It made his father tired too, and David wondered how he found the energy to get up each morning, make breakfast for David, see him off to school before heading to work, come home, make tea, help David with any homework that was proving difficult, visit David's mother, return home again, kiss David good night and then read the paper for an hour before taking himself off to bed.

Once, David had woken up in the night, his throat very dry, and gone downstairs to fetch a drink of water. He heard snoring in the sitting room and peered in to find his father asleep in his armchair, the paper fallen apart around him and his head hanging unsupported over the edge of the chair. It was three o'clock in the morning. David hadn't been sure what to do, but in the end he woke his father up because he remembered how he himself had once fallen asleep awkwardly in the train on a long journey and his neck had hurt for days afterwards. His father had looked a little surprised, and just slightly angry, at being woken up, but he'd roused himself from the chair and gone upstairs to rest. Still, David was sure that it wasn't the first time he'd fallen asleep like that, fully clothed and nowhere near his bed.

So when David's mother died it meant that there was no more pain for her, but also no more long journeys to and from the big yellow building where people faded away to nothing, no more sleeping in chairs, no more rushed dinners. Instead, there was only the kind of silence that comes when someone takes away a clock to be repaired and after a time you become aware of its absence because its gentle, reassuring tick is gone and you miss it so.

But the sense of relief went away after only a few days, and then David felt guilty for being glad that they no longer had to do all the things his mother's illness had required of them, and in the months that followed the feeling did not fade. Instead it got worse and worse, and David began to wish that his mother was still in the hospital. If she had been there he would have visited her every day, even if it meant getting up earlier in the mornings to finish his homework, because now he couldn't bear to think of life without her.

School became more difficult for him. He drifted apart from his friends, even before summer came and its warm breezes scattered them like dandelion seeds. There was talk that all of the boys would be evacuated from London and sent to the countryside when school resumed in September, but David's father had promised him he would not be sent away like the others. After all, his father had said, it was just the two of them now, and they had to stick together.

His father employed a lady, Mrs Howard, to keep the house clean and do a little cooking and ironing. She was usually there when David came home from school, but Mrs Howard was too busy to talk to him. She was training with the A.R.P., the Air Raid Precautions wardens, as well as taking care of her own husband and children, so she didn't have time to chat with David or to ask him how his day had been.

Mrs Howard would leave just after four o'clock, and David's father would not return from work at the university until six at the earliest, and sometimes later than that. This meant that David was stuck in the empty house with only the wireless and his books for company. Sometimes, he would sit in the bedroom that his father and mother had once shared. Her clothes were still in one of the wardrobes, the dresses and skirts lined up in such neat rows that they almost looked like people themselves if you squinted hard enough. David would run his fingers along them and make them swish, remembering as he did so that they had moved in just such a way when his mother walked in them. Then he would lie back on the pillow to the left, for that was the side on which his mother used to sleep, and try to rest his head against the same spot on which she had once rested her head, the place obvious from the slightly dark stain upon the pillowcase.

This new world was too painful to cope with. He had tried so hard. He had kept to his routines. He had counted so carefully. He had abided by the rules, but life had cheated. This world was not like the world of his stories. In that world, good was rewarded and evil was punished. If you kept to the path and stayed out of the forest, then you would be safe. If someone was sick, like the old king in one of the tales, then his sons could be sent out into the world to seek the remedy, the Water of Life, and if just one of them was brave enough and true enough, then the king's life could be saved. David had been brave. His mother had been braver still. In the end, bravery had not been enough. This was a world that did not reward it. The more David thought about it, the more he did not want to be part of such a world.

He still kept to his routines, although not quite as rigidly as before. He was content merely to touch the doorknobs and taps twice, left hand first, then right hand, just to keep the numbers even. He still tried to put his left foot down first on the floor in the mornings, or on the stairs of the house, but that wasn't so difficult. He wasn't sure what would happen now if he didn't adhere to his rules to some degree. He supposed that it might affect his father. Perhaps, in sticking to his routines, he had saved his father's life, even if he hadn't managed to save his mother. Now that it was just the two of them it was important not to take too many chances.

And that was when Rose entered his life, and the attacks began.

The first time was in Trafalgar Square, when he and his father were walking down to feed the pigeons after Sunday lunch at the Popular Café in Piccadilly. His father said that the Popular was due to close soon, which made David sad as he thought it was very grand.

David's mother had been dead for five months, three weeks, and four days. A woman had joined them to eat at the Popular that day. His father had introduced her to David as Rose. Rose was very thin, with long, dark hair and bright red lips. Her clothes looked expensive, and gold and diamonds glittered at her ears and throat. She claimed to eat very little, although she finished most of her chicken that afternoon and had plenty of room for pudding afterwards. She looked familiar to David, and it emerged that she was an administrator of the not-quite-hospital in which his mother had died. His father told David that Rose had looked after his mother really, really well, although not, David thought, well enough to keep her from dying.

Rose tried to speak with David about school and his friends and what he liked to do with his evenings, but David could barely manage to respond. He didn't like the way that she looked at his father or the way she called him by his first name. He didn't like the way that she touched his hand when he said something funny or clever. He didn't even like the fact that his father was trying to be funny and clever with her to begin with. It wasn't right.

Rose held on to his father's arm as they strolled from the restaurant. David walked a little ahead of them, and they seemed content to let him go. He wasn't sure what was happening, or this was what he told himself. Instead he silently accepted a bag of seeds from his father when they reached Trafalgar Square, and used them to draw the pigeons to him. The pigeons bobbed obediently towards this new source of food, their feathers stained with the muck and soot of the city, their eyes vacant and stupid. His father and Rose stood nearby, talking quietly to each other. When they thought he wasn't looking, David saw them kiss briefly.

That was when it happened. One moment David's arm was outstretched, a thin line of seed spread along it and two rather heavy pigeons pecking away at his sleeve, and the next he was lying flat on the ground, his father's coat beneath his head and curious onlookers – and the odd pigeon – staring down at him, fat clouds scudding behind their heads like blank thought balloons. His father told him that he had fainted, and David supposed he must be right, except there were now voices and whispers in his head where no voices and whispers had been before, and he had a fading memory of a wooded landscape and the howling of wolves. He heard Rose ask if she could do anything to help, and David's father told her that it was all right, that he would take him home and put him to bed. His father hailed a cab to bring them back to their car. Before he left, he told Rose he would telephone her later.

That night, as David lay in his room, the whispers in his head were joined by the sound of the books. He had to put his pillow over his ears to drown out the noise of their chatter, as the oldest of the stories roused themselves from their slumbers and began to look for places in which to grow.

Dr Moberley's office was in a terraced house on a tree-lined street in the centre of London, and was very quiet. There were expensive carpets on the floors and the walls were decorated with pictures of ships at sea. An elderly secretary with very white hair sat behind a desk in the waiting room, shuffling papers, typing letters and taking telephone calls. David sat on a big sofa nearby, his father beside him. A grandfather clock ticked in the corner. David and his father didn't speak. Mostly it was because the room was so quiet that anything they said would have been overheard by the lady behind the desk, but David also felt that his father was angry with him.

There had been two more attacks since Trafalgar Square, each one longer than the last and each leaving David with more strange images in his mind: a castle with banners fluttering from the walls, a forest filled with trees that bled redly from their bark, and a half-glimpsed figure, hunched and wretched, who moved through the shadows of this strange world, waiting. David's father had taken him to see their family doctor, Dr Benson, but Dr Benson had been unable to find anything wrong with David. He sent David to a specialist at a big hospital, who shone lights in David's eyes and examined his skull. He asked David some questions, then asked David's father many more, some of them concerning David's mother and her death. David had then been told to wait outside while they talked, and when David's father came out he looked angry. That was how they had ended up at Dr Moberley's office.

Dr Moberley was a psychiatrist.

A buzzer sounded beside the secretary's desk and she nodded to David and his father.

'He can go in now,' she said.

'Off you go,' said David's father.

'Aren't you coming in with me?' asked David.

David's father shook his head, and David knew that he had already spoken with Dr Moberley, perhaps over the telephone.

'He wants to see you alone. Don't worry. I'll be here when you're finished.'

David followed the secretary into another room. It was bigger and grander than the waiting room, furnished with soft chairs and couches. The walls were lined with books, although they were not books like the ones David read. David thought that he could hear the books talking amongst themselves when he arrived. He couldn't understand most of what they were saying, but they spoke v-e-r-y s-l-o-w-l-y as if what they had to impart was very important or the person to whom they were speaking was very stupid. Some of the books appeared to be arguing among themselves in blah-blah-blah tones, the way experts sometimes talked on the wireless when they were addressing one another, surrounded by other experts whom they were trying to impress with their intelligence.

The books made David very uneasy.

A small man with grey hair and a grey beard sat behind an antique desk that looked too big for him. He wore rectangular glasses with a gold chain to keep him from losing them. A red and black bow tie was knotted tightly at his neck, and his suit was dark and baggy.

'Welcome,' he said. 'I'm Dr Moberley. You must be David.'

David nodded. Dr Moberley asked David to sit down, then flicked through the pages of a notebook on his desk, tugging on his beard while he read whatever was written on them. When he had finished, he looked up and asked David how he was. David said he was fine. Dr Moberley asked him if he was sure. David said that he was reasonably sure. Dr Moberley said David's dad was worried about him. He asked David if he missed his mum. David didn't answer. Dr Moberley told David that he was worried about David's attacks, and together they were going to try to find out what was behind them.

Dr Moberley gave David a box of pencils and asked him to draw a picture of a house. David took a lead pencil and carefully drew the walls and the chimney, then put in some windows and a door before he set to work adding little curved slates to the roof. He was lost in the act of drawing slates when Dr Moberley told him that was quite enough. Dr Moberley looked at the picture, then looked at David. He asked David if he hadn't thought of using coloured pencils. David told him that the drawing wasn't finished, and that once the tiles were added to the roof he planned to colour them red. Dr Moberley asked David, in the v-e-r-y s-l-o-w way that some of his books spoke, why the slates were so important.

David wondered if Dr Moberley was a real doctor. Doctors were supposed to be very clever. Dr Moberley didn't seem terribly clever. V-e-r-y s-l-o-w-ly, David explained that without slates on the roof, the rain would get in. In their way, they were just as important as walls. Dr Moberley asked David if he was afraid of the rain getting in. David told him that he didn't like getting wet. It wasn't so bad outside, especially if you were dressed for it, but most people didn't dress for rain indoors.

Dr Moberley looked a bit confused.

Next, he asked David to draw a tree. Again, David took the pencil, painstakingly drew the branches, then proceeded to add little leaves to each one. He was on only the third branch when Dr Moberley asked him to stop again. This time, Dr Moberley had the kind of expression on his face that David's father sometimes had when he managed to finish the crossword in the Sunday paper. Short of standing up and shouting 'Aha!' with his finger pointing in the air, the way mad scientists did in cartoons, he couldn't have looked more pleased with himself.

Dr Moberley then asked David a lot of questions about his home, his mum, and his dad. He asked again about the blackouts, and if David could remember anything of them. How did he feel before they happened? Did he smell anything strange before he lost consciousness? Did his head hurt afterwards? Did his head hurt before? Did his head hurt now?

But he did not ask the most important question of all, in David's view, because Dr Moberley chose to believe that the attacks caused David to black out entirely and that the boy could remember nothing of them before he regained consciousness. That wasn't true. David thought about telling Dr Moberley of the strange landscapes that he saw when the attacks came, but Dr Moberley had already begun asking about his mother again and David didn't want to talk about his mother, not any more and certainly not with a stranger. Dr Moberley asked about Rose too, and how David felt about her. David didn't know how to answer. He didn't like Rose and he didn't like his father being with her, but he didn't want to tell Dr Moberley that in case he told David's father about it.

By the end of the session, David was crying and he didn't even know why. In fact, he was crying so hard that his nose bled and the sight of the blood frightened him. He began to scream and shout. He fell on the floor and a white light flashed in his head as he started to tremble. He beat his fists on the carpet and heard the books tut-tutting their disapproval as Dr Moberley called for help and David's dad came rushing in and then everything went dark for what seemed like only seconds but was in fact a very long time indeed.

And David heard a woman's voice in the darkness, and he thought it sounded like his mother. A figure approached, but it was not a woman. It was a man, a crooked man with a long face, emerging at last from the shadows of his world.

And he was smiling.

III

Of the New House, the New Child and the New King

This is how things came to pass.

Rose was pregnant. His father told David as they ate chips by the Thames, boats bustling by and the smell of oil and seaweed mixing in the air. It was November 1939. There were more policemen on the streets than before, and men in uniform were everywhere. Sandbags were piled against windows, and great lengths of barbed wire lay coiled around like vicious springs. Humpbacked Anderson shelters dotted gardens, and trenches had been dug in parks. White posters could be seen on every available space: reminders of lighting restrictions, proclamations from the king, all of the instructions for a country at war.

Most of the children David knew had by now left the city, thronging train stations with little brown luggage labels tied to their coats on their way to farms and strange towns. Their absence made the city appear emptier and increased the sense of nervous expectancy that seemed to govern the lives of all who remained. Soon, it was said, the bombers would come, and the city was shrouded in darkness at night to make their task harder. The blackout made the city so dark that it was possible to pick out the craters of the moon, and the heavens were crowded with stars.

On their way to the river they saw more barrage balloons being inflated in Hyde Park. When these were fully inflated they would hang in the air, anchored by steel cables. The cables would prevent the German bombers from flying low, which meant that they would have to drop their payloads from a greater height. That way the bombers would not be as certain of hitting their targets.

The balloons were shaped like enormous bombs. David's father said it was ironic, and David asked him what he meant. His father said it was just funny that something that was supposed to protect the city from bombs and bombers should look like a bomb itself. David nodded. He supposed that it was strange. He thought of the men in the German bombers, the pilots trying to avoid the anti-aircraft fire from below, one man crouched over the bomb-sight while the city passed beneath him. He wondered if he ever considered the people in the houses and the factories before he released the bombs. From high in the air, London would look just like a model, with toy houses and minia-ture trees on tiny streets. Maybe that was the only way you could drop the bombs: by pretending that it wasn't real, that nobody would burn and die when they exploded below.

David tried to imagine himself in a bomber – a British one, perhaps a Wellington or a Whitley – flying over a German city, bombs at the ready. Would he be able to release the load? It was a war after all. The Germans were bad. Everybody knew that. They had started it. It was like a playground fight: if you started it then you were to blame, and you couldn't really complain about what happened afterwards. David thought that he would release the bombs, but he wouldn't think about the possibility that there might be people below. There would just be factories and shipyards, shapes in the darkness, and everyone employed in them would be safely tucked up in bed when the bombs fell and blew apart their places of work.

A thought struck him.

'Dad? If the Germans can't aim properly because of the balloons, then their bombs could drop just anywhere, right? I mean, they'll be trying to hit factories, won't they, but they won't be able to, so they'll just let them go and hope for the best. They're not going to go home and come back another night just because of the balloons.'

David's father didn't reply for a moment or two.

'I don't think they care,' he said at last. 'They want people to lose their spirit and their hope. If they blow up aeroplane factories or shipyards along the way, then so much the better. That's how a certain type of bully works. He softens you up before going in for the killer blow.'

He sighed. 'We need to talk about something, David, something important.'

They had just come from another session with Dr Moberley, during which David was asked again if he missed his mother. Of course he missed her. It was a stupid question. He missed her, and he was sad because of it. He didn't need a doctor to tell him that. He had trouble understanding what Dr Moberley was saying most of the time anyway, partly because the doctor used words that David didn't understand, but mostly because his voice was now almost entirely drowned out by the dronings of the books on his shelves.

The sounds made by books had become clearer and clearer to David. He understood that Dr Moberley couldn't hear the books speak, otherwise he couldn't have worked in his office without going mad. Sometimes, when Dr Moberley asked a question of which the books approved, they would all say 'Hmmmmm' in unison, like a male voice choir practising a single note. If he said something of which they disapproved, they would mutter insults at him.

'Charlatan!'

'Poppycock!'

'The man's an idiot.'

One book, with the name 'Jung' engraved on its cover in gold letters, grew so irate that it toppled itself from the shelf and lay on the carpet, fuming. Dr Moberley looked quite surprised when

23

it fell. David was tempted to tell him what the book was saying, but he didn't think it would be a very good idea to let Dr Moberley know that he heard books talking. David had heard of people being 'put away' because they were 'wrong in the head'. David didn't want to be put away. Anyway, he didn't hear the books talking all of the time now. It was only when he was upset or angry. David tried to stay calm, to think about good things as much as he could, but it was hard sometimes, especially when he was with Dr Moberley, or Rose.

Now he was sitting by the river, and his whole world was about to change again.

'You're going to have a little brother or sister,' David's father said. 'Rose is going to have a baby.'

David stopped eating his chips. They tasted wrong. He felt pressure building in his head, and for a moment he thought he might topple from the bench and suffer another of his attacks, but somehow he made himself stay upright.

'Are you going to marry Rose?' he asked.

'I expect so,' said his father. David had heard Rose and his father discussing the subject the previous week, when Rose had come to visit and David was supposed to be in bed. Instead, he had sat on the stairs and listened to them talking. He did that, sometimes, although he always went to bed when the talking ceased and he heard the smack of a kiss, or Rose laughing in a low, throaty way. The last time he'd listened, Rose had spoken about 'people' and how these 'people' were talking. She didn't like what they were saying. That was when the subject of marriage came up, but David didn't hear any more because his father left the room to put the kettle on and David only barely avoided being seen on the stairs. He thought his father might have suspected something because he came upstairs to check on David moments later. He kept his eyes closed and pretended to be asleep, which seemed to satisfy his father, but David was too nervous to go back to the stairs again.

'I just want you to know something, David,' his father was saying to him. 'I love you, and that will never change, no matter who else we share our life with. I loved your mum too, and I'll always love her, but being with Rose has helped me a lot these last few months. She's a nice person, David. She likes you. Try to give her a chance, won't you?'

David didn't reply. He swallowed hard. He had always wanted a brother or sister, but not like this. He wanted it to be with his mum and dad. This wasn't right. This wouldn't really be his brother or sister. It would come out of Rose. It wouldn't be the same.

His father placed his arm around David's shoulder. 'Well, do you have anything to say?' he asked.

'I'd like to go home now,' said David.

His father kept his arm around David for a second or two more, then let it drop. He seemed to sag slightly, as though someone had just let a little air out of him.

'Fine,' he said sadly. 'Let's go home then.'

Six months later, Rose gave birth to a boy, and David and his father left the house in which David had grown up and went to live with Rose and David's new half-brother, Georgie. Rose lived in a great big old house northwest of London, three storeys high with large gardens at front and back, and forest surrounding it. The house had been in her family for generations, according to David's father, and was at least three times as big as their own house. David had not wanted to move at first, but his father had gently explained the reasons to him. It was closer to his new place of work, and because of the war he was going to have to spend more and more time there. If they lived closer to it, then he would be able to see David more often, and perhaps even come home for his lunch sometimes. His father also told David that the city was going to become more dangerous, and that out here they would all be a little safer. The German planes were coming, and while David's father was sure that Hitler would be beaten in the end, things were going to get much worse before they got better.

David was not entirely sure what his father now did for a living. He knew that his dad was very good at maths, and that he had been a teacher at a big university until recently. Then he had left the university and gone to work for the government in an old country house outside the city. There were army barracks nearby and soldiers manned the gates that led to the house and patrolled its grounds. Usually when David asked his father about his work, he would just tell him that it involved checking figures for the government. But on the day that they finally moved from their house to Rose's, his father seemed to feel that David was owed something more.

'I know that you like stories and books,' his father said, as they followed the removal van out of the city. 'I suppose you wonder why I don't like them as much as you do. Well, I do like stories, in a way, and that's part of my job. You know how sometimes a story seems to be about one thing, but in fact it's about another thing entirely? There's a meaning hidden in it, and that meaning has to be teased out?'

'Like Bible stories,' said David. On Sundays, the priest would often explain the Bible story that had just been read out loud. David didn't always listen because the priest was very dull, but it was surprising what the priest could see in stories that seemed quite simple to David. In fact, the priest appeared to like making them more complicated than they were, probably because it meant that he could talk for longer. David didn't care much for church. He was still angry at God for what had happened to his mother, and for bringing Rose and Georgie into his life.

'But some stories aren't meant to have their meaning understood by just anyone,' David's father continued. 'They're meant for only a handful of people, and so the meaning is very carefully hidden. It can be done using words, or numbers, or sometimes both together, but the purpose is the same. It's to prevent anyone else who sees it from interpreting it. Unless you know the code, it has no meaning.

'Well, the Germans use codes to send messages. So do we. Some of them are very complicated, and some of them appear very simple, although often those are the most complicated of all. Someone has to try to figure them out, and that's what I do. I try to understand the secret meanings of stories written by people who don't want me to understand them.'

He turned to David and laid a hand on his shoulder. 'I'm trusting you with this,' he said. 'You must never tell anyone else what it is that I do.'

He raised a finger to his lips.

'Top secret, old chap.'

David imitated the gesture.

'Top secret,' he echoed.

And they drove on.

David's bedroom was at the very top of the house, in a little low room that Rose had chosen for him because it was filled with books and bookshelves. David's own books found themselves sharing the shelves with other books that were older or stranger than they were. He made space for his books as best he could and eventually settled on ordering the books on the shelves according to size and colour, because they looked better that way. It meant his books kept getting mixed up with those that were already there, so one book of fairy tales ended up squeezed between a history of communism and an examination of the last battles of the First World War. David had tried to read a little of the book on communism, mainly because he wasn't entirely sure what communism was (apart from the fact that his father seemed to think that it was something very bad indeed). He managed to get about three pages into it before he lost interest, its talk of 'workers' ownership of the means of production' and 'the predation of capitalists' almost putting him to sleep. The history of the First World War was a little better, if only for the many drawings of old tanks that had been cut out of an illustrated magazine and stuck between various pages. There was also a dull textbook of French vocabulary, and a book about the Roman Empire that had some very interesting drawings in it and seemed to take a lot of pleasure in describing the cruel things that the Romans did to people and that other people did to the Romans in return.

David's book of Greek myths, meanwhile, was the same size and colour as a collection of poetry nearby, and he would sometimes pull out the poems instead of the myths. Some of the poems weren't too bad, once he gave them a chance. One was about a kind of knight – except in the poem he was called a 'Childe' – and his search for a dark tower and whatever secret it contained. The poem didn't really seem to end properly, though. The knight reached the tower and, well, that was it. David wanted to know what was in the tower, and what happened to the knight now that he'd reached it, but the poet obviously didn't think this was important. It made David wonder about the kind of people who wrote poems. Anyone could see that the poem was really only getting interesting when the knight reached the tower, but that was the point at which the poet decided to go off and write something else instead. Perhaps he had meant to come back to it and had simply forgotten, or maybe he couldn't come up with a monster for the tower that was impressive enough. David had a vision of the poet, surrounded by bits of paper with lots of ideas for creatures crossed out or scribbled over.

~~Werewolf.~~
~~Dragon.~~
~~Really big dragon.~~
~~Witch.~~
~~Really big witch.~~
~~Small witch.~~

David tried to give a form to the beast at the heart of the poem, but found that he could not. It was more difficult than it appeared, for nothing quite seemed to fit. Instead, he could only conjure up a half-formed being that crouched in the cobwebbed corners of his imagination where all the things that he feared curled and slithered in the darkness.

David was aware of a change in the room as soon as he began to fill the empty spaces on the shelves, the newer books looking and sounding uneasy beside these other works from the past. Their appearance was intimidating, and they spoke to David in dusty, rumbling tones. The older books were bound in calfskin and leather, and some of them contained knowledge that had long been forgotten, or that was found to be incorrect as science and the process of discovery uncovered new truths. The books that held this old knowledge had never come to terms with this diminution of their worth. They were now lower than stories, for stories were intended, at some level, to be made up and untrue, but these other books had been born for greater things. Men and women had worked hard on their creation, filling them with the sum total of all that they knew and all that they believed about the world. That they were misguided, and the assumptions they made were now largely worthless, was almost impossible for the books to bear.

A great book that claimed that the end of the world, based on a close examination of the Bible, would occur in 1783, had largely retreated into madness, refusing to believe that the present date was any later than 1782, for to do so would be to admit that its contents were wrong and its existence therefore had no purpose beyond mere curiosity. A slim work on the current civilisations of Mars, written by a man with a large telescope and an eye that discerned the paths of canals where no canals had ever flowed, gabbled constantly about how the Martians had retreated below the surface and were now building great engines in secret. It currently occupied a position among a number of books on sign language for the deaf, which, fortunately, could not hear anything that was being said to them.

But David also discovered books that were similar to his own. There were thick, illustrated volumes of fairy stories and folk tales, the colours still rich and full within. It was to these works that David turned his attention in those first days in his new home, lying on a box seat at the window and staring down occasionally upon the forest beyond, as though expecting the wolves and witches and ogres from the stories to materialise suddenly below, for the descriptions in the books matched so accurately the woods bordering the house that it was almost impossible to believe they were not one and the same, an impression strengthened by the nature of the books' construction. Some of their stories had been added to by hand and the drawings within had been carefully created by someone with no small talent for their art. David could find no name upon the books to identify the author of the additions, and a number of the tales were unfamiliar to him while still retaining echoes of the tales he knew almost by heart.

In one story, a princess was forced to dance all night and sleep all day by the actions of a sorcerer, but instead of being rescued by the intervention of a prince or a clever servant, the princess died, only for her ghost to return and torment the sorcerer to such a degree that he threw himself into a chasm in the earth and was burned to death in its fires. A little girl was threatened by a wolf while walking through the forest, and as she fled from him she met a woodsman with an axe, but in this story the woodsman did not merely kill the wolf and restore the girl to her family, oh no. He cut off the wolf's head, then brought the girl to his cottage in the thickest, darkest part of the forest, and there he kept her until she was old enough to wed him, and she became his bride in a ceremony conducted by an owl, even though she had never stopped crying for her parents in all the years that he had kept her prisoner. And she had children by

him, and the woodsman raised them to hunt wolves and seek out people who strayed from the paths of the forest. They were told to kill the men and take what was valuable from their pockets, but to bring the women to him.

David read the stories by day and by night, his blankets drawn around him to protect him from the cold, for Rose's house was never warm. The wind found its way in through cracks in the window frames and the ill-fitting doors, rustling the pages of open books as though seeking from them some piece of knowledge that it desperately required for its own purposes. The great sweeps of ivy that covered the house, front and back, had broken through the walls over the decades, so that tendrils crept from the upper corners of David's room, or bound themselves to the underside of the windowsill. At first, David had tried to cut them with his scissors, discarding the remnants, but after a few days the ivy would return, seemingly thicker and longer than before, clinging ever more tenaciously to the wood and the plaster. Insects exploited the holes too, so that the boundary between the natural world and the world of the house became blurred and unclear. David found beetles congregating in the closet, and earwigs exploring his sock drawer. At night, he heard mice scurrying behind the boards. It was as if nature was claiming David's room as its own.

Worse, when he slept he dreamed more often of the creature he had named the Crooked Man, who walked through forests very like the one beyond David's window. The Crooked Man would advance to the edge of the tree line, staring out at an expanse of green lawn to where a house just like Rose's stood. He would speak to David in his dreams. His smile was mocking, and his words made no sense to David.

'We are waiting,' he would say. 'Welcome, Your Majesty. All hail the new king!'

IV

Of Jonathan Tulvey and Billy Golding,
and Men Who Dwell by Railway Tracks

David's room was curious in its construction. The ceiling was quite low and rather higgledy-piggledy, sloping in places where it should not have sloped and providing ample opportunity for industrious spiders to spin their webs. On more than one occasion, David, in his urge to explore the darker corners of the bookshelves, had found himself wearing strands of spider silk in his face and hair, causing the web's creator to scuttle into a corner and crouch balefully, lost in thoughts of arachnoid revenge. There was a wooden toy box in one corner of the room, and a large wardrobe in the other. Between them stood a chest of drawers with a mirror on top. The room was painted light blue so that on a bright day it seemed like part of the world outside, especially with the ivy poking through the walls and the occasional insect providing food for the spiders.

The single small window overlooked the lawn and the woods. If he stood on his box seat David could also see the spire of a church and the roofs of the houses in the nearby village. London lay to the southwest, but it might as well have been in Antarctica, so completely did the trees and the forest hide the house from the outside world. The window seat was David's favourite place in which to read. The books still whispered and spoke amongst themselves, but he was now able to hush them with a single word if his mood was right, and anyway they tended to remain quiet while he was reading. It was as if they were happy once he was consuming stories.

It was summer once again, so David had plenty of time to read. His father had tried to encourage him to make friends with the children who lived nearby, some of them evacuees from the city, but David did not want to mix with them, and they in turn saw something sad and distant in him that kept them away. Instead, the books took their place. The old volumes of fairy tales in particular, so strange and sinister with their hand-written additions and new paintings, had increased David's fascination with these stories. They still reminded him of his mother, but in a good way, and whatever reminded him of his mother equally helped to keep Rose and *her* son Georgie at a distance. When he was not reading, the seat gave him a perfect view of one of the property's other curiosities: the sunken garden set into the lawn close to where the trees began.

It looked a little like an empty swimming pool, with a set of four stone steps leading down to a rectangle of green, bordered by a flagstoned pathway. While the grass was regularly mown by Mr Briggs the gardener, who came every Thursday to tend the plants and lend nature a helping hand where necessary, the stone parts of the sunken garden had fallen into disrepair. There were large cracks in the walls, and in one corner the stonework had crumbled away entirely, leaving a gap big enough for David to squeeze through, if he had chosen to do so. David had never gone further than poking his head in, though. The space beyond was dark and musty, and filled with all kinds of hidden, scurrying things. David's father had suggested that the sunken garden might make a suitable site for an air-raid shelter, if they decided it should ever become necessary, but so far he had only managed to start piling sandbags and sheets of corrugated iron in the garden shed, much to the annoyance of Mr Briggs who now had to navigate his way around them every time he wanted to reach his tools. The sunken garden became David's own place outside the house, especially when he wanted to get away from the whispering of the books or from Rose's well-intentioned but unwelcome intrusions into his life.

David's relations with Rose were not good. While he tried always to be polite, as his father had asked him to be, he did not like her and resented the fact that she was now part of his world. It was not merely that she had taken, or was trying to take, the place of his mother, although that was bad enough. Her attempts to cook meals that he liked for dinner, despite the pressures of rationing, irritated him. She wanted David to like her, and that made him dislike her even more.

But David believed that her presence also distracted his father from the memory of David's mother. He was forgetting about her already, so tied up was he with Rose and the baby. Little Georgie was a demanding child. He cried a lot and always seemed to be ailing, so that the local doctor was a regular visitor to the house. His father and Rose doted on him, even as he deprived them of sleep almost every night, leaving them both short-tempered and weary. The result was that David was increasingly left to his own devices, which made him both grateful for the freedom offered by Georgie and resentful of the lack of attention to his own needs. In any case, it gave him more opportunities to read, and that was no bad thing.

But as David's fascination with the old books grew, so too did his desire to find out more about their former owner, for they had clearly belonged to someone who was just like him. He had at last found a name, Jonathan Tulvey, written inside the covers of two of the books and he was curious to learn something more about him.

So it was that one day David swallowed his dislike of Rose and went down to the kitchen where she was working. Mrs Briggs, the housekeeper, and wife of Mr Briggs the gardener, was visiting her sister in Eastbourne, so Rose was taking care of the chores for the day. From outside came the clucking of hens in the chicken run. David had helped Mr Briggs to feed them earlier, and to check the vegetable garden for damage from rabbits and the run for any holes that might allow a fox to enter. The week before, Mr Briggs had trapped and killed a fox near the house using a snare. The fox had almost been decapitated by the trap, and David had said something about feeling sorry for it. Mr Briggs had scolded him, pointing out that one fox would kill every hen they had if he managed to get into the run, but David had still been troubled by the sight of the dead animal, its tongue caught between its small, sharp teeth, its fur and flesh torn where it had tried to bite itself free from the snare.

David made himself a glass of Borwick's lemon barley before sitting at the head of the table and asking Rose how she was. Rose stopped washing the dishes and turned around to speak with him, her face bright with pleasure and surprise. David had planned to try very hard to be nice in the hope of finding out more from her, but Rose, unused to any conversation with him that did not centre on food or bedtime, or was not conducted in surly monosyllables, immediately embraced the chance to build bridges between them, so David's acting abilities were not stretched very far. She dried her hands on a dishcloth and took a seat beside him.

'I'm fine, thank you,' she said. 'A little tired, what with Georgie and all, but that will pass. It's been a little strange this last while. I'm sure you feel the same way, the four of us all thrown together suddenly like this. I'm glad that you're here, though. This house is too big for one person, but my parents wanted to keep it in the family. It was . . . important to them.'

'Why?' asked David. He tried to keep himself from sounding too interested. He didn't want Rose to realise that the only reason he was talking with her was to find out more about the house, and particularly his room and the books that it contained.

'Well,' she said, 'this house has been in our family for a very long time. My grandparents built it, and lived in it with their children. They hoped that there would always be children living in it.'

'Did they own the books in my room?' asked David.

'Some of them,' said Rose. 'Others belonged to their children: my father, his sister, and—'

She paused for a moment.

'Jonathan?' suggested David, and Rose nodded. She looked sad.

'Yes. Jonathan. Where did you learn his name?'

'It was written in some of the books. I was wondering who he was.'

'He was my uncle, my father's older brother, although I never met him. Your room was once his bedroom, and a lot of those books were his. I'm sorry if you don't like them. I thought it would be such a nice room for you. I know it's a bit dark, but it has all those shelves and, of course, the books. I should have been more thoughtful.'

David looked puzzled.

'But why? I do like it, and I like the books too.'

Rose turned away. 'Oh, it's nothing,' she said. 'It doesn't matter.'

'No,' said David. 'Please tell me.'

Rose relented.

'Jonathan disappeared. He was only fourteen. It was a long time ago, and my grandparents kept his room exactly as it had always been, because they hoped that he would come back to them. He never did. Another child disappeared with him, a little girl. Her name was Anna, and she was the daughter of one of my grandfather's friends. He and his wife died in a fire, and my grandfather took Anna to live with his family instead. Anna was seven. My grandfather thought it would be good for Jonathan to have a little sister and for Anna to have a big brother to take care of her. Anyway, they must have wandered off and, oh, I don't know, something happened to them and they were never seen again. It was just very, very sad. They searched for them for so long. They looked in the woods and the river, and they asked after them in all of the nearby towns. They even went to London and placed drawings and descriptions of them anywhere they could, but nobody ever came forward to say that they had seen them.

'In time, they had two more children, my father and his sister, Katherine, but my grandparents never forgot Jonathan, and never stopped hoping that he and Anna might some day come home. My grandfather in particular never recovered from their loss. He seemed to blame himself for what had happened. I suppose he thought he should have protected them. I think he died young because of it. When my grandmother was dying, she asked my father not to disturb the room, but to leave the books in their place just in case Jonathan should ever return. She never lost hope. She cared about Anna too, but Jonathan was her eldest son, and I don't think a day went by when she didn't stare out the window of her bedroom in the hope of seeing him walk up the garden path, older but still her son, with some wonderful tale to tell of his disappearance.

'My father did as she asked: he left the books as they were, and so did I, after my father and mother died. I always wanted a family of my own, and I suppose I just felt that Jonathan so loved his books that he would have liked to think that someday there might be another little boy or girl in there who would appreciate them, instead of them being left to decay, unread. Now it's your room, but if you'd like us to move you to another one, we can. There's lots of space.'

'What was Jonathan like? Did your grandfather ever tell you about him?'

Rose thought. 'Well, I was as curious as you are, and I would ask my grandfather about him. I made quite a study of Jonathan, I suppose. My grandfather said that he was very quiet. He liked to read, as you can tell, just like you. It's funny, in a way: he loved fairy stories but they scared him too, yet the ones that scared him the most were the ones he most enjoyed. He was afraid of wolves. I remember my grandfather telling me that, once. Jonathan would have nightmares in which wolves were chasing him, and not just ordinary wolves: because they came from the stories that he read, they could speak. They were clever, the wolves of his dreams, and dangerous. My grandfather tried to take his books away, his nightmares were so bad, but Jonathan hated being without them so my grandfather would always relent in the end and return them to him. Some of the books were very old. They were old when Jonathan owned them. I suppose a few of them might even have been valuable, except someone else had written in them once upon a time. There were stories and drawings that didn't belong. My grandfather thought that it might have been the work of the man who sold them to him. He was a bookseller in London, a strange character. He sold a lot of books for children, but I don't think he liked children themselves very much. I think he just liked scaring them.'

Rose was staring out the window now, lost in memories of her grandfather and her missing uncle.

'My grandfather went back to that bookshop after Jonathan and Anna disappeared. I suppose he thought that people who had children of their own would come to buy books there, and that perhaps either they or their children might know something about the missing pair. But when he got to the street in question, he found that the bookshop was gone. It was boarded up. Nobody lived or worked there any more, and no one could tell him what had happened to the little man who owned it. Perhaps he died. He was very old, my grandfather said. Very old, and very odd.'

The doorbell rang, breaking the spell of harmony between David and Rose. It was the postman, and Rose went to greet him. When she returned, she asked David if he would like something to eat, but David said no. Already, he was feeling angry with himself for lowering his defences against Rose, even if he had learned something as a result. He didn't want her to think that everything was now all right between them, because it wasn't, not at all. Instead, he left her alone in the kitchen and headed back to his bedroom.

On the way, he looked in on Georgie. The baby was fast asleep in his cot, his big gas helmet and the bellows for pumping air into it lying close by. It wasn't his fault that he was here, David tried to tell himself. Georgie didn't ask to be brought into the world. Still, David couldn't rouse himself to care terribly for him, and something tore inside him each time he saw his father holding the new arrival. He was like a symbol of all that was wrong, of all that had changed. After his mother had died, it had been just David and his father, and they had become closer as a result because they had only each other to rely upon. Now his father had Rose too, and a new son. But David, well, he didn't have anyone else. It was just himself.

David left the baby and returned to his garret, where he spent the rest of the afternoon flicking through Jonathan Tulvey's old books. He sat at the window and thought that Jonathan had sat in this seat, once upon a time. He had walked the same hallways, eaten in the same kitchen, played in the same living room, even slept in the same bed as David. Perhaps, somewhere back in time, he was still doing all of those things, and both David and Jonathan were now occupying the same space but at different stages in history, so that Jonathan passed like an unseen ghost through David's world, unaware that he shared his bed each night with a stranger. The thought made David shiver, but it also gave him pleasure to think that two boys who were so much alike might somehow share such a connection.

He wondered what could have happened to Jonathan and to the little girl, Anna. Perhaps they had run away, although David was old enough to understand that there was a great deal of difference between the kind of running away that happened in storybooks and the reality of what would face a boy of fourteen with a girl of seven in tow. It wouldn't have taken them long to become tired and hungry if something had made them leave, and to regret what they had done. David's father had told him that if he ever got lost he was to find a policeman, or ask a grown-up to find one for him. He wasn't to approach men who were by themselves, though. He was always to ask a lady, or a man and woman together, preferably ones with a child of their own. You couldn't be too careful, his father would say. Was that what happened to Jonathan and Anna? Had they talked to the wrong person, someone who didn't want to help them get home but instead had spirited them away, hiding them in a place where they would never be found? Why would someone do that?

As he lay on his bed, David knew there was an answer to that question. Before his mother had finally left for the not-quite-hospital, he had heard her discussing with his father the death of a local boy named Billy Golding, who had disappeared on his way home from school one day. Billy Golding didn't go to David's school and he wasn't one of David's friends, but David knew what he looked like because Billy was a very good foot-baller who played in the park on Saturday mornings. People said that a man from Arsenal had spoken to Mr Golding about Billy joining the club when he was older, but someone else said that Billy had just made that up and it wasn't true at all. Then Billy went missing and the police came to the park two Saturdays in a row to talk to anyone who might know something about him. They spoke to David and his father, but David couldn't help them and, after that second Saturday, the police didn't come back to the park again.

Then, a couple of days later, David heard in school that Billy Golding's body had been found down by the railway tracks.

That night, as he got ready for bed, he heard his mother and father talking in their bedroom and that was how he learned that Billy had been naked when he was discovered and that the police had arrested a man who lived with his mother in a clean little house not far from where the body was found. David knew from the way they were talking that something very bad had happened to Billy before he died, something to do with the man from the clean little house.

David's mother had made a special effort that night to walk from her room in order to kiss David. She hugged him very tightly and warned him again about talking to strange men. She told him that he must always come straight home from school, and that if a stranger ever approached him and offered him sweets or promised to give him a pigeon for a pet if he would just go with him, then David was to keep on walking as fast as he could, and if the man tried to follow him then David was to go up to the first house that he came to and tell them what was happening. Whatever else he did, he must never, ever go with a stranger, no matter what the stranger said. David told her he would never do that. A question came to him as he made the promise to his mother, but he did not ask it. She looked worried enough as it was and David didn't want her to worry so much that she wouldn't even let him go out to play. But the question stayed in his mind, even after she turned out the light and he was left alone in the darkness of his room. The question was:

But what if he made me go with him?

Now, in another bedroom, he thought of Jonathan Tulvey and Anna, and wondered if a man from a clean little house, a man who lived with his mother and kept sweets in his pockets, had made them go down with him to the railway tracks.

And there, in the dark, he had played with them, in his way.

That evening at dinner, his father was talking about the war again. It still didn't feel to David as if there was a war on. All of the fighting was happening far away, even if they did get to see some of it on newsreels when they went to the pictures. It was a lot duller than David had expected. War sounded quite exciting, but the reality, so far, had been very different. True, squadrons of Spitfires and Hurricanes often passed over the house, and there were always dogfights over the Channel. German bombers had been carrying out repeated raids on airfields to the south, even dropping bombs on St Giles, Cripplegate in the East End (which Mr Briggs described as 'typical Nazi behaviour' but which David's father explained, rather less emotively, as a botched effort to destroy the Thameshaven oil refinery). Nevertheless, David felt removed from it all. It wasn't as if it was happening in his own back garden. In London, people were taking items from crashed German planes as souvenirs, even though nobody was supposed to approach the wrecks, and Nazi pilots who bailed out provided regular excitement for the citizenry. Here, even though they were barely fifty miles from London, it was all very sedate.

His father folded the *Daily Express* beside his plate. The newspaper was thinner than it used to be, down to six pages. David's father said that was because they had started rationing paper. *The Magnet* had stopped printing in July, depriving David of Billy Bunter, but there was still the *Boy's Own* paper every month, which David always filed carefully alongside his *Aircraft of the Fighting Powers* books.

'Will you have to go and fight?' David asked his father, once dinner was over.

'No, I shouldn't think so,' his father replied. 'I'm more use to the war effort where I am.'

'Top secret,' said David.

His father smiled at him.

'Yes, top secret,' he said.

It still gave David a thrill to think that his father might be a spy, or at least know about spies. So far, it was the only interesting part of the war.

That night, David lay in his bed and watched the moonlight streaming through the window. The skies were clear, and the moon was very bright. After a time, his eyes closed, and he dreamt of wolves and little girls and an old king in a ruined castle, fast asleep on his throne. Railway tracks ran alongside the castle, and figures moved through the long grass that grew alongside. There was a boy and a girl, and the Crooked Man. They disappeared beneath the earth, and David smelled gum drops and bullseyes, and he heard a little girl crying before her voice was drowned out by the sound of an approaching train.

V

Of Intruders and Transformations

The Crooked Man finally crossed over into David's world at the start of September.

It had been a long, tense summer. His father spent more time at his place of work than he did at home, sometimes not sleeping in his own bed for two or three nights in a row. It was often too difficult for him to return to the house anyway once night fell. All of the road signs had been removed to thwart the Germans if they invaded, and on more than one occasion David's father had managed to get lost while driving home in daylight. If he tried driving at night with his headlamps off, who knew where he might end up?

Rose was finding motherhood difficult. David wondered if his own mother had found it as hard, and if David had been as demanding as Georgie seemed to be. He hoped not. The stress of the situation had caused Rose's tolerance for David and his moods to sink lower and lower. They barely talked to each other now, and David could tell that his father's patience with both of them was almost extinguished. At dinner the night before, he had exploded when Rose took an innocuous remark of David's as an insult and the two of them had begun to bicker.

'Why can't you two just find a way to get along, for crying out loud!' his father had shouted. 'I don't come home for this. I can get all the tension and shouting matches I want at work.'

Georgie, seated in his high chair, started to cry.

'Now look what you've done,' said Rose. She threw her napkin down on the table and went to Georgie.

David's father buried his head in his hands.

'So it's all my fault,' he said.

'Well it's not mine,' replied Rose.

Simultaneously, their eyes turned towards David.

'What?' he said. 'You're blaming me? Fine!'

He stomped away from the table, leaving his dinner unfinished. He was still hungry, but the stew was mainly vegetables with some nasty pieces of cheap sausage spread through it to break the monotony. He knew that he'd have to eat the rest of it tomorrow, but he didn't care. It wasn't going to taste any worse reheated than it did already. As he headed for his room, he expected to hear his father's voice demanding that he return and finish his food, but nobody called him back. He sat down hard on his bed. He couldn't wait for the summer holidays to be over. A place had been found for David in a school not far from the house, which would at least be better than spending every day with Rose and Georgie.

David was not seeing Dr Moberley quite as often, mainly because nobody had time to take him into London. Anyway, the attacks had stopped, or so it appeared. He no longer fell to the ground or experienced blackouts, but something far stranger and more unsettling was now occurring, stranger even than the whisperings of the books, to which David had grown almost accustomed.

David was experiencing waking dreams. That was the only way he could find to describe them to himself. It felt like those moments late in the evening when you were reading or listening to the wireless and you grew so tried that for an instant you fell asleep and began dreaming, except obviously you didn't realise you'd fallen asleep so that the world suddenly seemed to become very strange. David would be playing in his room, or reading, or walking in the garden, and everything would shimmer. The walls would disappear, the book would fall from his hands, the garden would be replaced by hills and tall, grey trees. He would find himself in a new land, a twilight place of shadows and cold winds, heavy with the smell of wild animals. Sometimes, he would even hear voices. They were somehow familiar as they called to him, but as soon as he tried to concentrate on them the vision would end and he would be back in his own world.

The strangest thing of all was that one of them sounded like his mother's voice. It was the one that spoke loudest and clearest. She called to him from out of the darkness. She called to him, and she told him that she was alive.

The waking dreams were always strongest near the sunken garden, but David found them so disturbing that he tried to stay away from that part of the property as much as possible. In fact, so troubled was David by them that he was tempted to tell Dr Moberley about them, if his father could make time for an appointment. Perhaps he would finally tell him about the whispering of the books too, David thought. The two might be linked, but then he thought of Dr Moberley's questions about David's mother, and remembered once again the threat of being 'put away'. When David talked to him about missing his mother, Dr Moberley would speak in turn about grief and loss, about how it was natural yet you had to try to get over it. But being sad about your mother dying was one thing; hearing her voice crying out from the shadows of a sunken garden, claiming to be alive behind the decaying brickwork, was quite another. David wasn't sure how Dr Moberley would respond to that. He didn't want to be put away, but the dreams were frightening. He wanted them to stop.

It was one of his last days at home before school recommenced. Tiring of the house, David went for a walk in the woods at the back of the property. He picked up a big stick and scythed at the long grass. He found a spider's web in a bush and tried to tempt the spider out with fragments of twigs. He dropped one close to the centre of the web, but nothing happened. David realised it was because the twig wasn't moving. It was the struggles of the insect that alerted the spider, which made David think that perhaps spiders were a lot cleverer than anything so small had a right to be.

He looked back at the house and saw the window of his bedroom. The ivy growing on the walls almost surrounded the frame, making his room look more than ever like a part of the natural world. Now that he saw it from a distance, he noticed the ivy was thickest at his window, yet it had barely touched any of the others on this side of the house. It had not spread across the lower parts of the wall either, the way ivy usually did, but had climbed straight and true along a narrow path to David's window. Like the beanstalk in the fairy tale that led Jack to the giant, the ivy seemed to know precisely where it was going.

And then a figure moved inside David's room. He saw a shape pass by the glass, dressed in forest green. For a moment, he was certain that it must be Rose, or perhaps Mrs Briggs. But then David remembered that Mrs Briggs had gone down to the village while Rose rarely entered his room, and if she did she always asked his permission first. It wasn't his father either. The person in the room was the wrong shape for him. In fact, David thought, whoever was in his room was the wrong shape, full stop. The figure was slightly hunched, as though it had become so used to sneaking about that its body had contorted, the spine curving, the arms like twisted branches, the fingers clutching, ready to snatch at whatever it saw. Its nose was narrow and curved, and it wore a crooked hat upon its head. It disappeared from sight for a moment before it reappeared holding open one of David's books. The figure flicked through the pages before it found something that interested it, whereupon it paused and appeared to start reading.

Then, suddenly, David heard Georgie crying in his nursery.

The figure dropped the book and listened. David saw its fingers extend into the air, as if Georgie were hanging before it like an apple ready to be plucked from the tree. It seemed to be debating with itself as to what to do next, for David saw its left hand move to its pointed chin and stroke it softly. While it was thinking, it glanced over its shoulder and down towards the woods below. It saw David, and froze for an instant before dropping to the floor, but in that moment David saw coal-black eyes set in a pale face so long and thin that it seemed to have been stretched on a rack. Its mouth was very wide and its lips were very, very dark, like old, sour wine.

David ran for the house. He burst into the kitchen, where his father was reading the newspaper.

'Dad, there's someone in my room!' he said.

His father looked up at him curiously.

'What do you mean?'

'There's a *man* up there,' insisted David. 'I was walking in the woods, and I looked up at my window and he was there. He wore a hat, and his face was really long. Then he heard the baby crying and he stopped whatever he was doing and listened. He saw me looking at him, and he tried to hide. Please, Dad, you've got to believe me!'

His father's brow furrowed and he put the paper down.

'David, if you're joking . . .'

'I'm not, honestly!'

He followed his father up the stairs, the stick still clutched in his hand. The door to his room was closed, and David's father paused before opening it. Then he reached down and twisted the knob. The door opened.

For a second, nothing happened.

'See,' said David's father. 'There's nothing—'

Something struck his father in the face and he shouted loudly. There was a panicked fluttering, and a banging as whatever it was bounced against the walls and the window. Once the initial shock had gone away, David peered around his father and saw that the intruder was a magpie, its feathers a blur of black and white as it tried to escape from the room.

'Stay outside and keep the door closed,' said his father. 'They're vicious birds.'

David did as he was told, although he was still frightened. He heard his father open the window and shout at the magpie, forcing it towards the gap, until finally he could hear the bird no longer and his father opened the door, sweating slightly.

'Well, that gave both of us a fright,' he said.

David looked into the room. There were some feathers on the floor, but that was all. There was no sign of the strange little man he had seen. He went to the window. The magpie was perched on the crumbling stonework of the sunken garden. It seemed to be staring back at him.

'It was only a magpie,' said his father. 'That's what you saw.'

David was tempted to argue, but he knew his father would tell him that he was being silly if he insisted that something else had been in here, something far bigger and far nastier than a magpie. Magpies didn't wear crooked hats, or reach out for crying babies. David had seen its eyes, and its hunched body, and its long, grasping fingers.

He looked back at the sunken garden. The magpie was gone.

His father sighed theatrically.

'You still don't believe that it was only a magpie, do you?' he said.

He went down on his knees and checked under the bed. He opened the wardrobe and looked in the bathroom next door. He even peered behind the bookcases, where there was a gap barely large enough to accommodate David's hand.

'See?' said his father. 'It was just a bird.'

But he could see that David remained unconvinced so, together, they searched all of the rooms on the top floor and then the floors below, until it became clear that the only people

50

in the house were David, his father, Rose, and the baby. Then David's father left him and returned to his newspaper. Back in his room, David picked up a book from the floor by his window. It was one of Jonathan Tulvey's storybooks, and it lay open at the tale of Red Riding Hood. The story was illustrated by a picture of the wolf towering over the little girl, Grandma's blood on its claws, its teeth bared to consume her granddaughter. Someone, presumably Jonathan, had scribbled over the figure of the wolf with a black crayon, as though disturbed by the threat it represented. David closed the book and returned it to its shelf. As he did so, he noticed the silence in his room. There was no whispering. All the books were quiet.

I suppose a magpie could have dislodged that book, thought

David, but a magpie couldn't enter a room through a locked window. Someone else had been there, of that he was sure. In the old stories, people were always transforming themselves, or being transformed, into animals and birds. Couldn't the Crooked Man have changed himself into a magpie in order to escape discovery?

He hadn't gone far, though, oh no. He had flown only as far as the sunken garden, and then he had disappeared.

As David lay in bed that night, caught between sleeping and waking, his mother's voice carried to him from the darkness of the sunken garden, calling his name, demanding that she not be forgotten.

And David knew then that the time was quickly approaching when he would have to enter that place and face at last what lay within.

VI

Of the War, and the Way Between Worlds

David and Rose had their worst fight the next day.

It had been building for a long time. Rose was breast-feeding Georgie, which meant that she was forced to rise during the night in order to take care of his needs. But even after he was fed, Georgie would toss and turn and cry, and there was little that David's father could do to help even when he was around. This sometimes led to arguments with Rose. They usually began with a little thing – a dish that his father forgot to put away, or dirt tracked through the kitchen on the soles of his shoes – and quickly developed into shouting matches that would end with Rose in tears and Georgie echoing his mother's cries.

David thought that his father looked older and more tired than before. He worried about him. He missed his father's presence. That morning, the morning of the big fight, David stood at the bathroom door and watched his father shave.

'You work really hard,' he said.

'I suppose so.'

'You're tired all the time.'

'I'm tired of you and Rose not getting along.'

'Sorry,' said David.

'Hmmmph,' said his father.

He finished shaving, wiped the lather from his face with water from the sink, then dried himself with a pink towel.

'I don't see you that much any more,' said David, 'that's all. I miss having you around.'

His father smiled at him, then cuffed him gently on the ear. 'I know,' he said. 'But we all have to make sacrifices, and there are men and women out there who are making much greater sacrifices than we are. They're putting their lives at risk every day and I have a duty to do all I can to help them. It's important that we find out what the Germans are planning and what they suspect about our people. That's my job. And don't forget that we're lucky here. They're having a much harder time of it in London.'

The Germans had struck hard at London the day before. At one point, according to David's father, there had been a thousand aircraft battling over the Isle of Sheppey. David wondered what London looked like now. Was it filled with burnt-out buildings, with rubble where streets used to be? Were the pigeons still in Trafalgar Square? He supposed that they were. The pigeons weren't clever enough to move somewhere else. Perhaps his father was right and they were lucky to be away from it, but a part of David thought again that it must be quite exciting to live in London now. Frightening, sometimes, but exciting.

'In time, it will come to an end, and then we can all go back to living normal lives,' said his father.

'When?' asked David.

His father looked troubled. 'I don't know. Not for a while.'

'Months?'

'Longer, I think.'

'Are we winning, Dad?'

'We're holding on, David. At the moment, that's the best we can do.'

David left his father to get dressed. They all ate breakfast together before his father left, but Rose and his dad said little to each other. David knew that they had been squabbling again, so when his father left for work he decided to stay out of Rose's way even more than usual. He went to his room for a while and played with his soldiers, then later lay in the shade at the back of the house to read his book.

It was there that Rose found him. Although his book was open upon his chest, David's attention was focused elsewhere. He was staring at the far end of the lawn, where the sunken garden lay, his eyes fixed on the hole in the brickwork as though expecting to see movement within.

'So there you are,' said Rose.

David looked up at her. The sun was in his eyes, so he was forced to squint. 'What do you want?' he asked.

He hadn't meant it to come out the way it did. It sounded as if he was being disrespectful and rude, but he wasn't, or no more than he ever was to Rose. He supposed that he could have asked, 'What can I do for you?', or even have prefixed 'Yes' or 'Certainly' or just 'Hello' to what he had said, but by the time he thought of this it was too late.

Rose had red marks under her eyes. Her skin was pale, and he thought he saw more lines on her forehead and face than there had previously been. She was heavier too, but David supposed that this was to do with having the baby. He had asked his father about it, and his father had told him never, ever to mention it to Rose, no matter what. He had been very serious about it. In fact, he used the words 'more than our lives are worth' to stress how important it was that David keep such opinions to himself.

Now Rose, fatter and paler and more tired, was standing beside David, and even with the sun in his eyes he could see the anger rising in her.

'How *dare* you speak to me like that!' she said. 'You sit around all day with your head buried in your books and you contribute nothing to life in this house. You can't even keep a civil tongue in your head. Who do you think you are?'

David was about to apologise, but he didn't. What she was saying wasn't fair. He had offered to help with things but Rose nearly always turned him down, mostly because he seemed to catch her when Georgie was acting up, or when she had her hands full with something else. Mr Briggs took care of the garden, and David always tried to assist him with the sweeping and raking, but that was out-of-doors where Rose couldn't see what he was doing. Mrs Briggs did all of the cleaning and most of the cooking, but whenever David tried to lend her a hand she shooed him out of the room, claiming that he was just one more thing for her to trip over. It had simply seemed to him that the best option was to stay out of everyone's way as much as possible. And anyway, these were the last days of his summer holidays. The village school had postponed opening for a couple of days because of a shortage of teachers, but his father seemed certain that David would be behind his new desk by the start of the following week at the very latest. From then until half-term he would be in school during the day and doing homework in the evenings. His working day would be nearly as long as his father's. Why shouldn't he take it easy while he could? Now his anger was growing to match Rose's. He stood up and saw that he was just as tall as she was. The words poured from his mouth almost before he knew that he was speaking them, a mixture of half-truths and insults and all of the rage that he had suppressed since the birth of Georgie.

'No, who do *you* think you are?' he said. 'You're not my mother, and you can't talk to me like that. I didn't want to come here to live. I wanted to be with my dad. We were doing just fine by ourselves, and then you came along. Now there's Georgie too, and you think I'm just someone who's in your way. Well, you're in *my* way, and you're in my dad's way. He still loves my mum, just like I do. He still thinks of her, and he's never going to love you the way he loved her, not ever. It doesn't matter what you do or what you say. He still loves her. He. Still. Loves. *Her.*'

Rose hit him. She struck him on the cheek with the palm of her hand. It wasn't a hard slap, and she pulled the blow as soon as she realised what she was doing, but the impact was still enough to rock David on his heels. His cheek smarted, and his eyes watered. He stared, open-mouthed with shock, then brushed past Rose and ran to his room. He didn't look back, not even when she called after him and said that she was sorry. He locked the door behind him and refused to open it to her when she knocked on it. After a while, she went away and did not return.

David stayed in his room until his father came home. He heard Rose speak to him in the hallway. His father's voice grew louder. Rose tried to calm him down. There were footsteps on the stairs. David knew what was coming.

The door to his room was almost blown off its hinges by the force of his father's fists upon it.

'David, open this door. Open it *now*.'

David did as he was told, turning the key once in the lock, then stepped back hurriedly as his father entered. His father's face was almost purple with fury. He raised his hand as if to hit David, then seemed to think better of it. He swallowed once, took a deep breath, then shook his head. When he spoke again, his voice was strangely calm, which worried David more than the previous show of anger.

'You have no right to speak to Rose in that way,' said his father. 'You will show respect to her, just as you show respect to me. Things have been hard for all of us, but that does not excuse your behaviour today. I haven't decided yet what I'm going to do with you, or how you're to be punished. If it wasn't already too late, I'd pack you off to boarding school and then you'd realise just how fortunate you are to be here.'

David tried to speak. 'But Rose hi—'

His father raised his hand. 'I don't want to hear about it. If you open your mouth again, it will go hard with you. For now you will stay in your room. You will not go outside tomorrow. You will not read and you will not play with your toys. Your door will remain open and if I catch you reading or playing then, so help me, I will take a belt to you. You will sit there on your bed and you will think about what you said and about how you're going to make it up to Rose when you're eventually allowed to return to life with civilised people. I'm disappointed in you, David. I brought you up to behave better than that. We both did, your mum and I.'

With that, he left. David sank back on his bed. He didn't want to cry, but he couldn't stop himself. It wasn't fair. He had been wrong to talk to Rose that way, but she had been wrong to hit him. As his tears fell, he became aware of the murmuring of the books on the shelves. He had grown so used to it that he had almost ceased to notice it, like birdsong or the wind in the trees, but now it was growing louder and louder. A burning smell came to him, like matches igniting and tram wires sparking. He clenched his teeth as the first spasm came, but there was nobody to witness it. A great fissure appeared in his room, ripping apart the fabric of this world, and he saw another realm beyond. There was a castle, with banners waving from its battlements and soldiers marching in columns through its gates. Then that castle was gone and another took its place, this one surrounded by fallen trees. It was darker than the first, its shape unclear, and was dominated by a single great tower that pointed like a finger towards the sky. Its topmost window was lit, and David felt a presence there. It was at once both strange and familiar. It called to him in his mother's voice. It said:

David, I am not dead. Come to me, and save me.

David did not know how long he had been unconscious, or if sleep had at some point taken over, but his room was dark when he opened his eyes. There was a coppery taste in his mouth and he realised that he had bitten his tongue. He wanted to go to his father and tell him of the attack but he felt certain there would be very little sympathy for him from that quarter. Anyway, there was not a sound to be heard in the house, so he assumed that everyone was in bed. The waning moon shone upon the rows of books but they were now quiet again, apart from the occasional snore that arose from the duller, more boring volumes. There was a history of coal mining, abandoned and unloved upon a high shelf, that was particularly uninteresting and had the nasty habit of snoring very loudly and then coughing thunderously, at which point small clouds of black dust would appear to rise from its pages. David heard it cough now, but he was also aware of a certain wakefulness among some of the older books, the ones that contained the strange, dark fairy stories he loved so much. He sensed that they were waiting for an event to occur, although he could not tell what it might be.

David was certain that he had been dreaming, although he could not quite recall the substance of the dream. Of one thing he was sure: the dream had not been a pleasant one, but all that remained was a lingering sense of unease and a tingling on the palm of his right hand, as though it had been stroked with poison ivy. There was something of the same sensation on the side of his face, and he could not shake off the feeling that something unpleasant had touched him while he was lost to the world.

He was still wearing his day clothes. He climbed out of bed and undressed in the dark, changing into clean pyjamas. He returned to his bed and wrestled with his pillow, turning this way and that in an effort to find a comfortable position in which to go to sleep, but no rest came. As he lay with his eyes closed, he noticed that his window was open. He didn't like it to be open. It was hard enough to keep the insects out even when it was closed, and the last thing he wanted was for the magpie to return while he was sleeping.

David left his bed and carefully approached the window. Something curled over his bare foot and he raised it in fright. It was a tendril of ivy. There were shoots of it along the inner wall, and green fingers extended over the wardrobe and the carpet and the chest of drawers. He had spoken to Mr Briggs about it and the gardener had promised to get a ladder and trim back the ivy from the outside wall, but so far that hadn't happened. David didn't like touching the ivy. The way it was encroaching on his room made it seem almost alive.

David found his slippers and placed them on his feet before walking across the ivy to the glass. As he did so, he heard a woman's voice speak his name.

'David.'

'Mum?' he asked uncertainly.

'Yes, David. Listen. Don't be afraid.'

But David was afraid.

'Please,' said the voice. *'I need your help. I'm trapped here. I'm trapped in this strange place and I don't know what to do. Please come, David. If you love me, come across.'*

'Mum,' he said. 'I'm frightened.'

The voice spoke again, but it was fainter now.

'David,' it said, *'they're taking me away. Don't let them take me from you. Please! Follow me, and bring me home. Follow me through the garden.'*

And with that, David overcame his fear. He grabbed his dressing-gown and ran, as quickly and as quietly as he could, down the stairs and out on to the grass. He paused in the darkness. There was a disturbance in the night sky, a low, irregular put-putting noise that came from high above. David looked up and saw a distant glow, like a meteor falling. It was an aeroplane. He kept the light in view until he came to the steps that led into the sunken garden, taking them as fast as he could. He didn't want to pause, because if he paused he might think about what he was going to do, and if he began thinking about it he might become too afraid to act. He felt the grass crumple beneath his feet as he ran to the hole in the wall, even as the light in the sky grew brighter. The aeroplane was now flaming redly, and the noise of its sputtering engines tore through the night. David stopped and watched it descend. It was dropping faster, shedding burning shards as it came. It was too big to be a fighter. This was a bomber. He thought he could make out the shape of its wings and hear the desperate thrumming of the remaining engines as the plane fell to earth. It grew larger and larger, until at last it seemed to fill the sky, dwarfing their house, lighting up the dark with red and orange fire. It was heading straight for the sunken garden, flames licking at the German cross on its fuselage, as though something in the heavens above was determined to stop David from moving between realms.

The choice had been made for him. David could not hesitate. He forced himself through the gap in the wall and into the darkness, just as the world that he had left behind became an inferno.

VII

Of the Woodsman and the Work of His Axe

The bricks and mortar were gone. There was now rough bark beneath David's fingers. He was inside the trunk of a tree, an arched opening before him, beyond which lay shadowy woods. Leaves fell, descending in slow spirals to the forest floor. Thorny bushes and stinging nettles provided low cover, but there were no flowers that David could see. It was a landscape composed of greens and browns. Everything appeared to be illuminated by a strange half-light, as though dawn was just approaching or the day was at last drawing to its close.

David stayed in the darkness of the trunk, unmoving. His mother's voice was gone, and now there was only the barely heard sound of leaf glancing against leaf and the distant rushing of water over rocks. There was no sign of the German plane, no indication that it had even existed. He was tempted to turn back, to run to the house and wake his father in order to tell him of what he had seen. But what could he say, and why would his father believe him after all that had occurred that day? He needed proof, some token of this new world.

And so David emerged from the hollow of the tree trunk. The sky above was starless, the constellations hidden by heavy clouds. The air smelled fresh and clean to him at first, but as he breathed deeply he caught a hint of something else, something less pleasant. David could almost taste it on his tongue:

a metallic sensation composed of copper and decay. It reminded him of the day he and his father had found a dead cat by the side of the road, its fur torn and its insides exposed. The cat had smelled a lot like the night air in the new land. David shivered, and only partly from the cold.

Suddenly he was aware of a great roaring from behind him, and a sensation of heat at his back. He threw himself to the ground and rolled away as the trunk of the tree began to swell and distend, the hollow widening until it resembled the entrance to a great, bark-lined cave. Flames flickered deep within and then, like a mouth expelling a tasteless piece of food, it spat forth part of the burning fuselage of the German bomber, the body of one of its crew still trapped in the wreckage of the gondola beneath, its machine gun pointing at David. The wreckage tore a path through the undergrowth before it came to rest in a clearing, still spewing smoke and fumes as the flames fed upon it.

David stood, brushing leaves and dirt from his clothing. He tried to approach the burning plane. It was a Ju 88; he could tell from the gondola. He could see the remains of the gunner, now almost entirely wreathed in fire. He wondered if any of the crew had survived. The body of the trapped aviator lay pressed against the cracked glass of the gondola, his mouth grinning in his charred skull. David had never seen death up close before, not like this, not violent and smelly and turning to black. He could not help thinking of the German's final moments, trapped in the searing heat, his skin burning. He experienced a wave of pity for the dead man whose name he would never know.

Something whizzed by his ear like the warm passage of a night insect, followed almost immediately by a cracking noise. A second insect buzzed past but by then David was already lying flat on the ground, crawling for cover as the ammunition for its guns ignited. He found a depression in the earth and threw himself into it, covering his head with his hands and trying to keep himself as flat as he could until the hail of bullets had ceased. Only when he was certain that the ammunition was entirely spent did he dare to raise his head again. He stood warily and watched as flames and sparks shot into the skies above. For the first time, he got some sense of how huge were the trees in this forest, taller and wider than even the oldest of oaks in the woods back home. Their trunks were grey and entirely without branches until, at least one hundred feet above his head, they exploded into massive, mostly bare crowns.

A black, boxlike object had separated from the main body of the shattered plane and now lay, smoking slightly, not far from where David stood. It looked like an old camera, but with wheels on its side. He could make out the word *Blickwinkel* marked on one of the wheels. Beneath it was a label reading *Auf Farbglas Ein*.

It was a bomb-sight. David had seen pictures of them. This was what the German flyers used to pick out their targets on the ground. Perhaps that had even been the task of the man who now lay burning in the wreckage, for the city would have passed beneath him as he lay prone in the gondola. Some of David's pity for the dead man seeped away. The bomb-sight made what they had been doing seem more real, somehow, more awful. He thought of the families huddled in their Anderson shelters, the children crying and the adults hoping that whatever descended would strike far away from them; or the crowds gathered together in the Underground stations, listening to the explosions, dust and dirt falling on their heads as the bombs shook the ground above.

And they would be the lucky ones.

He kicked out hard at the bomb-sight, connecting with a perfect right-foot shot, and felt a surge of satisfaction as he heard the sound of broken glass from within and knew that the delicate lenses had shattered.

Now that the excitement was over, David put his hands in the pockets of his dressing-gown and tried to take in a little more of his surroundings. Some four or five steps beyond where he was, four bright purple flowers stood tall above the grass. They were the first signs of real colour he had seen so far. Their leaves were yellow and orange, and the hearts of the flowers themselves looked to David like the faces of sleeping children. Even in the murk of the forest, he thought he could discern their closed eyelids, the slightly opened mouths, the twin holes of their nostrils. They were unlike any blooms that he had ever seen before. If he could take one and give it to his father, then he might be able to convince him that this place truly existed.

David approached the flowers, dead leaves crunching beneath his feet. He was almost upon them when the lids of the nearest one opened, revealing small yellow eyes. Then its lips parted and it emitted a shriek. Instantly, the other flowers awoke and then, almost as one, they closed their leaves around themselves, revealing hard, barbed undersides that glistened faintly with a sticky residue. Something told David that it would be a bad idea to touch those barbs. He thought of nettles, and poison ivy. They were bad enough, but who knew what poisons the plants here might use to defend themselves?

David's nose wrinkled. The wind was blowing the smell of the burning aircraft away from him, and its stench had now been replaced by another. The metallic smell that he had detected earlier was stronger here. He took a few steps deeper into the forest and saw an uneven formation under the fallen leaves, spots of blue and red suggesting something lay barely concealed beneath. It was roughly the shape of a man. David drew closer and saw clothing, and fur beneath it. His brow furrowed. It was an animal, an animal wearing clothes. It had clawed fingers and legs like those of a dog. David tried to glimpse its face, but there was none. Its head had been cleanly severed from the body, and recently too, for a long spray of arterial blood still lay upon the forest floor.

David covered his mouth so that he would not be sick. The sight of two corpses in as many minutes was making his stomach churn. He stepped away from the body and turned back towards his tree. As he did so, the hole in the trunk disappeared before his eyes, the tree returning to its previous size and the bark seeming to grow over the gap while he watched, entirely covering the passage back to his own world. It became just one more in a forest of great trees, each hardly different from the next. David touched his fingers to the wood, pressing and knocking, hoping to find some way of reopening the portal, but nothing happened. He almost cried, but he knew that if he began crying all would be lost. He would be just a small boy, powerless and afraid, far from home. Instead, he looked around him and found the tip of a large, flat rock erupting from the dirt. He dug it free and, using its sharpest edge, chipped at the trunk of the tree: once, then again, over and over until the bark fragmented and fell to the ground. David thought that he felt the tree shudder, the way a person might if he had suddenly experienced a severe shock. The whiteness of the inner pulp turned to red, and what looked very much like blood began to seep from the wound, flowing down the channels and crevasses of the bark and dripping onto the ground beneath.

A voice said: 'Don't do that. The trees don't like it.'

David turned. There was a man standing in the shadows a short distance from him. He was big and tall, with broad shoulders and short, dark hair. He wore brown boots of leather that came almost to his knees and a coat made from skins and hides. His eyes were very green, so that he seemed almost like a part of the forest itself given human form. Over his right shoulder, he carried an axe.

David dropped the stone. 'I'm sorry,' he said. 'I didn't know.'

The man regarded him silently. 'No,' he said at last. 'I don't suppose you did.'

He advanced towards David, and the boy instinctively took a couple of steps back until he felt his hands graze the tree. Once again, it seemed to shiver beneath his touch, but the feeling was less pronounced than before, as though it were gradually recovering from the injury it had received and was certain now, in the presence of the approaching stranger, that no such hurt would be visited on it again. David was not so reassured by the man's approach: after all, he had an axe, the kind of axe that looked as if it could sever a head from a body.

Now that the man had emerged from the shadows, David was able to examine his face more closely. He thought that the man looked stern, but there was kindness there too, and the boy felt that here was someone who could be trusted. He began to relax a little, although he kept a wary eye on the big axe.

'Who are you?' said David.

'I might ask you the same question,' said the man. 'These woods are in my care, and I have never seen you in them before. Still, in answer to you, I am the Woodsman. I have no other name, or none that matters.'

The Woodsman approached the burning aeroplane. The flames were dying down now, leaving the framework exposed. It looked like the skeleton of some great beast, abandoned to the fire after the roasted meat had been stripped from its bones. The gunner could no longer be seen clearly. He had become just another dark shape in a tangle of metal and machine parts. The Woodsman shook his head in wonder, then walked away from the wreckage and returned to David. He reached past the boy and laid his hand upon the trunk of the wounded tree. He looked closely at the damage David had inflicted upon it, then patted the bark as one might pat a horse or a dog. Kneeling down, he removed some moss from the nearby stones, which he packed into the hole.

'It's all right, old fellow,' he said to the tree. 'It will heal soon enough.'

Far above David's head, the branches moved for a moment, even though all of the other trees remained still. The Woodsman returned his attention to David.

'And now,' he said, 'it's your turn. What is your name, and what are you doing here? This is no place for a boy to be wandering alone. Did you come in this . . . *thing*?'

He gestured towards the aeroplane.

'No, that followed after me. My name is David. I came through the tree trunk. There was a hole, but it disappeared. That was why I was chipping at the bark. I was hoping to cut my way back in, or at least to mark the tree so I would be able to find it again.'

'You came *through* the tree?' he asked. 'From where did you come?'

'A garden,' said David. 'There was a little gap in a corner, and I found a way through from there to here. I thought I heard my mother's voice, and I followed it. Now the way back is gone.'

The Woodsman pointed again at the wreckage. 'And how did you come to bring that with you?'

'There was fighting. It fell from the sky.'

If the Woodsman was surprised by this information, he didn't show it.

'There is the body of a man inside,' said the Woodsman. 'Did you know him?'

'He was the gunner, one of the crew. I'd never seen him before. He was a German.'

'Well, he is a dead German now.'

The Woodsman touched his fingers to the tree once again, lightly tracing its surface as though hoping to find the tell-tale cracks of a doorway beneath his skin. 'As you say, there is no longer a door here. You were right to try to mark this tree, though, even if your methods were clumsy.'

He reached into the folds of his jacket and removed a small ball of rough twine. He unravelled it until he was satisfied that he had the correct length, then tied it around the trunk of the tree. From a small leather bag he produced a grey, sticky substance that he smeared on the twine. It didn't smell at all nice.

'It will keep the animals and birds from gnawing upon the rope,' explained the Woodsman. He picked up his axe. 'You'd better come with me,' he said. 'We'll decide what to do with you tomorrow, but for now we need to get you to safety.'

David didn't move. He could still smell blood and decay on the air, and now that he had seen the axe at close quarters he thought he spotted drops of red along its length. There were red marks too on the man's clothing.

'Excuse me,' he said, as innocently as he could, 'but if you care for the woods, why do you need an axe?'

The Woodsman looked at David with what might almost have been amusement, as though he saw through the boy's efforts to conceal his concern yet was impressed by his guile nonetheless.

'The axe isn't for the woods,' said the Woodsman. 'It's for the things that live in the woods.'

He raised his head and sniffed the air. He pointed the axe in the direction of the headless corpse.

'You smelled it,' he said.

David nodded.

'I saw it, too. Did you do that?'

'I did.'

'It looked like a man, but it wasn't.'

'No,' said the Woodsman. 'Not a man. We can talk about it later. You have nothing to fear from me, but there are other creatures that we both have reason to fear. Come now. Their time is near, and the heat and the smell of burning flesh will draw them to this place.'

David, realising that he had no other choice, followed the Woodsman. He was cold, and his slippers were damp, so the Woodsman gave him his jacket to wear and raised David up onto his back. It had been a long time since someone had carried David upon his back. He was too heavy for his father now, but the Woodsman did not appear troubled by the burden. They passed through the forest, the trees seeming to stretch endlessly before them. David tried to take in the new sights, but the Woodsman moved quickly and it was all David could do to hang on. Above their heads, the clouds briefly parted, and the moon was revealed. It was very red, like a great hole in the skin of the night. The Woodsman picked up the pace, his long strides eating up the forest floor.

'We must hurry,' he said. 'They'll be coming soon.'

And as he spoke, a great howling arose from the north, and the Woodsman began to run.

VIII

*Of Wolves, and
Worse-Than-Wolves*

The forest passed in a blur of grey and brown and fading winter green. Briars tore at the Woodsman's jacket and the bottoms of David's pyjamas, and on more than one occasion David had to duck down to prevent his face from being raked by high bushes. The howling had ceased, but the Woodsman had not slowed his pace, not for a moment. Neither did he speak, so David too stayed silent. He was frightened, though. He tried to look back over his shoulder once, but the effort almost caused him to lose his balance and he did not try again.

They were still in the depths of the forest when the Woodsman stopped and seemed to be listening. David almost asked him what was wrong, but then thought better of it and remained quiet, trying to hear what it was that had caused the Woodsman to pause. He felt a prickling sensation at his neck as his hairs stood on end, and was certain that they were being watched. Then, faintly, he heard a brushing of leaves to his right, and a snapping of twigs to his left. There was movement around them, as though presences in the undergrowth were trying to close in on them as softly as possible.

'Hold on tight,' said the Woodsman. 'Almost there.'

He sprinted to his right, leaving the easy ground and breaking through a thicket of ferns, and instantly David heard the woods erupt into noise behind them as the pursuit recommenced in

earnest. A cut opened on his hand, dripping blood onto the ground, and a large hole was ripped in his pyjamas from the knee to the ankle. He lost a slipper, and the night air bit at his bare toes. His fingers ached with the cold and the effort of holding on tightly to the Woodsman, but he did not release his grip. They passed through another patch of bushes and now they were on a rough trail that wound its way down a slope towards what looked like a garden beyond. David glanced behind him and thought he saw two pale orbs gleaming in the moonlight, and a patch of thick fur.

'Don't look back,' said the Woodsman. 'Whatever you do, don't look back.'

David faced forward again. He was terrified, and very sorry that he had followed the voice of his mother into this place. He was just a boy wearing pyjamas, one slipper, and an old blue dressing-gown under a stranger's jacket, and he did not belong anywhere but in his own bedroom.

Now the trees were thinning, and David and the Woodsman emerged into a patch of lovingly tended land, sown with row upon row of vegetables. Before them stood the strangest cottage that David had ever seen, surrounded by a low wooden fence. The dwelling was built of logs hewn from the forest, with a door at the centre, a window on either side, and a sloping roof with a stone chimney-stack at one end, but that was where any resemblance to a normal cottage ended. Its silhouette against the night sky was like that of a hedgehog, for it was covered in spikes of wood and metal, where sharpened sticks and rods of iron had been inserted between, or through, the logs. As they drew closer, David could also make out pieces of glass and jagged stone in the walls and even on the roof, so that it shone in the moonlight as though sprinkled with diamonds. The windows were heavily barred and great nails had been driven through the door from the inside, so that to fall heavily against it would be to risk instant impalement. This was not a cottage: this was a fortress.

They passed through the fence and were approaching the safety of the house when a form appeared from behind its walls. It resembled a large wolf in shape, except that it wore an ornate shirt of white and gold on its upper body, and bright red breeches on its lower half. And then, as David watched, it rose on its hind legs and stood like a man, and it became clear that this was more than an animal. Its ears were roughly human in shape, although tufted with points of hair and adorned with gold hoops, while its muzzle was shorter than a wolf's. Its lips were drawn back from its fangs, and it growled at them in warning, but it was in its eyes that the struggle between wolf and man was clearest. These were not the eyes of an animal. They were cunning but also self-aware, and filled with hunger and desire.

Other similar creatures were now emerging from the forest, some wearing clothing, mostly tattered jackets and torn trousers, and they too rose up and stood on their hind legs, but there were many more who were just like ordinary wolves. They were smaller and stayed on all fours, and looked savage and unthinking to David. It was the ones who bore traces of men upon them that frightened David the most.

The Woodsman lowered David to the ground.

'Stay close to me,' he said. 'If anything happens, run for the cottage.'

He patted David on the lower back, and David felt something fall into the pocket of the jacket. As discreetly as he could, he allowed his hand to drift towards the pocket, trying to pretend it was the cold that made him seek its comfort. He put his hand inside and felt the shape of a large iron key. David closed his fist upon it and held it as though his very life depended on it, which, he was starting to realise, might well be the case.

The wolf-man by the house regarded David intently, and so terrifying was his gaze that David was forced to look to the ground, to the back of the Woodsman's neck, anywhere but into those eyes that were both familiar and alien. The wolf-man touched a long claw to one of the spikes on the cottage's walls, as though testing its power to harm, and then it spoke. Its voice was deep and low, and filled with spittle and growls, but David could clearly understand every word that it said.

'I see you have been busy, Woodsman,' it said. 'You have been fortifying your lair.'

'The woods are changing,' the Woodsman replied. 'There are strange creatures abroad.'

He shifted the axe in his hands in order to improve his grip upon it. If the wolf-man noticed the implicit threat, he did not show it. Instead he merely growled in agreement, as if he and the Woodsman were neighbours whose paths had crossed unexpectedly while walking in the evening.

'The whole land is changing,' said the wolf-man. 'The old king can no longer control his kingdom.'

'I am not wise enough to judge such matters,' said the Woodsman. 'I have never met the king, and he does not consult with me about the care of his realm.'

'Perhaps he should,' said the wolf-man. He seemed almost to smile, except there was no friendliness to it. 'After all, you treat these woods as though they were your own kingdom. You should not forget that there are others who would contest your right to rule them.'

'I treat all living creatures in this place with the respect they deserve, but it is in the order of things that man should rule over all.'

'Then perhaps it is time for a new order to rise,' said the wolf-man.

'And what order would that be?' asked the Woodsman. David could hear mockery in his tone. 'An order of wolves, of predators? The fact that you walk on hind legs doesn't make you a man, and the fact that you wear gold in your ear doesn't make you a king.'

'There are many kingdoms that might exist, and many kings,' said the wolf-man.

'You will not rule here,' said the Woodsman. 'If you try, I will kill you and all of your brothers and sisters.'

The wolf-man opened its jaws and snarled. David trembled, but the Woodsman did not move an inch.

'It seems that you have already begun. Was that your handiwork back in the forest?' asked the wolf-man, almost carelessly.

'These are my woods. My handiwork is all over them.'

'I am referring to the body of poor Ferdinand, my scout. He appears to have lost his head.'

'Was that his name? I never had a chance to ask. He was too intent upon tearing out my throat for us to engage in idle chit-chat.'

The wolf-man licked his lips.

'He was hungry,' he said. 'We are all hungry.'

His eyes flicked from the Woodsman to David, as they had done for much of the conversation, but this time they lingered a little longer on the boy.

'His appetites will no longer trouble him,' said the Woodsman. 'I have relieved him of their burden.'

But Ferdinand was forgotten. The wolf-man's attention was now entirely focused on David.

'And what have you found on your travels?' said the wolf-man. 'It seems that you have discovered a strange creature of your own, new meat from the forest.'

A long, thin thread of saliva dripped from its muzzle as it spoke. The Woodsman placed a protective hand on David's shoulder, drawing him closer, while his right hand held firmly on to the axe.

'This is my brother's son. He has come to stay with me.'

The wolf-man tilted its head and the hackles on its back rose high. It sniffed the air.

'You lie!' it growled. 'You have no brother, no family. You live alone in this place, and you always have. This is no child of our land. He brings with him new scents. He is . . . *different*.'

'He is mine, and I am his guardian,' said the Woodsman.

'There was a fire in the forest. Something strange was burning there. Did it come with him?'

'I do not know anything about it.'

'If you do not, then perhaps the boy does, and he can explain to us where this came from.'

The wolf-man nodded to one of its fellows, and a dark shape flew through the air and landed close to David.

It was the head of the German gunner, all cindery black and charred red. His flight helmet had melted into his scalp, and once again David glimpsed his teeth still locked in their death grimace.

'There was little eating on him,' said the wolf-man. 'He tasted of ash, and sour things.'

'Man does not eat man,' said the Woodsman in disgust. 'You have shown your true nature through your actions.'

The wolf-man ignored him.

'You cannot keep the boy safe. Others will learn of him. Give him to us, and we will offer him the protection of the pack.'

But the wolf-man's eyes gave the lie to its words, for everything about the beast spoke of hunger and want. Its ribs stuck out against its grey fur, visible beneath the white of its shirt, and its limbs were thin. The others with it were also starving. They were now slowly closing in on David and the Woodsman, unable to resist the promise of food.

Suddenly, there was a blur of movement to the right and one of the lower order of wolves, overcome by its appetites, leaped. The Woodsman spun, the axe rose, and there was a single sharp yelp before the wolf fell dead upon the ground, its head almost severed from its body. A howling arose from the assembled pack, the wolves twisting and turning in excitement and distress. The wolf-man stared at the fallen animal, then turned on the Woodsman, every sharp tooth in its mouth visible. David thought that it must certainly fall upon them, and then the rest would follow and they would be torn apart, but instead the side of the creature that bore traces of something human seemed to overcome the animal half, and it brought its rage under control. It rose once again on its hind legs and shook its head.

'I warned them to keep their distance, but they are starving,' it said. 'There are new enemies, and new predators who compete with us for food. Still, this one was not like us, Woodsman. We are not animals.'

The Woodsman and David were backing towards the cottage, trying to get closer to the promise of safety that it offered.

'Do not fool yourself, beast,' said the Woodsman. 'There is no "us". I have more in common with the leaves on the trees and the dirt on the ground than I do with you and your kind.'

Already, some of the wolves had advanced and begun to feed on their fallen comrade, but not the ones who wore clothes. They looked longingly at the corpse but, like their leader, they tried to maintain a veneer of self-control. It did not run deep, however. David could see their nostrils twitching at the scent of blood, and he felt certain that were the Woodsman not there to protect him, the wolf-men would have already torn him to pieces. The lower wolves were cannibals, content to feed upon their own kind, but the appetites of the ones that resembled men were much worse than those of the rest.

The wolf-man considered the Woodsman's answer. Masked by the Woodsman's body, David had already taken the key from his pocket and was quietly preparing to insert it into the lock.

'If there is no bond between us,' it said, thoughtfully, 'then my conscience is clear.'

It looked to the assembled pack, and howled.

'It is time,' it snarled, 'to *feed*.'

David fitted the key into the hole just as the wolf-man fell to all fours, its body crouching and ready to spring.

A sudden yelp of warning came from one of the wolves at the edge of the forest. The animal turned to face some threat as yet unseen, and it drew the attention of the rest of the pack, so that even their leader was distracted for crucial seconds. David risked a glance and saw a shape moving against the trunk of a tree, coiling around it like a snake. The wolf backed away, whining softly. While it was distracted, a length of green ivy extended itself from a low branch and looped around the wolf's neck. It cinched tight upon the fur and then yanked the wolf high into the air, the animal's legs kicking in vain as it began to choke.

Now the whole forest appeared to come alive in a blur of twisting strands of green, the tendrils curling around legs and muzzles and throats, hauling wolves and wolf-men into the air or trapping them upon the ground, drawing tighter and tighter around them until all struggles ceased. The wolves immediately began to fight back, snapping and snarling, but they were powerless against an enemy like this, and those that could were already trying to retreat. David felt the key turn in the lock as the pack leader's head jerked to and fro, torn between its desire for flesh and its urge to survive. Lengths of ivy were moving in its direction now, creeping across the damp earth of the vegetable patch. It had to choose quickly between fight and flight. With a final growl of fury at the Woodsman and David, the wolf-man turned tail and ran south, even as the Woodsman pushed David through the gap and into the safety of the cottage, the door closing firmly behind them and sealing off the sounds of howling and dying from the edge of the forest.

IX

Of the Loups and How They Came into Being

David moved to one of the barred windows as a soft orange glow crept through the little cottage. The Woodsman had made sure that the door was securely bolted and the wolves had fled before piling logs into the stone fireplace and preparing the fire. If he was troubled by what had occurred outside then he wasn't showing it. In fact, he seemed remarkably calm, and some of that calm had spread to David. He should have been terrified, even traumatised. After all, he had been threatened by talking wolves, witnessed an attack by living ivy, and the charred head of a German flyer had landed at his feet, half gnawed by sharp teeth. Instead, he was merely bewildered, and more than a little curious.

David's fingers and toes tingled. His nose began to run in the growing warmth, and he discarded the Woodsman's jacket. He wiped his nose on the sleeve of his dressing-gown and then felt a little ashamed. The dressing-gown, now looking decidedly sorry for itself, was the only item of outer clothing that he possessed, and it seemed unwise to add to its current state of disrepair in any way. Apart from the gown, he had one slipper, a pair of torn, muddy pyjama bottoms, and a pyjama shirt which, compared with the other items, was almost as good as new.

The window at which he stood had been blocked by internal

shutters behind the bars, with a narrow horizontal slit to allow those inside to see out. Through the slit he watched the corpses of wolves being dragged into the forest, some leaving trails of blood behind.

'They are growing ever bolder and more cunning, and that makes them harder to kill,' said the Woodsman. He had joined David at the window. 'A year ago they would not have risked such an attack upon me or any other under my protection, but now there are more of them than ever before, and their numbers are swelling with each passing day. Soon they may try to make good on their promise to take the kingdom.'

'The ivy attacked them,' said David. He still could not quite believe what he had seen.

'The forest, or this forest at least, has ways of protecting itself,' said the Woodsman. 'Those beasts are unnatural, a threat to the order of things. The forest wants no part of them. It is to do with the king, I think, and the fading of his powers. This world is coming apart, and it grows stranger every day. The Loups are the most dangerous creatures yet to have arisen, for they have the worst of man and beast fighting for supremacy within them.'

'Loups?' said David. 'Is that what you call those wolf things?'

'They are not wolves, although wolves run with them. Neither are they men, although they walk on two legs when it suits their purposes, and their leader decks himself in jewels and fine clothes. He calls himself Leroi, and he is as intelligent as he is ambitious, and as cunning as he is cruel. Now he would war with the king. I hear stories from travellers through these woods. They talk of great packs of wolves moving across the land, white wolves from the north and black wolves from the south, all heeding the call of their brothers, the greys, and their leaders, the Loups.'

And while David sat by the fire, the Woodsman told him a story.

The Woodsman's First Tale

Once upon a time there was a girl who lived on the outskirts of the forest. She was lively and bright, and wore a red cloak, for that way if she ever went astray she could easily be found, since a red cloak would always stand out against the trees and bushes. As the years went by, and she became more woman than girl, she grew more and more beautiful. Many men wanted her for their bride, but she turned them all down. None was good enough for her, for she was cleverer than every man she met and they presented no challenge to her.

Her grandmother lived in a cottage in the forest, and the girl would visit her often, bringing her baskets of bread and meat and staying with her for a time. While her grandmother slept, the girl in red would wander among the trees, tasting the wild berries and strange fruits of the woods. One day, as she walked in a dark grove, a wolf came. It was wary of her and tried to pass without being seen, but the girl's senses were too acute. She saw the wolf, and she looked into its eyes and fell in love with the strangeness of it. When it turned away, she tracked it, travelling deeper into the forest than she had ever gone before. The wolf tried to lose her in places where there were no trails to follow, no paths to be seen, but the girl was too quick for it, and mile after mile the chase continued. At last, the wolf grew weary of the pursuit, and it turned to face her. It bared its fangs and growled a warning, but she was not afraid.

'Lovely wolf,' she whispered. 'You have nothing to fear from me.'

She reached out her hand and placed it upon the wolf's head. She ran her fingers through its fur, and calmed it. And the wolf saw what beautiful eyes she had (all the better to see him with), and what gentle hands (all the better to stroke him with), and what soft, red lips (all the better to taste him with). The girl leaned forward, and she kissed the wolf. She cast off her red cloak and put her basket of flowers aside, and she lay with the animal. From their union came a creature that was more human than wolf. He was the first of the Loups, the one called Leroi, and more followed after him.

In time, other women came, lured by the girl in the red cloak. She would wander the forest paths, enticing those who passed her way with promises of ripe, juicy berries and spring water so pure that it could make skin look young again. Sometimes she travelled to the edge of a town or village, and there she would wait until a girl walked by and she would draw her into the woods with false cries for help.

But some went with her willingly, for there are other women who dream of lying with wolves.

None was ever seen again, because the Loups turned on those who had created them and fed upon them in the moonlight.

And that is how the Loups came into being.

When his tale was done, the Woodsman went to an oak chest in the corner by the bed and found a shirt that would fit David, as well as a pair of trousers that were just a little too long, and shoes that were just a little too loose, although the addition of an extra pair of coarse wool socks made them wearable. The shoes were leather and had clearly not been worn in a great many years. David wondered where they had come from, for they had obviously belonged to a child once, but when he tried to ask the Woodsman about them he just turned away and busied himself with laying out bread and cheese for them to eat.

While they ate, the Woodsman questioned David more closely about how he came to enter the forest, and about the world that he had left behind. There was so much to tell, but the Woodsman seemed less interested in talk of war and flying machines than he was in David and his family, and the story of his mother.

'You say that you heard her voice,' he said. 'Yet she is dead, so how can this be?'

'I don't know,' said David. 'But it was her. I know it was.'

The Woodsman looked doubtful. 'I have seen no woman pass through the woods for a long time. If she is here, she found another way into this world.'

In return, the Woodsman told David much about the place in which he now found himself. He spoke of the king, who had reigned for a very long time but had lost control of his kingdom as he grew old and tired and was now a virtual recluse in his castle to the east. He spoke more of the Loups and their desire to reign over others as men did, and of new castles that had appeared in distant parts of the kingdom, dark places of hidden evil.

And he spoke of a trickster, the one who had no true name and was unlike any other creature in the kingdom, for even the king feared him.

'Is he a crooked man?' asked David, suddenly. 'Does he wear a crooked hat?'

The Woodsman stopped chewing his bread. 'And how would you know that?' he said.

'I've seen him,' said David. 'He was in my bedroom.'

'That is him,' said the Woodsman. 'He steals children, and they are never seen again.'

And there was something so sad and yet so angry about the way the Woodsman spoke of the Crooked Man that David wondered if Leroi, the leader of the Loups, was wrong. Perhaps the Woodsman did have a family, once, but something very bad had happened and now he was entirely alone.

X

Of Tricksters and Trickery

David slept that night upon the Woodsman's bed. It smelled of dried berries and pine cones and the animal scent of the Woodsman's leathers and furs. The Woodsman dozed in a chair by the fire, his axe close to hand and his face cast in flickering shadows by the light of the dying flames.

It took David a long time to get to sleep, even though the Woodsman assured him that the cottage was secure. The slits in the windows had been covered up, and there was even a metal plate, pierced with small holes, set part of the way up the chimney to prevent the creatures of the forest from entering that way. The woods beyond were silent, but it was not the quiet of peace and rest. The Woodsman told David that the forest changed at night: half-formed creatures, beings from deep beneath the ground, colonised it once the dim light faded, and most of the nocturnal animals were dead or had learned to be even warier of predation than before.

The boy was aware of a strange mixture of feelings. There was fear, of course, and an aching regret that he had ever been foolish enough to leave the security of his own home and enter this new world. He wanted to return to the life he knew, however difficult it might be, but he also wanted to see a little more of this land, and he had not yet found an explanation for the sound of his mother's voice. Was this what happened to the dead? Did they travel into this land, perhaps on the way to another place? Was his mother trapped here? Could a mistake have been made? Maybe she wasn't meant to die, and now she was trying to hold on here in the hope that someone would find her and bring her back to those whom she loved. No, David could not return, not yet. The tree was marked and he would find his way home, once he had discovered the truth about his mother and the part this world now played in her existence.

He wondered if his father had missed him yet, and the thought made his eyes water. The impact of the German plane would have woken everyone, and the garden was probably already sealed off by the army or the A.R.P. David's absence would have been quickly noticed. They would be looking for him at this very moment. He felt a kind of satisfaction in the knowledge that, by his absence, he had made himself more important in his father's life. Now perhaps his dad would be worried more about him and less about work and codes and Rose and Georgie.

But what if they didn't miss him? What if life became easier for them now that he was gone? His father and Rose could start a new family, untroubled by the remnant of the old, except once a year, perhaps, when the anniversary of his disappearance came around. In time, though, even that would fade, and then he would be largely forgotten, remembered only in passing just as the memory of Rose's uncle, Jonathan Tulvey, had been resurrected only by David's own questions about him.

David tried to push such thoughts aside and closed his eyes. At last he fell asleep, and he dreamt of his father, and of Rose and his new half-brother, and of things that burrowed up from beneath the earth, waiting for the fears of others to give them shape.

And in the dark corners of his dreams a shadow capered, and it threw its crooked hat in the air with glee.

*   *   *

David woke to the sound of the Woodsman preparing food. They ate hard white bread at the little table by the far wall and drank strong black tea from crudely made mugs. Outside, only the faintest trace of light showed in the sky. David assumed that it was very early in the morning indeed, so early that the sun had not yet dawned, but the Woodsman said the sun had not been truly visible for a very long time and this was as much light as was ever seen in the world. It made David wonder if he had somehow travelled far to the north, to a place where night lasted for months and months in winter, but even in the Arctic north the long, dark winters were balanced by days of endless light in summer. No, this was no northern land. This was Elsewhere.

After they had eaten, David washed his face and hands in a bowl and tried to clean his teeth with his finger. When he had finished, he performed his little rituals of touching and counting, and it was only when he became aware of a silence in the room that he realised the Woodsman was watching him quietly from his chair.

'What are you doing?' asked the Woodsman.

It was the first time that the question had ever been posed to David, and he was stumped for a moment as he tried to provide a plausible excuse for his behaviour. In the end, he settled on the truth.

'They're rules,' he said simply. 'They're my routines. I started doing them to try to keep my mother from harm. I thought that they would help.'

'And did they?'

David shook his head.

'No, I don't think so. Or maybe they did, but just not enough. I suppose you think they're strange. I suppose you think *I'm* strange for doing them.'

He was afraid to look at the Woodsman, fearful of what he might see in the man's eyes. Instead he stared into the bowl and saw his reflection distort upon the water.

89

Eventually the Woodsman spoke. 'We all have our rituals,' he said softly. 'But they must have a purpose and provide an outcome that we can see and take some comfort from, or else they have no use at all. Without that, they are like the endless pacings of a caged animal. If they are not madness itself, then they are a prelude to it.'

The Woodsman stood and showed David his axe.

'See here,' he said, pointing with his finger at the blade. 'Every morning, I make certain that my axe is clean and keen. I look to my house and check that its windows and doors remain secure. I tend to my land, disposing of weeds and ensuring that the soil is watered. I walk through the forest, clearing those paths that need to be kept open. Where trees have been damaged, I do my best to repair what has been harmed. These are *my* rituals, and I enjoy doing them well.'

He laid a hand gently on David's shoulder, and David saw understanding in his face. 'Rules and routines are good, but they must give you satisfaction. Can you truly say you gain that from touching and counting?'

David shook his head. 'No,' he said, 'but I get scared when I don't do them. I'm afraid of what might happen.'

'Then find some that allow you to feel secure when they are done. You told me that you have a new brother: look to him each morning. Look to your father, and your stepmother. Tend to the flowers in the garden, or in the pots upon the window sill. Seek others who are weaker than you are, and try to give them comfort where you can. Let these be your routines, and the rules that govern your life.'

David nodded, but he turned his face from the Woodsman's to hide what might be read upon it. Perhaps the Woodsman was right, but David could not bring himself to do those things for Georgie and Rose. He would try to take on some other, easier duties, but to keep safe these intruders into his life was beyond him.

The Woodsman took David's old clothes – his torn dressing-gown, his dirty pyjamas, his single muddy slipper – and placed them in a rough sack. He slung the sack over his shoulder and unlocked the door.

'Where are we going?' said David.

'We're going to return you to your own land,' said the Woodsman.

'But the hole in the tree has disappeared.'

'Then we will try to make it appear again.'

'But I haven't found my mother,' said David.

The Woodsman looked at him sadly. 'Your mother is dead. You told me so yourself.'

'But I heard her! I heard her voice.'

'Perhaps, or something like it,' said the Woodsman. 'I don't pretend to know every secret of this land, but I can tell you that it is a dangerous place, and becoming more so with every day that passes. You must go back. The Loup Leroi was right about one thing: I can't protect you. I can barely protect myself. Now come: this is a good time to travel, for the night beasts are in their deepest sleep, and the worst of the daylight ones are not yet awake.'

So David, perceiving that he had little choice in the matter, followed the Woodsman from the cottage and into the forest. Time and again the Woodsman would stop and listen, his hand raised as a signal to David that he should remain silent.

'Where are the Loups and the wolves?' David asked eventually, after they had walked for perhaps an hour. The only signs of life that he had seen were birds and insects.

'Not far away, I fear,' replied the Woodsman. 'They will scavenge for food in other parts of the forest where they are less at risk of attack, and in time they will try once again to steal you away. That is why you must leave here before they return.'

David shivered at the thought of Leroi and his pack descending upon him, their jaws and claws tearing at his flesh.

He was beginning to understand the cost that might have to be paid in searching this place for his mother, but it seemed as if the decision to return home had already been made for him, at least for now. He could always come back here again, if he chose. After all, the sunken garden still remained, assuming the German plane had not entirely destroyed it when it crashed.

They came to the glade of enormous trees through which he had first entered the Woodsman's world. As they reached it, the Woodsman stopped so suddenly that David almost ran into him. Cautiously, he peered around the man's back in order to glimpse what it was that had caused him to stop.

'Oh no,' gasped David.

Every tree, as far as the eye could see, was marked with string, and every string, David's nose told him, was daubed with the same, foul-smelling substance that the Woodsman had used to keep the animals from gnawing at it. There was no way of telling which tree was the one that marked the doorway from David's world to this one. He walked on a little, trying to find the hollow from which he had emerged, but every tree was similar, every bark smooth. It seemed even the hollows and gnarls that made each one distinctive had been filled in or altered, and the little path that once wound through the forest was now entirely gone, so the Woodsman had no bearings to follow. Even the wreckage of the German bomber was nowhere to be seen, and the furrow that it had carved through the earth had been filled in. It should have taken hundreds of hours, and the work of many, many hands, to achieve such an end, thought David. How could it have been done in a single night, and without leaving even one footprint upon the ground?

'Who would so such a thing?' he asked.

'A trickster,' said the Woodsman. 'A crooked man in a crooked hat.'

'But why?' said David. 'Why didn't he just take away the string that you had tied. Wouldn't that have worked just as well?'

The Woodsman thought for a moment before answering. 'Yes,' he said, 'but it wouldn't have been so amusing to him, and it wouldn't have made such a good story.'

'A story?' asked David. 'Whatever do you mean?'

'You're part of a story,' said the Woodsman. 'He likes to create stories. He likes to store up tales to tell. This will make a very good story.'

'But how will I get home?' asked David. Now that his means of returning to his own world was gone he suddenly wanted very much to be there, whereas when it had seemed that the

Woodsman was trying to force him to return against his will, David had wanted nothing more than to stay in the new land and look for his mother. It was all very peculiar.

'He doesn't want you to get home,' said the Woodsman.

'I've never done anything to him,' said David. 'Why is he trying to keep me here? Why is he being so mean?'

The Woodsman shook his head. 'I don't know,' he said.

'Then who does?' said David. He almost shouted in frustration. He was starting to wish there was someone around who knew a little more than the Woodsman. The Woodsman was fine for decapitating wolves and giving unwanted advice, but he didn't seem to be keeping up with developments in the kingdom.

'The king,' said the Woodsman at last. 'The king might know.'

'But I thought you told me that he wasn't in control any more, that no one had seen him in a long time.'

'That doesn't mean he isn't aware of what's happening,' said the Woodsman. 'They say that the king has a book, a Book of Lost Things. It is his most prized possession. He keeps it hidden in the throne room of his palace, and no one is permitted to look upon it but him. I have heard it said that it contains in its pages all of the king's knowledge, and that he turns to it in times of trouble or doubt to give him guidance. Perhaps there is an answer within it to the question of how to get you home.'

David tried to read the expression on the Woodsman's face. He wasn't sure why, but he had a strong feeling that the Woodsman wasn't telling him the entire truth about the king. Before he could question him further, the Woodsman tossed the sack containing David's old clothes into a copse of bushes and started to walk back in the direction from which they had come.

'It will be one fewer thing to carry on our journey,' he said. 'We have a long way to go.'

With a last, longing look at the forest of anonymous trees, David turned and followed the Woodsman back to the cottage.

When they were gone, and all was quiet, a figure emerged from the beneath the spreading roots of a great and ancient tree. Its back was hunched, its fingers were twisted, and it wore a crooked hat upon its head. It moved quickly through the undergrowth until it came to a thicket dotted with swollen, frost-sweetened berries, but it ignored the fruits in favour of the rough, dirty sack that lay amid the leaves. It reached inside, removed the top of David's pyjamas, and held the clothing to its face, sniffing deeply.

'Boy lost,' it whispered to itself, 'and child lost to come.'

And with that it grabbed the sack and was swallowed up by the shadows of the forest.

XI

Of the Children Lost in the Forest and What Befell Them

David and the Woodsman returned to the cottage without incident. There they packed food into two leather bags and filled a pair of tin canteens from the stream that ran behind the house. David saw the Woodsman kneel by the water's edge and examine some marks on the damp ground, but he said nothing to David about them. David glanced at them in passing and thought that they looked like the tracks left by a big dog, or a wolf. There was a little water at the bottom of each, so David knew that they were recent.

The Woodsman armed himself with his axe, a bow and a quiver of arrows, and a long knife. Finally, he took a short-bladed sword from a storage chest. After only the slightest pause to blow some of the dust from it, he gave the sword to David, and a leather belt upon which to wear it. David had never held a real sword before, and his knowledge of swordsmanship did not extend much further than playing pirates with wooden sticks, but having the sword at his side made him feel stronger and braver.

The Woodsman locked the cottage, then laid his hand flat upon the door and lowered his head, as though praying. He looked sad and David wondered if, for some reason, the Woodsman thought that he might not see his home again. Then they moved into the forest, heading northeast, and kept up a steady pace while the sickly luminescence that passed for daylight lit their way. After a few hours, David grew very tired. The Woodsman allowed him to rest, but only for a little while.

'We must be clear of the woods before nightfall,' he told David, and the boy did not have to ask him why. Already he feared to hear the silence of the woods shattered by the howling of wolves and Loups.

As they walked, David had a chance to examine his surroundings. He was unable to name any of the trees that he saw, although aspects of some were familiar to him. A tree that looked like an old oak had pine cones dangling beneath its evergreen leaves. Another was the size and shape of a large Christmas tree, the bases of its silver leaves dotted with clusters of red berries. Most of the trees, though, were bare. Occasionally, David would catch sight of some of the childlike flowers, their eyes wide and curious, although at the first sign of the approaching Woodsman and boy they would draw their leaves protectively around themselves and quake gently until the threat had passed.

'What are those flowers called?' he asked.

'They have no name,' said the Woodsman. 'Sometimes, children stray from the path and become lost in the forest, and they are never seen again. They die there, consumed by beasts or slain by evil men, and their blood soaks into the ground. In time, one of these flowers will spring up, often far from where the child breathed its last. They cluster together, just like frightened children might. They are the forest's way of remembering them, I think. The forest feels the loss of a child.'

David had learned that the Woodsman generally did not speak unless spoken to first, so it was left to him to ask questions, which the Woodsman would answer as best he could. He tried to give David some sense of the geography of this place: the king's castle lay many miles to the east, and the area in between was sparsely populated, with only the occasional settlement to disturb the landscape. A deep chasm separated the Woodsman's forest from the territories further to the east, and they would have to cross it to continue their journey to the king's castle. To the south was a great, black sea, but few ever ventured far upon it. It was the domain of sea beasts, dragons of the waters, and constantly wracked by storms and huge waves. North and west lay ranges of mountains, but they were impassable for most of the year, their peaks topped with snow.

While they walked, the Woodsman spoke more to David of the Loups.

'In the old days, before the coming of the Loups, wolves were predictable creatures,' he explained. 'Each pack, rarely numbering more than fifteen or twenty, had a territory where it would live and hunt and breed. Then the Loups began to appear, and everything changed. The packs began to grow; allegiances were formed; territories were extended, or ceased to have meaning at all; and cruelty raised its head. In the past, perhaps half of all wolf pups died. They needed more food than their parents, for their size, and if food was scarce then they starved. Sometimes they were killed by their own parents, but only if they showed signs of disease or madness. For the most part, wolves were fine guardians, sharing their kills with the young, giving them care and affection.

'But the Loups brought a new way of dealing with the young: only the strongest are now fed, never more than two or three to a litter, and sometimes not even that. The weak are eaten. In that way, the pack itself remains strong, but it has altered their nature. Now they turn upon one another, and there is no loyalty between them. Only the rule of the Loups keeps them under control. Without the Loups, they would be as they once were, I think.'

The Woodsman told David how to tell the females from the males. The females had narrower muzzles and foreheads. Their necks and shoulders were thinner, their legs shorter, yet they were faster when young than males of a similar age and for that reason made better hunters and deadlier enemies. In normal wolf packs the females were often the leaders, but once again the Loups had usurped this natural order of things. There were females among them, but it was Leroi and his lieutenants who made the important decisions. Perhaps that was one of their weaknesses, suggested the Woodsman. Their arrogance had led them to turn their backs on thousands of years of female instinct. Now they were driven only by the desire for power.

'Wolves will not give up on prey,' said the Woodsman, 'not unless they are exhausted. They can run for ten or fifteen miles at speeds far faster than a man can travel, and trot for five miles more before they have to rest. The Loups have slowed them somewhat, for they mostly choose to walk on two legs and are no longer as fleet as they once were, but on foot we are still no match for them. We must hope that, when we reach our destination tonight, horses are to be found. There is a man who deals in them, and I have money enough to buy us a mount.'

They followed no trails. Instead, they relied upon the Woodsman's knowledge of the forest, although as they travelled further and further from his home he stopped more frequently, examining growths of moss and the shapes the wind had carved from the trees in order to satisfy himself that they had not strayed. In all that time they passed only one other dwelling, and that lay in brown ruins. It appeared to David to have melted rather than fallen into disrepair, and only its stone chimney remained standing, blackened but intact. He could see where molten droplets had cooled and hardened upon the walls, and the buckled spaces where the windows had collapsed in upon themselves. The route they were taking brought him close enough to touch the structure, and now it was clear that there were chunks of a lighter substance embedded in the walls. He rubbed his hand upon the door frame, then chipped away at it with a nail. He recognised the texture, and the faint smell that arose.

'It's chocolate,' he exclaimed. 'And gingerbread.'

He broke off a large piece and was about to taste it when the Woodsman knocked it from his hands.

'No,' he said. 'It may look and smell sweet, but it hides its own poison yet.'

And he told David another story.

The Woodsman's Second Tale

Once upon a time, there were two children, a boy and a girl. Their father died and their mother married again, but their step-father was an evil man. He hated the children and resented their presence in his home. He came to despise them even more when the crops failed and famine came, for they ate valuable food, food that he would rather have kept for himself. He begrudged them every meagre bite that he was forced to give them, and as his own hunger grew he began to suggest to his wife that they might eat the children and thereby save themselves from death, since she could always give birth to more children when times improved. His wife was horrified, and she feared what her new husband might do to her offspring when her back was turned. Yet she realised that she could no longer afford to feed them herself, so she took them deep, deep into the forest, and there she abandoned them to fend for themselves.

The children were very frightened, and cried themselves to sleep that first night, but in time they grew to understand the forest. The girl was wiser and stronger than her brother, and it was she who learned to trap small animals and birds, and to steal eggs from nests. The boy preferred to wander or to daydream, waiting for his sister to provide whatever she could catch to feed them both. He missed his mother and wanted to return to her. Some days he did nothing but cry from dawn until dusk. He wanted his old life back and made no effort to embrace the new.

One day, he did not return when his sister called his name. She went in search of him, leaving a trail of blossoms behind so that she would be able to find her way back to their small supply of food, until she came to the edge of a clearing and there she saw the most extraordinary house. Its walls were made of chocolate and gingerbread. Its roof was slated with slabs of toffee, and the glass in its windows was formed from clear sugar. Embedded in its walls were almonds and fudge and candied fruits. Everything about it spoke of sweetness and indulgence. Her brother was picking nuts from the walls when she found him, and his mouth was dark with chocolate.

'Don't worry, there's nobody home,' he said. 'Try it. It's delicious.'

He held out a piece of chocolate to her, but she did not take it at first. Her brother's eyelids were half closed, so overcome was he by the wonderful taste of the house. His sister tried to open the door, but it was locked. She peered through the glass, but the curtains were drawn and she could not see inside. She did not want to eat, for something about the house made her uneasy, but the smell of the chocolate was too much for her and she allowed herself to nibble on a piece. It tasted even better than she had imagined and her stomach cried out for more. So she joined her brother and together they ate and ate until they had consumed so much that, in time, they fell into a deep sleep.

When they awoke, they were no longer lying on the grass beneath the trees of the forest. Instead, they were inside the house, trapped in a cage that hung from the ceiling. A woman was fuelling an oven with logs. She was old and foul-smelling. Piles of bones lay stacked on the floor by her feet, the remains of the other children who had fallen prey to her.

'Fresh meat!' she whispered to herself. 'Fresh meat for old Gammer's oven!'

The little boy began to cry, but his sister hushed him. The woman approached and peered at them through the bars of the cage. Her face was covered with black warts, and her teeth were worn and crooked like old gravestones.

'Now which of you will be first?' she asked.

The boy tried to hide his face, as though by doing so he might avoid the attentions of the old woman. But his sister was braver.

'Take me,' she said. 'I am plumper than my brother, and will make a better roast for you. While you eat me you can fatten him up, so that he will feed you for longer when you cook him.'

The old woman cackled with joy.

'Clever girl,' she cried. 'Although not so clever as to avoid Gammer's plate.'

She opened the cage and reached in, grabbing the girl by the scruff of the neck and dragging her out. Then she locked the cage once again and brought the girl to the oven. It was not yet hot, but it soon would be.

'I will never fit in there,' said the girl. 'It's too small.'

'Nonsense,' said the old woman. 'I've put bigger than you in there, and they've cooked just fine.'

The girl looked doubtful.

'But I have long limbs, and fat upon them. No, I will never manage to get into that oven. And if you do manage to squeeze me in, you'll never get me out again.'

The old woman took the girl by the shoulders and shook her.

'I was wrong about you,' she said. 'You're an ignorant, foolish girl. Look, I'll show you how big this oven is.'

She climbed up and stuck her head and shoulders into the mouth of the oven.

'See?' she said, and her voice echoed within. 'There's room to spare for me, let alone a little girl.'

And while the old woman's back was turned, the little girl ran at her and with a great push she shoved her into the oven and slammed the door closed. The old woman tried to kick it open again but the girl was too sharp for her, slamming the bolt on it (for the old woman did not want a child to break free once the *roasting had begun) and leaving her trapped inside. Then she fed more logs into the fire and slowly the old woman began to cook, all the time screaming and wailing and threatening the girl with the most awful of tortures. So hot was the oven that the fats of the old woman's body began to melt, creating a stench so terrible that the little girl felt ill. Still the old woman fought, even as her skin parted from her flesh, and her flesh from her bones, until at last she died. Then the little girl drew wood from the fire and scattered burning logs around the cottage. She led her brother away by the hand as the house melted behind them, leaving only the chimney standing tall, and they never went back there again.*

In the months that followed, the girl grew happier in the forest. She built a shelter, and over time the shelter became a little house. She learned to fend for herself, and as the days went by she thought less and less of her old life. But her brother was never content and yearned always to be back with his mother. After a year and a day, he left his sister and returned to his old home, but by then his mother and his stepfather were long gone and no one could tell him where they were. He came back to the forest, but not to his sister, for he was jealous and resentful of her. Instead, he found a path in the woods that was well tended and cleared of roots and briars, the bushes beside it heavy with juicy berries. He followed it, eating some of the berries as he went, never noticing that the path behind him was disappearing with every step that he took.

And after a time he came to a clearing, and in the clearing was a pretty little house, with ivy on the walls and flowers by the door and a trail of smoke rising from its chimney. He smelled bread baking, and a cake lay cooling on the windowsill. A woman appeared at the door, bright and merry as his mother had once been. She waved to him, inviting him to draw nearer, and he did.

'Come in, come in,' she said. 'You look tired, and berries are not enough to fill a growing boy. I have food roasting over the

fire, and a soft place for you to rest. Stay as long as you wish, for I have no children, and have long wanted a son to call my own.'

The boy cast the berries aside as the path behind him vanished for ever, and he followed the woman into the house, where a great cauldron bubbled on the fire, and a sharp knife lay waiting on the butcher's block.

And he was never seen again.

XII

Of Bridges and Riddles, and the Many Unappealing Characteristics of Trolls

The light was changing as the Woodsman's story ended. He looked up at the sky, as if in hope that darkness might be held back for a little longer, and suddenly he stopped walking. David followed his gaze. Above their heads, just at the level of the forest's crown, David saw a black shape circling and thought that he heard a distant cawing.

'Damnation,' hissed the Woodsman.

'What is it?' asked David.

'A raven.'

The Woodsman removed his bow from his back and nocked an arrow to its string. He knelt, sighted, and released the arrow. His aim was true. The raven jerked in the air as the arrow pierced its body, then tumbled to the ground not far from where David stood. It was dead, the tip of the arrow red with its blood.

'Foul bird,' said the Woodsman, as he lifted the corpse and pulled the arrow through its body.

'Why did you kill it?' asked David.

'The raven and the wolf hunt together. This one was leading the pack to us. They would have fed our eyes to it as its reward.'

He looked back in the direction they had come.

'They will have to rely on scent alone now, but they are closing on us, make no mistake. We must hurry.'

They continued on their way, moving at a slight trot, as though they themselves were tired wolves at the end of a hunt, until they reached the edge of the forest and emerged onto a high plateau. Ahead of them lay a great chasm, hundreds of feet deep and a quarter of a mile wide. A river, thin as a length of silver thread, wound through it, and David heard the cries of what might have been birds echoing from the canyon's walls. Carefully, he peered over the edge of the crevasse in the hope of getting a better look at what was making the noise. He glimpsed a shape, much larger than any bird that he had ever seen, gliding through the air, supported by the updraughts from the canyon. It had bare, almost human legs, although its toes were strangely elongated and curved like a bird's talons. Its arms were stretched wide and from them hung the great folds of skin that served as its wings. Its long white hair flowed in the wind, and as David listened he heard it start to sing. The creature's voice was very high and very beautiful, and its words were clear to him:

> What falls is food,
> What drops will die,
> Where lives the Brood,
> Birds fear to fly.

Its song was taken up and echoed by other voices, and David could make out many more of the creatures moving through the canyon. The one nearest to him performed a loop in the air, at once both graceful and strangely menacing, and David caught sight of its naked body. He looked away immediately, ashamed and embarrassed.

It had a female form: old, and with scales instead of skin, yet still a woman's for all that. He risked another look and saw the creature descending now in decreasing circles, until suddenly its wings folded in, streamlining its form, and it fell rapidly, its clawed feet extended as it seemed to head directly for the canyon wall. It struck the stone and David saw something struggle in its claws: it was a little brown mammal of some kind, scarcely bigger than a squirrel. Its paws flailed at the air as it was plucked from the rocks. Its captor changed direction and headed for an outcrop beneath David in order to feed, shrieking in triumph. Some of its rivals, alerted by its cries, approached in the hope of stealing its meal, but it struck at the air with its wings in warning and they drifted away. David had an opportunity to examine its features as it hovered: it resembled a human, but was longer and thinner, with a lipless mouth that left its sharp teeth permanently exposed. Now those teeth tore into its prey, ripping great chunks of bloody fur from its body as it fed.

'The Brood,' said the Woodsman from nearby. 'Harpies. Another new evil that blights this part of the kingdom.'

'Harpies,' said David.

'You've seen such creatures before?' asked the Woodsman.

'No,' said David. 'Not really.'

But I've read about them. I've seen them in my book of Greek myths. For some reason, I don't think they belong in this story, yet here they are . . .

David felt ill. He moved away from the edge of the canyon, which was so deep that it was giving him vertigo.

'How do we get across?' he asked.

'There is a bridge about a half-mile downriver,' said the Woodsman. 'We'll make it before the light fades.'

He led David along the canyon, keeping close to the edge of the forest so that there was no danger of them losing their footing and falling into that awful abyss where the Brood waited. David could hear the beating of their wings and, on more than one occasion, he thought he saw one of the creatures briefly ascend above the rim of the canyon and regard them balefully.

'Don't be afraid,' said the Woodsman. 'They are cowardly things. Were you to fall, they would pluck you from the air and tear you apart as they fought over you, but they would not dare to attack you on the ground.'

David nodded, but he did not feel reassured. In this land, it seemed that hunger inevitably overwhelmed cowardice, and the harpies of the Brood, as thin and emaciated as the wolves, looked very hungry indeed.

After they had walked for a little while, their footsteps echoed by the beating of the harpies' wings, they saw a pair of bridges spanning the gorge. The bridges were identical. They were made from rope, with uneven slats of wood for the base, and they did not look terribly safe to David. The Woodsman stared at them in puzzlement.

'Two bridges,' he said. 'There was only ever one bridge at this spot.'

'Well,' said David, matter-of-factly, 'now there are two.' It didn't seem like such a terrible imposition to have a choice of two ways to cross. Perhaps this was a busy place. After all, there didn't seem to be any other way to get across the chasm, unless you were able to fly and were prepared to take your chances with the harpies.

He heard flies buzzing nearby and followed the Woodsman to a small clearing just out of sight of the chasm. The remains of a cottage and some stables stood there, but it was clear that the property was deserted. Outside one of the stables lay the remains of a horse, most of the meat already picked from its bones. David watched as the Woodsman peered into the stables, then looked through the open doorway of the house itself. With his head lowered, he walked back to David.

'The horse dealer is gone,' he said. 'It looks as if he fled with whatever horses survived.'

'The wolves?' asked David.

'No, something else did this.'

They returned to the chasm. One of the harpies hung in the air nearby, watching them, her wings beating a fast cadence to keep her in place. She stayed in that position for just an instant too long, for suddenly her body jerked and the barbed silver tip of a harpoon shot through her chest, a length of rope anchoring the shaft to a point lower down on the canyon wall. The harpy grasped the harpoon, as if she could somehow wrest her body from it and escape, but then the beating of her wings began to fail and she plummeted, twisting and turning until the rope reached the end of its length and she was brought up short, her body striking against the rock with a dull, thudding sound. From the edge of the chasm, David and the Woodsman watched the dead harpy's body being hauled up towards a hollow in the wall, the barbs of the harpoon preventing the corpse from sliding off. Finally, the body reached the entrance to the cave and was pulled inside.

'Ugh,' said David.

'Trolls,' said the Woodsman. 'That explains the second bridge.'

He approached the twin structures. Between them was a slab of stone into which words had been crudely, if laboriously, carved.

> One lies in truth,
> One's truth is lies.
> One path is death,
> One path is life.
> One question asked,
> The path to guide.

'It's a riddle,' said David.

'But what does it mean?' asked the Woodsman.

The answer quickly became apparent. David had never seen a troll before, although he had always been fascinated by their presence in stories. In his mind, they existed as shadowy figures who lived beneath bridges, testing travellers in the hope of eating them when they failed. The figures that climbed over the lip of the canyon, flaming torches in their hands, were not quite what he had expected. They were smaller than the Woodsman, but very broad, and their skin was similar to that of an elephant, tough and wrinkled. Raised plates of bone, like those on the backs of some dinosaurs, ran along their spines, but their faces were those of apes; very ugly apes, admittedly, and ones that seemed to be suffering from severe acne, but apes nonetheless. Each troll took up a position in front of one of the bridges and smiled unpleasantly. They had small red eyes that glowed sinisterly in the light of the torches.

'Two bridges, and two paths,' said David. He was thinking aloud, but he caught himself before he gave anything away to the two trolls and resolved to keep his thoughts to himself until he had come to some conclusion. The trolls already had all the advantages. He didn't want to give them any more.

The riddle clearly meant that one bridge was unsafe, and to take it would lead to death at the hands of either the harpies or the trolls themselves, or, assuming both parties failed to act quickly enough, by falling a very long distance and landing hard on the rocks below. Actually, David thought both bridges looked pretty ramshackle, but he had to assume that the riddle had some truth to it. Otherwise, well, there was hardly any point in having a riddle at all.

One lies in truth, one's truth is lies. David knew that one. He'd encountered it somewhere before, probably in a story. Oh, he had it! One could tell only lies, and the other could tell only the truth. So you could ask one troll which bridge to follow, but he – or she, as David wasn't entirely sure if the trolls were male or female – might not be telling the truth. There was a solution to it as well, except that David couldn't remember it. What was it?

The light faded entirely at last, and a great howling arose from the forest. It sounded very close.

'We have to cross,' said the Woodsman. 'The wolves have found our trail.'

'We can't cross until we've chosen a bridge,' explained David. 'I don't think those trolls will let us pass unless we do, and if we try to force our way through and choose the wrong one—'

'Then we won't have to worry about the wolves,' the Woodsman said, finishing the sentence for him.

'There's a solution,' said David. 'I know there is. I just have to recall how it goes.'

They heard a thrashing in the woods. The wolves were drawing ever nearer.

'One question,' muttered David.

The Woodsman hefted his axe in his right hand and with his

left drew his knife. He was facing the line of trees, ready to take on whatever emerged from the woods.

'Got it!' said David. 'I think,' he added, softly.

He approached the troll on the left. It was slightly taller than the other, and smelled slightly better, which wasn't saying much.

David took a deep breath.

'If I asked the other troll to point to the right bridge, which bridge would it choose?' he asked.

There was silence. The troll knitted its brow, causing some of the sores upon its face to ooze unpleasantly. David didn't know how recently the bridge had been constructed, or how many other travellers had passed this way, but he got the feeling the troll had never been asked that question before. Finally, the troll seemed to give up trying to understand David's logic and pointed to its left.

'It's the one on the right,' said David to the Woodsman.

'How can you be sure?' he asked.

'Because if the troll I asked is the liar, then the other troll is the truth-teller. The truth-teller would point to the correct bridge, but the liar would lie about it, so if the truthful one would have pointed to the bridge on the right, then the liar would lie about it and tell me that it was the one on the left.

'But if the troll I asked has to tell the truth, then the other is the liar, and he would point to the wrong bridge. Either way, the one on the left is the false bridge.'

Despite the approach of the wolves, the presence of the bewildered trolls, and the shrieking of the harpies, David couldn't help but grin with pleasure. He'd remembered the riddle and recalled the solution. It was like the Woodsman had said: someone was trying to create a story and David was a part of it, but the story was itself made up of other stories. David had read about trolls and harpies, and lots of old stories had woodsmen. Even talking animals, like the wolves, cropped up in them.

'Come on,' said David to the Woodsman. He approached the bridge on the right and the troll standing before it stepped to one side to allow David to pass. David put a foot on the first of the boards and held on tight to the ropes. Now that his life depended on his choice, he felt less certain of himself, and the sight of the harpies gliding just beneath his feet made him even more anxious. Still, he had chosen now and there was no going back. He took a second step, then another, always keeping a grip on the rope supports and trying not to look down. He was making good progress when he realised that the Woodsman was not following. David stopped on the bridge and looked back.

The forest was alive with wolf eyes. David could see them shining in the torchlight. Now they were moving, emerging from the shadows, advancing slowly on the Woodsman, the more primitive ones leading, the others, the Loups, staying back, waiting for their lesser brothers and sisters to overpower the armed man before they approached. The trolls had vanished, clearly realising that there was little point in discussing riddles with wild animals.

'No!' cried David. 'Come on! You can make it.'

But the Woodsman did not move. Instead, he called out to David.

'Go now, and go quickly. I will hold them off for as long as I can. When you get to the other side, cut the rope. Do you hear me? Cut the rope!'

David shook his head. 'No,' he repeated. He was crying. 'You have to come with me. I need you to come with me.'

And then, almost as one, the wolves pounced.

'Run!' shouted the Woodsman, as his axe swung and his knife flashed. David saw a fine spray of blood fountain into the air as the first wolf died, and then they were all around the Woodsman, snapping and biting, some trying to find a way past him to pursue the boy. With one last look over his shoulder,

David ran. He was still not quite halfway across the bridge and it swung sickeningly with each movement that he made. The pounding of his feet echoed through the gorge. Soon, it was joined by the sound of paws on wood. David looked to his left and saw that three of his pursuers had taken the other bridge in the hope of cutting him off on the far side, for they could not find a way around the Woodsman, who was guarding the first bridge. The wolves were gaining ground quickly. One of them, the Loup bringing up the rear, wore the remains of a white dress, and droplets of gold dangled from its ears. Saliva dripped from its jaws as it ran, and it licked at it with its tongue.

'Run,' it said, in a voice that was almost girlish, 'for all the good that it will do you.' It snapped at the air. 'You'll taste just as good on the other side.'

David's arms ached from holding on to the ropes, and the swaying of the bridge made him feel dizzy. The wolves were already almost level with him. He would never make it to the other side before they did.

And then some of the slats on the false bridge collapsed, and the lead wolf plunged through the hole. David heard the whistling of a harpoon, and the wolf was speared through its belly and yanked towards the trolls in the canyon wall.

The other wolf stopped in its tracks so suddenly that the female Loup almost knocked it over from behind. A great hole, six or seven feet wide at least, now gaped where their brother had broken through. More harpoons shot across the air: the trolls were no longer prepared to wait for their prey to fall. The wolves had set foot on the wrong bridge and in doing so had doomed themselves. Another barbed tip found its mark, and the second wolf was pulled through the gaps in the ropes, writhing in torment upon the steel as it died. Now only the Loup remained. It tensed its body and leaped across the hole in the bridge, landing safely on the other side. It slid for a moment, then recovered itself before it rose on its hind legs and, now out of range of the trolls' weapons, howled in triumph, even as a shadow descended upon it.

The harpy was larger than any of the others that David had seen, taller and stronger and more ancient than the rest. It hit the Loup with enough force to send it toppling over the support ropes, and only the firm grasp of the harpy's claws, which had buried themselves deep in the Loup's flesh as they struck, prevented it from tumbling to its death. The Loup's paws flailed and its jaws snapped at empty space as it tried to bite the harpy, but the fight was already lost. As David watched in horror, a second harpy joined the first, sinking its claws into the Loup's neck. The two monstrous females pulled in opposite directions, their wings beating rapidly, and the Loup was torn in two.

The Woodsman was still trying to hold back the pack, but he was fighting a losing battle. David saw him slash and cut again and again at what seemed like a moving wall of fur and fangs, until finally he fell, and the wolves descended upon him.

'No!' cried David, and although he was overcome by rage and sadness, he somehow found it in himself to begin running again, even as he saw two Loups leap over the Woodsman's body to lead a pair of wolves onto the bridge. He could hear their paws rattling the struts, and the weight of their bodies made the bridge sway. David reached the far side of the chasm, drew his sword, and faced the approaching animals. They were now more than halfway across, and closing fast. The four support ropes of the bridge were fixed to a pair of thick poles set deep into the stone beneath David's feet. David took his sword and swung at the first of the ropes, cutting partly through it. He struck again, and the rope shot away, causing the bridge to topple suddenly to the right and sending the two wolves into the canyon. David heard the harpies cry with delight, and the beating of their wings grew louder.

There were still two Loups on the bridge, and they had somehow managed to hook their limber paws around the remaining support rope. Now, standing on their two hind legs, and keeping to the ropes on the left, they were continuing to close on David. He brought his sword down on the second rope, and heard the Loups whine in alarm. The bridge shook, and strands unravelled beneath his blade. He laid the sword edge on the rope, looked to the Loups, then raised his arms and slashed with all the force that he could muster. The rope broke, and now there was nothing for the Loups to hold on to and only the wooden slats of the bridge beneath their feet. With loud yelps, they fell.

David stared over at the far side of the chasm. The Woodsman was gone. There was a trail of blood on the ground where he had been dragged into the forest by the wolves. Only their leader, the dandy Leroi, remained. He stood upright in his red trousers and his white shirt, staring at David with undisguised hatred. He raised his head and howled for the lost members of his pack, but he did not leave. Instead, he continued to watch David until the boy at last left the bridge and disappeared over a small rise, crying softly for the Woodsman who had saved his life.

XIII

Of Dwarfs and Their Sometimes Irascible Nature

David was on a raised white road, paved with gravel and stones. It was not straight but wound according to the obstacles it encountered: a small stream here, a rocky outcrop there. A ditch ran along each side, and from there an area of weed and grass led to the tree line. The trees were smaller and more scattered than in the forest he had recently left, and he could see the outlines of small hills rising beyond them. He was suddenly very tired. Now that the chase was over, all of his energy was gone. He wanted very badly just to fall asleep, but he was afraid to do so out in the open, or to remain too close to the chasm. He needed to find shelter. The wolves would not forgive him for what had happened at the bridges. They would find another way to cross, and then they would seek out his trail once again. Instinctively, he raised his eyes to the sky, but he could see no birds following his path from above, no traitorous ravens waiting to reveal his presence to the hunters at his back.

To give himself some energy, he ate a little bread from his bag and drank deeply from his water. It made him feel better for a moment, but the sight of the bag and the carefully packed food reminded him of the Woodsman. His eyes grew teary again, but he refused to allow himself the luxury of crying. He got to his feet, put his pack on his shoulder, and almost fell over a dwarf who had just climbed up on the road from the low ditch on the left.

'Mind where you're going,' said the dwarf. He was about three feet tall and wore a blue tunic, black trousers, and black boots that came up to his knees. There was a long blue hat on his head, at the end of which was a little bell that no longer made any noise. His face and hands were grubby with dirt and he carried a pickaxe over one shoulder. His nose was quite red, and he had a short white beard. The beard appeared to have pieces of food trapped in it.

'Sorry,' said David.

'So you should be.'

'I didn't see you.'

'Oh, and what's that supposed to mean?' said the dwarf. He waved his pick threateningly. 'Are you sizeist? Are you saying I'm *small*?'

'Well, you are small,' said David. 'Not that there's anything wrong with that,' he added hurriedly. 'I'm small too, compared to some people.'

But the dwarf was no longer listening and had instead commenced shouting at a column of squat figures heading for the road.

'Oy, Comrades!' said the dwarf. 'Bloke over here says I'm small.'

'Bloody cheek!' said a voice.

'Hold him till we get there, Comrade,' said another, who then appeared to reconsider. 'Hang on, how big is he?'

The dwarf examined David. 'Not very big,' he said. 'Dwarf and a half. Dwarf and two-thirds at most.'

'Right, we'll 'ave him,' came the reply.

Suddenly, it seemed as if David was surrounded by short, unhappy men muttering about 'rights' and 'liberties' and having enough of 'this sort of thing'. They were all filthy and they all wore hats with broken bells. One of them kicked David in the shin.

'Ow!' said David. 'That hurt.'

'Now you know how our feelings, er, feel,' said the first dwarf.

A small, grubby hand tugged at David's pack. Another tried to steal his sword. A third appeared to be poking him in his soft places just for the fun of it.

'That's enough!' shouted David. 'Stop it!'

He swung his pack wildly and was pleased to feel it connect with a pair of dwarfs, who immediately fell into the ditch and rolled around in a theatrical manner for some time.

'What did you do that for?' asked the first dwarf. He looked quite shocked.

'You were kicking me.'

'Was not.'

'Were so too. And someone tried to steal my bag.'

'Did not.'

'Oh, this is just ridiculous,' said David. 'You did and you know it.'

The dwarf lowered his head and kicked idly at the road, sending a little puff of white dust into the air.

'Oh, all right then,' it said. 'Maybe I did. Sorry.'

'That's all right,' said David.

He reached down and helped the dwarfs raise their two fellows from the ditch. Nobody was badly hurt. In fact, now that it was all over, the dwarfs seemed rather to have enjoyed the whole encounter.

'Reminder of the Great Struggle, that was,' said one. 'Right, Comrade?'

'Absolutely, Comrade,' replied another. 'The workers must resist oppression at every turn.'

'Um, but I wasn't really oppressing you,' David said.

'But you could have, if you'd wanted to,' said the first dwarf. 'Right?'

He looked up at David quite pathetically. David could tell that he really, really would have liked someone to try unsuccessfully to oppress him.

'Well, if you say so,' said David, just to make the dwarf happy.

'Hurrah!' shouted the dwarf. 'We have resisted the threat of oppression. The workers will not be shackled!'

'Hurrah!' shouted the other dwarfs in unison. 'We have nothing to lose but our chains.'

'But you don't have any chains,' said David.

'They're *metaphorical* chains,' explained the first dwarf. He nodded once, as if he had just said something very profound.

'If you say so,' said David. He wasn't certain what a metaphorical chain was, exactly. In fact, David wasn't entirely sure what the dwarfs were talking about at all. Still, there were seven of them altogether, which seemed about right.

'Do you have names?' asked David.

'Names?' said the first dwarf. '*Names?* Course we have names. I—' he gave a little, self-important cough, 'am Comrade Brother Number One. These are Comrade Brothers Numbers Two, Three, Four, Five, Six and Eight.'

'What happened to Seven?' asked David.

There was an embarrassed silence.

'We don't talk about Former Comrade Brother Number

Seven,' said Comrade Brother Number One, eventually. 'He has been officially excised from the Party's records.'

'He went to work for his mum,' explained Comrade Brother Number Three, helpfully.

'A capitalist!' spat Brother Number One.

'A baker,' Brother Number Three corrected him.

He stood on his tiptoes and whispered to David.

'We're not allowed to talk to him now. We can't even eat his mum's buns, not even the day-old ones that she sells for half price.'

'I heard that,' said Brother Number One. 'We can make our own buns,' he added huffily. 'Don't need buns made by a class traitor.'

'No, we can't,' said Brother Number Three. 'They're always hard, and then *she* complains.'

Instantly, the dwarfs' relative good humour disappeared. They picked up their tools and prepared to leave.

'Got to be on our way,' said Brother Number One. 'Pleasure to have met you, Comrade. Er, you are a comrade, aren't you?'

'I suppose so,' said David. He wasn't sure that he was, but he wasn't about to risk getting into another fight with the dwarfs. 'Can I still eat buns if I'm a comrade?'

'As long as they're not baked by Former Comrade Brother Number Seven—'

'Or his mum,' added Brother Number Three sarcastically.

'—you can eat anything you like,' concluded Brother Number One, as he raised a finger of warning to Brother Number Three.

The dwarfs started marching back down the ditch on the other side of the road, following a rough trail that led into the trees.

'Excuse me,' said David. 'I don't suppose I could stay with you for the night, could I? I'm lost, and very tired.'

Comrade Brother Number One paused.

'She won't like it,' said Brother Number Four.

'Then again,' said Brother Number Two, 'she's always complaining that she has nobody to talk to. Might put her in a good mood to see a new face.'

'A good mood,' said Brother Number One wistfully, as though it was a wonderful flavour of ice cream that he'd tasted a long, long time ago. 'Right you are, Comrade,' he said to David. 'Come with us. We'll see you straight.'

David was so happy, he could have skipped.

While they walked, David learned more about the dwarfs. At least, he thought that he might be learning more about them, but he didn't quite catch everything he was being told. There was a lot of stuff about 'workers' ownership of the methods of production' and 'the principles of the Second Congress of the Third Committee' but not the Third Congress of the Second Committee, which had apparently ended in a fight over who was going to wash the cups afterwards.

David had some idea of who 'she' might be as well, but it seemed polite to check, just in case.

'Does a lady live with you?' he asked Brother Number One.

The buzz of conversation from the other dwarfs instantly ceased.

'Yes, unfortunately,' said Brother Number One.

'All seven of you?' David continued. He wasn't sure why, but there was something slightly odd about a woman who lived with seven little men.

'Separate beds,' said the dwarf. 'No funny business.'

'Gosh, no,' said David. He tried to wonder what funny business the dwarf could be referring to, then decided that it might be better not to think about it. 'Er, her name wouldn't be Snow White, would it?'

Comrade Brother Number One stopped suddenly, causing a minor pile-up of comrades behind him.

'She's not a friend of yours, is she?' he asked suspiciously.

'Oh no, not at all,' said David. 'I've never met the lady. I might have heard about her, that's all.'

'Huh,' said the dwarf, apparently satisfied, and started walking again. 'Everybody's heard of her: "Ooooh, Snow White who lives with the dwarfs, eats them out of house and home. They couldn't even kill her right." Oh yes, everybody knows about Snow White.'

'Er, kill her?' asked David.

'Poisoned apple,' said the dwarf. 'Didn't go too well. We underestimated the dose.'

'I thought it was her wicked stepmother who poisoned her,' said David.

'You don't read the papers,' said the dwarf. 'Turned out the wicked stepmother had an alibi.'

'We should really have checked first,' said Brother Number Five. 'Seems she was off poisoning someone else at the time. Chance in a million, really. It was just bad luck.'

Now it was David's turn to pause. 'So you mean *you* tried to poison Snow White?'

'We just wanted her to nod off for a while,' said Brother Number Two.

'A *very* long while,' said Number Three.

'But why?' said David.

'You'll see,' said Brother Number One. 'Anyway, we feed her an apple: chomp-chomp, snooze-snooze, weep-weep, "Poor Snow White, we-will-miss-her-so-but-life-goes-on". We lay her out on a slab, surround her with flowers and little weeping bunny rabbits, you know, all the trimmings, then along comes a bloody prince and kisses her. We don't even *have* a prince round here. He just appeared out of nowhere on a bleeding white horse. Next thing you know he's climbed off and he's onto Snow White like a whippet down a rabbit hole. Don't know what he thought he was doing, gadding about randomly kissing strange women who happened to be sleeping at the time.'

'Pervert,' said Brother Number Three. 'Ought to be locked up.'

'Anyway, so he ponces in on his white horse like a big perfumed tea cosy, getting involved in affairs that are none of his business, and next thing you know she wakes up and – oooooh! – was she in a bad mood. The prince didn't half get an earful, and that was after she clocked him one first for "taking liberties". Five minutes of listening to that and, instead of marrying her, the prince gets back on his horse and rides off into the sunset. Never saw him again. We blamed the local wicked stepmother for the whole apple business, but, well, if there's a lesson to be learned from all this, it's to make sure that the person you're going to wrongfully blame for doing something bad is actually available for selection, as it were. There was a trial, we got suspended sentences on the grounds of provocation combined with lack of sufficient evidence, and were warned that if anything ever happened to Snow White again, if she even chipped a nail, we'd be for it.'

Comrade Brother Number One did an impression of choking on a noose, just in case David didn't understand what 'it' meant.

'Oh,' said David. 'But that's not the story I heard.'

'Story!' The dwarf snorted. 'You'll be talking about "happily ever after" next. Do we look happy? There's no happily ever after for us. Miserably ever after, more like.'

'We should have left her for the bears,' said Brother Number Five, glumly. 'They know how to do a good killing, do the bears.'

'Goldilocks,' said Brother Number One, nodding approvingly. 'Classic that, just classic.'

'Oh, she was awful,' said Brother Number Five. 'You couldn't blame them, really.'

'Hang on,' said David. 'Goldilocks ran away from the bears' house and never went back there again.'

He stopped talking. The dwarfs were now looking at him as if he might have been a bit slow.

'Er, didn't she?' he added.

'She got a taste for their porridge,' said Brother Number One, tapping the side of his nose gently as though confiding a great secret to David. 'Couldn't get enough of it. Eventually, the bears just got tired of her and, well, that was that. *"She ran away into the woods and never went back to the bears' house again."* A likely story!'

'You mean . . . they killed her?' asked David.

'They ate her,' said Brother Number One. 'With porridge. That's what "ran away and was never seen again" means in these parts. It means "eaten".'

'Um, and what about "happily ever after"?' asked David, a little uncertainly. 'What does that mean?'

'Eaten quickly,' said Brother Number One.

And with that they reached the dwarfs' house.

XIV

Of Snow White, Who is Very Unpleasant Indeed

'*You're late!*'

David's eardrums rang like bells as Comrade Brother Number One opened the front door of the cottage and cried, very nervously, 'Coo-ee, we're home!' in that singsong voice that David's father had sometimes used on David's mother when he got back late from the pub and knew he was in trouble.

'Don't "we're home" me,' came the reply. 'Where have you been? I'm *starvin'*. Me stomach's like an empty barrel.'

David had never heard a voice quite like it. It was a woman's voice, but it managed to be both deep and high at the same time, like those huge trenches that were supposed to lie at the bottom of the ocean, only not quite so wet.

'Ooooooh, I can 'ear it rumbling,' said the voice. ''Ere, you, listen to it.'

A big white hand reached out and grabbed Brother Number One by the scruff of the neck, lifting him off his feet and yanking him inside.

'Oh, yeph,' said Brother Number One, after a moment or two. His voice sounded muffled. 'I can hear iff now.'

David allowed the other dwarfs to enter the cottage ahead of him. They walked like prisoners who had just been told that the executioner had a little extra time on his hands and could fit in a few more beheadings before he went home for his tea. David cast a lingering glance back at the dark forest and wondered if he shouldn't just take his chances outside.

'Close that door!' said the voice. 'I'm freezin'. Me teeth are chatterin'.'

David, feeling that he had no other choice, stepped into the cottage and closed the door firmly behind him.

Standing before him was the biggest, fattest lady that David had ever seen. Her face was caked with white make-up. Her hair was black, held back by a brightly coloured cotton band, and her lips were painted purple. She wore a pink dress large enough to house a small circus. Brother Number One was pressed hard against its folds, the better to hear the strange noises that the great stomach beneath was currently making. His little feet almost, but not quite, touched the ground. The dress was decorated with so many ribbons and buttons and bows that David was quite at a loss as to how the lady could remember which ones actually released her from the dress and which were merely for show. Her feet were squashed into a pair of silk slippers that were at least three sizes too small, and the rings on her fingers were almost lost in her flesh.

'Who are you, then?' she said.

'He'ph comfany,' said Brother Number One.

'Company?' said the lady, dropping Brother Number One like an unwanted toy. 'Well, why didn't you say you were bringin' company?' She patted her hair and smiled, exposing lipstick-smeared teeth. 'I'd have dressed up. I'd have put me face on.'

David heard Brother Number Three whisper to Brother Number Eight. The words 'anything' and 'improvement' were barely audible. Unfortunately, they were still too loud for the lady's liking and Brother Number Three received a smack across the head for his trouble.

'Careful,' she said. 'Cheeky sod.'

She then extended a large pale hand towards David and gave a little curtsy.

'Snow White,' she said. 'Pleased to make your acquaintance, I'm sure.'

David shook hands and watched with alarm as his fingers were swallowed up in Snow White's marshmallow palm.

'I'm David,' he said.

'That's a nice name,' said Snow White. She giggled and buried her chin in her chest. The action created so many ripples of fat that her head looked as if it was melting. 'Are you a prince?'

'No,' said David. 'Sorry.'

Snow White looked disappointed. She released David's hand, and tried to play with one of her rings, but the ring was so tight that it wouldn't budge.

'A nobleman, maybe?'

'No.'

'Son of a nobleman, with a great inheritance waiting for you on your eighteenth birthday?'

David pretended to think about the question.

'Er, no again,' he said.

'Well, what are you then? Don't tell me you're another one of their *booorrrrinng* friends come here to talk about workers and oppression. I warned them, I did: no more talk about revolutions, not until I've had me tea.'

'But we *are* oppressed,' protested Brother Number One.

'Of course you're oppressed!' said Snow White. 'You're only three feet tall. Now go and get me tea started, before I lose me good humour. And take your boots off. I don't want you lot puttin' muck on me nice clean floor. You only cleaned it yesterday.'

The dwarfs removed their boots and left them at the door along with their tools, then queued to wash their hands in the little sink before preparing the evening meal. They sliced bread and cut vegetables while two rabbits roasted over the open fire. The smell made David's mouth water.

'I suppose you'll be wantin food an' all,' said Snow White to David.

'I am very hungry,' David admitted.

'Well, you can share their rabbit. You ain't 'avin any of mine.'

Snow White plopped herself down in a big chair by the fire. She puffed her cheeks and sighed loudly.

'I 'ate it 'ere,' she said. 'It's so *booorrrinnng*.'

'Why don't you just leave?' asked David.

'Leave?' said Snow White. 'And where would I leave to?'

'Don't you have a home?' said David.

'Me dad and stepmum moved away. They say their place is too small for me. Anyway, they're just *booorrinnnng*, and I'd rather be bored here than bored with 'em.'

'Oh,' said David. He wondered if he should bring up the subject of the court case and the dwarfs' attempt to poison Snow White. He was very interested in it, but he wasn't sure that it would be polite to ask. After all, he didn't want to get the dwarfs into any more trouble than they were already in.

In the end, Snow White made the decision for him. She leaned forward and whispered, in a voice like two rocks rubbing together: 'Anyway, they 'ave to look after me. Judge told them they 'ad to, on account of how they tried to poison me.'

David didn't think he'd want to live with someone who had already tried to poison him once, but he supposed that Snow White wasn't worried about the dwarfs trying again. If they did, they'd be killed, although the look on Brother Number One's face made David suspect that death might almost be welcomed - after living with Snow White for a while.

'But don't you want to meet a handsome prince?' he asked.

'I've met a handsome prince,' said Snow White. She stared dreamily out of the window. 'He woke me with a kiss, but then he 'ad to leave. He told me he'd be back, though, once he'd gone off and killed some dragon or other.'

'Should have stayed here and taken care of the one we have first,' muttered Brother Number Three. Snow White threw a log at him.

'See what I 'ave to put up with?' she said to David. 'I'm left alone all day while they work down't mine, and then I 'ave to listen to them complain as soon as they get home. I don't even know why they bother with all that minin'. They never seem to find anything!'

David saw the dwarfs exchange some looks when they heard what Snow White was saying. He even thought he heard Brother Number Three give a little laugh, until Brother Number Four kicked him in the shin and told him to be quiet.

'So I'm going to stay 'ere with this lot with until me prince returns,' said Snow White. 'Or until another prince comes along and decides to marry me, whichever happens first.'

She bit a hangnail from her little finger, chewed it for a moment, then spat it into the fire.

'Now,' she said, bringing the subject to a close. '*WHERE'S. ME. TEA?*'

Every cup, pot, pan and plate in the cottage rattled. Dust fell from the ceiling. David saw a family of mice evacuate their mousehole and leave through a crack in the wall, never to return.

'I always get a bit shouty when I'm 'ungry, me,' said Snow White. 'Right, somebody 'and me that rabbit . . .'

They ate in silence, apart from the slurping, scraping, chewing and belching coming from Snow White's end of the table. She really did eat an awful lot. She stripped her own rabbit to the bone and then began picking meat from Brother Number Six's plate without even a by-your-leave. She devoured an entire loaf of bread, and half a block of very smelly cheese. She drank tankard after tankard of the ale the dwarfs brewed in their shed, and polished it all off with two chunks of fruitcake baked by Brother Number One, although she complained when a raisin chipped one of her teeth.

'I told you it was a bit dry,' whispered Brother Number Two to Brother Number One. Brother Number One just scowled.

Once there was nothing left to eat, Snow White staggered from the table and flopped down in her chair by the fire, where she instantly fell asleep. David helped the dwarfs to clear the table and wash the dishes, then joined them in a corner where they all began smoking pipes. The tobacco reeked as if someone was burning old, damp socks. Brother Number One offered to share his pipe with David, but David very politely declined.

'What do you mine?' he asked.

There was some coughing from a number of the dwarfs, and David noticed that none of them wanted to catch his eye. Only Brother Number One seemed willing to try to answer the question.

'Coal, sort of,' he said.

'Sort of?'

'Well, it's a kind of coal. It's stuff that used to be, sort of, in a way, coal.'

'It's coal*ish*,' said Brother Number Three helpfully.

David considered this. 'Do you mean diamonds?'

Seven small figures instantly leaped on him. Brother Number One covered David's mouth with a little hand and said: 'Don't say that word in here. Ever.'

David nodded. Once the dwarfs were sure that he understood the gravity of the situation, they climbed off him again.

'So you haven't told Snow White about the, er, coal*ish* stuff,' he said.

'No,' said Brother Number One. 'Never, um, quite got round to it.'

'Don't you trust her?'

'Would you?' asked Brother Number Three. 'Last winter, when food was hard to come by, Brother Number Four woke up to find her nibbling on his foot.'

Brother Number Four nodded solemnly to let David know that this was nothing less than the truth.

'Still have the marks,' he said.

'If she found out the mine was working, she'd take us for every gem we were worth,' continued Brother Number Three. 'Then we'd be even more oppressed than we are already. And poorer.'

David looked round the cottage. It really wasn't very much to write home about. There were two rooms: the one in which they now sat, and a bedroom that Snow White had taken for her own. The dwarfs slept together in one bed in a corner beside the fire, three at one end and four at the other.

'If she wasn't around, we could do the place up a bit,' said Brother Number One. 'But if we start spending money on it then she'll get suspicious, so we have to keep it the way it is. We can't even buy another bed.'

'But aren't there people nearby who know about the mine? Doesn't anybody suspect?'

'Oh, we've always let people know that we make a little from mining,' said the dwarf. 'Just enough to keep us going. It's hard work, mining, and nobody wants to do it unless they're sure of getting wealthy from it. As long as we keep our heads down and don't go wild spending money on fancy clothes or gold chains –'

'Or beds,' said Brother Number Eight.

'Or beds,' agreed Brother Number One, 'then everything will be fine. It's just that none of us is getting any younger, and it would be nice to take things a bit easier and perhaps treat ourselves to some luxuries.'

The dwarfs looked at Snow White snoring in her chair, and all of them sighed as one.

'Actually, we're hoping to bribe someone to take her off our hands,' admitted Brother Number One at last.

'You mean, pay someone to marry her?' asked David.

'He'd have to be really desperate, of course, but we'd make it worth his while,' said Brother Number One. 'Well, I'm not sure there are enough diamonds in the whole land to make living with her worthwhile, but we'd give him enough to ease the burden. He could buy some really nice earplugs, and a really big bed.'

By now some of the dwarfs were nodding off. Brother Number One took a long stick and nervously approached Snow White.

'She doesn't like being woken up,' he explained to David. 'We find this is easiest for everyone.'

He poked at Snow White with the end of the stick. Nothing happened.

'I think you'll have to do it harder,' said David.

This time, the dwarf gave her a good strong prod. It seemed to work, because Snow White grabbed the stick and gave it a sharp tug, almost launching Brother Number One straight into the fireplace before he remembered to let go and landed in the coal scuttle instead.

'Unk,' said Snow White. 'Arfle.'

She wiped some drool from her mouth, rose from her chair, and staggered to her bedroom. 'Bacon in the morning,' she said. 'Four eggs. And a sausage. No, make that eight sausages.'

With that, she slammed the door behind her, fell on her bed, and was immediately sound asleep.

David sat curled up in the chair by the fire. The house rumbled with the snoring of Snow White and the dwarfs, a complex arrangement of snorts, whistles and dusty coughs. David thought of the Woodsman, and the trail of blood leading into the woods. He remembered Leroi, and the look in the Loup's eyes. David knew that he could not afford to remain with the dwarfs for longer than one night. He had to keep moving. He had to get to the king.

He rose from his chair and walked to the window. He could see nothing outside, so thick and heavy was the darkness. He listened, but he could hear only the hooting of an owl. He had not forgotten what had brought him to this place, but his mother's voice had not come to him again since he had entered the new world. Only if she called to him would he be able to find her.

'Mum,' he whispered. 'If you're out there, I need your help. I can't find you if you don't guide me.'

But there was no reply.

He went back to his chair and closed his eyes. He fell asleep and dreamed of his bedroom at home, and of his father and his new family, but they were not alone in the house. In his dream, the Crooked Man stalked the hallway until he came to Georgie's bedroom, where he stood for a long time looking at the child before departing the house and returning to his own world.

XV

Of the Deer-Girl

Snow White was still snoring in her bed when David and the dwarfs departed the next morning, and the spirits of the little men seemed to lift significantly the further behind they left her. They walked with him as far as the white road, then they all stood around rather awkwardly as everyone tried to find the best way to say goodbye.

'We can't tell you where the mine is, obviously,' said Brother Number One.

'Obviously,' said David. 'I quite understand.'

'Because it's secret, like.'

'Yes, of course.'

'Don't want every Tom, Dick and Harry snooping around it.'

'That seems very sensible.'

Brother Number One tugged pensively at his ear.

'It's just beyond the big hill on the right,' he said quickly. 'There's a trail that leads up to it. It's well hidden, mind, so you'll need to keep watching out for it. It's marked by an eye carved in a tree. At least, we think it's carved. You never can tell with those trees. Just in case, you know, you ever need a little company.' Brother Number One's face brightened. 'Ha!' he said. 'A "little company!" See what I did there? You know, a little company, like friends, and a *little company*, like a band of dwarfs. See?'

David did see, and laughed dutifully.

'Now remember,' said Brother Number One, 'if you come across a prince or a young nobleman, in fact if you see anyone who looks desperate enough to marry a difficult woman for money, you send him to us, right? Make sure he waits on this road until we appear. We don't want him making his own way to the cottage and, well, you know . . .'

'Being scared off,' finished David for him.

'Yes, quite. Well, good luck, and stay on the road. There's a village about a day's walk from here, and there's bound to be someone there who can help you on your way, but don't be tempted to stray from the path, no matter what you see. There's a lot of nasty things in these woods, and they have their ways of luring folk into their clutches, so mind how you go.'

And with that the little company of the little company was lost to David as the dwarfs disappeared into the forest. He heard them singing a song as they marched, one that Brother Number One had made up for them as they went on their way to work. It didn't have much of a tune, and Brother Number One seemed to have encountered some difficulty in finding suitable rhymes for 'collectivisation of labour' and 'oppression by the capitalist running dogs', but David was still sad when the song faded away and he was left alone on the silent road.

He had quite liked the dwarfs. He often had no idea what they were talking about, but for a group of homicidal, class-obsessed small people, they were really pretty good fun. After they departed, he felt very vulnerable. Although this was clearly a major road, David appeared to be the only person travelling upon it. Here and there he found traces of others who had passed this way – the remains of a fire, now long cold; a leather strap, gnawed at one end by a hungry animal – but that was as close as it appeared he was going to come to another human being that day. The constant twilight, which altered significantly only early in the morning and late in the evening, sapped his energy and subdued his spirits, and he found his attention drifting. At times, he seemed to fall asleep on his feet, for he had flashes of dreams, visions in which Dr Moberley stood over him and seemed to be speaking to him, and periods of darkness during which he thought that he heard his father's voice. Then he would awaken suddenly as his feet strayed from the path, his legs almost tangling beneath him as he moved from stone to grass.

He realised that he was very hungry. He had eaten with the dwarfs that morning but now his stomach was rumbling and aching. There was still food in his pack, and the dwarfs had added to his supplies by giving him some pieces of dried meat, but he had no idea how far he might have to travel before he reached the castle of the king. Even the dwarfs were of no help there. As far as David could tell, the king didn't have very much to do with the running of his kingdom at all. Brother Number One told David that someone had once come to the cottage claiming to be a royal tax collector, but after an hour in the company of Snow White, he left without his hat and never returned again. The only facts about the king that Brother Number One could confirm were that there was a king (probably) and that there was a castle, somewhere at the end of the road on which David was travelling, although Brother Number One had never seen it. And so David walked on, his mind drifting, his stomach hurting, and the road glowing whitely before him.

It was during one of his near-tumbles into the ditch that David saw apples hanging from a tree in a clearing near the edge of the road. They looked green and almost ripe, and he felt his mouth begin to water. He remembered the dwarfs' injunction, their warning that he should remain on the path always and not be tempted by the gifts of the forest. But what harm could it do to take some apples from a tree? He would still be able to see the road from it, and with the help of a fallen branch he could probably dislodge enough fruit to keep him going for a day, perhaps more. He stopped and listened, but heard nothing. The forest was quiet.

David left the road. The ground was soft, and his feet made an unpleasant squelching noise with each step that he took. As he drew nearer to the tree, he saw the fruit at the farthest ends of the branches was smaller and less ripe than the apples higher up at the heart of the tree, where each one was as big as a man's fist. He could reach them if he climbed up, and climbing trees was something at which David excelled. It was the work of only a few minutes to scale the trunk, and soon he was seated on a thick branch, munching on an apple that tasted incredibly sweet to him. It had been weeks since he'd eaten an apple, not since a local farmer had quietly slipped Rose a couple 'for the little 'uns'. Those apples had been small and sour, but these were wonderful. The juice trickled down his chin, and the flesh was firm in his mouth.

He devoured the last of the first apple and discarded the core, then picked another. He ate this one more slowly, recalling his mother's warnings about eating too many apples. They gave you stomach pains, she had said. David supposed that stuffing yourself with too much of anything was a recipe for feeling ill, but he wasn't sure how that applied if you hadn't eaten for hours. All he knew for certain was that the fruit tasted good and his stomach was grateful for it.

He was halfway through the second apple when he heard a disturbance in the forest below. Something was approaching fast from his left. He could see movement in the bushes, and a flash of tan hide. It looked like a deer, although David could not see its head, and it was clearly fleeing from some threat. Instantly, David thought of the wolves. He cowered closer to the trunk of the tree and tried to shield himself with it. Even as he did so, he wondered if the wolves would detect his scent upon the ground as they passed, or if the lure of the deer might be enough to blind their senses to it.

Seconds later, the deer broke from cover and entered the clearing beneath David's tree. It paused for a moment, as if uncertain of which direction to take, and in that moment he got his first clear look at its head. The sight made him gasp, for it was not the head of a deer but that of a young girl with blond hair and dark green eyes. He could see where her human neck ended and the body of the deer began, because a red welt marked the place where the two beings had been joined. The girl glanced up, startled by the sound, and her eyes met David's.

'Help me!' she begged. 'Please.'

And then the sounds of pursuit drew nearer, and David saw a horse and rider bearing down upon the clearing, the rider's bow drawn and ready to release its arrow. The deer-girl heard them too, for her back legs tensed and she bounded forward towards the cover of the forest. She was still in mid-air when the arrow struck her neck. The blow threw her body to the right, where it lay twitching upon the ground. The deer-girl's mouth opened and closed as she tried to speak her final words. Her back legs kicked at the dirt, her body trembled, and then she stopped moving.

The rider trotted into the clearing on a huge black horse. He was hooded and dressed in the colours of the autumn forest, all greens and ambers. In his left hand he held a short bow, and a quiver of arrows hung across his shoulder. He dismounted from the horse, drew a long blade from a scabbard at his saddle, and approached the body on the ground. He raised the blade and struck once, then again, at the neck of the deer-girl. David looked away after the first blow, his hand against his mouth and his eyes squeezed shut. When he dared to glance back, the girl's head had been severed from the deer's body and the hunter was carrying it by the hair, dark blood dripping from the neck onto the forest floor. Using the hair, he tied the head to the horn of his saddle so that it hung against the flank of his horse, then placed the carcass of the deer across its back before preparing to remount. His left foot was already raised when he paused and stared at the ground. David followed his gaze and saw the discarded core of the apple at the horse's hoofs. The hunter lowered his foot and stared at the core, then in one swift move-ment drew an arrow from his quiver and nocked it to the bow. The tip of the arrow was raised towards the apple tree and came to rest pointing straight at David.

'Come down,' said the hunter, his voice muffled slightly by a scarf across his mouth. 'Come down or I'll shoot you down.'

David had no choice but to comply. He felt himself start to cry. He tried desperately to stop himself but he could smell the deer-girl's blood on the air. His only hope was that the hunter had enjoyed his sport for the day and might see fit to spare him as a result.

David reached the base of the tree. He was tempted for an instant to run and take his chances in the forest, but it was an idea that he rejected almost immediately. A hunter who could kill a leaping deer with an arrow while riding on horseback would surely be able to hit a fleeing boy with greater ease. He had no choice but to hope for mercy from the hunter, but as he stood before the hooded figure he looked into the deer-girl's sightless eyes and wondered if there was any hope of mercy from someone who could do such a thing.

'Lie down,' said the hunter. 'On your belly.'

'Please, don't hurt me,' said David.

'Lie down!'

David knelt on the ground before forcing himself to lie flat. He heard the hunter approach and then his arms were wrenched behind his back and his wrists bound with coarse rope. His sword was taken from him. His legs were tied at the ankles and he was lifted into the air and slung over the back of the great horse, his body lying beside that of the deer, his left side resting painfully against the saddle. But David did not think about the pain, not even when they began to trot and the ache in his side became a regular, rhythmic pounding, like the blade of a dagger being forced between his ribs.

No, all that David could think about was the head of the deer-girl, for her face rubbed against his as they rode, her warm blood smeared his cheek, and he saw himself reflected in the dark green mirrors of her eyes.

XVI

Of the Three Surgeons

They rode for what seemed to David like an hour, perhaps more. The hunter did not speak. David felt dizzy from hanging across the horse, and his head hurt. The smell of the deer-girl's blood was very strong and as their journey drew on, the touch of her skin against his grew colder and colder.

At last they came to a long stone house in the forest. It was plain and unadorned, with narrow windows and a high roof. To one side was a large stable, and there the rider tethered his horse. There were other animals here too. A doe stood in a stall, chewing on some straw and blinking at the new arrivals, alongside chickens in a wire run and rabbits in hutches. Nearby a fox clawed at the bars of its cage, its attention torn between the hunter and the tasty prey just beyond its reach.

The hunter dismounted and detached the deer-girl's head from the saddle. With his other hand he lifted David and slung him over his shoulder, then carried him to the house. The deer-girl's head made a soft thudding noise against the door as the hunter raised the latch, and then they entered and David was thrown to the stone floor. He landed on his back and lay there, dazed and frightened, as, one by one, lamps were lit, and he was at last able to see the hunter's lair.

The walls were covered with heads, each mounted upon a wooden board and fixed to the stone. Many of the heads came from animals – deer, wolves, even a Loup, which seemed to have been given pride of place at the centre of the display on one wall – but others were human. Some came from young adults, and three came from very old men, but most belonged to children, boys and girls, their eyes replaced with glass orbs that glittered in the lamplight. There was a fireplace at one end of the room, and a single pallet bed beside it. Against another wall stood a small desk and a single chair. David turned his head and saw dried meat hanging from hooks at the other end of the room. He could not tell if it came from animals or people.

But the room was dominated by two great oak tables, so huge that they must have been assembled within the house itself, piece by piece. They were stained with blood, and from where he lay David could see chains and manacles attached, and leather restraints. To one side of the tables was a rack of knives and blades and surgical tools, all clearly old but kept keen and clean. Above the table hung an array of metal and glass tubes on ornate frames, some as thin as needles, the others as thick as David's arm.

Bottles of all shapes and sizes, some filled with clear liquid, the rest used to store body parts, stood on shelves. One bottle was filled almost to the top with eyeballs. They seemed alive to David, as though being wrenched from their sockets had not deprived them of the capacity to see. Another contained a woman's hand, a gold ring upon its wedding finger, red varnish flaking slowly from its nails. A third contained half a brain, its inner workings exposed and marked by coloured pins.

And there were worse things than those, oh much worse . . .

He heard footsteps approaching. The hunter stood over him, the hood now lowered and the scarf removed to reveal the face beneath. It was the face of a woman. Her skin was ruddy and unadorned, her mouth slim and unsmiling. Her hair was tied loosely upon her head. It was black and white and silver, like the fur of an old badger. While David watched, she released her tresses, so that they fell in an avalanche across her shoulders and down her back. She knelt and gripped David's face with her right hand, turning his head back and forth as she examined his skull. She then released his face and tested his neck, and the muscles in his arms and legs.

'You'll do,' she said, more to herself than to David, and then left him to lie upon the floor while she worked on the head of the deer-girl. She did not say another word to him until, many hours later, her work was complete. She raised David and placed him upon a low chair before displaying to him the fruits of her labours.

The deer-girl's head had been mounted upon a piece of dark wood. Her hair had been washed and spread out upon the block, held in place by a thin glue. Her eyes had been removed and replaced with ovals of green and black glass. Her skin had been coated with a waxy substance to preserve it, and her head made a hollow sound when the huntress rapped upon it with her knuckles.

'She's pretty, don't you think?' said the huntress.

David shook his head, but said nothing. This girl had had a name once. She'd had a mother and father, maybe sisters and brothers. She would have played and loved and been loved in return. She might have grown up and given birth to children of her own. Now all of that was lost.

'You disagree?' asked the huntress. 'Perhaps you feel sorry for her. But think: in years to come she would have grown old and ugly. Men would have used her. Children would have burst forth from her. Her teeth would have rotted from her head, her skin would have wrinkled and aged, and her hair would have grown thin and white. Now, she will always be a child, and she will always be beautiful.'

The huntress leaned forward. She touched her hand to David's cheek, and for the first time she smiled. 'And soon, you too will be like her.'

David twisted his head away.

'Who are you?' he asked. 'Why are you doing this?'

'I am a hunter,' she replied simply. 'A hunter must hunt.'

'But she was a little girl,' said David. 'A girl with the body of an animal, but still a girl. I heard her speak. She was frightened. And then you killed her.'

The huntress stroked the deer-girl's hair.

'Yes,' she said, softly. 'She lasted longer than I expected. She was more cunning than I thought. Perhaps a fox's body might have been more appropriate, but it is too late now.'

'*You* made her that way?' David said. Even though he was frightened, his disgust at what the huntress had done suffused every word. The huntress looked surprised at the venom in his voice and seemed to feel that some justification of her actions was required.

'A hunter is always seeking new prey,' she said. 'I grew tired of hunting beasts, and humans make poor game. Their minds are sharp, but their bodies are weak. And then I thought how wonderful it would be if I could combine the body of an animal with the intelligence of a human. What a test it would be for my skills! But it was hard, so hard, to create such hybrids: both animals and people would die before I could bring them together. I could not stem the bleeding for long enough to make the union possible. Their brains died, their hearts stopped, and all my hard work would turn to nothing, drop by red drop.

'And then I had some good fortune. Three surgeons were travelling through the forest, and I came upon them and captured them and brought them here. They told me of a salve they had created, one that could fuse a severed hand back upon its wrist, or a leg to its torso. I made them show me what they could do. I cut the arm from one of them and the others repaired it, just as they said they could. Then I cut another in half, and his friends made him whole again. Finally, I severed the head of the third, and they fixed it again upon his neck.

'And they became the first of my new prey', she said, pointing to the heads of three elderly men on the wall, 'once they had told me how to make the salve for myself. Now each prey is different, for each child brings something of itself to the animal with which it is fused.'

'But why children?' asked David.

'Because adults despair,' she answered, 'while children do not. Children accommodate themselves to their new bodies and their new lives, for what child has not dreamed of being an animal? And, in truth, I prefer to hunt children. They make better sport, and better trophies for my wall, because they are so beautiful.'

The huntress stepped back and regarded David carefully, as though only now becoming aware of the nature of his questions.

'What is your name, and where have you come from?' she asked. 'You are not from these lands. I can tell from your scent and your speech.'

'My name is David. I came from another place.'

'What place?'

'England.'

'*Eng-land*,' repeated the huntress. 'And how did you get here?'

'There was a passageway between my land and this one. I came through, but now I can't get back.'

'So sad, so sad,' said the huntress. 'And are there many children in Eng-land?'

David did not reply. The huntress grabbed his face and dug her nails into his skin.

'Answer me!'

'Yes,' he said, reluctantly.

The huntress released him.

'Perhaps I will make you show me the way. There are so few children here now. They do not wander as they once did. This one —' She gestured at the head of the deer-girl '— was the last that I had, and I had been saving her. Now, though, I have you.

So . . . Should I use you as I used her, or should I make you take me to Eng-land?'

She stepped away from David and thought for a time.

'I am patient,' she said, at last. 'I know this land, and I have weathered its changes before. The children will come again. Soon it will be winter, and I have food enough to keep me. You will be my last hunt before the snow descends. I will make you a fox, because I think you are even brighter than my little deer. Who knows, you may escape me and live out your life in some hidden part of the forest, although none has yet managed it. There is always hope, my David, always hope. Now, sleep, for tomorrow we begin.'

With that, she cleaned David's face with a cloth and kissed him softly on the lips. Then she carried him to the great table and chained him there in case he tried to escape during the night, before extinguishing all of the lamps. In the firelight she undressed herself, then lay naked upon her pallet and fell asleep.

But David did not sleep. He thought about his situation. He recalled his old tales and returned to the memory of the Woodsman telling him of the gingerbread house. In every story, there was something to be learned.

And, in time, he began to plan.

XVII

Of Centaurs and the Vanity
of the Huntress

Early the next morning, the huntress awoke and dressed. She
roasted some meat on the fire and ate it with a tea made from
herbs and spices, then came to David and raised him up. His
back and limbs ached from the hard table and the constraints
placed upon his movement by the chains, and he had slept only
a little, but he now had a sense of purpose. Up to this point, he
had been largely dependent upon the goodwill of others – the
Woodsman, the dwarfs – for his care and safety. Now he was on
his own, and the possibility of survival lay entirely in his own hands.

The huntress gave him some of the tea, then tried to make
him eat the meat, but he would not open his mouth to it. It
smelled strong and gamy.

'It is venison,' she said. 'You must eat. You will need your
strength.'

But David kept his mouth tightly closed. He could think only
of the deer-girl, and the feel of her skin against his. Who knew
what child had once been part of this animal's body, human and
beast becoming one? Perhaps this was even the flesh of the deer-
girl, torn bloodied from her body to provide fresh fare for the
huntress's breakfast. He could not, would not, eat of it.

The huntress gave up and offered David bread instead. She
even freed one of his hands so that he could feed himself. While
he ate, she brought the caged fox from the stables and laid it

on the table beside David. The fox watched the boy, almost as though it were aware of what was to come. While they regarded each other, the huntress began to assemble all that she would need. There were blades and saws, swabs and bandages, long needles and lengths of black thread, tubes and vials, and a jar of clear, viscous lotion. She attached bellows to some of the tubes – 'to keep the blood flowing, just in case' – and adjusted the restraints so that they would fit the small legs of the fox.

'So what do you think of your new body to come?' she said to David once her preparations were complete. 'It is a fine fox, young and nimble.'

The fox tried to bite at the wire of its cage, revealing sharp white teeth.

'What will you do with my body and its head?' asked David.

'I will dry your flesh, and add it to my winter store. I have found that while it is possible successfully to fuse the head of a child with the body of an animal, the opposite does not hold true. Animal brains are unable to adjust to the new bodies. They cannot move properly and make poor prey. In the beginning, I would set them free for fun and nothing more, but now I do not even waste my time doing that. Still, they are out in the forest, those that have survived. They are sickly creatures. Sometimes, I kill them out of pity when they cross my path.'

'I was thinking about what you said last night,' said David carefully, 'about how all children dream of being animals.'

'And is it not true?' asked the huntress.

'I think so,' said David. 'I always wanted to be a horse.'

The huntress looked interested.

'And why a horse?'

'In the stories that I read when I was little, I came across a creature called a centaur. It was half horse and half man. Instead of a horse's neck, it had the torso of a man, so it could hold a bow in its hands. It was beautiful and strong, and it was the perfect hunter because it combined all of the strength and speed of a horse with the skill and cunning of a person. You were fast on your mount yesterday, but you were still not one with your horse. I mean, doesn't your horse trip sometimes, or move in ways that you hadn't expected? My father used to ride as a boy, and he told me that even the finest of horsemen can be unsaddled. If I was a centaur, then I would be the best of both horse and man in one, and if I hunted, then nothing would ever be able to escape me.'

The huntress looked from the fox to David, then back again. She turned away from them and walked to her desk. She found a scrap of paper and a quill pen, and began drawing. From where he sat, David saw diagrams, and figures, and the shapes of horses and men, drawn with all the care of an artist. He did not disturb the huntress. He simply watched her patiently, and when he looked to the fox, he found that it was watching her too. So boy and fox remained that way, united in anticipation, until at last the huntress's work was done.

She rose, returned to the great operating tables, and without another word bound David's free hand once again so that he could not move. He felt a moment of panic. Perhaps his plan had not worked and she was now about to operate on him, severing his head and transplanting it to the body of a wild animal, creating a new being out of blood and salve and agony. Would she decapitate him with a single sweep of an axe, or cut and saw her way through gristle and bone? Would she give him something to put him to sleep, so that before he closed his eyes he would be one thing and when he woke he would be another entirely, or was there a part of her that enjoyed the infliction of pain? As her hands worked upon him, he wanted to cry out, but he did not. Instead, he was quiet, swallowing his fear, and his self-discipline was rewarded.

Once he was secure, the huntress put on her hooded cloak and left the house. After a few minutes had gone by, David heard the clopping of a horse's hoofs, and then they faded as she rode

off into the forest, leaving David alone with the fox, two beasts
on the verge of becoming one.

David dozed for a while but woke to the huntress returning. This
time, the horse's hoofs sounded very close. The door to the house
opened and the huntress appeared, leading her mount by the
reins. At first, the horse seemed reluctant to enter, but she spoke
softly to it and eventually it followed her through the door. David
could see the horse's nose responding to the smells in the house,
and he thought its eyes looked panicked. She tethered it to a
ring in the wall, then approached David.

'I will make a bargain with you,' she said. 'I have been thinking
about this creature, this *centaur*. You are right: such a beast
would be the perfect hunter. I wish to become one. If you help
me, I give you my word that I will set you free.'

'How do I know that you won't kill me as soon as you become
a centaur?' David asked.

'I will destroy my bows and arrows, and I will draw you a
map to guide you back to the road. Even if I chose to pursue
you, what threat would I pose without a bow with which to hunt?
In time I will make more, but by then you will be long gone, and
if you ever pass through my forest again I will give you free
passage in recognition of all that you have done for me.'

Then the huntress leaned over and whispered in David's ear.
'But if you do not agree to help me, then I will make you one
with the fox, and I guarantee that you will not live out this day.
I will chase you through these forests until you fade from exhaus-
tion, and when you can run no longer, I will skin you alive and
wear you on cold winter days. You may live or die. The choice
is yours.'

'I want to live,' said David.

'Then we are agreed,' said the huntress. With that, she fed
her bows and arrows to the fire and drew David a detailed map
of the forest showing him the way back to the road, which he

tucked carefully into his shirt. The huntress then instructed him in what he had to do. She brought from the stable a pair of huge blades, heavy and sharp as guillotines, and raised them above the operating tables using a system of ropes and pulleys. The huntress adjusted one of these so that it would sever her body in half when it fell, then showed David how to apply the salve immediately so that she would not bleed to death before her torso could be attached to the horse's body. She went over the procedures with him again and again, until he knew them by rote. Then the huntress stripped herself naked, took a long, heavy blade in her hands, and with two strokes severed her horse's head from its body. There was a great deal of blood at first, but David and the huntress quickly poured the salve over the exposed flesh of the horse's neck, the wounds smoking and sizzling as the mixture did its work. Instantly the ejections from the veins and arteries ceased. The horse's body rested on the floor, its heart still beating, while its head lay nearby, the eyes rolling in the sockets, the tongue lolling from its mouth.

'We don't have long,' said the huntress. 'Hurry, hurry!'

She lay on the table beneath the blade. David tried not to look at her nakedness and instead concentrated on the preparations for the release of the blade, as he had been instructed. While he checked the ropes once again, the huntress gripped his arm. In her right hand, she held a sharp knife.

'If you try to run away, or if you betray me, this knife will leave my hand and find your body before you can get an arm's length from me. Do you understand?'

David nodded. One of his ankles was tied to the leg of the table. He couldn't have run far, even if he wanted to take his chances. The huntress released her grip on him. Beside her stood one of the glass jars containing the miraculous salve. It would be David's task to pour it on her wounded body, then haul her from the table to the floor. From there, he would help her crawl to the horse. Once the two wounds were touching, he would have to pour more salve, causing the huntress and the horse to fuse together, creating one living creature.

'Then do it, and be quick.'

David stepped back. The rope holding the guillotine in place was taut. To avoid any accidents, he simply had to sever it with his sword blade, causing it to drop down on the huntress and sever her body into two pieces.

'Ready?' asked David.

He set the blade to the rope. The huntress gritted her teeth.

'Yes. Do it! Do it now!'

David raised the blade above his head and brought it down on the rope with all of his strength. The rope snapped and the blade fell, cutting the huntress in two. She screamed in agony, writhing upon the table as the blood poured from both halves of her being.

'The salve!' she cried. 'Apply it quickly!'

But instead David raised the blade again and cut off the huntress's right hand. It fell to the floor, the knife still held tightly in its grasp. Finally, with a third stroke David broke the rope binding him to the table. He jumped over the horse's body and ran for the door, while all the time the huntress's screams of rage and pain filled the room. The door was locked, but the key remained in the keyhole. David tried to turn it, but it would not move.

Behind him, the huntress's screams rose in pitch, followed

suddenly by a smell of burning. David turned to see the the great wound in her upper body smoking and bubbling as the salve repaired her injuries. Her right arm, too, was covered in the salve, and she was pouring more on the floor so that it pooled over the wrist of her severed hand, healing the wound. Using the stump and the power of her left hand, she forced herself off the table and onto the floor.

'Come back here!' she hissed. 'We're not done yet. I'll eat you alive.'

She touched her stump to her right hand, then doused both with salve. Instantly, the two halves reconnected, and she raised the knife to her mouth, clasping the blade between her teeth. The huntress began to pull herself across the floor, drawing closer and closer to David. Her hand touched the end of his trouser leg as the key turned in the lock and the door opened. David pulled his leg free and ran out into the open air, then stopped dead.

He was not alone.

The clearing before the house was filled with an assemblage of creatures with the bodies of children and the heads of beasts. There were foxes and deer and rabbits and weasels, the features of the smaller animals sitting incongruously on the larger human shoulders, their necks narrowed by the actions of the salve. The hybrids moved awkwardly, as though not in control of their own limbs. They shuffled and staggered, their faces filled with confusion and pain. Slowly, they approached the house, just as the huntress dragged herself through the doorway and on to the grass. The knife dropped from her mouth and she grasped it in her fist.

'What are you doing here, you foul creatures? Get away from this place. Go back to skulking in the shadows.'

But the beasts did not respond. They just kept shambling forwards, their gaze fixed on the huntress. The huntress looked up at David. She was frightened now.

'Take me back inside,' she said. 'Quickly, before they reach me. I forgive you for all that you have done. You are free to go. Only do not leave me here with . . . *them.*'

David shook his head. He moved away from her as a creature with the body of a boy but the head of a squirrel twitched its nose at him.

'Don't desert me,' cried the huntress. She was now almost surrounded, the knife striking out feebly at thin air as the beasts she had created encircled her.

'Help me!' she shouted to David. 'Please help me.'

And then the animals fell upon her, tearing and biting, ripping and shredding, as David turned away from the grisly sight and fled into the forest.

XVIII
Of Roland

David walked for many hours through the forest, trying as best he could to follow the huntress's map. There were trails marked upon it that either had ceased to exist or had never existed in the first place. Cairns of stones that had been used for generations as primitive signposts were often obscured by long grass, overgrown by moss, or had been demolished by passing animals or vindictive travellers, so that David was forced again and again to go back over old ground, or slash at the undergrowth with his sword in order to find the markers. From time to time he wondered if the huntress had been planning to trick him by constructing a false map, a ruse that would have left him trapped in her forest, easy prey for her once she became a centaur.

Then, suddenly, he glimpsed a thin line of white through the trees, and moments later he was standing on the edge of the forest with the road before him. David had no idea where he was. He could have been back at the dwarfs' crossing or further east along the road, but he didn't care. He was just glad to be out of the woods and once again on the path that would take him to the king's castle.

He walked on, until the weak light of that world began to fade. It was very disconcerting, this absence of proper daylight. It made him feel sad for much of the time – even sadder, he was sure, than he would already have felt under the circumstances.

He sat on a rock and ate a piece of dry bread and some of the dried fruit that the dwarfs had pressed upon him, washed down with cool water from the little brook that always ran alongside the path.

He wondered what his dad and Rose were doing. He supposed that they must be very worried about him by now, but he had no idea what would happen if they looked in the sunken garden, or even if anything remained of the garden itself. He recalled the fires of the burning bomber illuminating the night sky, and the desperate roar of its engines as it descended. It must have torn the garden apart when it struck, scattering bricks and aeroplane parts across the lawn and setting fire to the trees beyond. Perhaps the crack in the wall through which David escaped had collapsed in the aftermath of the crash, and the path from his world to this one was no more. There would be no way for his father to know if David had been in the garden when the plane fell, or what had become of him if he was there when it happened. He imagined men and women sifting through the remains of the plane, searching for charred bodies in the wreckage, fearful of finding one that was smaller than the rest . . .

Not for the first time, David worried about whether he was doing the right thing by moving further and further away from the doorway through which he had entered this world. If his father, or someone else, found a way through and came looking for him, then wouldn't they arrive at the same place? The Woodsman had seemed so certain that the best thing to do was to travel to the king, but the Woodsman was gone. He hadn't been able to save himself from the woods, and he had not been able to protect David. The boy was alone.

David glanced down the road. He couldn't go back now. The wolves were probably still looking for him, and even if he did manage to find his way to the chasm he would then have to seek out another bridge. There was nothing for it but to keep going in the hope that the king might be able to help him. If his father came looking for him, well, David just hoped that he would keep himself safe. But just in case he or someone else came this way, David took a flat rock from beside the brook and, using a sharp stone, carved his name upon it and an arrow pointing in the direction he was taking. Beneath it, he wrote: 'To see the king.' He made a little cairn of rocks by the side of the road, just like the ones used to mark the forest trails, and placed his message on top of it. It was the best that he could do.

As he was packing away the remains of his food, he spied a figure approaching on a white horse. David was tempted to hide, but he knew that if he could see the horseman, then the horseman could also see him. The rider drew nearer, and David could see that he was wearing a silver breastplate decorated with twin symbols of the sun, and he had a silver helmet upon his head. A sword hung from one side of his saddle, and a bow and a quiver of arrows from the other: the weapons of choice in this world, or so it seemed. A shield, also bearing the device of the twin suns, hung from his saddle. He pulled up his horse when he was alongside David and stared down at the boy. He reminded David of the Woodsman, because there was something similar about the horseman's face. Like the Woodsman, he looked both serious and kind.

'And where are you going, young man?' he asked David.

'I'm going to see the king,' said David.

'The king?' The horseman did not look very impressed. 'What use would the king be to anyone?'

'I'm trying to get home. I was told that the king had a book, and in that book might be a way for me to return to where I'm from.'

'And where would that be?'

'England,' said David.

'I don't think I've heard that name before,' said the horseman. 'I can only suppose that it is far from here. Everywhere is far from here,' he added, almost as an afterthought.

He shifted slightly on his horse and glanced around him, scanning the trees, the hills beyond them, and the road ahead and behind.

'This is no place for a boy to be walking alone,' he said.

'I came across the chasm two days ago,' said David. 'There were wolves, and the man who was helping me, the Woodsman, was—'

David broke off. He didn't want to say aloud what had befallen the Woodsman. He saw again his friend falling beneath the weight of the wolf pack, and the trail of blood that led into the forest.

'You crossed the chasm?' said the horseman. 'Tell me, was it you who cut the ropes?'

David tried to read the expression on the horseman's face. He didn't want to get into trouble, but he supposed he must have caused no end of harm by destroying the bridge. Still, he did not want to lie, and something told him that the horseman would call him on it if he did.

'I had to,' he said. 'The wolves were coming. I had no choice.'

The horseman smiled. 'The trolls were most unhappy,' he said. 'They will have to rebuild the bridge now if they are to continue their game, and the harpies will harass them at every turn.'

David shrugged his shoulders. He didn't feel sorry for the trolls. Forcing travellers to gamble their lives on the solution to a silly riddle wasn't a decent way to behave. He hoped that the harpies would decide to eat some of the trolls for dinner, although he didn't imagine trolls would taste very nice.

'I came another way, so your antics did not interfere with my plans,' said the horseman. 'But it seems to me that a young man who manages to irritate trolls and escape from both harpies and wolves might be worth having around. I'll make a bargain with you: I will take you to the king if you will accompany me for a time. I have a task to complete, and will have need of a squire to help me along the way. It should not require more than a few days of service, and in return I will make sure that you have safe passage to the royal court.'

It didn't seem to David as if he had very much choice in the matter. He didn't believe that the wolves would forgive him for the deaths he had caused at the bridge, and by now the pack must surely be on his trail. He had been lucky at the bridge. He might not be so fortunate a second time. Travelling alone on this road, he was always at the mercy of those, like the huntress, who might wish to do him harm.

'I'll go with you, then,' he said. 'Thank you.'

'Good,' said the horseman. 'My name is Roland.'

'And I am David. Are you a knight?'

'No, I am a soldier, nothing more.'

Roland reached down and offered David his hand. When David took it, he was instantly lifted off the ground and hoisted onto the back of Roland's horse.

'You look tired,' said Roland, 'and I can afford to spare a little dignity by sharing my horse with you.'

He tapped the horse's flanks with his heels, and they took off at a trot.

David was not used to sitting on a horse. He found it hard to adjust to her movements, so that his bottom bounced against the saddle with painful regularity. It was only when Scylla – for that was the horse's name – broke into a gallop that he began to enjoy the experience. It was almost like floating along the road, and even with the added burden of David on her back, Scylla's hoofs ate up the ground beneath her feet. For the first time, David began to fear the wolves a little less.

They had been riding for some time when the landscape around them began to change. The grass was charred, the ground broken and churned up as though by great explosions. Trees had been cut down, the trunks sharpened to points and driven into the ground in what looked like an effort to create defences against some enemy. There were pieces of armour scattered upon the earth, and battered shields and shattered swords. It seemed they were gazing on the aftermath of a great battle, but there were no bodies that David could see, although blood soaked the ground, and the muddy pools that pitted the battlefield were more red than brown.

And in the midst of it all was something that did not belong, something so strange that it caused Scylla to halt in her tracks and worry at the ground with one of her hoofs. Even Roland stared at it with undisguised fear. Only David knew what it was.

It was a Mark V tank, a relic of the Great War. Its squat six-pounder gun still protruded from the turret on its left, but it bore no markings of any kind. In fact, it was so clean, so pristine, that it looked to David as if it had just rolled out of a factory somewhere.

'What is it?' asked Roland. 'Do you know?'

'It's a tank,' said David.

He realised that this was unlikely to make the nature of the thing any more understandable to Roland, so he added: 'It's a machine, like a big, um, covered cart in which men can travel. This,' he pointed at the six-pounder, 'is a gun, a kind of cannon.'

David clambered up onto the body of the tank, using the rivets for handholds and footholds. The hatch was open. Inside he could see the system of brakes and gears by the driver's seat, and the workings of the big Ricardo engine, but there was no sign of a crew. Once again, it seemed as if it had never been used. From his perch atop the tank, David looked around and could find no tracks on the muddy field. It was as if the Mark V had just appeared there from out of nowhere.

He climbed down, jumping the last couple of feet so that he landed on the ground with a splash. Blood and mud instantly stained his trousers, and he was reminded again that they were standing in a place where men had been injured and, almost certainly, had died.

'What happened here?' he asked Roland.

The horseman shifted in the saddle, still uneasy in the presence of the tank.

'I do not know,' he said. 'A battle of some kind, from the signs. The fight was recent. I can still smell blood on the air, but where are the bodies of the fallen? And if they were buried, then where are the graves?'

A voice spoke from behind them. It said: 'You are looking in the wrong place, travellers. There are no bodies on the field. They are elsewhere.'

Roland turned Scylla, drawing his sword as he did so. He helped David to climb up behind him. As soon as he was settled, David reached for his own small sword and pulled it from its scabbard.

The remains of an old wall, all that was left of some larger structure now long gone from this world, stood by the roadside. Upon the stones sat an old man. He was completely bald, and thick blue veins ran across his exposed scalp like rivers on a map of some barren, cold place. His eyes were criss-crossed with blood-vessels, and the sockets seemed too big for them, so that the red flesh beneath his skin hung loose and exposed under each eyeball. His nose was long, and his lips were pale and dry. He wore an old brown robe, rather like a monk's habit, that ended just above his ankles. His feet were bare and his toenails were yellow.

'Who fought here?' asked Roland.

'I did not ask them their names,' said the old man. 'They came, and they died.'

'To what purpose? They must have been fighting for some cause.'

'No doubt. I am sure that they believed their cause was the right one. *She*, unfortunately, did not.'

The smell from the battlefield was making David queasy, and it added to his sense that the old man was not to be trusted. Now the way he spoke of the 'she' who had done this, and the manner in which he smiled at the mention of her, made it very clear to David that the men who had died here had died very badly indeed.

'And who is "she"?' asked Roland.

'She is the Beast, the creature that lives beneath the ruins of a tower deep in the forest. She has slept for a long time, but now she is awake once more.' The old man made a gesture towards the trees at his back. 'They were the king's men, trying to maintain control over a dying kingdom, and they paid the price. They made their stand here and were overwhelmed. They retreated to the cover of the woods behind me, dragging their dead and injured with them, and there she had her way with them.'

David cleared his throat. 'How did the tank get here?' he asked. 'It doesn't belong.'

The old man grinned, revealing purple gums dotted with ruined teeth. 'Perhaps the same way you did, boy,' he replied. 'You don't belong here either.'

Roland urged Scylla towards the forest, always keeping his distance from the old man. Scylla was a brave horse, and after only a moment's hesitation she did her master's bidding.

The smell of blood and decomposition grew stronger. There was a copse of broken, stunted bushes ahead, and David knew that this was the true source of the stench. Roland told David to dismount, then instructed him to keep his back against a tree and his eyes on the old man, who remained upon the little wall, watching them over his shoulder.

David knew that Roland didn't want him to see what lay beyond the bushes, but he could not resist the urge to look as he heard the soldier parting the foliage to enter the copse. David caught a brief glimpse of bodies hanging from trees, the remains reduced to little more than bloodied bones. He quickly looked away –

And found himself staring straight into the eyes of the old man. David had no idea how he had moved so quickly and so silently from his perch on the wall, but now here he was, so close that the boy could smell his breath. It stank of sour berries. David grasped the sword more tightly in his hand, but the old man did not even blink.

'You are a long way from home, boy,' said the old man. He raised his right hand and touched his fingers to a stray strand of David's hair. David shook his head furiously and pushed at the old man. It was like pushing at a wall. He might have looked frail, but he was far stronger than David.

'Do you still hear your mother calling?' he said. He put his left hand to his ear as though trying to catch the sound of a voice on the air. '*Da-vid*,' he sang, in a high voice. '*Oh, Da-vid.*'

'Stop it!' said David. 'You stop it now.'

'Or you'll do what?' said the old man. 'A little boy, far, far from home, crying for his dead mother. What can you do?'

'I'll hurt you,' said David. 'I mean it.'

The old man spat on the ground. The grass sizzled where the spittle landed. The liquid expanded, forming a frothy pool on the ground.

And in the pool David saw his father, and Rose, and baby Georgie. They were all laughing, even Georgie, who was being tossed high in the air by his father, just as David had once been.

'They don't miss you, you know,' said the old man. 'They don't miss you one little bit. They're glad that you're gone. You made your father feel guilty because you reminded him of your mother, but he has a new family now and with you out of the way he no longer has to worry about you or your feelings. He has forgotten you already, just as he has forgotten your mother.'

The image in the pool changed, and David saw the bedroom

his father shared with Rose. Rose and his father were standing beside the bed, kissing each other. Then, as David watched, they lay down together. David looked away. His face was stinging, and he felt a great rage rising up inside him. He didn't want to believe it, and yet the evidence was before him in a pool of steaming spittle ejected from the mouth of a poisonous old man.

'See,' said the old man. 'There's nothing for you to go back to now.'

He laughed, and David struck at him with the sword. He was not even aware that he was doing it. He was just so angry, and so sad. He had never felt so betrayed. Now it was as if control of his body had been taken over by something else, something outside himself, so that he seemed to have no will of his own. His arm rose of its own volition and slashed at the old man, tearing through his brown robe and drawing a line of red across the skin beneath.

The old man retreated. He put his fingers to the wound on his chest. They came back red. His face began to change. It extended and assumed the shape of a half-moon, the chin curving up so sharply that it almost met the tip of his crooked nose. Clumps of rough black hair sprouted from his skull. He cast aside the robe and David saw a green and gold suit, tied with an ornate gold belt, and a gold dagger that twisted like the body of a snake. There was a rip in the fabric of the suit where David's sword had cut through the beautiful material, and black blood glistened in the wound. Last of all, a flat black disc appeared in the man's hand. He flicked with it at the air, and it became a crooked hat, which he placed upon his head.

'You,' said David. 'You were in my room.'

The Crooked Man hissed at David, and the dagger at his waist wriggled and writhed as though it really were a snake. His face was contorted with fury and pain.

'I have walked through your dreams,' he said. 'I know

166

everything that you think, everything that you feel, everything that you fear. I know what a nasty, jealous, hateful child you are. And despite all that, I was still going to help you. I was going to help you find your mother, but then you cut me. Ooooh, you're a horrid boy. I could make you very sorry, so sorry you'd wish you'd never been born, but—'

The tone of his voice suddenly changed. It became quiet and reasonable, which frightened David even more.

'I won't, because you'll have need of me yet. I can take you to the one you seek, and then I can get you both home. I'm the only one who can. And I'll just ask for one small thing in return, so small that you won't even miss it . . .'

But before he could proceed, he was disturbed by the sound of Roland returning. The Crooked Man wagged a finger in David's face.

'We'll talk again, and perhaps you'll be a little more appreciative when we do!'

The Crooked Man began spinning in a circle, and he spun so fast and so hard that he dug a hole in the earth and disappeared from view, leaving only the brown robe behind. His spittle had dried into the ground, and the images from David's world could no longer be seen.

David felt Roland arrive beside him, and the two of them peered into the dark hole left by the Crooked Man.

'Who, or what, was that?' asked Roland.

'He disguised himself as the old man,' said David. 'He told me that he could help me to get back home, and that he was the only one who could. I think he was the one the Woodsman spoke of. He called him a trickster. He's a crooked man.'

Roland saw the dark blood dripping from the blade of David's sword.

'Did you cut him?'

'I was angry,' said David. 'It happened before I could stop myself.'

167

Roland took the sword from David's hands, plucked a large green leaf from a bush and used it to clean the blade.

'You must learn to control your impulses,' he said. 'A sword wants to be used. It wants to draw blood. That is why it was forged, and it has no other purpose in the world. If you do not control it, then it will control you.'

He handed the sword back to David. 'Next time you see that man, don't just cut him: kill him,' said Roland. 'Whatever he may say, he means you no good.'

They walked together to where Scylla stood nibbling at the grass.

'What did you see back there?' asked David.

'Much the same as you saw, I suspect,' said Roland. He shook his head in mild annoyance at the fact that David had disobeyed his instructions. 'Whatever killed those men sucked the flesh from their bones, then left their remains hanging from trees. The forest is filled with bodies, as far as the eye can see. The ground is still wet with blood, but they injured this "Beast", or whatever it is, before they died. There is a foul substance on the ground, black and putrid, and the tips of some of their spears and swords have been melted by it. If it can be wounded, then it can be killed, but it will take more than a soldier and a boy to do it. This is none of our concern. We ride on.'

'But –' said David. He wasn't sure what to say. It wasn't like this in the stories. Soldiers and knights slew dragons and monsters. They weren't afraid, and they didn't run away from the threat of death.

Roland was already astride Scylla. His hand was outstretched, waiting for David to take it. 'If you have something to say, then say it.'

David tried to find the right words. He did not want to offend Roland.

'These men all died, and whatever killed them is still alive, even if it is wounded,' he said. 'It will kill again, won't it? More people will die.'

'Perhaps,' said Roland.

'So shouldn't something be done?'

'What would you suggest: that we hunt it down with one-and-a-half swords to our names? This life is filled with threats and danger, David. We face those that we have to face, and there will be times when we must make the choice to act for a greater good, even at risk to ourselves, but we do not lay down our lives needlessly. Each of us has only one life to live, and one life to give. There is no glory in throwing it away where there is no hope. Now, come. The twilight grows thicker. We need to find a place to shelter for the night.'

David hesitated for a moment more, then took Roland's hand and was hoisted into the saddle. He thought of all those dead men, and wondered at the kind of creature that could inflict such harm upon them. The tank still stood in the midst of the battlefield, marooned and alien. Somehow, it had found its way from his world to this one, but without a crew and apparently without even being driven to that spot.

As they left the slaughter behind, he remembered the visions in the Crooked Man's pool of spittle, and the words that had been spoken to him:

'They don't miss you one little bit. They're glad that you're gone.'

It couldn't be true, could it? And yet David had seen the way his father doted on Georgie, and the way he looked at Rose and held her hand as they walked, and he guessed at the things they did together when the bedroom door closed each night. What if he found a way to return home and they didn't want him back? What if they really were happier without him?

But the Crooked Man had told him that he could make things right, that he could restore David's mother to him and bring them both home in return for just one small favour. And David wondered what that favour might be, even as Roland spurred Scylla, urging her on.

Meanwhile, far to the west, out of sight and out of hearing, a chorus of triumphant howls rose into the air.

The wolves had found another bridge across the chasm.

XIX

Of Roland's Tale and the Wolf Scout

Roland was reluctant to pause for the night. He was anxious to continue his quest and deeply concerned about the wolves that were pursuing David, but Scylla was tiring and David was so exhausted that he could barely hold on to Roland's waist. Eventually, they came to the ruins of what looked like a church, and there Roland agreed to rest for a few hours. He would not allow a fire, even though it was cold, but he gave David a blanket in which to wrap himself, and allowed him to sip from a silver flask. The liquid inside burned David's throat before filling him with a dull warmth. He lay down and stared at the sky. The spire of the church loomed over him, its windows as empty as the eyes of the dead.

'The new religion,' said Roland dismissively. 'The king tried to make others understand it when he still had the will to do so, and the power to enforce that will. Now he broods in his castle, and his chapels lie empty.'

'What do you believe in?' asked David.

'I believe in those whom I love and trust. All else is foolishness. This god is as empty as his church. His followers choose to attribute all of their good fortune to him, but when he ignores their pleas or leaves them to suffer, they say only that he is beyond their understanding and abandon themselves to his will. What kind of god is that?'

Roland spoke with such anger and bitterness that David wondered if he had once followed the 'new religion', only to turn his back upon it when something bad happened to him. David had felt that way himself at times as he sat in church in the weeks and months after his mother's death, listening to the priest talking of God and how much He loved his people. He had found it hard to equate the priest's God with the one who had left his mother to die slowly and painfully.

'And who do you love?' he asked Roland.

But Roland pretended not to hear him.

'Tell me about your home,' he said. 'Talk to me of your people. Talk to me of anything but false gods.'

And so David told Roland of his mother and his father, of the sunken garden, of Jonathan Tulvey and his old books, of hearing his mother's voice and following it into this strange land, and, finally, of Rose and the arrival of Georgie. As he spoke, he could not hide his resentment of Rose and her baby. It made him feel ashamed, and more like a child than he wished to appear in front of Roland.

'That is hard indeed,' said Roland. 'So much has been taken from you, but so much has been given too, perhaps.'

He did not say any more, for fear that the boy might think he was preaching to him. Instead, Roland lay back against Scylla's saddle, and told David a tale.

Roland's First Tale

Once upon a time, there was an old king who promised his only son in marriage to a princess in a land far away. He bade his son farewell, and entrusted to him a golden cup that had been in his family for many generations. This, he told his son, would be part of his dowry to the princess, and a symbol of the bond between her family and their own. A servant was ordered to travel with the prince and to care for his every need, and so the two men set out together for the princess's lands.

After they had travelled for many days, the servant, who was jealous of the prince, stole the goblet from him while he was sleeping and dressed himself in the prince's finest clothing. When the prince awoke, the servant made him vow, on pain of his own death and the deaths of all those whom he loved, that he would inform no man of what had transpired, and told him that in future the prince would serve him in all things. And so the prince became the servant, and the servant the prince, and in that way they came to the castle of the princess.

When they arrived, the false prince was treated with great cere-mony and the true prince was given a job herding pigs, for the false prince told the princess that he was a bad and unruly servant and could not be trusted. So her father sent the true prince out to herd swine and sleep on mud and straw, while the impostor ate the finest food and rested his head on the softest of pillows.

But the king, who was a wise old man, heard others speak well of the swineherd, of how gracious were his manners and how kind he was to the animals under his charge and to the servants whom he met, and he went to him one day and asked him to tell him something of himself. But the true prince, bound by his vow, informed the king that he was unable to obey his command. The king grew angry, for he was not used to being disobeyed, but the true prince fell to his knees and said:

'I am bound by a death vow not to tell any man the truth about myself. I beg you to forgive me, for I mean Your Majesty no disrespect, but a man's word is his bond, and without it he is no better than an animal.'

So the king thought for a time, and then he said to the true prince: 'I can see that the secret you keep inside is troubling to you, and perhaps you would feel happier once you have spoken it aloud. Why don't you tell it to the cold hearth in the servants' quarters, and then you may rest easier because of it.'

The true prince did as the king asked, but the king hid in the darkness behind the hearth and he heard the true prince's tale. That night, he held a great banquet, for the princess was due to marry the impostor the next day, and he invited the true prince to sit on one side of his throne as a masked guest, and on the other side he placed the false prince. And he said to the false prince: 'I have a test of your wisdom, if you will agree to take it.' The false prince agreed readily, and the king told him the tale of an impostor who took on the identity of another man, and as a result claimed all the wealth and privileges that were due to another. But the false prince was so arrogant, and so certain of his position, that he did not recognise the tale as being about himself.

'What would you do with such a man?' asked the king.

'I would strip him naked and place him inside a barrel studded with nails,' said the false prince. 'Then I would tie the barrel behind four horses, and I would drag it through the streets until the man inside was ripped to death.'

'Then that shall be your punishment', said the king, 'for such is your crime.'

And the true prince was restored to his position, and he married the princess and lived happily ever after, while the false prince was torn to pieces in a barrel of nails, and nobody wept for him, and nobody spoke his name after he was gone.

When the story was done, Roland looked at David.

'What did you think of my tale?' he asked.

David's brow was furrowed. 'I think I read a story like it once before,' he said. 'But my story was about a princess, not a prince. The ending was the same though.'

'And did you like the ending?'

'I did when I was little. I thought that was what the false prince deserved. I liked it when the bad were punished.'

'And now?'

'It seems cruel.'

'But the false prince would have done the same to another, had it been in his power to do so.'

'I suppose so, but that doesn't make the punishment right.'

'So you would have shown mercy?'

'If I was the true prince, then, yes, I think so.'

'But would you have forgiven him?'

David thought about the question.

'No, he did wrong, so he deserved some punishment. I would have made him herd the pigs and live the way the true prince had been forced to live, and if he ever hurt one of the animals, or hurt another person, then the same thing would be done to him.'

Roland nodded approvingly. 'That is a fit punishment, and merciful. Sleep now,' he said. 'We have wolves snapping at our heels, and you must rest while you can.'

David did as he was told. With his head upon his pack, he closed his eyes and instantly fell fast asleep.

He did not dream, and he awoke only once before the false dawn that marked the coming of day. He opened his eyes and thought that he heard Roland speaking softly to someone. When he glanced over at the soldier, he saw that he was staring at a small silver locket. Inside was a picture of a man, younger than Roland and very handsome. It was to this image that Roland was whispering, and although David could not understand everything that was said, the word 'love' was spoken clearly more than once.

Embarrassed, David drew his blanket closer to his head to block out the words until he fell asleep again.

Roland was already up and moving about when David woke again. He washed himself in a brook, ate a little food, and almost began to perform one of his counting routines, but he stopped himself, remembering the Woodsman's advice, and instead cleaned his sword and sharpened its blade against a rock. He checked that his belt was still strong and that the loop holding the scabbard in place was undamaged, then asked Roland to teach him how to saddle Scylla and tighten her reins and bridle. Roland did so, and also taught him how to check the horse's legs and hoofs for any signs of injury or discomfort.

David wanted to ask the soldier about the picture in the locket, but he did not want Roland to think that he had been spying on him in the night. Instead, he asked the other question that had been troubling him since the two had first met, and by doing so was given an answer to the mystery of the man in the locket.

'Roland,' David asked, as the soldier placed the saddle on Scylla's back once again. 'What task have you set yourself?'

Roland drew the straps tight around the horse's belly.

'I had a companion,' he said, without looking at David. 'His name was Raphael. He wanted to prove himself to those who doubted his courage and spoke ill of him behind his back. He heard a tale of a woman bound to sleep by an enchantress in a chamber filled with treasures, and vowed to release her from her curse. He set out from my land to find her, but he never returned. He was closer to me than a brother. I vowed that I would discover what had befallen him, and avenge his death if such had been his fate. The castle in which she lies is said to move with the cycles of the moon. It now rests at a place not more than two days' ride from here. After we have discovered the truth within its walls, I will take you to see the king.'

David climbed onto Scylla's back, and then Roland led the horse by the reins back to the road, testing the ground in front for any hidden hollows that might injure his mount. David was growing used to Scylla and the rhythm of her movements, although he still ached from the long ride of the day before. He held on to the horn of the saddle and they left the ruins of the church as the first faint light of morning scratched at the sky.

But they did not leave unobserved. In a patch of brambles beyond the ruins, a pair of dark eyes watched them. The wolf's fur was very dark, and its face had more of man than beast about it. It was the fruit of the union between a loup and a she-wolf, but it favoured its mother in looks and instincts. It was also the largest and most ferocious of its kind, a mutant of sorts, big as a pony with jaws capable of encircling a man's chest. The scout had been sent on by the pack to look for signs of the boy. It had picked up his scent on the road, following it to a little house deep in the woods. There it had almost met its end, for the dwarfs had set traps around their home: deep pits with sharpened poles at their base, disguised with sticks and sods of grass. Only the wolf's reflexes had prevented it from falling to its death, and it had been more careful in its approaches thereafter. It had found the boy's spoor mingled with that of the dwarfs, and had traced it back to the road. It had then lost the track for a time until it reached a little stream, where it was replaced by the odour of a horse. This told the wolf that the boy was no longer on foot, and probably not alone. It marked the place with its urine, as it had marked each step of its hunt, so that the pack might follow it more easily.

The scout knew what Roland and David could not: the pack had ceased its advance shortly after crossing the chasm, for more wolves were arriving to join its march upon the king's castle. The scout had been entrusted by Leroi with the task of finding the boy. If possible, it was to bring him back to the pack for Leroi to deal with. If this could not be achieved, then it was to kill him and return with only a token – the boy's head – to prove that the deed had been done. The scout had already decided the head would be sufficient. It would feed on the rest of the boy: it was a long time since it had eaten fresh man-flesh.

The wolf hybrid had again detected traces of the boy by the

battlefield, along with the stench of something unknown that stung its delicate nose and made its eyes water. The starving scout had fed upon the bones of one of the soldiers, sucking the marrow from deep within, and its belly was now fuller than it had been in many months. Its energy renewed, it had followed the horse's scent once more, and arrived at the ruins just in time to see the boy and the rider depart.

With its massive back legs, the scout was capable of long, high leaps, and its bulk had driven many a rider from the saddle of a horse, forcing him to the ground and allowing the scout to tear his throat out with its long, sharp teeth. Taking the boy would be easy. If the scout judged its leap right, it could have the boy in its jaws and be ripping him apart before the horseman even realised what was happening. Then the scout would flee, and if the horseman chose to follow, well, it would draw him straight into the jaws of the waiting pack.

The rider was leading his mount at a slow pace, carefully negotiating low branches and thick patches of briar. The wolf shadowed them, waiting for its chance. Ahead of the horseman was a fallen tree, and the wolf guessed that the horse would pause there for a moment as it tried to work out the best way to overcome the obstacle. The wolf would seize the boy when the horse stopped. Quietly, it padded on, overtaking the horse so that it would have time to find the best position from which to strike. It reached the tree and found, in the bushes to its right, a slab of elevated stone perfect for its purpose. Saliva dripped from its jaws, for it was already tasting the boy's blood in its mouth. The horse came into view, and the scout tensed, ready to strike.

A sound came from behind the wolf: the faintest hint of metal against stone. It turned to face the threat, but not quickly enough. It saw the flash of a blade, and felt a burning deep in its throat, so deep that it could not even make a sound of pain or surprise. It began to smother in its own blood, its legs giving out beneath it as it fell on the rock, its eyes bright with panic as it began to die. Then that brightness began to fade, and the scout's body trembled and spasmed, until finally it lay still.

In the darkness of its pupil, the Crooked Man's face was reflected. With the blade of his sword, he cut off the scout's nose and placed it in a little leather pouch on his belt. It was another trophy for his collection, and its absence would give Leroi and the pack pause when they found the remains of their brother. They would know who they were dealing with, oh yes, for no other mutilated his prey in this way. The boy was his, and his alone. No wolf would feed upon his bones.

So the Crooked Man watched as David and Roland passed by, Scylla pausing for a second before the fallen tree, just as the scout had guessed she would, then jumping it with a single leap and taking the rider and the boy towards the road beyond.

The Crooked Man descended into the briars and thorns, and was gone.

XX

*Of the Village,
and Roland's Second Tale*

David and Roland encountered no one on the road that morning. It still surprised David that so few should walk upon it. After all, the road was well kept and it seemed to him that others must use it to get from here to there.

'Why is it so quiet?' he asked. 'Why are there no people?'

'Men and women fear to travel, for this world has grown passing strange,' said Roland. 'You saw what was left of those men yesterday, and I have told you of the sleeping woman and the enchantress who binds her. There have always been dangers in these lands, and life has never been easy, but now there are new threats and no one can tell where they have come from. Even the king is uncertain, if the stories from his court are true. They say his time is almost done.'

Roland raised his right hand and pointed to the northeast. 'There is a settlement beyond those hills, and there we will spend our last night before we reach the castle. Perhaps we will learn more from those who live there of the woman and of what fate might have befallen Raphael.'

After another hour had gone by, they came upon a party of men emerging from the woods. The men carried dead rabbits and voles tied to sticks. They were armed with sharpened staffs and short, crude swords. When they saw the horse approaching, they raised their weapons in warning.

'Who are you?' called one. 'Come no closer until you have identified yourselves.'

Roland reined in Scylla while they were still out of reach of the men's staffs.

'I am Roland. This is my squire, David. We are heading for the village, in the hope that we may find food and rest there.'

The man who had spoken lowered his sword. 'Rest you may find,' he said, 'but little food.' He raised one of the sticks of dead animals. 'The fields and forests are almost bare of life. This is all we have for two days of hunting, and we lost a man for it.'

'Lost him how?' asked Roland.

'He was bringing up the rear. We heard him cry out, but when we went back his body was gone.'

'You saw no trace of what took him?' asked Roland.

'None. The earth was disturbed where he had stood, as though some creature had burst through from below, but above there was only blood and some filthy stuff that did not come from any animal we know. He was not the first to die in such a way: we have lost others, but have yet to see the thing responsible. Now we venture out only in numbers, and we wait, for most believe that it will soon attack us in our beds.'

Roland looked back down the road, in the direction from which he and David had come.

'We saw the remains of soldiers, about half a day's ride from here,' said Roland. 'From their insignia, it appears that they were the king's men. They had no luck against this Beast, and they were well-trained and well-armed. Unless your fortifications are high and strong, you might be advised to leave your homes until the threat has passed.'

The man shook his head. 'We have farms, livestock. We live where our fathers lived, and their fathers too. We will not abandon all that we have worked so hard to build.'

Roland said nothing more, but David could almost hear what he was thinking:

Then you will die.

David and Roland rode alongside the men, talking with them and sharing what was left of the spirits in Roland's flask. The men were grateful for the kindness, and in return they confirmed the changes in the land and the presence of new creatures in the forests and fields, all of them hostile and hungry. They spoke too of the wolves, who had become ever more daring of late. The hunters had trapped and killed one of their leaders during their time in the woods: a Loup, an interloper from far away. Its fur was a perfect white, and it wore breeches made from the skin of a seal. Before it died it told them that it had travelled from the distant north, and others were coming who would avenge its death at their hands. It was as the Woodsman had told David: the wolves wanted the kingdom for themselves, and they were assembling an army with which to seize it.

As they rounded a bend in the road, the settlement was revealed to them. It was surrounded by clear space upon which cattle and sheep grazed. A wall of tree trunks had been built as protection, the tops sharpened to white points, and elevated platforms behind allowed men to watch all the approaches. Thin streams of smoke were rising from the houses within, and the spire of another church was visible above the top of the wall. Roland did not look pleased to see it.

'Here, perhaps, they still practise the new religion,' he said to David softly. 'For the sake of peace, I will not trouble them with my views.'

A cry went up from inside the walls as they drew closer to the village, and the gates were opened to admit them. Children gathered to greet their fathers, and women arrived to kiss sons and husbands. They stared curiously at Roland and David, but before anyone had a chance to question them a woman began wailing and crying, unable to find the one whom she sought among the hunters. She was young and very pretty, and in between her sobs she called a name over and over again: 'Ethan! Ethan!'

The leader of the hunters, whose name was Fletcher, approached David and Roland. His wife hovered nearby, grateful that her husband had returned safely.

'Ethan was the man that we lost along the way,' he said. 'They were to have been married. Now, she does not even have a grave at which to mourn him.'

The other women gathered around the weeping woman, trying to console her. They brought her to one of the little houses nearby, and the door closed behind them.

'Come,' said Fletcher. 'I have a stable behind my home. You may sleep there, if you wish, and I will feed you from my table for tonight. After that, I will have just enough to feed my own family, and you must ride on.'

Roland and David thanked him and followed him through the narrow streets until they came to a wooden cottage, its walls painted white. Fletcher showed them to the stable and pointed out where they could find water, and fresh straw and a few stale oats for Scylla. Roland removed Scylla's saddle and made sure that she was comfortable before he and David washed themselves in a trough. Their clothes smelled, and although Roland had other garments that he could wear, David had none. When she heard this, Fletcher's wife brought David some of her son's old clothes, for he was now seventeen and had a wife and son of his own. Feeling much better than he had in a long time, David went with Roland to Fletcher's house, where the table was laid and Fletcher and his family were waiting for them. Fletcher's son looked a lot like his father, for he also had long red hair, although his beard was not as thick and lacked the grey that marked the older man's. His wife was small and dark, and said little, all of her attention fixed on the baby in her arms. Fletcher had two more children, both girls. They were younger than David, although not by much, and they cast sly glances at him and giggled softly.

Once Roland and David were seated, Fletcher shut his eyes, bent his head, and gave thanks for the food – David noticed that Roland neither closed his eyes nor prayed – before inviting all at the table to eat.

The conversation drifted from village matters to the hunting trip and the disappearance of Ethan, before finally reaching Roland and David, and the purpose of their journey.

'You are not the first to have passed through here on the way to the Fortress of Thorns,' said Fletcher, once Roland had told him of his quest for it.

'Why do you call it that?' asked Roland.

'Because that is what it is: a keep is surrounded entirely by thorny creepers. Even to approach its walls is to risk being torn apart. You will need more than a breastplate to breach them.'

'You have seen it, then?'

'A shadow passed across the village perhaps a month ago. When we looked up to see what it was, we saw the castle moving through the air without sound or support. Some of us followed it and saw where it had landed, but we did not dare approach. Such things are best left alone.'

'You said others have tried to find it,' said Roland. 'What happened to them?'

'They did not return,' replied Fletcher.

Roland reached beneath his shirt and took out the locket. He opened it and showed the image of the young man to Fletcher. 'Was he one of those who did not come back?'

Fletcher examined the picture in the locket. 'Yes, I recall him,' he said. 'He watered his horse here and drank ale at the inn. He left before nightfall, and that was the last we saw of him.'

Roland closed the locket and placed it near to his heart once more. He did not speak again until they had finished their meal.

When the table was cleared, Fletcher invited Roland to take a seat by the fire and they shared some tobacco.

'Tell us a story, Father,' said one of the little girls, who had seated herself at Fletcher's feet.

'Yes, please do, Father!' echoed the other.

Fletcher shook his head. 'I have no more stories to tell. You have heard them all. But perhaps our guest might have a tale that he could share with us?'

He looked enquiringly at Roland, and the faces of the little girls turned towards the stranger. Roland thought for a moment, then he laid down his pipe and began to speak.

Roland's Second Tale

Once upon a time there was a knight named Alexander. He was all that a knight should be. He was brave and strong, loyal and discreet, but he was also young, and anxious to prove himself by feats of daring. The land in which he lived had been at peace for a very long time, and Alexander had been given few opportunities to gain greater renown in battle. So one day he informed his lord and master that he wished to travel to new and strange lands, to test himself and find out if he was truly worthy to stand alongside the greatest of his fellow knights. His lord, recognising that Alexander would not be content until he was granted permission to leave, gave him his blessing, and so the knight prepared his horse and weapons and set out alone to seek his destiny, without even a squire to tend to his needs.

In the years that followed, Alexander found the adventures of which he had long dreamed. He joined an army of knights that journeyed to a kingdom far to the east, where they marched against a great sorcerer named Abuchnezzar, who had the power to turn men to dust with his gaze, so that their remains blew like ash across the fields of his victories. It was said that the sorcerer could not be slain by the arms of men, and all those who had attempted to kill him had died. Yet the knights believed that there might still prove to be a way to end his tyranny, and the promise of great rewards from the true king of the land, who was in hiding from the sorcerer, spurred them on.

The sorcerer met the knights with his ranks of vicious imps on the empty plain before his castle, and there a fierce and bloody combat commenced. As his comrades fell to the claws and teeth of demons, or were transformed into ash by the sorcerer's gaze, Alexander battled his way through the enemy's ranks, hiding always behind his shield and never looking in the direction of the sorcerer, until at last he was within earshot of him. He called Abuchnezzar's name, and when the sorcerer turned his gaze towards Alexander, the knight quickly spun his shield around so that its inner surface faced his enemy. Alexander had stayed awake all through the previous night polishing the shield so that it now shone brightly in the hot midday sun. Abuchnezzar looked upon it and saw his own reflection, and in that instant he was turned to ash, and his army of imps vanished into thin air and were never seen in the kingdom again.

The king was true to his word and lavished gold and jewels upon Alexander, and offered him the hand of his daughter in marriage so that Alexander might become the heir to his kingdom. Yet Alexander turned down all these things and asked only that word might be sent back to his own lord telling him of the great deed he had performed. The king promised that it would be done, and so Alexander left him and continued on his travels. He killed the oldest and most terrible dragon in the western lands and made a cloak from its skin. He used the cloak to guard himself against the heat of the underworld, where he journeyed to rescue the son of the Red Queen, who had been abducted by a demon. With every feat that he accomplished, word was sent back to his lord, and so Alexander's reputation grew and grew.

Ten years passed and Alexander became weary of wandering. He bore the painful scars of his many adventures, and he felt certain that his reputation as the greatest of knights was now secure. He decided to return to his own lands and so began his long journey home. But a band of thieves and brigands fell upon him on a dark road and Alexander, worn down by battles uncountable, was barely able to fight them off, suffering grievous injuries at their hands. He rode on, but he was weak and ailing. Upon a hill before him he spied a castle, and he rode to its gates and called out for help, for it was the custom in those lands that people offered help to strangers in need, and that a knight in particular should never be turned away without being given all that was in the power of another to offer him.

But there was no reply, even though a light burned in the upper reaches of the castle. Alexander called out again, and this time a woman's voice said:

'I cannot help you. You must leave this place and seek comfort elsewhere.'

'I am wounded,' answered Alexander. 'I fear that I may die if my injuries are not tended to.'

But the woman again replied: 'Go. I cannot help you. Ride on. In a mile or two you will reach a village, and there they will see to your wounds.'

With no choice but to do as she said, Alexander turned his horse away from the castle gates and prepared to follow the road to the village. As he did so, his strength failed him. He fell from his horse and lay upon the cold, hard ground, and the world grew dark around him.

When he awoke, he found himself on clean sheets in a large bed. The room in which he lay was very lavish, but layered with dust and cobwebs, as though it had not been used in a very long time. He rose and saw that his wounds had been cleaned and dressed. His weapons and armour were nowhere to be seen. There was food by his bedside, and a jug of wine.

He ate and drank, then dressed himself in a robe that hung from a hook on the wall. He was still weak, and he ached when he walked, but he was no longer at risk of death. He tried to leave the room, but the door was locked. Then he heard the woman's voice again. It said:

'I have done more than I wished for you, but I will not allow you to roam my house. None has entered this place in many years. It is my domain. When you are strong enough to travel, then I will open the door and you must leave and never return.'

'Who are you?' asked Alexander.

'I am the Lady,' she said. 'I no longer have any other name.'

'Where are you?' asked Alexander, for her voice seemed to come from somewhere beyond the walls.

'I am here,' she said.

At that moment, the mirror on the wall to his right shimmered and grew transparent, and through the glass he saw the shape of a woman. She was dressed all in black and was seated on a great throne in an otherwise empty room. Her face was veiled, and her hands were concealed by velvet gloves.

'Can I not look upon the face of the one who has saved my life?' asked Alexander.

'I choose not to allow it,' the Lady replied.

Alexander bowed, for if it was the Lady's will, then so it should be.

'Where are your servants?' asked Alexander. 'I would like to be sure that my horse is being tended to.'

'I have no servants,' said the Lady. 'I have looked to your horse myself. He is well.'

Alexander had so many questions to ask that he was not sure where to begin. He opened his mouth but the Lady raised a hand to silence him.

'I will leave you now,' she said. 'Sleep, for I wish you to recover quickly and be gone from this place as soon as you can.'

The mirror shimmered and the Lady's image was replaced

with Alexander's own. With nothing else to do, Alexander returned to his bed and slept.

The next morning, he awoke to find fresh bread beside him, and a jug of warm milk. He had heard no one enter during the night. Alexander drank some of the milk, and while he ate the bread he walked to the mirror and gazed upon it. Although the image did not change, he was certain that the Lady was behind the glass, watching him.

Now Alexander, like many of the greatest knights, was not merely a warrior. He could play both the lute and the lyre. He could compose poems, and even paint a little. He had a love of books, because in books was recorded the knowledge of all those who had gone before him. And so, when next the Lady appeared in the glass that night, he asked for some of these things in order to pass the time while he recovered from his injuries. When he woke up the next morning, he was greeted by a pile of old books, a slightly dusty lute, and a canvas, paints and some brushes. He played the lute, then began to work his way through the books. There were volumes of history and philosophy, astronomy and morals, poetry and religion. As he read them in the days that followed, the Lady began to appear more often behind the glass, questioning him about all that he had read. It was clear to him that she had read them all many times and knew their contents intimately. Alexander was surprised. In his own land, women were not allowed access to such books, yet he was grateful for the conversation. The Lady then asked him to play for her on the lute, and he did so, and it seemed to him that the sounds he made pleased her.

Thus the days turned to weeks, and the Lady spent more and more time on the other side of the glass, talking with Alexander of art and books, listening to him play and enquiring after what it was that he was painting. Alexander refused to show it to her and obtained a promise from her that she would not look upon it while he slept, for he did not want her to see it until it was *finished. And although Alexander's wounds had almost healed, the Lady no longer seemed to wish him to leave, and Alexander no longer wanted to leave: he was falling in love with the strange, veiled woman behind the glass. He spoke to her of the battles he had fought, and the reputation he had gained from his conquests. He wanted her to understand that he was a great knight, a knight worthy of a great lady.*

After two months had passed, the Lady came to Alexander and sat in her usual place.

'Why do you look so sad?' she asked, because it was clear to her that the knight was unhappy.

'I cannot finish my painting,' he said.

'Why? Do you not have brushes and paints? What more do you need?'

Alexander turned the canvas away from the wall, so that the Lady might see the image upon it. It was a painting of the Lady herself, yet the face was blank, for Alexander had yet to look upon it.

'Forgive me,' he said. 'I am in love with you. In these months we have spent together I have learned so much about you. I have never met a woman like you, and I fear that if I leave here I may never do so again. Can I hope that you might feel the same way about me?'

The Lady lowered her head. She seemed about to speak, but then the mirror shimmered and she disappeared from view.

Days went by, and the Lady did not reappear. Alexander was left alone to wonder if he had offended her by what he had said and done. Each night he slept soundly, and each morning food appeared, but he never caught sight of the Lady who brought it.

Then, after five days, he heard the key turning in the lock of his door and the Lady entered. She was still veiled and still dressed all in black, but Alexander sensed something different about her.

'I have thought about what you said,' she told him. 'I, too,

have feelings for you. But tell me, and tell me truly: do you love me? Will you always love me, no matter what may occur?'

Somewhere deep in Alexander, the hastiness of youth still lived, and he answered, almost unthinkingly: 'Yes, I will always love you.'

Then the Lady raised her veil, and Alexander looked upon her face for the first time. It was the face of a woman crossed with that of a beast, a wild thing of the woods, like a panther or a tigress. Alexander opened his mouth to speak, but he could not, so shocked was he by what he saw.

'My stepmother made me this way,' said the Lady. 'I was beautiful, and she envied me my beauty, so she cursed me with the features of an animal and told me that I would never be loved. And I believed her, and I hid myself away in shame, until you came.'

The Lady advanced towards Alexander, her hands outstretched, and her eyes were filled with hope and love and a flicker of fear, for she had opened herself to him as she had never before opened herself to another human being, and now her heart lay exposed as it would before a sharp blade.

But Alexander did not come to her. He backed away, and in that moment his fate was sealed.

'Foul man!' cried the Lady. 'Fickle creature! You told me that you loved me, but you love only yourself.'

She raised her head and bared her sharp teeth at him. The tips of her gloves split as long claws emerged from her fingers. She hissed at the knight, then sprang upon him, biting him, scratching him, ripping him with her claws, the taste of his blood warm in her mouth, the feel of it hot upon her fur.

And she tore him apart in the bedchamber, and she wept as she consumed him.

The two little girls looked shocked when Roland finished his tale. He rose, thanked Fletcher and his family for the meal, then indicated to David that they should leave. At the door, Fletcher laid a hand gently on Roland's arm.

'A word, if you please,' he said. 'The elders are worried. They believe that the village has been marked by the Beast of which you spoke, and fear that it is nearby.'

'Do you have weapons?' asked Roland.

'We do, but you have seen the best of them. We are farmers and hunters, not soldiers,' said Fletcher.

'Perhaps that is fortunate,' said Roland. 'The soldiers did not fare so well against it. You may have better luck.'

Fletcher looked at him quizzically, unable to tell if Roland was being serious or was taunting him. Even David was not sure.

'Are you jesting with me?' asked Fletcher.

Roland laid his hand upon the older man's shoulder. 'Only a little,' he said. 'The soldiers approached the Beast's destruction as they would that of another army. They fought of necessity on unfamiliar ground, against an enemy that they did not understand. They had time to build some defences – we saw what was left of them – but they were not strong enough to hold. They were forced to retreat into the forest and there they were finished off. Whatever it is, this creature is big, and heavy: I saw where its bulk had flattened trees and shrubs. I doubt if it can move fast, but it is strong and can withstand the injuries inflicted by spears and swords. Out in the open, the soldiers were no match for it.

'But you and your fellows are in a different position. This is your land, and you know it. You need to look upon this thing as you would a wolf or a fox that is threatening your animals. You must lure it to a place of your own choosing, and there trap it and kill it.'

'You're suggesting a decoy? Livestock, perhaps?'

Roland nodded. 'That might work. It is coming. It likes the taste of meat, and there is little of that between the site of its last meal and this village. You may huddle here and hope that your walls can withstand it, or you can plan for its destruction, but you may have to sacrifice more than some cattle to achieve that end.'

'What do you mean?' asked Fletcher. He looked fearful.

Roland wet his finger in a flask of water, then knelt and drew a circle on the stone floor, leaving a small gap instead of completing it.

'This is your village,' said Roland. 'Your walls are built to repel an attack from outside.' He drew arrows pointing away from the circle. 'But what if you were to allow your enemy in, and then close the gates behind it?' Roland completed the circle, and this time he drew arrows pointing inwards. 'Then your walls become a trap.'

Fletcher stared at the drawing, which was already drying upon the stone, fading away to nothing.

'And what do we do once it's inside?' he asked.

'Then you set fire to the village, and everything within,' said Roland. 'You burn it alive.'

That night, as Roland and David slept, a great blizzard arose, and the village and all that surrounded it was blanketed with snow. The snow continued to fall throughout the day, so thickly that it was impossible to see more than a few feet ahead. Roland decided that they would have to stay in the village until the weather improved, but neither he nor David had food left, and the villagers had barely enough for themselves. So Roland asked to meet the elders, and he spent time with them in the church, where the villagers always gathered to discuss matters of great importance. He offered to help them kill the Beast if they would give shelter to him and to David. David sat at the rear of the church as Roland told them of his plan, and the arguments for and against it went back and forth. Some of the villagers were unwilling to sacrifice their houses to the flames, and David didn't really blame them. They wanted to wait in the hope that the walls and defences would save them when the Beast came.

'And if they do not hold?' asked Roland. 'What then? By the time you realise they have failed you, it will be too late to do anything but die.'

In the end, a compromise was suggested. As soon as the weather cleared, the women, children and old men would leave the village and take shelter in the caves in the nearby hills. They would bring with them everything of value, even their furniture, leaving only the shells of the houses behind. Barrels of pitch and oil would be stored in the cottages near the heart of the village. If the Beast attacked, the defenders would try to repel it or kill it from behind the walls. If it broke through, they would retreat, drawing it into the centre. There the fuses would be lit, but only as a last resort. The villagers took a vote and all agreed that this was the best plan.

Roland stormed out of the church. David had to run to catch up with him.

'Why are you so angry?' asked David. 'They consented to most of your plan.'

'Most isn't enough,' said Roland. 'We don't even know what we're facing. What we do know is that trained soldiers, armed with hardened steel, couldn't kill this thing. What hope do farmers have against it? Had they listened to me, then the Beast might have been defeated without any loss of life to them. Now men will die needlessly because of sticks and straw, because of hovels that could be rebuilt in weeks.'

'But it's their village,' said David. 'It's their choice.'

Roland slowed down, then stopped. His hair was white with snow. It made him look much older than he was.

'Yes,' he said, 'it's their village. But our fortunes are now tied up with theirs, and if this fails then there is a good chance that we may die alongside them for our troubles.'

The snow fell, and the fires burned in the cottages, and the wind carried the smell of smoke into the darkest depths of the forest.

And in its lair the Beast smelled it upon the air, and began to move.

XXI

Of the Coming of the Beast

All that day and the next, preparations were made for the evacuation of the village. The women, children and old men gathered up everything that they could carry, and every cart and every horse was pressed into service, except for Scylla, for Roland would not let her out of his sight. Instead, he rode along the wall, both inside and out, checking it for weaknesses. He did not look pleased by what he saw. The snow still fell, numbing fingers and freezing feet. It made the task of reinforcing the village's defences harder and the men grumbled amongst themselves, asking if all these preparations were really necessary and suggesting that they might have been better off fleeing with the women and children. Even Roland seemed to have his doubts.

'We might as well set splinters and firewood against this creature,' David heard him tell Fletcher. They had no idea from which direction the attack would come, so over and over again Roland instructed the defenders in their lines of retreat if the wall was breached and in their tasks once the Beast was in the village. He did not want the men to panic and flee blindly when the creature broke through – as he was sure it would – or all would be lost, but he had little faith in their willingness to stand and face the Beast if the tide of battle turned against them.

'They are not cowards,' Roland told David while they sat by

a fire and rested, drinking milk still warm from the cow. All around them men were sharpening staffs and sword blades, or using oxen and horses to drag tree trunks into the compound in order to support the walls from within. There was little conversation now, as the day was drawing to a close and night was approaching. Everyone was tense and frightened. 'Each of these men would lay down his life for his wife and children,' Roland continued. 'Faced by bandits or wolves or wild beasts they would meet the threat, and live or die according to the outcome. But this is different: they don't know or understand what they are about to confront, and they are not disciplined or experienced enough to fight as one. While they will all stand together, each in his way will face this thing alone. They will be united only when the courage of one falters and he runs, and the others follow after him.'

'You don't have much faith in people, do you?' said David.

'I don't have much faith in anything,' Roland replied. 'Not even in myself.'

He drank the last of his milk, then cleaned the cup in a bucket of cold water.

'Come now,' he said. 'We have sticks to sharpen, and blunt swords to make keen.'

He smiled emptily. David did not smile back.

It had been decided that they would marshal the main part of their little force near the gates, in the hope that this would draw the Beast to them. If it breached the defences it would be lured into the centre of the village, where the trap would be sprung. They would then have one chance, and one chance only, to contain it and to kill it.

When not even the barest sliver of pale moon was visible in the sky, a final convoy of people and animals quietly left the village, with a small escort of men to make sure that they reached the caves safely. Once the men had returned, a formal watch was placed upon the walls, each man taking it in turn to spend a few hours guarding the approaches. Altogether, they numbered about forty souls, and David. Roland had asked David if he wished to enter the caves with the others, but, although he was frightened, David said that he wanted to stay. He was not sure why. Perhaps partly it was because he felt safer with Roland, who was the only person he trusted in this place, but he was also curious. David wanted to see the Beast, whatever it was. Roland seemed to know this and, when the villagers asked him why he had allowed David to stay, he told them that David was his squire and was as valuable to him as his sword or his horse. His words made David blush with pride.

They tethered an old cow in the clearing before the gates, hoping that it would lure the Beast, but nothing happened on that first night of the watch, or the second, and the men grew ever more grouchy and tired. The snow kept falling and freezing, falling and freezing. The watchers on the walls found it hard to see the forest because of the blizzard. A few began muttering amongst themselves.

'This is foolishness.'

'This creature is as cold as we are. It will not attack us in this weather.'

'Perhaps there is no Beast at all. What if Ethan was attacked by a wolf, or a bear? We have only this vagabond's word that he saw the bodies of soldiers.'

'The blacksmith is right. What if all of this is a trick?'

It was Fletcher who tried to make them see reason.

'And what purpose would such a trick serve?' he asked them. 'He is one man, with a boy by his side. He cannot murder us in our sleep and we have nothing worth stealing. If he is doing it for food, then there is precious little of it for him here. Have faith, my friends, and be patient and watchful.'

Their grumblings ceased, but they were still cold and unhappy, and they missed their wives and their families.

David spent all of his time with Roland, sleeping beside him during their periods of rest and walking the perimeter with him when their time came to take the watch. Now that the defences had been strengthened as well as they could be, Roland took time to talk and joke with the men, shaking them awake when they dozed and encouraging them when their spirits grew low. He knew that this was the hardest time for them, for the watch was both dull and hard on their nerves. Watching him move among them, and seeing the way in which he had supervised the defence of the village, David wondered if Roland really was only a soldier, as he claimed. He seemed more like a leader to David, a natural captain of men, yet he was riding alone.

On the second night, they sat in the light of a big fire, huddled beneath thick cloaks. Roland had told David that he was free to sleep in one of the cottages nearby, but none of the others had chosen to do so and David did not want to appear weaker than he already was by taking up the offer, even if his refusal meant sleeping outdoors, cold and exposed. Thus he chose to remain with Roland. The flames illuminated the soldier's features, casting shadows across his skin, enhancing the bones in his cheeks and deepening the darkness in the sockets of his eyes.

'What do you think happened to Raphael?' David asked him.

Roland did not answer. He just shook his head.

David knew that he should probably remain silent, but he did not want to. He had questions and doubts of his own, and somehow he knew that Roland shared them. It was not chance that had brought them together. Nothing in this place seemed bound by the rules of chance alone. There was a purpose to all that was happening, a pattern behind it, even if David could catch only glimpses of it in passing.

'You think he's dead, don't you?' he said softly.

'Yes,' answered Roland. 'I know it in my heart.'

'But you have to find out what happened to him.'

'I will know no peace until I do.'

'But you may die as well. If you follow his path, you could end up just as he did. Aren't you afraid of dying?'

Roland took a stick and poked at the fire, sending sparks flying upwards into the night. They fizzled out before they got very far, like insects that were already being consumed by the flames even as they struggled to escape them.

'I am afraid of the pain of dying,' he said. 'I have been wounded before, once so badly that it was feared I would not survive. I can recall the agony of it, and I don't wish to endure it again.

'But I feared more the death of others. I did not want to lose those whom I loved, and I worried about them while they were alive. Sometimes, I think that I concerned myself so much with the possibility of their loss that I never truly took pleasure in the fact of their existence. It was part of my nature, even with Raphael. Yet he was the blood in my veins, the sweat on my brow. Without him, I am less than I once was.'

David stared into the flames. Roland's words resonated within him. That was how he had felt about his mother. He had spent so long being terrified at the thought of losing her that he had never really enjoyed the time they spent together towards the end.

'And you?' said Roland. 'You're only a boy. You don't belong here. Aren't you frightened?'

'Yes,' said David. 'But I heard my mother's voice. She's here, somewhere. I have to find her. I have to bring her back.'

'David, your mother is dead,' said Roland gently. 'You told me so.'

'Then how can she be here? How can I have heard her voice so clearly?'

But Roland had no answer, and David's frustration grew.

'What is this place?' he demanded. 'It has no name. Even you can't tell me what it's called. It has a king, but he might as well not exist. There are things here that don't belong: that tank, the German plane that followed me through the tree, the harpies. It's all wrong. It's just . . .'

His voice trailed off. There were words forming in his brain like a dark cloud building on a clear summer's day, filled with heat and fury. The question came to him, and he was almost surprised to hear his own voice ask it.

'Roland, are you dead? Are we dead?'

Roland looked at him through the flames.

'I don't know,' he replied. 'I think I am as alive as you are. I feel cold and warmth, hunger and thirst, desire and regret. I am conscious of the weight of a sword in my hand, and my skin bears the marks of the armour that I wear when I remove it at night. I can taste bread and meat. I can smell Scylla upon me after a day in the saddle. If I were dead, such things would be lost to me, would they not?'

'I suppose so,' said David. He had no idea how the dead felt once they passed from one world to the next. How could he? All he knew was that his mother's skin had been cold to the touch, but David could still sense the warmth of his own body. Like Roland, he could smell and touch and taste. He was aware of pain and discomfort. He could feel the heat from the fire, and he was sure that if he put his hand to it his skin would blister and burn.

And yet this world remained a curious mix of the strange and the familiar, as though by coming here he had somehow altered its nature, infecting it with aspects of his own life.

'Have you ever dreamed of this place?' he asked Roland. 'Have you ever dreamed of me, or of anything else in it?'

'When I met you on the road, you were a stranger to me,' said Roland, 'and although I knew there was a village here, I had never seen it until now, for I have never travelled these roads before. David, this land is as real as you are. Do not start believing that it is some dream conjured up from deep within yourself. I have seen the fear in your eyes when you speak of the wolf packs and the creatures that lead them, and I know that they will eat you if they find you. I smelled the decay of those men on the battlefield. Soon we will face whatever wiped them out, and we may not survive the encounter. All of these things are real. You have endured pain here. If you can endure pain, then you can die. You can be killed here, and your own world will be lost to you forever. Never forget that. If you do, you are lost.'

Perhaps, thought David.

Perhaps.

It was deep in the third night when a cry went up from one of the lookouts at the gates.

'To me, to me!' said the young man whose job it was to watch the main road to the settlement. 'I heard something, and I saw movement on the ground. I am certain of it.'

Those who were sleeping awoke and joined him. Those who were far from the gates heard the cry and were about to come running too, but Roland called to them and ordered them to stay where they were. He arrived at the gates and began to climb a ladder to the platform at the top of the walls. Some of the men were already waiting for him, while others stood on the ground and stared through the slits that had been cut into the tree trunks at eye level. Their torches hissed and sputtered as the snow fell upon them and melted instantly.

'I can see nothing,' said the blacksmith to the young man. 'You woke us for no good reason.'

They heard the cow lowing nervously. It rose from its sleep and tried to pull itself free from the post to which it was tethered.

'Wait,' said Roland. He took an arrow from a pile against the wall, each one with a rag soaked in oil at its tip. He touched the wrapped point to one of the torches, and it exploded into flame. He took careful aim, and fired towards where the guard on the wall said that he had seen movement. Four or five of the men did the same, their arrows sailing like dying stars through the night air.

For a moment, there was nothing to be seen but falling snow and shadowy trees. Then something moved, and they saw a massive yellow body erupting from beneath the earth, ridged like that of a great worm, each ridge embedded with thick black hairs, each hair ending in a razor-sharp barb. One of the arrows had lodged itself in the creature and a foul smell of burning flesh arose, so horrible that the men covered their noses and mouths to block the stink. Black fluid bubbled from the wound, spitting in the heat of the arrow's flame. David could see the shafts of broken arrows and spears stuck in its skin, relics of its earlier encounter with the soldiers. It was impossible to tell how long it was, but the exposed part of its body was ten feet high at least. They saw the Beast twist and turn as it pulled itself free from the dirt, and then a terrible face was revealed. It had clusters of black eyes like a spider, some small, some large, and a sucking mouth beneath them that was lined with row upon row of sharp teeth. Between eyes and mouth, openings like nostrils quivered as it smelled the men in the village and the blood that flowed in their veins. There were two arms at either side of its jaws, each ending in a series of three hooked claws with which it could pull its prey into its maw. It did not seem able to make any sound from its mouth, but there was a wet, sucking noise as it began to move across the forest floor, and clear, sticky strands of mucus dripped from its upper body as it raised itself up like a huge, ugly caterpillar reaching for a tasty leaf. Its head was now twenty feet above the ground, revealing its lower body and the twin rows of black, spiny legs with which it propelled itself along the ground.

'It's higher than the wall!' yelled Fletcher. 'It won't need to break through. It can just climb over!'

Roland didn't reply. Instead, he told all of the men to light arrows and aim for the Beast's head. A rain of flames shot towards the creature. Some missed their mark, while more bounced off the great ridges on its body. But still others struck home, and

David saw an arrow land in one of the creature's eyes, bursting it instantly. The smell of rotting, burning flesh grew stronger. The Beast shook its head in pain, then began to close on the walls. They could now clearly see how big it was: thirty feet long from its jaws to its rear. It was moving much faster than even Roland had expected, and only the thick snow prevented it from moving faster still. Soon it would be upon them.

'Keep firing for as long as you can, then retreat once you've drawn it to the walls!' cried Roland. He grabbed David's arm. 'Come with me. I need your help.'

But David could not move. He was drawn by the dark eyes of the Beast, unable to tear his gaze from it. It was as though a fragment of his own nightmares had somehow come to life, a thing that lay in the shadows of his imagination finally given form.

'David!' shouted Roland. He shook the boy's arm, and the spell was broken. 'Come now. We have little time.'

They climbed down from the platform and headed for the gates. These consisted of two thick masses of planks, locked from within by half a tree trunk that could be raised by pressing hard upon one end. When they reached the trunk, Roland and David began to push down with all of their strength.

'What are you doing?' shouted the blacksmith. 'You'll damn us to death!'

And then the great head of the Beast appeared above the blacksmith, and one of its clawed arms shot out and grasped the man, lifting him high into the air and straight into its waiting jaws. David looked away, unable to watch the blacksmith die. The other defenders were using spears and swords now, stabbing at the Beast's body and hacking at its sides. Fletcher, who was bigger and stronger than any of the others, raised a sword and with a single blow tried to sever one of the Beast's arms from its body, but it was as thick and hard as the trunk of a small tree and the sword barely broke its skin. Still, the pain distracted it for long enough to allow the villagers to begin their retreat from the walls, just as David and Roland managed to raise the barrier from the gates.

The Beast was attempting to climb over the wall, but Roland had instructed the men to force sticks tipped with hooks through the gaps if the Beast got close enough. They tore at the Beast's flesh, and it writhed and twisted upon them. The hooks slowed it down, but it continued to try to push itself over the defences, even at the cost of great injury to itself. Just then, Roland opened the gates and appeared outside the walls. He drew an arrow and fired it at the side of the Beast's head.

'Hey!' shouted Roland. 'This way. Come on!'

He waved his arms, then fired again. The Beast pulled its body from the wall and flopped to the ground, the ooze from its wounds staining the snow black. It turned on Roland, pushing itself through the gates, its arms trying to grab him as he ran ahead of it, its head thrusting forward, its jaws snapping at his heels. It paused as it crossed the threshold, taking in the twisting streets, the fleeing men. Roland waved his torch.

'Here!' he cried. 'Here I am!'

Roland dropped the torch and loosed another arrow, barely missing the Beast's jaws, but it was no longer interested in him. Instead, its nostrils opened and closed as it lowered its head, sniffing, searching. David, hiding in the shadows outside the blacksmith's forge, saw his face reflected in the depths of its eyes as the Beast found him. Its jaws opened, dripping saliva and blood, and then one of its great claws swiped the roof from the forge as it reached for the boy. David threw himself backwards just in time to avoid being swept up in the Beast's grasp. Dimly, he heard Roland's voice.

'Run, David! You must lure it for us!'

David rose to his feet and began to sprint through the narrow streets of the village. Behind him, the Beast crushed the walls and roofs of cottages as it followed him, its head lunging at the little figure fleeing before it, its claws raking at the air. Once

David stumbled and the claws tore at the clothes on his back as he rolled out of their reach and got to his feet again. Now he was just a stone's throw from the centre of the village. There was a square around the church, where markets had been held in happier times. Channels had been dug through it by the defenders so that the oil would flow into the square, surrounding the Beast. David raced across the open space towards the doors of the church, the Beast just feet behind him. Roland was already in the doorway, urging David forward.

Suddenly, the Beast stopped. David turned and stared at it. In the nearby houses, the men were preparing to send the oil into the channels, but they too ceased what they were doing and watched the Beast. It began to shudder and shake. Its jaws grew impossibly wide and its body writhed as though in great pain. Suddenly it fell to the ground as its belly started to swell. David could see movement inside. A shape pressed itself against the Beast's skin from within.

She. The Crooked Man had said the Beast was a female.

'It's giving birth!' shouted David. 'You have to kill it now!'

It was too late. The Beast's belly split open with a great ripping sound and her offspring began to pour out, miniatures of herself, each as big as David, their eyes clouded and unseeing but their jaws snapping and hungry for food. Some were chewing their way out of their own mother, eating her flesh as they freed themselves from her dying body.

'Pour the oil!' shouted Roland to the other men. 'Pour it, then light the fuses and run!'

Already the young were pushing themselves across the square, the instincts to hunt and kill strong within them. Roland pulled David inside the church and locked the door behind them. Something thrust against it from outside, and the door trembled in its frame.

Roland took David by the hand and led him towards the bell tower. They ascended the stone steps until they reached the chamber where the bell itself hung, and from there they looked down upon the square.

The Beast was still lying on her side, but she had stopped moving. If she was not already dead, then she soon would be. Some of her offspring continued to feed on her, chewing at her insides and gnawing at her eyes. Others were squirming across the square, or searching the surrounding cottages for food. The oil was running through the channels, but the young did not seem troubled by it. In the distance, David saw the surviving defenders running for the gates, desperate to escape the creatures.

'There are no flames,' cried David. 'They haven't lit the fires!'

Roland drew an oil-soaked arrow from his quiver.

'Then we will have to do it for them,' he said.

He lit the arrow from his flaming torch, then aimed for one of the channels of oil below. The arrow shot from the bow and struck the black stream. Instantly, flames arose, the fire racing across the square, following the patterns that had been cut into it. The offspring in its path began to burn, sizzling and writhing as they died. Roland took a second arrow and fired into a cottage through its window, but nothing happened. Already David could see some of the young trying to escape from the square and the flames. They could not be allowed to return to the forest.

Roland nocked a final arrow to his bow, drew it against his cheek, and released it. This time there was a loud explosion from inside the cottage, and its roof was lifted off by the force of the blast. Flames shot up into the air, followed by more explosions as the system of barrels that Roland had placed inside the houses ignited one after the other, showering burning liquid all over the square and killing everything within reach. Only Roland and David were saved, high in their perch in the bell tower, for the flames could not reach the church. There they stayed, the stink of the burning creatures and the smell of acrid smoke filling the air, until there was only the dying crackle of the flames and the soft hiss of snow melting in fire to disturb the silence of the night.

XXII

Of the Crooked Man and the Sowing of Doubt

David and Roland left the village next morning. By then the snow had ceased falling, and although thick drifts still masked the lay of the land it was possible to pick out the route that the concealed road took between the tree-covered hills. The women, children and old men had returned from their hiding places in the caves. David could hear some of them crying and wailing as they stood before the smouldering ruins of what were once their homes, or mourning those who had been lost, for three men had died fighting the Beast. Others had gathered in the square where the horses and oxen were once again being pressed into service, this time to haul away the charred carcasses of the Beast and her foul offspring.

Roland had not asked David why he thought the Beast had chosen to pursue him through the village, but David had seen the soldier looking at him thoughtfully as they prepared to depart. Fletcher, too, had seen what occurred, and David knew that he also was curious. David was not sure how he would answer the question if it was asked. How could he explain his sense that the Beast was familiar to him, that there was a corner of his imagination where the creature had found an echo of herself? What frightened him most of all was the feeling that he had somehow been responsible for its creation, and the deaths of the soldiers and the villagers were now on his conscience.

When Scylla was saddled, and they had scraped together some food and found fresh water, Roland and David walked through the village to the gates. Few of the inhabitants came to wish them well. Most chose instead to turn their backs upon the departing travellers or stared balefully at them from the ruins. Only Fletcher seemed truly sorry to see them go.

'I apologise for the behaviour of the rest,' he said. 'They should show more gratitude for what you have done.'

'They blame us for what happened to their village,' said Roland to Fletcher. 'Why should they be grateful to those who took the roofs from above their heads?'

Fletcher looked embarrassed.

'There are those who say that the Beast followed you, and that you should never have been allowed to enter the village in the first place,' he said. He glanced at David quickly, unwilling to meet his eye. 'Some have spoken about the boy and how the Beast pursued him. They say that he is cursed, and we are well rid of both of you.'

'Are they angry with you for bringing us here?' asked David, and Fletcher was thrown slightly by the boy's solicitude.

'If they are, then they will soon forget. Already we are planning to send men into the forest to cut down trees. We will rebuild our homes. The wind saved most of the houses to the south and west, and we will share our living spaces with one another until we have rebuilt. In time, they will come to realise that, had it not been for you, there would be no village at all, and many more would have died in the jaws of the Beast and her young.'

Fletcher handed Roland a sack of food.

'I can't take this,' said Roland. 'You will all have need of it.'

'With the Beast dead, the animals will return, and we will have prey to hunt once again.'

Roland thanked him and prepared to turn Scylla to the east.

'You are a brave young man,' Fletcher said to David. 'I wish there was something more that I could give to you, but all I could find was this.'

In his hand he held what looked like a blackened hook. He gave it to David. It was heavy, and had the texture of bone.

'It is one of the Beast's claws,' said Fletcher. 'If anyone ever questions your bravery, or you feel your courage ebb, take it in your hand and remember what you did here.'

David thanked him and stored the claw in his pack. Then Roland spurred Scylla on and they left the ruins of the village behind them.

They rode in silence through the twilight world, its appearance rendered more spectral yet by the fallen snow. Everything seemed to glow with a blueish tinge, and the land appeared both brighter and yet more alien. It was very cold and their breath hung heavily in the air. David felt the little hairs in his nostrils freeze and the moisture from his breath formed crystals of ice upon his eyelashes. Roland rode slowly, taking care to keep Scylla away from ditches and drifts for fear that she might injure herself.

'Roland,' said David at last. 'There's something that's been bothering me. You told me that you were just a soldier, but I don't think that's true.'

'Why do you say that?' asked Roland.

'I saw how you gave orders to the villagers and how they obeyed you, even the ones who weren't sure they liked you. I have seen your armour and your sword. I thought that the decoration on them was just bronze or coloured metal, but when I looked more closely I could see that it was gold. The sun symbol on your breastplate and your shield is made of gold, and there is gold on your scabbard and on the hilt of your sword. How can that be, if you are just a soldier?'

Roland did not answer for a time, then he said: 'I was once more than a soldier. My father was lord of a vast estate and I was his eldest son and heir. But he did not approve of me or of the way that I lived my life. We argued, and in a fit of anger he banished me from his presence and from his lands. It was not long after our fight that my quest for Raphael began.'

David wanted to ask more, but he sensed that whatever lay between Roland and Raphael was private and very personal. To pursue it further would have been rude and hurtful to Roland.

'And you?' asked Roland. 'Tell me more about yourself and your home.'

And David did. He tried to explain some of the wonders of his own world to Roland. He told him of aeroplanes and the wireless, of cinemas and cars. He spoke of the war, of the conquest of nations and the bombing of cities. If Roland thought these things were extraordinary, he did not show it. He listened to them the way an adult might listen to a child's constructed tales, impressed that a mind could create such fantasies but reluctant to share their creator's belief in them. He seemed more interested in what the Woodsman had told David of the king, and of the book that held his secrets.

'I, too, have heard that the king knows a great deal about books and stories,' said Roland. 'His realm may be falling to pieces around him, but he always has time for talk of tales. Perhaps the Woodsman was right to try to lead you towards him.'

'If the king is weak, as you say, then what will happen to his kingdom when he dies?' asked David. 'Does he have a son or a daughter who will succeed him?'

'The king has no children,' said Roland. 'He has ruled for a very long time, since before I was born, but he has never taken a wife.'

'And before him?' asked David, who had always been interested in kings and queens and kingdoms and knights. 'Was his father king?'

Roland struggled to remember.

'There was a queen before him, I think. She was very, very old, and she announced that a young man, one whom nobody had ever seen before but who was soon to come, would rule the realm in her place. That was what happened, according to those who were alive then. Within days of the young man's arrival, he was king, and the queen went to her bed and fell asleep and never woke again. They say that she seemed almost . . . grateful to die.'

They came to a stream, frozen over by the intense cold, and there they decided to rest for a short while. Roland used the hilt of his sword to break the ice so that Scylla could drink from the water. David wandered along the edge of the stream while Roland ate. He was not hungry. Fletcher's wife had given him great slabs of home-made bread and jam for breakfast that morning, and they were still sitting in his stomach. He sat on a rock and dug in the snow for stones to throw at the ice. The snow was deep, and soon his arm was buried up to the elbow. His fingers touched some pebbles—

And a hand shot out of the snow and gripped him just above the elbow. It was white and thin, with long, jagged nails, and with enormous force it pulled him from the rock and into the snow. David opened his mouth to yell for help, but a second hand appeared and clamped itself across his lips. He was dragged deep beneath the drift, the snow falling on top of him so that he could no longer see the trees and sky above, the hands never loosening their hold upon him. He felt hard ground at his back and was overcome by a terrible sense of suffocation, and then the earth, too, collapsed and he found himself in a hollow of dirt and stone. The hands released him and a light shone through the darkness. Tree roots hung down from above, gently caressing his face, and David saw the openings of three tunnels, their mouths converging on this one spot. Yellowing bones lay in one corner, the flesh that once covered them long since rotted or consumed. There were worms and beetles and spiders all around, scurrying and fighting and dying in the damp, cold ground.

And there was the Crooked Man. He squatted in a corner, one of those pale hands that had dragged David down now holding a lamp while the other gripped a huge black beetle. As David watched, the Crooked Man put the struggling insect into his mouth, head first, and bit it in half. He chewed on the beetle, all the time watching David. The bottom half of the insect kept moving for a few seconds, then stopped. The Crooked Man offered it to David. David could see part of its insides. They were white. He felt very sick.

'Help me!' he shouted. 'Roland, please help me!'

But there was no reply. Instead, the vibrations of his cries merely dislodged dirt from the roof of the hollow. It fell on his head and into his mouth. David spat it out, then prepared to shout again.

'Oh, I wouldn't do that,' said the Crooked Man. He picked at his teeth and extracted a long, black beetle leg that had lodged close to his gums. 'The ground here isn't stable, and with all that snow above, well, I don't like to think what would happen if it came down on top of you. You'd die, I expect, and not very pleasantly.'

David closed his mouth. He did not want to be buried alive down there with the insects and the worms and the Crooked Man.

The Crooked Man worked on the lower half of the beetle, removing its back to expose its innards entirely.

'Are you sure you don't want any?' he asked. 'They're very good: crunchy on the outside, soft on the inside. Sometimes, though, I find that I don't want crunchy. I just want soft.'

He lifted the insect's body to his mouth and sucked at its flesh, then threw the husk into a corner.

'I thought that you and I should have a talk,' he said, 'without the risk of your, um, "friend" up there interrupting us. I don't think you've fully grasped the nature of your predicament. You still seem to think that allying yourself with every passing stranger will help you, but it won't, you know. I'm the reason you're still alive, not some ignorant Woodsman or disgraced knight.'

David couldn't bear to hear the men who had helped him dismissed like that.

'The Woodsman wasn't ignorant,' he said. 'And Roland argued with his father. He isn't a disgrace to anyone.'

The Crooked Man grinned unpleasantly. 'Is that what he told you? Tut, tut. Have you seen the picture he carries in his locket? Raphael, isn't that the name of the one whom he seeks? Such a nice name for a young man. They were very close, you know. Oooh, very close.'

David didn't know quite what the Crooked Man meant, but the way he spoke made David feel dirty and soiled.

'Perhaps he would like *you* to be his new friend,' continued the Crooked Man. 'He looks at you in the night, you know, when you're asleep. He thinks you're beautiful. He wants to be close to you, and closer than close.'

'Don't talk about him that way,' warned David. 'Don't you dare.'

The Crooked Man sprang from the corner, leaping like a frog, and landed in front of David. His bony hand grasped the boy's jaw painfully, the nails digging into his skin.

'Don't tell me what to do, *child*,' he said. 'I could tear your head off if I chose, and use it to adorn my dinner table. I could bore a hole in your skull and stick a candle in it, once I'd eaten my fill of whatever was inside – which wouldn't be much, I expect. You're not a very bright boy, are you? You enter a world you don't understand, chasing the voice of someone you know is dead. You can't find your way back again, and you insult the only person who can help you to return, namely me. You are a very rude, ungrateful and ignorant little person.'

With a snap of his fingers, the Crooked Man produced a long, sharp needle, threaded with coarse black string made from what looked like the knotted legs of dead beetles.

'Now why don't you work on your manners before you force me to sew your lips shut?'

He released his grip on David's face, then patted his cheek gently.

'Let me show you a proof of my good intentions,' he purred. He reached into the leather pouch at his belt and drew from it the snout that he had severed from the wolf scout. He dangled it in front of David.

'It was following you, and it found you as you emerged from the church in the forest. It would have killed you, too, had I not intervened. Where it went, others will follow. They are on your trail, and growing ever greater in number. More and more of them are transforming now, and they cannot be stopped. Their time is coming. Even the king knows it, and he does not have the strength to stand in their way. It would be well for you to be back in your own world before they find you again, and I can help you. Tell me what I want to know and you will be safe in your bed before night-fall. All will be well in your house, and your problems will have been solved. Your father will love you, and you alone. This I can promise if you answer just one question.'

David didn't want to bargain with the Crooked Man. He couldn't be trusted, and David felt certain that he was keeping many things from him. No deal made with him could ever be simple or without cost. Yet David also knew that much of what he was saying was true: the wolves were coming, and they would not stop until they found David. Roland would not be able to kill them all. Then there was the Beast: terrible though she was, she was only one of the horrors that this land seemed to conceal. There would be others, perhaps worse than the Loups or the Beast. Wherever David's mother now was, in this world or another, she appeared beyond his reach. He could not find her. He had been foolish ever to think he could, but he had wanted so badly for it to be true. He had wanted her to be alive again. He missed her. Sometimes he would forget her, but in forgetting he would remember her again and the ache for her would return with a vengeance. Still, the answer to his loneliness did not lie in this place. It was time to go home.

And so David spoke:

'What do you want to know?' he said.

The Crooked Man leaned towards him, and whispered. 'I want you to tell me the name of the child in your house,' he said. 'I want you to name for me your half-brother.'

David's fear was replaced by puzzlement.

'But why?' he said. He didn't understand. If the Crooked Man was the same figure he had seen in his bedroom, then wasn't it possible that he had been in other parts of the house too? David remembered how he had awoken at home with the unpleasant sensation that something or someone had touched his face while he was asleep. A strange smell had sometimes hung about Georgie's bedroom (stranger, at least, than the smell that usually came from Georgie). Could that have been an indication of the Crooked Man's presence? Was it possible that the Crooked Man had failed to hear Georgie's name spoken during his incursions into their house, and why was it so important to him to know the name anyway?

'I just want to hear it from your lips,' said the Crooked Man. 'It's such a small thing, such a tiny, tiny favour. Tell me, and all this will be over.'

David swallowed hard. He so badly wanted to go home. All he had to do was speak Georgie's name. What harm could that do? He opened his mouth to speak, but the next name spoken was not Georgie's but his own.

'David! Where are you?'

It was Roland. David heard the sound of digging from above. The Crooked Man hissed his displeasure at the intrusion.

'Quickly!' he said to David. 'The name! Tell me the name!'

Dirt fell on David's head, and a spider scurried across his face.

'Tell me!' shrieked the Crooked Man, and then the ceiling of earth over David's head fell in, blinding and burying him. Before his sight failed, he saw the Crooked Man scurry for one of the tunnels to escape the collapse. There was soil in David's mouth and nose. He tried to breathe, but it caught in his throat. He was drowning in dirt, until strong hands gripped his shoulders and pulled him into the clean, crisp air above. His vision cleared, but he was still choking on clay and bugs. Roland's hands pumped at David's body, forcing the earth and insects from his throat. David coughed up dirt and blood and bile and crawling things as his airway cleared, then lay on his side in the snow. The tears froze on his cheeks, and his teeth were chattering.

Roland knelt by his side. 'David,' he said. 'Talk to me. Tell me what happened.'

Tell me. Tell me.

Roland touched his hand to David's face, and David felt himself recoil. Roland, too, registered his response, for instantly he withdrew his hand and moved away from the boy.

'I want to go home,' David whimpered. 'That's all. I just want to go home.'

And he curled into himself upon the snow and cried until he had no more tears left to shed.

XXIII
Of the March of the Wolves

David sat on Scylla's back. Roland was not riding with him but once more led the horse by her reins along the road. There was an unspoken tension between Roland and David, and while the boy was able to recognise both Roland's hurt and its source, he could not find a way to connect the two with an apology. The Crooked Man had hinted at something about the relationship between Roland and the lost Raphael that David felt might be true, but he was less convinced by the implication that Roland now had similar feelings for David himself. Deep down, he was certain that it was false; Roland had shown him nothing but kindness, and if there had been any ulterior motive to his actions, it would have revealed itself long before now. He was sorry that he had recoiled from Roland's touch of solicitude, but to make the admission would have forced him to acknowledge that, even for just the blink of an eye, the Crooked Man's words had found their mark.

It had taken David a long time to recover himself. His throat hurt when he spoke, and he could still taste dirt in his mouth even after he had washed it out with icy water from the stream. It was only after riding in silence for a long time that he was able to tell Roland of what had taken place beneath the ground.

'And that is all he asked of you?' said Roland, when David had repeated to him most of what had been uttered. 'He wanted you to tell him your half-brother's name?'

David nodded. 'He told me I could go back home if I did.'

'Do you believe him?'

David thought about the question. 'Yes,' he said. 'I think he could show me the way, if he wanted to.'

'Then you must decide for yourself what to do. Remember, though, that nothing comes without cost. The villagers learned that as they sifted through the remains of their homes. There is a price to be paid for everything, and it is a good idea to find out that price before you make the agreement. Your friend the Woodsman called this fellow a trickster, and if that is what he is, then nothing he says is entirely to be trusted. Be careful in striking a bargain with him, and listen closely to his words, for he will say less than he means, and conceal more than he reveals.'

Roland did not look back at David as he spoke, and these were the last words that they exchanged for many miles. When they stopped to rest that night, they sat at opposite sides of the small fire Roland had made, and they ate in silence. Roland removed the saddle from Scylla's back and placed it against a tree, far from the spot where he had laid out David's blanket.

'You can rest easy,' he said. 'I am not tired, and I will keep watch on the forest while you rest.'

David thanked him. He lay down and closed his eyes, but he could not sleep. He thought of wolves and Loups, of his father and Rose and Georgie, of his lost mother and the offer that the Crooked Man had made. He wanted to leave this place. If all that was required was to share Georgie's name with the Crooked Man, then perhaps that was what he should do. But the Crooked Man would not come back now that Roland was keeping watch, and David felt his anger at Roland begin to grow. Roland was using him: his promise of protection and of guidance to the king's castle had come at too great a cost. David was being dragged along on a quest for a man whom he had never met, a man for whom only Roland had feelings, and those feelings, if the Crooked Man was to be believed, were not natural. There were names for men like Roland where David came from. They were among the worst names that a man could be called. David had always been warned to keep away from such people, and now here he was keeping company with one of them in a strange land. Well, soon their ways would part. Roland reckoned that they would reach the fortress the following day, and there they would finally learn the truth of Raphael's fate. After that, Roland would lead him to the king, and then their arrangement would be over.

While David slept, and Roland brooded, the man named Fletcher knelt at the walls of his village, his bow in his hand, a quiver of arrows by his side. Others crouched alongside him, their faces lit by torches once again, just as they had been when they prepared to face the Beast. They gazed out at the forest before them, for even in the darkness it was clear to them that it was no longer empty and still. Shapes moved between the trees, thousands upon thousands of them. They padded on all fours, grey and white and black, but among them were those that walked on two legs, dressed like men but with faces that bore traces of the animals they once were.

Fletcher shivered. This, then, was the wolf army of which he had heard. He had never seen so many animals moving as one before, not even when he had looked to the late summer skies and witnessed the migration of birds. Yet they were now more than animals. They moved with a purpose beyond merely the desire to hunt or breed. With the Loups at their head to impose discipline and plan the campaign, they represented a fusion of all that was most terrifying about men and wolves. The king's forces would not be strong enough to defeat them on a field of battle.

One of the Loups emerged from the pack and stood at the edge of the forest, staring at the men hunched behind the defences of their little village. He was more finely dressed than the others, and even from this distance Fletcher could tell that he seemed more human than the others, although he could not yet be mistaken for a man.

Leroi: the wolf who would be king.

During the long wait for the coming of the Beast, Roland had shared with Fletcher what he knew of the wolves and the Loups, and how David had bested them. Although Fletcher wished the soldier and the boy only health and happiness, he was very glad that they were no longer within the walls of the village.

Leroi knows, thought Fletcher. He knows they were here, and if he suspected they were still with us, he would attack with the full force of his legions.

Fletcher raised himself to his feet and stared across the open ground to the place where Leroi stood.

'What are you doing?' whispered someone from close by.

'I will not cower before an animal,' said Fletcher. 'I will not give that *thing* the satisfaction.'

Leroi nodded, as though in understanding of Fletcher's gesture, then slowly drew a clawed finger across his throat. He would be back once the king was dealt with, and then they would see how brave Fletcher and the others truly were. With that, Leroi turned away to rejoin the pack, leaving the men to watch impotently as the great wolf army passed through the woods on its way to seize the kingdom.

XXIV

Of the Fortress of Thorns

David awoke the next morning to find Roland gone. The fire was dead and Scylla was no longer tethered to her tree. David rose and found where the horse's tracks disappeared into the forest. He felt concern at first, then a kind of relief, followed by anger at Roland for abandoning him without even a word of goodbye and, finally, the first twinge of fear. Suddenly, the prospect of confronting the Crooked Man alone again was not so appealing, and the possibility of the wolves coming across him was less appealing yet. He drank from his canteen. His hand was shaking. It caused him to spill water over his shirt. He wiped at it and caught the jagged end of a fingernail on the coarse material. A thread unravelled, and as he tried to free it his nail tore still further, causing him to yelp in pain. He threw the canteen at the nearest tree in a fit of rage, then sat down hard on the ground and buried his head in his hands.

'And what purpose did that serve?' said Roland's voice.

David looked up. Roland was watching him from the edge of the woods, seated high on Scylla's back.

'I thought you'd left me,' said David.

'Why would you think that?'

David shrugged. Now he was ashamed of his display of petulance and for his doubts about Roland. He tried to hide it by going on the attack.

'I woke up and you were gone,' he replied. 'What was I supposed to think?'

'That I was scouting the way ahead. I did not leave you for very long, and I believed that you were safe here. There is stone not far below this ground, so our friend could not use his tunnels against you, and at all times I was within earshot. You had no reason to doubt me.'

Roland dismounted and walked to where David sat, leading Scylla behind him.

'Things have not been the same with us since that foul wretch dragged you beneath the ground,' said Roland. 'I think I may have some inkling of what he said to you about me. My feelings for Raphael are mine, and mine alone. I loved him, and that is all anyone needs to know. The rest is no business of any man's.

'As for you, you are my friend. You are brave and you are both stronger than you look and stronger than you believe yourself to be. You are trapped in an unfamiliar land with only a stranger for company, yet you have defied wolves, trolls, a beast that had destroyed a force of armed men, and the tainted promises of the one you call the Crooked Man. Through it all I have never yet seen you in despair. When I agreed to take you to the king, I thought you would be a burden on me, but instead you have proved yourself worthy of respect and trust. I hope that I in turn have proved myself worthy of *your* respect and trust, for without it we are both lost. Now, will you come with me? We have almost reached our destination.'

He extended his hand to David. The boy took it, and Roland raised him to his feet.

'I'm sorry,' said David.

'You have nothing to be sorry about,' said Roland. 'But gather your belongings, for the end is near.'

They rode for only a short time, but as they travelled the air around them changed. The hairs on David's head and arms stood on end.

He could feel the static when he touched his hand to them. The wind blew a strange scent from the west, musty and dry, like the interior of a crypt. The land rose beneath them until they came to the brow of a hill, and there they paused and looked down.

Before them, like a stain upon the snow, was the dark shape of a fortress. David thought of it as a shape rather than a fortress itself, because there was something very peculiar about it. He could make out a central tower, and walls and outbuildings, but they were slightly blurred, like the lines of a watercolour painting made on damp paper. It stood at the centre of the forest, but all of the trees around it had been felled as though by some great explosion. Here and there David saw the glinting of metal upon its battlements. Birds hovered above it, and the dry smell grew stronger.

'Carrion birds,' said Roland, pointing. 'They feed upon the dead.'

David knew what he was thinking: Raphael had entered that place, and had not returned.

'Perhaps you should stay here,' said Roland. 'It will be safer for you.'

David looked around. The trees here were different from the others he had seen. They were twisted and ancient, their barks diseased and pitted with holes. They looked like old men and women frozen in agony. He did not want to remain alone among them.

'Safer?' queried David. 'There are wolves following me, and who knows what else lives in these woods? If you leave me here, I'll just follow you on foot anyway. I might even be useful to you. I didn't let you down in the village when the Beast came after me, and I won't let you down now,' he said with determination.

Roland did not argue with him. Together they rode towards the fortress. As they moved through the forest, they heard voices whispering. The sounds seemed to come from within the trees, emerging through the openings in their trunks, but whether they were the voices of the trees themselves or those of unseen beings that dwelt within them David could not say. Twice he believed he saw movement in the holes, and once he was certain that eyes had stared back at him from deep inside the tree, but when he told Roland, the soldier said only: 'Don't be afraid. Whatever they are, they have nothing to do with the fortress. They are not our concern, unless they choose to make themselves so.'

Nevertheless he slowly withdrew his sword as he rode and let it hang by Scylla's side, his right hand fixed upon its hilt.

The forest was so thick with trees that the fortress was lost from sight as they passed through them, so it came as something of a shock to David when they finally emerged into the blasted landscape of fallen trunks. The force of the explosion, or whatever it was, had torn the trees from the ground, so that their roots lay exposed above deep hollows. At the epicentre lay the fortress, and now David could see why it had appeared blurred from a distance. It was completely covered by brown creepers that wound around the central tower and covered the walls and battlements, and from the creepers emerged dark thorns, some easily a foot long and thicker than David's wrist. It might have been possible to attempt to climb the walls using the creepers, but make even the slightest misstep and an arm or a leg or, worse, the head or the heart would be impaled upon the waiting spikes.

They rode around the perimeter of the fortress until they came to the gates. They were open, but the creepers had formed a barrier across the entrance. Through the gaps between the thorns, David could see a courtyard, and a closed door at the base of the central tower. A suit of armour lay on the ground before it, but there was no helmet, and no head.

'Roland,' said David. 'That knight . . .'

But Roland was not looking at the gates, or at the knight.

His head was raised, and his eyes were fixed on the battlements. David followed his gaze and discovered what it was that had gleamed upon the walls from a distance.

The heads of men had been impaled upon the topmost thorns, facing out over the gates. Some still wore their ornate helmets, although their face-guards were raised or torn off so that their expressions could be seen, while others had no armour left at all. Most were little more than skulls and, while there were three or four that were still recognisable as men, they looked as though they had no flesh left on their faces, just a thin covering of grey, papery skin over the bone. Roland examined each one in turn until, at last, he had stared into the faces of every dead man at the battlements. He looked relieved when he was done.

'Raphael is not among those that I can identify,' he said. 'I see neither his face nor his armour.'

He dismounted and approached the entrance. Drawing his sword, he sliced off one of the thorns. It fell to the ground, and instantly another grew in its place, even longer and thicker than the one that had been severed. It grew so fast that it almost stabbed Roland in the chest before he managed, just in time, to duck out of its way. Roland next tried to hack through the creeper itself, but his sword inflicted only the slightest of cuts, and the damage once again repaired itself before his eyes.

Roland stepped back and returned his sword to its sheath.

'There must be a way inside,' he said. 'How else did that knight gain entry before he died? We will wait. We will wait, and we will watch. In time, perhaps it will reveal its secrets to us.' They settled down after building a small fire and kept silent, uneasy vigil on the Fortress of Thorns.

Night fell, or the greater darkness that merely deepened the shadows of the day and served as eventide in this strange world. David looked to the sky and saw a faint glow of moonlight. The whispering from the forest, which had continued while they circled the castle, abruptly ceased with the coming of the moon. The carrion birds disappeared.

David and Roland were alone.

A light appeared in the topmost window of the tower, and then was blocked as a figure passed before the opening. It paused and seemed to stare down upon the man and boy below, then disappeared.

'I saw it,' said Roland, before David could open his mouth.

'It looked like a woman,' said David.

It was the enchantress, he thought, watching over the sleeping lady in the tower. The moonlight shone on the armour of the dead men impaled on the battlements, reminding him of the danger he and Roland now faced. They must all have been armed when they approached the fortress, yet still they had died. The body of the knight that lay inside the gates was huge, taller than Roland by a foot at least, and almost as broad as him again. Whoever guarded the tower was strong and fast and very, very cruel.

Then, as they watched, the creepers and thorns blocking the gates began to move. They unravelled slowly, creating an entrance through which a man could pass. It gaped like an open mouth, the long spikes poised like teeth waiting to bite.

'It's a trap,' said David. 'It must be.'

Roland stood.

'What choice do I have?' he said. 'I must discover what happened to Raphael. I have not come all this way to sit on the ground and stare at walls and thorns.'

He placed his shield on his left arm. He did not look frightened. In fact, he looked happier to David than he had at any point since they had met. He had travelled from his own land to find an answer to his friend's disappearance, tormented by what might have befallen him. Whatever now happened within the fortress walls, and whether he lived or died as a result, he would at last discover the truth about the end of Raphael's journey.

'Stay here, and keep the fire burning,' said Roland. 'If I have not returned by daybreak, take Scylla and ride as fast as you can from this place. Scylla is as much your horse now as mine, for I think she loves you just as she loves me. Remain on the road, and it will lead you eventually to the castle of the king.'

He smiled down at David.

'It has been an honour to travel these roads with you. If we do not see each other again, I hope that you find your home and the answers you seek.'

They shook hands. David did not shed a tear. He wanted to be as brave as he thought Roland to be. It was only later that he wondered if Roland was truly brave. He knew that Roland now believed Raphael was dead, and that he wanted revenge upon whomever had killed him. But he also felt, as Roland prepared to walk towards the waiting fortress, that this man did not want to live without Raphael, and that death, for him, would be preferable to a life alone.

David accompanied Roland to the gates. As they approached, Roland gazed up at the waiting thorns in apprehension, as though he feared they might close upon him as soon as he was within their reach. But they did not move, and Roland passed through the gap without incident. He stepped over the armour of the knight and pushed open the door of the tower. He glanced back at David, raised his sword in a final farewell, and walked into the shadows. The creepers on the gates twisted and the thorns extended, restoring the barrier across the entrance to the courtyard, and then all was still once more.

The Crooked Man watched what had transpired from his perch on the topmost branch of the tallest tree in the forest. The presences that dwelt within the tree trunks did not trouble him: they were more scared of the Crooked Man than of almost any other being that lived in this land. The thing in the fortress was ancient and cruel, but the Crooked Man was older and crueller still. He stared at the boy seated by the fire, Scylla standing close by, untethered, as she was a brave, intelligent horse and would not easily take fright or abandon her rider. The Crooked Man was tempted to approach David once again and ask him for the child's name, but he thought better of it. A night alone at the edge of the forest, facing the Fortress of Thorns and watched over by the heads of dead knights, would make him more willing to treat with the Crooked Man come morning.

For the Crooked Man knew that the knight Roland would never come out of the fortress alive, and that David was, once more, alone in the world.

Time passed slowly for David. He fed the fire with sticks and waited for Roland to return. Sometimes, he felt Scylla nuzzle his neck gently, reminding him that she was close. He was glad of the horse's presence. Her strength and her loyalty were reassuring to him.

But tiredness began to overcome him, and his mind played tricks on him. He would fall asleep for a second or two and instantly begin to dream. He glimpsed flashes of home, and incidents from the last few days replayed themselves in distorted form, their stories overlapping as wolves and dwarfs and the young of the Beast all became part of the same tale. He heard the voice of his mother crying out for him, as she sometimes had when the pain became too great for her in her last days, and then her face was replaced by Rose's, just as his place in his father's affections had been taken by Georgie.

But was that true? He realised suddenly that he missed Georgie, and the feeling was so surprising to him that he gasped aloud in his sleep. He remembered the way the baby would smile at him, or grasp his finger in his chubby fist. True, he was noisy and smelly and demanding, but all babies were like that. It wasn't Georgie's fault, not really.

The image of Georgie faded and David saw Roland, sword in hand, advancing down a long, dark hallway. He was inside the tower, but the tower itself was a kind of illusion, and hidden within it were a great many rooms and corridors, each one containing traps for the unwary. Roland entered a large circular chamber, and in his dream David saw Roland's eyes widen in disbelief and the walls ran red as something in the shadows called David's name . . .

David sat up abruptly. He was still by the fire, but the flames had almost died out. Roland had not returned. David got up and walked towards the gates. Scylla whinnied nervously as he moved away but did not follow him. David stood before the gates, reached out and touched a finger warily to one of the thorns. Immediately, the creepers retreated, the thorns retracted, and an opening in the barrier was revealed. David looked back at Scylla and the dying embers of the fire. I should go now, he thought. I should not even wait for the dawn. Scylla will take me to the king, and he will help me.

But still he lingered before the gates. Despite what Roland had told him to do if he did not return, David did not want to abandon his friend. And as he stood facing the thorns, uncertain of how to proceed, he heard a voice calling to him.

'*David,*' it whispered. '*Come to me, please come to me.*'

It was his mother's voice.

'*This is the place to which I was brought,*' the voice continued. '*When the sickness took me I fell asleep, and I passed from our world to this one. Now she watches over me. I cannot awake, and I cannot escape. Help me, David. If you love me, please help me . . .*'

'Mum,' said David. 'I'm afraid.'

'*You've come so far, and you've been so brave,*' said the voice. '*I've been watching you in my dreams. I'm so proud of you, David. Just a few steps more. Just a little more courage, that's all I ask.*'

David reached inside his pack and found the claw of the Beast. He slipped it into his pocket and thought of Fletcher's words. He had been brave once, and he could be brave again for his mother. The Crooked Man, still watching from the trees, realised what was happening and began to move. He leaped from his perch, descending from branch to branch and landing like a cat upon the ground, but he was too late. David had passed into the fortress, and the barrier of thorns had closed behind him.

The Crooked Man howled with rage, but David, already lost to the fortress, did not hear him.

XXV

Of The Enchantress and What Became of Raphael and Roland

The courtyard was cobbled with black and white stones stained by droppings from the carrion birds that hovered above the fortress by day. Carved steps led up to the battlements; racks of weapons stood beside them, but the spears, swords and shields were rusted and useless. Some of the weaponry had fantastic designs, intricate spirals and delicate interwoven chains of silver and bronze that were echoed on the hilts of the swords and the faces of the shields. David could not equate the beauty of the craftsmanship with the sinister place that now held them. It suggested that the fortress had not always been as it now was. It had been taken over by a malevolent entity, a cuckoo that had turned it into a spiked, creepered nest, and its original inhabitants had either died or fled when it came.

Now that he was inside, David could see signs of damage: hollow pits, mostly, where the walls and courtyard had absorbed the force of cannon fire. It was clear that the fortress was very old, yet the fallen trees surrounding it suggested that what Roland had heard and what Fletcher claimed to have seen, however strange, was in fact the case. The fortress could move through the air, travelling to new locations with the cycles of the moon.

Beneath the walls were stables, but they were empty of hay and bore no trace of the healthy animal smells such places built up over time. Instead there were only the bones of horses left to starve after the deaths of their masters, and the lingering stench from within was a reminder of their slow decay. Across from them, and at either side of the central tower, were what might once have been guards' quarters and kitchens. Carefully, David peered through the windows of each, but all were entirely devoid of life. There were bare bunks in the guards' building and cold, empty ovens in the kitchens. Plates and mugs lay upon the tables, as though a meal had been disturbed and those who were eating had never been given the chance to return to their food.

David walked to the door of the tower. The body of the knight lay at his feet, a sword still gripped in his great hand. The sword had not rusted, and the knight's armour still shone. In addition, he wore a sprig of some white flower tucked into a hole in his shoulder armour. It had not yet withered fully, so David guessed that his body had not been lying there for very long. There was no blood on his neck or on the ground around him. David did not know a great deal about the mechanics of cutting off a man's head, but he imagined that there would be some blood at least. He wondered who the knight was and whether he, like Roland, bore a device on his breastplate to identify him. The huge knight was lying chest down, and David wasn't sure that he would be able to turn him over. Still, he decided that the identity of the dead knight should not remain unknown, just in case he found a way to tell anyone of what had happened to him.

David knelt and took a deep breath to prepare himself for the effort of moving the body, then pushed hard against the armour. To his surprise, the knight's remains moved quite easily. True, the armour was heavy, but not as heavy as it should have been with the body of a man inside. Once he had managed to turn the knight over, David could see the sign of an eagle on his breastplate, a snake writhing in its talons. He rapped upon the armour with the knuckles of his right hand. The sound echoed within; it was like tapping on a dustbin. It seemed that the suit of armour was empty.

But, no, that was not the case, for David had both heard and felt something move as he rolled the armour, and when he examined the hole at the top, where the head had been separated from the body, he saw bone and skin within. The top of the spinal column was white where the head had been severed from the body, but even here there was no blood. Somehow, the knight's remains had been reduced to a husk inside the armour, rotting away to almost nothing so quickly that the flower he wore, perhaps for luck, had not yet had time to die.

David considered fleeing the fortress, but he knew that even if he tried to do so, the thorns would not part for him. This was a place to be entered but not to be left, and despite his doubts he had heard, once again, his mother's voice calling to him. If she was truly here, then he could not abandon her now.

David stepped over the fallen knight and entered the tower. A set of stairs wound upwards in a spiral. He listened intently, but could hear no sound from above. He wanted to call his mother's name, or to cry out for Roland, but he was afraid of alerting the presence in the tower to his approach. Perhaps, though, whatever waited in the tower already knew that he was in the fortress and had parted the thorns to enable him to enter. Still, it seemed wiser to be quiet than to be noisy, and so he did not speak. He recalled the figure that had passed across the lighted window, and the tale of the enchantress who kept a woman in thrall, dooming her to an eternal, ageless sleep in a chamber of treasures unless she could be awakened by a kiss. Could that woman be his mother? The answer lay above.

He drew his sword and started to climb. There were small, narrow windows every ten steps and these allowed a little light to filter into the tower, enabling David to see where he was going. He counted a dozen such windows before he reached the stone floor at the top of the tower. A hallway stretched before him, with open doorways on either side. From outside, the tower appeared to be twenty or thirty feet wide, but the corridor in front of him was so long that the end of it was lost in shadow. It must have been hundreds of feet in length, lit by flaming torches set into the walls, yet somehow it was contained within a tower only a fraction of that size.

David walked slowly down the hallway, glancing into each room as he did so. Some were bedrooms, opulently furnished with enormous beds and velvet drapes. Others contained couches and chairs. One housed a grand piano and nothing else. The walls of another were decorated with hundreds of similar versions of one painting: a picture of two male children, identical twins, with a painting of themselves in the background that was an exact replica of the picture they occupied, so they were being watched by infinite versions of themselves.

Halfway down the hall was a vast dining room, dominated by a huge oak table with one hundred chairs around it. Candles were lit along its length, and their light shone upon a great feast: there were roast turkeys and geese and ducks, and a huge pig with an apple in its mouth as the centrepiece. There were platters of fish and cold meats, and vegetables steamed in big pots. It all smelled so wonderful that David was drawn into the room, unable to resist the urgings of his growling stomach. Someone had started carving one of the turkeys, for its leg had been removed and slivers of white meat had been cut from its breast and now lay, tender and moist, on a china plate. David picked up one of the biggest pieces and was about to take a great bite from it when he saw an insect crawling across the table. It was a large red ant, and it was making its way towards a fragment of skin that had fallen from the turkey. It clasped the crisp, brown morsel in its jaws and prepared to carry it away, but suddenly it seemed to totter on its feet, as though its burden was heavier than it had expected. It dropped the skin, wobbled a little more, then ceased moving entirely. David poked at it with his finger, but the insect did not respond. It was dead.

David dropped his piece of turkey on the table and quickly

wiped his fingers clean. Now that he looked more closely, he could see that the table was littered with the remains of dead insects. The corpses of flies and beetles and ants dotted the wood and the plates, all poisoned by whatever was contained in the food. David backed away from the table and returned to the hallway, his appetite entirely gone.

But if the dining room disgusted him, the next room into which he looked was more troubling still. It was his bedroom in Rose's house, perfectly re-created down to the books on the shelves, although neater than David's room had ever been. The bed was made, but the pillows and sheets were slightly yellowed and covered in a thin layer of dust. There was dust on the shelves as well, and when David stepped inside, he left footprints on the floor. Ahead of him was the window facing onto the garden. It was open, and noises could be heard from outside, the sounds of laughter and singing. He walked over to the glass and looked out. In the garden below, three people were dancing in a circle: David's father, Rose, and a boy whom David did not recognise but whom he knew instantly to be Georgie. Georgie was older now, perhaps four or five, but still a chubby child. He was smiling widely as his parents danced with him, his father holding his right hand and Rose his left, the sun shining down upon them from a perfect blue sky.

'Georgie Porgie, pudding and pie,' they sang to him, 'kissed the girls and made them cry!'

And Georgie laughed with joy as bees buzzed and birds sang.

'*They have forgotten you,*' said the voice of David's mother. '*This was once your room, but nobody comes in here now. Your father did, in the beginning, but then he resigned himself to the fact that you were gone and found pleasure instead in his other child and his new wife. She is pregnant again, although she does not yet know it. There will be a sister for Georgie, and then your father will have two children once more and there will be no more need for memories of you.*'

The voice came from everywhere and nowhere, from within David and from the hallway outside, from the floor beneath his feet and the ceiling above his head, from the stones in the walls and the books on the shelves. For a moment, David even saw the speaker reflected in the glass of the window, a faded vision of his mother standing behind him and looking over his shoulder. When he turned round there was nobody there, but still her reflection remained in the glass.

'*It does not have to be that way,*' said his mother's voice. The lips of the image in the glass moved, but they appeared to be saying other words, for their motions did not quite match the words that David heard. '*Remain brave and strong for just a little longer. Find me here and we can have our old life back again. Rose and Georgie will be gone, and you and I will take their places.*'

Now the voices from the garden below had changed. They were no longer singing and laughing. When he looked down, David saw his father mowing the lawn, and his mother clipping a rose bush with a pair of secateurs, carefully beheading each branch and tossing the red flowers into a basket at her feet. And seated on a bench between them, reading a book, was David.

'*Do you see how it can be? Now come, we have been apart too long. It is time that we were together again. But be careful: she will be watching and waiting. When you find me, do not look left or right, but keep your eyes only on my face and everything will be well.*'

The image disappeared from the glass and the figures vanished from the garden below. A cold wind arose, raising dust ghosts in the room, obscuring everything within. The dust made David cough and his eyes watered. He backed out of the room and bent over in the hallway, hacking and spitting.

A noise came from nearby: the sound of a door slamming and locking. He spun round and a second door slammed and locked, then another. The door to each room that he had passed was shutting firmly. Now his bedroom door was suddenly sealed in his face, and all of the doors ahead of him began to close as well. Only the torches on the walls lit his way, and then they began to be extinguished, starting with those nearest the stairs. There was total darkness behind him, and it was advancing quickly. Soon, the entire hallway would be drowned in blackness.

David ran, trying desperately to stay ahead of the approaching shadows, his ears ringing with the sound of slamming doors. He was moving as quickly as he could, his feet slapping upon the hard stone floor, but the lights were dying faster than he could run. He saw the torches just behind him die, then the ones at either side, and finally those ahead fizzled out. He kept running, hoping that somehow he could catch up with them, that he would not be left alone in the dark. Then the last torches faded, and the darkness was complete.

'No!' shouted David. 'Mum! Roland! I can't see. Help me!'

But nobody replied. David stood still, uncertain of what to do. He did not know what lay ahead, but he knew that the stairs were behind him. If he turned back, following the wall, he could find them again, but he would be abandoning his mother, and Roland too, if he was still alive. If he went forward, he would be stumbling blindly into the unknown, easy prey for the 'she' of whom his mother's voice had spoken, the enchantress who guarded this place with thorns and creepers and who reduced men to husks in armour and heads on battlements.

David glimpsed a tiny light in the distance, like a firefly suspended in the blackness, and his mother's voice said:

'David, don't be afraid. You're almost there. Don't give up now.'

He did as he was told and the light grew stronger and brighter, until he saw that it was a lamp hanging from the ceiling. Slowly, the outline of an archway became clear beneath it. David drew nearer and nearer, so that at last he stood at the entrance to a great chamber, its domed ceiling supported by four enormous stone pillars. The walls and pillars were covered by thorned creepers far thicker than those that guarded the walls and gates of the fortress, the thorns so long and sharp that some were taller than David himself. Between each set of pillars a bronze lantern hung from an ornate iron frame, and their light shone upon chests of coins and jewellery, on goblets and gilded picture frames, on swords and shields, all gleaming with gold and precious stones. It was a treasure greater than most men could imagine, but David barely glanced at it. Instead, his attention was drawn by a raised stone altar at the centre of the room. A woman lay upon the altar, still as the dead. She was dressed in a red velvet dress with her hands folded across her chest. As David looked more closely, he saw the rise and fall of her breathing. This, then, was the sleeping lady, the victim of the enchantress's spell.

David entered the chamber, and the flickering glow of the lamps caught something bright and shiny high up on the thorned wall to his right. He turned, and his stomach cramped so hard at what he saw that he bent over in pain.

Roland's body was impaled on one of the great thorns ten feet above the floor. The point had passed through his chest and erupted from his breastplate, destroying the image of the twin suns. There was a trace of blood upon his armour, but not much. Roland's face was thin and grey, his cheeks hollow and the skull sharp beneath the skin. Beside Roland's body was that of another, also wearing the armour of the twin suns: Raphael. Roland had discovered the truth about his companion's disappearance at last.

And they were not alone. The vaulted chamber was dotted with the remains of men, like drained flies set in a web of thorns. Some of them had been there for a very long time, for their armour had rusted to red and brown, and those that had heads were no more than skeletons.

David's anger overcame his fear, and his rage put paid to thoughts of flight. In that moment, he became more man than boy, and his passage into adulthood began in earnest. He walked slowly towards the sleeping woman, turning constantly in slow circles so that no hidden threat could creep up on him unawares. He remembered his mother's warning not to look right or left, but the sight of Roland impaled upon the wall made him want to confront the enchantress and kill her for what she had done to his friend.

'Come out,' he shouted. 'Show yourself!'

But nothing moved in the chamber, and no one answered his challenge. The only word he heard, half real, half imagined, was '*David*', spoken in his mother's voice.

'Mum,' he said, in reply. 'I'm here.'

He was now at the stone altar. A flight of five steps led up to the sleeping woman. He climbed them slowly, still aware of the unseen threat, the killer of Roland and Raphael and of all those men who hung, pierced and hollow, from the walls. At last, he reached the altar and looked down upon the face of the sleeping woman. It was his mother. Her skin was very white, but there was a hint of pink at her cheeks, and her lips were full and moist. Her red hair glowed like fire against the stone.

'*Kiss me*,' David heard her say, although her mouth remained still. '*Kiss me, and we will be together again.*'

David placed his sword by her side and leaned over to kiss her cheek. His lips touched her skin. She was very cold, colder even than when she had lain in her open coffin, so cold that the touch of her was painful to him. It numbed his lips and stilled his tongue, and his breath turned to crystals of ice that sparkled like tiny diamonds in the still air. As he broke the contact with her, his name was called again, but this time it was a man's voice, not a woman's.

'David!'

He looked round, trying to find the source of the sound. There was movement upon the wall. It was Roland. His left hand waved feebly, then gripped the thorn that protruded from his chest, as though by doing so he might concentrate the last of his strength and say what needed to be said. His head moved, and with a final great effort he forced the words from his lips.

'David,' he whispered. 'Beware!'

Roland lifted his right hand and his index finger pointed at the figure on the altar. Then his body sagged on the thorn as the life passed from him at last.

David looked down at the sleeping woman, and her eyes opened. They were not the eyes of David's mother. Her eyes were brown and loving and kind. These eyes were black, devoid of colour, like lumps of coal set in snow. The face of the sleeping woman had also changed. She was no longer David's mother, although he still knew her. Now she was Rose, his father's lover. Her hair was black, not red, and it pooled like liquid night. Her lips opened, and David saw that her teeth were very white and very sharp, the canines longer than the rest. He took a step back, almost falling from the dais as the woman sat up on her stone bed. She stretched like a cat, her spine curving and her arms tensing. The shawl around her shoulders fell away, exposing an alabaster neck and the tops of her breasts. David saw drops of blood upon them, like a necklace of rubies frozen against her skin. The woman turned upon the stone, allowing her bare feet to drape over the side. Those deep black eyes regarded David, and her pale tongue licked at the points of her teeth.

'Thank you,' she said. Her voice was soft and low, but there was a hissing undertone to her words, as though a snake had been given the power of speech. 'Ssssuch a handsssome boy. Sssssuch a brave boy.'

David retreated, but with each step he took the woman advanced another to match it, so that the distance between them remained always the same.

'Am I not beautiful?' she asked. Her head tilted slightly, and her face looked troubled. 'Am I not pretty enough for you? Come, kisssss me again.'

She was Rose, but Not-Rose. She was night without the promise of dawn, darkness without hope of light. David reached for his sword, then realised that it still lay on the altar. To get to it, he would have to find a way past the woman, and he knew instinctively that if he tried to slip by her, she would kill him. She seemed to guess what he was thinking, because she glanced back at the sword.

'You have no need of it now,' she said. 'Never hassss one ssso young come ssso far. Ssso young, and ssso beautiful.'

One slim finger, its nail etched in blood, touched itself to her lips.

'Here,' she whispered. 'Kissss me here.'

David saw his reflection drown in her dark eyes, sinking in the depths of her, and knew what his fate would be. He spun on his heel and jumped the last steps, twisting awkwardly on his right ankle as he landed. The pain was bad, but he was not going to let it hinder him. On the floor ahead of him lay the sword of one of the dead knights. If he could just get to it—

A figure glided over his head, the hem of its gown brushing against his hair, and the woman appeared before him. Her feet were not touching the ground. She hung in the air, red and black, blood and night. She was no longer smiling. She opened her lips, exposing her fangs, and her mouth gaped larger than before, with row upon row of sharp teeth like the inside of a shark's jaws. Her hands reached for David.

'I will have my kisss,' she said, as her nails sank into his shoulders and her head moved towards David's lips.

David reached into the pocket of his jacket. His right hand sliced through the air and the claw of the Beast tore a jagged red line across the woman's face. The wound gaped, but no blood flowed from it for she had no blood in her veins. She shrieked and pressed her hand to the wound as David struck again, slashing from left to right and blinding her instantly. The woman attacked him with her fingernails, catching his hand and sending the Beast's claw flying from it. David ran for the doorway to the chamber, no thought now except to get back to the pitch-black hall and find his way to the stairs. But the creepers twisted and turned, blocking the way out and trapping him in the room with Not-Rose.

She still hung in the air, her hands now outstretched from her sides, her eyes and face ruined. David moved away from the entrance, trying to get to the fallen sword again. The woman's sightless eyes followed him.

'I can *sssssmell* you,' she said. 'And you will pay for what you have done to me.'

She flew towards David, her teeth snapping and her fingers clutching at the air. David darted to his right then back to his left in the hope that he could fool her and reach the sword, but she was too clever for him and cut him off. She moved back and forth before him, so quickly that she was little more than a blur in the air, always advancing, sealing off any avenue of escape and forcing him back against the thorns until at last she was only a few feet away from him. David felt sharp pains at his neck and back. He was standing against the tips of the thorns, long and sharp as spears. There was nowhere left for him to go. The woman's hand snatched at the air, missing his face by an inch.

'Now,' she hissed, 'you are mine. I will love you and you will die loving me in return.'

Her spine stretched and her mouth opened so wide that her skull split almost in half, the rows of teeth braced to tear David's throat open. She shot forward and David threw himself to the floor, waiting until she was almost upon him before he moved. Her dress covered his face, so that he heard but did not see what happened next. There was a sound like a rotten fruit being punctured, and a foot kicked once at his head and then was still.

David rolled out from beneath the folds of red velvet. The thorns had pierced the woman through the heart and the side. Her right hand, too, had been impaled, but her left hand was free. It trembled against a creeper, the only part of her that moved. David could see her face. She no longer looked like Rose. Her hair had turned to silver, and her skin was old and wrinkled. A dank, musty smell came from the wounds in her body. Her lower jaw hung loosely on her wrinkled chest. Her nostrils quivered as she smelled David, and she tried to speak. At first, her voice was so faint that he could not hear what she said. He leaned in closer, still wary of her even though he knew that she was dying. Her breath stank of decay, but this time he understood her words.

'Thank you,' she whispered, and then her body sagged against the thorns and crumbled to dust before his eyes.

And as she disappeared, the creepers began to wither and die, and the remains of the dead knights fell clattering to the ground. David ran to where Roland lay. His body had been almost drained of blood. David felt like crying for him, but no tears would come. Instead he dragged Roland's remains up the steps to the stone bed and, with some effort, laid him to rest upon it. He did the same for Raphael, placing his body by Roland's side. He put their swords at their chests and folded their hands across the hilts, the way that he had seen dead knights laid out in his books. He retrieved his own sword and returned it to its scabbard, then took one of the lamps from its stand and used it to find his way back to the stairs of the tower. The long corridor with its many rooms was now no more, and only dusty stones and crumbling walls remained. When he got outside, he saw that here, too, the creepers and thorns had withered away, and all that was left was an old fortress, ruined and decayed. Beyond its gates, Scylla stood waiting for him by the ashes of the fire. She neighed with joy as she saw him approach. David put his hand against her brow and whispered in her ear, so that she might know what had happened to her beloved master. Only then did he climb into the saddle and turn her towards the forest and the road east.

All was quiet as they passed through the trees, for the things that dwelt within them heard David coming and were afraid. Even the Crooked Man, who had returned to his perch among the topmost branches, now looked at the boy in a new way, and tried to work out how he might best use this latest development to his advantage.

XXVI

Of Two Killings
and Two Kings

David and Scylla followed the road to the east. David's eyes stared straight ahead, but they noticed little of what was before them. Scylla's head hung lower than it previously had, as though she too were mourning the passing of her master in her soft, dignified way. Snow sparkled in the eternal dusk, and icicles hung like frozen tears from the bushes and the trees.

Roland was dead. So too was David's mother. He had been a fool to imagine otherwise. Now, as the horse plodded through this cold, dark world, David admitted to himself, perhaps for the first time, that he had always known his mother was gone. He had just wanted to believe otherwise. It was like the routines that he had employed while she was ill in the hope that they might keep her alive. They were false hopes, dreams without foundation, insubstantial as the voice he had followed to this place. He could not change the world that he had left, and this world, while taunting him with the possibility that things could be different, had ultimately frustrated him. It was time to go home. If the king could not help him, then he might yet be forced to make a deal with the Crooked Man. All he had to do was speak Georgie's name aloud to him.

But hadn't the Crooked Man told him that everything could be restored to the way it was? That was a lie. His mother was dead and the life of which she had been a part was gone for ever. Even if he went back, it would be to a place in which she was only a memory. Home was now a house shared with Rose and Georgie, and the best would have to be made of that, for his sake as much as theirs. If the Crooked Man's promise could not be kept, then what others might he break? It was as Roland had warned:

He will say less than he means, and conceal more than he reveals.

Any deal made with the Crooked Man would be filled with potential traps and perils. David would just have to hope that the king was able and willing to help him, allowing him to avoid any further contact with the trickster. But what he had heard so far about the king caused him doubt. Roland had clearly thought little of him, and even the Woodsman had admitted that the king's grasp of his kingdom was not what it once was. Now, faced with the threat of Leroi and his wolf army, perhaps the king would be tested beyond endurance. His kingdom would be taken from him by force, and he would die in Leroi's jaws. With the burden of that knowledge on his shoulders, would he even have time for the problems of a boy lost in the world?

And what of the book itself, the Book of Lost Things? What could be contained in its pages that would help David to return home: a map to another hollow tree, perhaps, or a spell capable of magicking him back? But if the book had magical properties, then why couldn't the king use it to protect his kingdom? David hoped that the king wasn't like the Great Oz, all smoke and mirrors and good intentions, but without any real power to back him up.

So lost was David in his own thoughts, and so used was he to an empty road, that he failed to see the men until they were almost upon him. There were two of them, dressed mostly in rags, with scarves covering their faces so that only their eyes were visible. One carried a short sword, the other a bow with an arrow nocked at its string, ready to fire. They dashed from the undergrowth, casting aside the white furs with which they had camouflaged themselves, and stood in front of David, their weapons raised.

'Halt!' cried the man with the sword, and David stopped Scylla just a few feet from where they stood.

The one with the bow squinted down the length of his arrow, then eased the pressure on the string as he lowered the weapon.

'Why, it's just a boy,' he said. His voice was hoarse, and rumbled with menace. He lowered the scarf from his face, revealing a mouth distorted by a vertical scar that cut across his lips. His companion threw back the hood from his head. Most of his nose had been cut off. All that was left was a mess of scarred cartilage with two holes in the centre.

'Boy or not, that's a fine horse he's riding,' he said. 'He has no business with such an animal. He probably stole it himself, so there's no sin in relieving him of what wasn't his to begin with.'

He reached for Scylla's reins, but David pulled the horse back a step.

'I didn't steal her,' he said softly.

'What?' said the thief. 'What did you say, boy? We'll have none of your lip, or you won't live long enough to regret the day you met us.'

He brandished his sword at David. It was primitive and crudely made, and David could see the marks of the whetstone upon its blade. Scylla neighed and stepped further away from the threat.

'I said,' David repeated, 'that I didn't steal her, and she's not going anywhere with you. Now get away from us.'

'Why, you little—'

The swordsman snatched at Scylla's reins once again, but this time David raised her up on her hind legs, then urged her onwards and down. One of her hoofs struck the swordsman on the forehead, and there was a hollow, cracking sound as the man fell dead to the ground. His fellow bandit was so shocked that he failed to respond quickly enough. He was still trying to lift his bow when David urged Scylla on, his own sword now drawn and extended. He slashed at the archer and the very tip of his sword caught the man's throat, slicing through the rags to the flesh beneath. The bandit stumbled and his bow fell. He raised his hand to his neck and tried to speak, but only a wet, gurgling sound emerged. Blood fountained through his fingers and scattered itself upon the snow. The front of his clothing was already drenched with red as he dropped to his knees beside his dead companion, the flow slowly starting to ease as his heart began to fail.

David turned Scylla so that she was facing the dying man.

'I warned you!' shouted David. He was crying now, crying for Roland and his mother and his father, crying even for Georgie and Rose, for all of the things that he had lost, both those that could be named and those that could only be felt. 'I asked you to leave us alone, but you wouldn't. Now look at what it's brought you. You idiots. You stupid, *stupid* men!'

The bowman's mouth opened and closed and his lips formed words, but no sounds emerged. His eyes were fixed on the boy. David saw them narrow, as if the bowman could not quite understand what was being said or what was happening to him as he knelt in the snow, his blood pooling around him.

Then, slowly, they grew wide and calm as death gave him an explanation.

David climbed down from Scylla's back and checked her legs to make sure that she had not injured herself during the confrontation. She seemed unhurt. There was blood on David's sword. He thought of wiping it clean with the ragged clothing of one of the dead men, but he did not want to touch the bodies. Neither did he want to clean it on his own clothes, for then their blood would be on him. He opened his pack and found a piece of old muslin in which Fletcher had wrapped some cheese and used the material to get rid of the blood. He tossed the bloodied cloth onto the snow before kicking the bodies of the dead men into the ditch by the side of the road. He was too weary to try to hide them better. Suddenly, he felt a rumbling in his stomach. There was a sour taste in his mouth, and his skin was slick with sweat. He stumbled away from the bodies and vomited behind a rock, retching over and over until all that he had left to bring up was foul gas.

He had killed two men. He hadn't meant to, not really, but now they were dead because of him. The killings of the Loups and wolves at the canyon, even what he had done to the huntress in her cottage and the enchantress in her tower, had not affected him in this way. He had caused the deaths of the others, true, but he had dispatched at least one of these men by tearing through his flesh with the point of a sword. Scylla's hoofs had accounted for the other, but David had been in the saddle when it happened and had raised her up and urged her on. He hadn't even had to think about what he was doing; it had just come naturally to him, and it was this capacity for harm that disturbed him more than anything else.

He wiped his mouth clean with snow, then remounted Scylla and continued on his way, leaving behind him the deed, if not the memory of it. As he rode, thick flakes began to descend, settling on his clothing and on Scylla's head and back. There was no wind. The snow fell straight and slow, adding another layer to the drifts and covering roads, trees, bushes and bodies, the living and the dead as one beneath its veil. The corpses of the thieves were soon shrouded in white, and there they would have remained, unmourned and undiscovered, until the coming of spring, had not a wet muzzle traced their scent and revealed their remains. The wolf gave a low howl, and the forest came alive as the pack descended, tearing flesh and gnawing bones, the weak left to fight for scraps while the strong and fast filled their bellies. Yet there were too many now to be fed on so meagre a meal.

The pack had swollen so that it was many thousands strong: white wolves from the far north, who blended into the winter landscape so perfectly that only the darkness of their eyes and the redness of their jaws gave them away; black wolves from the east, said by old wives to be the spirits of witches and demons inhabiting the form of beasts; grey wolves from the forests to the west, bigger and slower than the rest, who kept to their own and did not trust the rest; and, finally, the Loups, who dressed like men and hungered like wolves and wanted to rule like kings. They stayed apart from the pack, watching from the edge of the forest as their more primitive brethren snapped and fought over the entrails of the dead bandits. A female approached them from the road. In her jaws she held a scrap of muslin, marked with drying blood. The taste of the blood had made her mouth water, and it was all that she could do not to chew it and swallow it as she walked. Now she dropped it at the feet of their leader and stepped back obediently. Leroi lifted the rag to his nose and sniffed it. The smell of the dead men's blood was strong and sharp, but he could still detect traces of the boy's scent.

Leroi had last smelled the boy in the fortress courtyard, led there by his scouts. They had refused to climb the stairs of the tower, disturbed by what they sensed within, but Leroi had ascended, more as a display of courage for his followers than out of any great desire to discover what lay above. With its enchantments vanquished, the tower was now merely an empty shell behind ruined walls. All that was left of its former self was a stone chamber at the very top, littered with the husks of dead men and a scattering of dust that had once been some-thing not quite human. At its centre was the raised dais, with the bodies of Roland and Raphael resting upon it. Leroi recog-nised Roland's scent, and knew that the boy's protector was now dead. He had been tempted to tear apart the bodies of the two knights, to desecrate their resting place, but he knew that this was what an animal would do and he was no longer an animal. He left the bodies as they were and, although he would never have admitted it to his lieutenants, he was happy to depart the chamber and the tower. There were things in it that he did not understand here, and they made him uneasy.

He stood with the bloodied rag in his claws and felt a degree of admiration for the boy whom he was hunting. How quickly you have grown, thought Leroi. Not so long ago you were a frightened child, and now you triumph where armed knights failed. You take the lives of men and wipe your blade clean to make it ready for the next killing. It is almost a pity that you have to die.

Leroi was growing more like a man and less like a wolf with each day that passed, or so he told himself. He still had wiry hair on his body, and his ears were pointed, his teeth sharp, but his muzzle was little more than a swelling around his mouth, and the bones of his face were re-forming to make him look more human and less lupine. He rarely walked on all fours, except when the necessity for speed arose or when the excitement of the hunt briefly overwhelmed him. That was one of the benefits of having so many to call upon: while the horse's odour was strong, much stronger than that of the boy or of the man, the recent snowfalls had meant that it was frequently lost to them, but by using large numbers of scouts the scent was quickly found again each time. They had tracked him to the village, and Leroi had been tempted to attack it with the full strength of his pack, but they had picked up the spoor of the horse and the man heading east and they knew then that the pair were no longer in the village. Some of his Loups had still counselled an assault, for the pack was hungry, but Leroi decided that it would only waste valuable time. It suited him also to keep the appetite of the pack sharp, as hunger would increase their savagery when it came time to attack the king's castle. He recalled the man standing at the village's defences, defying the wolf army. Leroi had admired the gesture, just as he admired many aspects of men's natures. This was one of the reasons why he was so comfortable with his own transformation, but it would not prevent him from returning to the village and making an example of the man who had tried to face him down.

The pack had lost some ground when the boy and the man had left the road, because Leroi had assumed that they would continue directly to the castle of the king, and half a day had been wasted before he realised his mistake. It was then only David's good fortune that had caused the pack to miss him as he left the Fortress of Thorns, for the wolves had been wary of the forest, uncertain of the hidden beings that lived within the trees, and had skirted its deepest depths in their approach to the fortress. Once Leroi was sure that nobody remained alive inside, he sent a dozen scouts to follow David's trail through the forest while the main pack headed east towards the king's castle using a longer but safer route. When the pack was reunited with the scouts, only three remained alive. Seven had been killed by the creatures that lived in the trees. The other two – and this interested Leroi greatly – had been found with their throats cut and their snouts hacked off.

'The crooked one is protecting the boy,' one of Leroi's most trusted lieutenants had growled upon hearing the news. He, too, was becoming like a man, although in him the transformation was slower and less pronounced.

'He thinks that he has found a new king,' replied Leroi. 'But we are here to bring an end to the rule of the human kings. The boy will never claim the throne.'

He barked an order and his Loups began to gather the pack, snarling and biting at those who did not respond quickly enough. Their time was near. The castle was less than a day's march away, and once they reached it there would be meat enough for all and the bloody rule of the new king Leroi would begin.

Leroi might have been becoming something more than an animal and less than a man, but deep, deep inside he would always remain a wolf.

XXVII

Of the Castle,
And the King's Greeting

The day passed, a poor, sluggish thing that departed almost grate-
fully as night took its place. David's spirits were low, and his
back and legs ached from hours in the saddle. Still, he had
managed to adjust the stirrups so that his feet fitted comfortably
in them, and he had learned how to hold the reins properly from
watching Roland, so he now looked more at ease on Scylla than
ever before, even if the horse remained too big for him. The snow
had dwindled to a few flurries, and soon would cease entirely.
The land seemed to luxuriate in its silence and its whiteness,
knowing that the snow had rendered it more beautiful than
before.

They came to a bend in the road. Ahead of them, the horizon
was lit by a soft, yellow glow, and David knew that they were
close to the king's castle. He felt a sudden surge of energy and
urged Scylla on, even though they were both weary and hungry.
Scylla broke into a trot, as though already smelling hay and fresh
water and a warm stable in which to rest, but almost as quickly
David reined her in again and listened carefully. He had heard
something, like the sound of the wind, except that the night was
still. Scylla seemed to sense it too, for she whinnied and pawed
at the ground. David patted her flank, trying to calm her even
as he felt himself grow tense.

'Hush, Scylla,' he whispered.

The noise came again, clearer now. It was the howling of a wolf. There was no way of telling how near it was, for the snow muffled all sound, but it was close enough to be heard and that was too close for David's liking. There was movement from the forest to his right and he drew his sword, already imagining white teeth and a pink tongue and snapping jaws. Instead, the Crooked Man emerged. He had his slim, curved blade in his hand. David pointed his own sword at the approaching figure and stared down its length, the tip focused on the Crooked Man's throat.

'Put down your sword,' said the Crooked Man. 'You have nothing to fear from me.'

But David kept his sword exactly where it was. He was pleased to see that his arm did not tremble. The Crooked Man did not appear surprised.

'Very well, then,' he said. 'As you wish. The wolves are coming. I don't know how long I can hold them off, but it should be long enough to allow you to reach the castle. Stay on the road, and don't be tempted by short cuts.'

More howls came, closer now.

'Why are you helping me?' asked David.

'I've been helping you all along,' replied the Crooked Man. 'You were just too wilful to understand. I have shadowed your path and saved your life, all so you could reach the castle. Now go to the king. He is expecting you. Go!'

And with that, the Crooked Man bounded away from David, skirting the edge of the forest, his blade making a whistling sound as he sliced at the air, already killing wolves in his mind. David watched him until he was out of sight, then, with no other choice but to do as he was advised, he urged Scylla towards the light ahead. The Crooked Man observed him from a hollow at the base of an old oak. It had been so much more difficult than he had anticipated, but the boy would soon be where he was supposed to be, and the Crooked Man would be one step closer to his reward.

'Georgie, Porgie, pudding and pie,' he sang. He licked his lips. 'Georgie pudding, and Georgie pie.' He giggled, then covered his mouth to stifle the laugh. He was not alone. Harsh breathing came from close by, and a plume of breath formed in the darkness. The Crooked Man curled up into a ball, only his knife hand remaining outstretched, half buried beneath the snow.

And as the wolf scout passed by, he slit it from throat to tail, and its entrails steamed in the chill night air.

The road twisted and turned, narrowing as David drew closer to his destination. Sheer faces of rock rose up on either side of him, creating a canyon in which the pounding of Scylla's hoofs echoed, for the snow had not fallen as thickly here, the ground being sheltered by the walls. Then David was clear of the canyon and before him stretched a valley with a river running through it. By its banks, about a mile or so distant, stood a great castle with high, thick walls and many towers and buildings. Lights shone in its windows and fires were lit upon its battlements. David could see soldiers on guard. As he watched, the portcullis was raised and a group of twelve horsemen emerged. They crossed the drawbridge and headed towards David, riding fast. Still fearful of the wolves, David rode down to meet them. As soon as they saw him, the horsemen spurred on their horses until they reached him and surrounded him, the men at the rear turning to face the canyon, spears at the ready in case any threat should appear from that direction.

'We have been waiting for you,' announced one of the men. He was older than the others, and he bore the scars of old battles upon his face. Grey-brown hair curled from beneath his helmet and he wore a silver breastplate studded with bronze under his dark cloak. 'We are to bring you to the safety of the king's chambers. Come now.'

David rode with them, hemmed in on all sides by armed

riders so that he felt at once both protected and a prisoner. They arrived at the drawbridge without incident and passed into the castle, the portcullis instantly lowering behind them. Servants came and helped David to dismount. They wrapped him in a cloak of soft, black fur and gave him a hot, sweet drink in a silver cup to warm him. One of them took Scylla by the reins. David was about to stop him when the leader of the horsemen intervened.

'They will take good care of your horse, and she will be stabled close to where you sleep. I am Duncan, Captain of the King's Guard. Have no fear. You are safe with us as an honoured guest of the king.'

He asked David to follow him. David did so, staying behind him as they left the outer courtyard and moved deeper into the castle. There were more people here than he had seen in his entire travels so far, and he was an object of interest to all of them. Serving girls stopped and whispered about him behind their hands. Old men bowed slightly as he passed, and small boys looked at him with something like awe.

'They have heard a great deal about you,' said Duncan.

'How?' asked David.

But all Duncan would say was that the king had his ways.

Down stone corridors they went, past spitting torches and luxuriously furnished chambers. Now the servants were replaced by courtiers, serious men with gold around their necks and papers in their hands. They stared at David with a mixture of expressions: happiness, worry, suspicion, even fear. Finally, Duncan and David arrived at a pair of great doors, carved with images of dragons and doves. Soldiers stood guard at either side, each armed with pikes. As David and Duncan approached, the soldiers opened the doors for them, revealing a large room lined with marble pillars, its floors covered with beautifully woven carpets. Tapestries hung from the walls, giving the chamber a feeling of warmth. They depicted battles and weddings, funerals and coronations. There were more courtiers here, and more soldiers, forming two lines between which David and Duncan passed, until they found themselves at the foot of a throne raised upon three stone steps. On the throne sat an old, old man. A gold crown lay on his brow, inset with red jewels, but it appeared to weigh heavily upon him, and the skin was red and raw where the metal touched his forehead. His eyes were half closed, and his breathing was very shallow.

Duncan fell to one knee and bowed his head. He tugged at David's leg as a hint that he should do the same. David, of course, had never been before a king and was not sure how to behave, so he followed Duncan's example, only peering up from under the fringe of his hair so that he could see the old man.

'Your Majesty,' said Duncan. 'He is here.'

The king stirred, and opened his eyes a little wider.

'Come closer,' he said to David.

David wasn't sure if he was supposed to rise to his feet or stay kneeling and just shuffle along. He didn't want to offend anyone or get in any trouble.

'You may stand,' said the king. 'Come, let me see you.'

David stood and approached the dais. The king beckoned him with a wrinkled finger, and David climbed the steps until he was facing the old man. With a great effort, the king leaned forward and gripped David's shoulder, his entire upper body seeming to rest upon the boy. He weighed hardly anything at all, and David was reminded of the drained husks of the knights in the fortress of thorns.

'You have come a long way,' said the king. 'Few men could have achieved what you have managed to accomplish.'

David did not know how to respond. 'Thank you' didn't seem right, and anyway he didn't feel particularly proud of himself. Roland and the Woodsman were both dead, and the bodies of the two thieves lay somewhere on the road, hidden by snow. He wondered if the king knew about them too. The king seemed to know a great deal for someone who was supposed to be losing control of his kingdom.

In the end, David settled upon saying, 'I'm happy to be here, Your Majesty,' and he imagined the ghost of Roland being impressed by this act of diplomacy.

The king smiled and nodded, as if it were not possible that someone could be unhappy to be in his company.

'Your Majesty,' said David. 'I was told that you could help me to get home. I was told that you had a book, and in it—'

The king raised a wrinkled hand, its back a chaos of purple veins and brown spots.

'All in good time,' he said. 'All in good time. For now, you must eat and you must rest. In the morning, we will talk again. Duncan will show you to your quarters. You will not be far from here.'

With that, David's first audience with the king was over. He retreated backwards from the high throne, because he thought that turning his back on the king might be considered rude. Duncan nodded at him approvingly, then rose and bowed to the king. He guided David to a small door to the right of the throne. From there, a set of stairs led up to a gallery overlooking the chamber, and David was shown into one of the rooms leading off it. The room was enormous, with a huge bed at one end, a table and six chairs in its centre, a fireplace at the other end, and three small windows that overlooked the river and the road to the castle. A change of clothing lay on the bed and there was food on the table: hot chicken, potatoes, three kinds of vegetables, and fresh fruit for pudding. There was also a jug of water, and what smelled to David like hot wine in a stone pot. A large tub had been placed before the fire, with a pan of glowing coals beneath it to heat the water.

'Eat all you wish, and then sleep,' said Duncan. 'I will come for you in the morning. If there is anything that you need, ring the bell by your bedside. The door will not be locked, but please do not leave this room. You do not know the castle and we would not wish you to get lost.'

Duncan bowed to him, then left. David took off his shoes. He ate nearly all of the chicken and most of the fruit, and he tried the hot wine but didn't care for it. In a little closet beside his bed he found a wooden bench with a round hole cut in it, which passed for a toilet. The smell was terrible, even with the bouquets of flowers and herbs that had been hung from hooks on the wall. David did what he had to do as quickly as possible, holding his breath for the entire time, then dashed out and closed the door firmly behind him before breathing again. He took off his clothes and sword and washed in the tub, then dressed himself in a stiff cotton nightshirt. Before he climbed into bed, he went to the door and opened it softly. The throne room beneath was now empty of guards, the king no longer present. A guard was, however, walking along the gallery, his back to David, and David could see another guard at the opposite side. The thick walls blocked out all sound, so it was as if he and the guards were the only people alive in the castle. David closed the bedroom door and fell, exhausted, into bed. Within seconds, he was sound asleep.

David woke suddenly, and for a few moments he was unsure of where he was. He thought that he was back in his own bed, and he looked around for his books and his games, but they were nowhere to be seen. Then, quickly, everything came back to him. He sat up and saw that fresh wood had been stacked on the fire while he was sleeping. The remains of his supper and the plates that he had used had all been taken away. Even the tub and hot pan had been removed, all without waking him from his slumbers.

David had no idea how early or late it was, but he guessed that it was the middle of the night. The castle felt as if it was asleep, and when he glanced out of his window he saw a wan moon wreathed by wisps of cloud. Something had woken him. He had been dreaming of home, and in his dream he heard voices that did not belong in the house. At first, he had simply tried to incorporate them into his dream, the same way that the tolling of his alarm clock sometimes became the ringing of a telephone in his dream if he was very tired and very deep in sleep. Now, as he sat on his soft bed, surrounded by pillows, the low murmur of two men talking was clearer to him, and he was sure that he heard his name being spoken. He pushed back the covers on the bed and crept to the door. He tried listening at the keyhole, but the voices were too muffled to understand clearly, so he opened the door as quietly as he could and peered outside.

The guards who had been patrolling the gallery were gone. The voices were coming from the throne room below. Keeping to the shadows, David hid himself behind a large silver urn filled with ferns and looked down on the two men. One of them was the king, but he was not seated on his throne. He was sitting on the stone steps, wearing a purple dressing-gown over a nightshirt of white and gold. His head was entirely bald on top and dotted with more brown spots. Lengths of white hair hung loosely over his ears and the collar of his gown, and he trembled in the cold of the great hall.

The Crooked Man sat upon the king's throne, his legs crossed and his fingers steepled before him. He seemed unhappy with something that the king had said, for he spat on the stone floor in disgust. David heard the spittle hiss and sizzle where it landed.

'It cannot be rushed,' said the Crooked Man. 'A few more hours will not kill you.'

'Nothing, it seems, will kill me,' said the king. 'You promised an end to this. I need to rest, to sleep. I want to lie in my crypt and decay to dust. You promised me that I would be allowed to die at last.'

'He thinks the book will help him,' said the Crooked Man. 'When he finds out that it had no value, he will listen to reason and then we will both have our reward from him.'

The king shifted position and David saw that he had a book upon his lap. It was bound in brown leather and looked very old and ragged. The king's fingers brushed lovingly across its cover, and his face was a mask of sadness.

'The book has value to *me*,' he said.

'Then you can take it to the grave with you,' said the Crooked Man, 'for it will be useless to anyone else. Until that time, leave it where its presence can taunt him.'

The king stood painfully and tottered down the steps. He walked to a small alcove in the wall and laid the book carefully upon a gold cushion. David had not noticed it before because drapes had been drawn across the recess during his meeting with the king.

'Don't worry, Your *Majesty*,' said the Crooked Man, his voice full of sarcasm. 'Our bargain is almost concluded.'

The king frowned. 'It was no bargain,' he said, 'not for me, and not for the one whom you took to secure it.'

The Crooked Man vaulted from the throne and, in a single bound, landed inches from the king. But the old man did not cower or try to move away.

'You concluded no bargain that you did not wish to conclude,' said the Crooked Man. 'I gave you what you desired, and I made clear what was expected of you in return.'

'I was a child,' said the king. 'I was angry. I did not understand the harm that I was doing.'

'And you think that excuses you? As a child you saw things only in black and white, good and bad, what gave you pleasure and what brought you pain. Now you see everything in shades of grey. Even the care of your own kingdom is beyond you, so unwilling are you to decide what is right and wrong or even to admit that you can tell the difference. You knew what you were agreeing to on the day that we made our bargain. Regrets have clouded your memory and now you seek to blame me for your own weaknesses. Mind your tongue, old man, or else I will be forced to remind you of the power that I still wield over you.'

'What can you do to me that you have not already done?' asked the king. 'All that is left is death, and you continue to deny that to me.'

The Crooked Man leaned so close to the king that their noses touched.

'Remember, and remember well: there are easy deaths and there are hard deaths. I can make your passing as peaceful as an afternoon snooze, or as painful and lengthy as your withered body and brittle bones will allow. Never forget that.'

The Crooked Man turned away and walked to the wall behind the throne. A tapestry of a unicorn hunt billowed briefly in the torchlight, and then there was only the king, alone in his throne room. The old man went to the alcove, opened the book once more and stared for a time at whatever was revealed in its pages, then closed it again and left through a doorway beneath the gallery. David was now alone. He waited for the guards to return, but they did not come. When five minutes had passed, and all was still quiet, he took the stairs down to the throne room and padded softly across the flagstones to where the book lay.

So this was the book of which the Woodsman and Roland had spoken. This was the Book of Lost Things. Yet the Crooked Man had declared it to be of no value, even though the king appeared to treasure it more than his crown. Perhaps the Crooked Man was wrong, thought David. Maybe he simply did not understand what was contained within its pages.

David reached out and opened the book.

XXVIII

Of the Book of Lost Things

The first page to which David opened the book was decorated with a pencil drawing of a big house: there were trees, and a garden, and long windows. A smiling sun shone in the sky and stick figures of a man, a woman, and a little boy held hands beside the front door. David turned another page and found a ticket stub for a show at a London theatre. Underneath it, a child's hand had written 'My first play!' Across from it was a postcard of a seaside pier. It was a very old postcard, and looked more brown-and-white than black-and-white. David turned more pages and saw flowers stuck down, and a tuft of dog hair ('Lucky, A Good Dog') and photographs and drawings and a piece of a woman's dress and a broken chain, painted to look like gold but with the base metal showing through. There was a page from another book, depicting a knight slaying a dragon, and a poem about a cat and a mouse, written in a boy's hand. The poem wasn't very good, but at least it rhymed.

David couldn't understand it. All of these things belonged in his world, not this one. They were tokens and souvenirs of a life not unlike his own. He read further, and came to a series of diary entries. Most of them were short, describing days at school, trips to the seaside, even the discovery of a particularly large and hairy spider in a garden web. The tone of them changed as they went on, the entries growing longer and more detailed, but also bitter and angry. They spoke of the arrival of a little girl, a potential sister, into a family, and of a boy's rage at the attention being paid to the new arrival. There was regret, and nostalgia for a time when it had been just 'me and my mummy and daddy'. David felt a kinship with the boy, but also a dislike for him. His anger at this girl, and at his parents for bringing her into his world, was so intense that it veered into pure hatred.

'I would do anything to be rid of her', read one entry. 'I would give away all of my toys, and every book that I ever owned. I would give up my savings. I would sweep the floors every day for the rest of my life. I would sell my soul if she would just GO AWAY!!!!'

But the final entry was the shortest of them all. It said simply: 'I have decided. I will do it.'

Glued to the last page was a photograph of a family, its four members standing beside a vase of flowers in a photographic studio. There was a father with a bald head and a pretty mother wearing a white dress decorated with lace. At her feet sat a boy dressed in a sailor suit, who scowled at the camera as though the photographer had just said something nasty to him. Beside him, David could just make out the hem of a dress and a pair of small black shoes, but the rest of the girl's image had been scraped away.

David turned back to the very first page and saw what was written there. It read:

Jonathan Tulvey. His Book.

David closed the book with a snap and hastily stepped away from it. Jonathan Tulvey: Rose's great-uncle who had disappeared along with his little adopted sister and had never been seen again. This was Jonathan's book, a relic of his life. He remembered the old king, and the loving way in which he had touched the volume.

'*The book has value to* me.'

Jonathan was the king. He had made a bargain with the Crooked Man, and in return he had become the ruler of this land. Perhaps he had even passed through the same portal that David had used to come here. But what was the arrangement, and what had happened to the little girl? Whatever bargain he had made with the Crooked Man had cost him dearly in the end. The old king, pleading to be allowed to die, was living proof of this.

A sound came from above. David shrank back against the wall as a guard appeared on the gallery, resuming his position now that the chamber was empty once again. There was no way David could get back to his bedroom without being seen. He looked around and tried to find another way out. He could take the doorway the king had used, but that would almost certainly mean being confronted by the guards. There was also the tapestry on the wall behind the throne. Somehow, the Crooked Man had found a way out through there, and David doubted that there would be guards where the Crooked Man had gone. David was also curious. For the first time, he felt that he knew more than the Crooked Man or the king thought he knew. It was time to try to use that knowledge.

Silently, he made his way to the tapestry and lifted it away from the wall. Behind it was a door. David pushed down on the handle and the door opened without a sound. Beyond lay a low-ceilinged passageway, lit by candles set in alcoves in the stonework. The roof of the passage was so low that it almost touched David's hair as he entered. He closed the door behind him and followed the passageway down, down, deep into the cold, dark places that lay beneath the castle. He passed disused dungeons, some still littered with bones, and a chamber that was filled with instruments of pain and torture: racks upon which to stretch prisoners until they screamed; thumbscrews with which to break their bones; spikes and spears and blades to pierce the flesh; and, in a far corner, an iron maiden, shaped like the mummies' coffins that David had seen in museums but with nails set into its lid and back so that anyone placed inside would face an agonising death. It made David feel queasy, and he passed through the chamber as quickly as he could.

At last he came to an enormous room dominated by a great hourglass. Each bulb of the glass was as tall as a house, but the top bulb was almost empty of sand. The wood and glass from which the hourglass had been constructed looked very old. Time, for someone or something, was draining away, and now it was almost gone.

Beside the hourglass room was a small alcove furnished with a simple bed, a stained mattress and an old, grey blanket resting upon it. On the wall across from the bed was an array of bladed weapons, daggers and swords and knives, all arranged in descending order of length. Another wall held a shelf covered in glass jars of different shapes and sizes. One of them seemed to glow faintly.

David's nose wrinkled at an unpleasant smell from close by. He turned to find the source and almost bumped his head against a garland of wolves' snouts hanging by a rope from the ceiling above, twenty or thirty in all, some still damp with blood.

'Who are you?' said a voice, and David's heart came close to stopping from the shock of hearing it. He tried to find the source of the sound, but there was nobody there.

'Does he know you're here?' said the voice again. It was the voice of a girl.

'I can't see you,' said David.

'But I can see you.'

'Where are you?'

'I'm over here, on the shelf.'

David followed the sound of the voice to the shelf of jars. There, in a green flask close to the edge, he saw a tiny little girl. Her hair was long and blond, and her eyes were blue. She shone with a pale light and wore a simple white nightdress. There was a hole in the gown at her left breast, with a large chocolate-coloured stain around it.

'You shouldn't be here,' said the little girl. 'If he finds you, he'll hurt you, just like he hurt me.'

'What did he do to you?' asked David.

But the little girl only shook her head and clenched her lips tightly, as though trying not to cry.

'What's your name?' asked David, trying to change the subject.

'My name is Anna,' said the little girl.

Anna.

'I'm David. How can I get you out of there?'

'You can't,' said the girl. 'I'm dead.'

David leaned in a little closer to the jar. He could see where the girl's small hands had touched the glass, but they left no fingerprints upon it. Her face was white and her lips were purple, and dark rings surrounded her eyes. The hole in her nightdress was clearer now, and David thought that the stain surrounding it might be dried blood.

'How long have you been here?' he said.

'I've lost count of the years,' she said. 'I was very young when

I came here. There was another little boy in this room when I arrived. I dream of him sometimes. He was like I am now, but he was very frail. He faded away when I was brought here, and I never saw him again. I've been growing weaker, though. I'm afraid. I'm scared that what happened to him is going to happen to me. I'll disappear, and then no one will ever know what became of me.'

She began to cry, but no tears fell, for the dead can no longer weep or bleed.

David placed his little finger against the jar, just where the girl's hand was touching it from the inside, so that only the glass separated them.

'Does anyone else know that you're here?' asked David.

She nodded.

'My brother sometimes comes, but he's very old now. Well, I call him my brother but he never was, not really. I just wanted him to be. He tells me that he's sorry. I believe him. I think he *is* sorry.'

Suddenly, everything began to make awful sense to David.

'Jonathan brought you here, and he gave you to the Crooked Man,' he said. 'That was the bargain he made.'

He sat down hard on the cold, uncomfortable bed.

'He was jealous of you,' he continued, speaking more softly now, talking as much to himself as to the girl in the jar, 'and the Crooked Man offered him a way to be free of you. Jonathan became king, and the one who preceded him, the old queen, was allowed to die. Perhaps, many years before, she had made a similar bargain with the Crooked Man, and the boy you saw in the jar when you came was her brother, or cousin, or some little boy next door who annoyed her so much that she dreamed of getting rid of him.'

And the Crooked Man heard her dreams, because that was where he wandered. His place was the land of the imagination, the world where stories began. The stories were always looking for a way to be told, to be brought to life through books and reading. That was how they crossed over from their world into ours. But with them came the Crooked Man, prowling between his realm and ours, looking for stories of his own to create, hunting for children who dreamed bad dreams, who were jealous and angry and proud. And he made kings and queens of them, cursing them with a kind of power, even if the real power lay always in his hands. And in return they betrayed the objects of their jealousy to him, and he took them into his lair deep beneath the castle . . .

David stood and returned to the girl in the jar.

'I know it's hard for you, but you have to tell me what happened to you when you came here. It's very important. Please, try.'

Anna screwed her face up and shook her head.

'No,' she whispered. 'It hurt. I don't want to remember it.'

'You must,' said David, and there was a new force to his voice. It sounded deeper, as though the man that he would become had briefly shown himself before his time. 'If it's not to happen again, you have to tell me what he did.'

Anna was trembling. Her lips were pressed as thin as paper, and her tiny fists were clenched so tightly that the bones threatened to break through her skin. At last, she released a moan of sorrow and anger and remembered pain, and the words poured out.

'We came through the sunken garden,' she began. 'Jonathan was always being so mean to me. He would tease me, when he spoke to me at all. He would pinch me and pull my hair. He would take me into the forest and try to lose me there, until I started to cry and he had to come back for me in case his parents heard me. He told me that if I ever said anything to them he would give me away to a stranger. He said that they wouldn't believe me anyway because he was their real child and I wasn't. I was just a little girl that they'd taken pity on, and if I disappeared then they wouldn't be sad for very long.

'But sometimes he could be so kind and gentle, as though he forgot that he was supposed to hate me, and the real Jonathan shone through instead. Perhaps that was why I followed him down to the garden that night, because he'd been so nice to me that day. He'd bought me sweets with his own money, and he'd shared his apple pudding with me after I dropped mine on the floor. He woke me in the night and told me that he had something to show me, something special and secret. Everyone else was asleep, and we sneaked down to the sunken garden, my hand in Jonathan's. He showed me a hollow place. I was scared. I didn't want to go inside. But Jonathan said that, if I did, I'd see a strange land, a fabulous land. He went first, and I followed. At first, I couldn't see anything at all. There was only darkness and spiders. Then I saw trees and flowers, and smelled apple blossom and pine. Jonathan was standing in a clearing, dancing around in circles, laughing and calling to me to join him.

'So I did.'

She fell silent for a moment. David waited for her to continue.

'There was a man waiting: the Crooked Man. He was sitting on a rock. He stared at me and licked his lips, then spoke to Jonathan.

'"Tell me," he said.

'"Her name is Anna," said Jonathan.

'"Anna," said the Crooked Man, as if he was trying out my name to see if he liked how it tasted. "Welcome, Anna."

'Then he jumped from the rock and wrapped me in his arms, and he began spinning round and round, just as Jonathan had done, but he spun so hard that he dug a hole in the ground and he dragged me down with him, through roots and dirt, through worms and beetles, into the tunnels that run under this world. He carried me for miles and miles, even though I cried and cried, until at last we came to these rooms.

'And then—'

She stopped.

'And then?' prompted David.

'He ate my heart,' she whispered.

David felt himself grow pale. He was so sickened that he thought he might faint.

'He put his hand inside me, tearing at me with his nails, then pulled it out and ate it in front of me,' she said. 'And it hurt, it hurt so much. I was in such pain that I left my own body to escape it. I could see myself dying on the floor, and I was being lifted up, and there were lights and voices. Then glass closed around me, and I was trapped in this jar and placed on this shelf, and I've been here ever since. The next time I saw Jonathan, he had a crown on his head and he called himself the king, but he didn't look happy. He looked frightened and miserable, and he's remained that way for all these years. As for me, I never sleep because I am never tired. I never eat because I am never hungry. I never drink because I never feel thirst. I just stay here, with no way to tell how many days or years have passed, except when Jonathan comes and I see the ravages of time on his face. Mostly, though, *he* comes. He looks older now, too. He's sick. As I fade, so he grows weaker. I hear him talking in his sleep. He is looking for another, someone to take Jonathan's place and someone to take mine.'

David saw, once again, that hourglass in the room beyond, its top half nearly empty of grains. Was it counting down the days, the hours, the minutes, until the end of the Crooked Man's life? If he was allowed to take another child, would the hourglass be turned upside down so that the great count of his existence could begin again? How many times had that glass been turned? There were many jars on the shelf, most of them thick with dust and mould. Had each one, at some point, held the spirit of some lost child?

A bargain: by naming the child to him, you doomed yourself. You became a ruler without power, haunted always by the betrayal of someone smaller and weaker than yourself, a brother, a sister, a friend whom you should have protected, someone who trusted you to stand up for them, who looked up to you, and who would, in turn, have been there for you as the years went by and childhood became adulthood. And once you had struck the bargain, there was no way back, for who could return to their old life knowing the terrible thing that they had done?

'You're coming with me,' said David. 'I'm not leaving you alone here for a minute longer.'

He lifted the jar from the shelf. There was a cork in the top, but David could not release it, no matter how hard he tried. His face grew puce from the effort, but all was in vain. He looked around and found an old sack in a corner.

'I'm going to put you in here,' he said, 'just in case someone sees us.'

'That's all right,' said Anna. 'I'm not afraid.'

David placed the jar carefully in the sack, then hung the sack over his shoulder. Just as he was about to leave, something caught his eye in a corner of the room. It was his pyjamas, his dressing-gown and a single slipper, the clothing discarded by the Woodsman before they had set out for the king. It seemed so long ago now, but here were tokens of the life that he had left behind. He did not like to think of them down there in the Crooked Man's lair. He gathered them up, went to the doorway and listened carefully. There was no sound to be heard. David took a deep breath to calm himself, and ran.

XXIX

Of the Crooked Man's Hidden Kingdom and the Treasures That He Kept There

The Crooked Man's lair was much larger, and much deeper, than David could have known. It ran far beneath the castle, and there were rooms that contained things much more terrifying than a collection of rusty torture implements, or the ghost of a dead girl trapped in a jar. This was the heart of the Crooked Man's world, the place where all things were born and all things died. He was there when the first men came into the world, erupting into being along with them. In a way, they gave him life and purpose, and in return he gave them stories to tell, for the Crooked Man remembered every tale. He even had a story of his own, although he had changed its details in crucial ways before it could be told. In his tale, it was the Crooked Man's name that had to be guessed, but that was his little joke. In truth, the Crooked Man had no name. Others could call him what they wished, but he was a being so old that the names given to him by men had no meaning for him: Trickster; the Crooked Man; Rumple—

Oh, but what was that name again? Never mind, never mind . . .

Only the names of children mattered to him, because there was one truth in the tale that the Crooked Man had given the world about himself: names did have a power, if they were used in the right way, and the Crooked Man had learned how to use them very well indeed. One enormous room in his lair was a testament to all that the Crooked Man knew: it was filled entirely with small skulls, each one bearing the name of a lost child, reminders that the Crooked Man had struck many bargains for the lives of children. He could remember the faces and voices of every one and sometimes, when he stood among their remains, he conjured up the memory of them so that the room was filled with their shades, a chorus of lost boys and girls weeping for their mummies and their daddies, a gathering of the forgotten and the betrayed.

The Crooked Man had treasures upon treasures, relics of stories told and stories yet to be told. A long crypt was used to store an array of thick glass cases, and in each case a body was suspended in yellowish liquid so that it would not decay. Come, look over here. Peer closely at this case, so closely that your breath creates a little cloud of moisture upon the glass and you can stare into the milky eyes of the fat, bald man within. It's as if he himself is breathing, although he has not taken or released a breath in a very long time. See how his skin is burst and burned? See how his mouth and throat, his belly and chest, are swollen and distended? Do you want to know his tale, for it is one of the Crooked Man's favourite stories. It is a nasty tale, a very nasty tale . . .

You see, the fat man's name was Manius, and he was very greedy. He owned so much land that a bird could take off from his first field and fly for a day and a night, yet still not reach the limits of Manius's property. He charged heavy rents to those who worked his fields and lived in his villages. Even to set foot on his land was to invite a charge, and in this way he became very wealthy, but he never had enough gold and was always seeking new ways to increase his fortune. If he could have charged a bee to take pollen from a flower, or a tree to grow roots in his soil, then he would have done so.

One day, while Manius walked in the largest of his orchards, he saw a disturbance in the ground and out popped the Crooked Man, who was busy extending his network of tunnels beneath the earth. Manius challenged him, for he saw that the Crooked Man's clothes, although dirtied by the soil, had gold buttons and gold trim, and the dagger at his belt gleamed with rubies and diamonds.

'This is my land,' Manius said. 'All that is above it and all that is below belongs to me, and you must pay me for the right of passage.'

The Crooked Man rubbed his chin thoughtfully. 'That seems only fair,' he said. 'I will pay you a reasonable price.'

Manius smiled and said, 'I have ordered a banquet to be prepared for myself tonight. We will weigh all the food on the table before I eat, and all that is left when I am done. You will pay me in gold the weight of all that I have eaten.'

'A bellyful of gold,' said the Crooked Man. 'It is agreed. I will come to you tonight, and I will give you all you can eat in gold.'

They shook hands on the deal and parted. That night, the Crooked Man sat and watched as Manius ate and ate. Manius consumed two whole turkeys and a full ham, bowl upon bowl of potatoes and vegetables, whole tureens of soup, great plates of fruit and cakes and cream, and glass after glass of the finest wines. The Crooked Man carefully weighed it all before the meal began, and weighed the meagre remains when the meal was over. The difference amounted to many, many pounds, or enough gold to purchase one hundred fields.

Manius belched. He felt very tired, so tired that he could barely keep his eyes open.

'Now where is my gold?' he asked, but the Crooked Man was growing blurry, and the room was spinning, and before he could hear the answer he was asleep.

When he awoke, he was chained to a chair in a dark dungeon. His mouth was held open by a metal vice, and a bubbling cauldron was suspended above his head.

The Crooked Man appeared before him. 'I am a man of my word,' he said. 'Prepare to receive your bellyful of gold.'

The cauldron tipped. Molten gold spilled into Manius's mouth and poured down his throat, scalding his flesh and burning his bones. The pain was beyond imagining, but he did not die, not immediately, because the Crooked Man had ways of delaying death to make his tortures last. The Crooked Man would pour a little gold, then allow it to cool before pouring a little more, and thus he continued until he had filled Manius so full of gold that it bubbled behind his back teeth. By then, of course, Manius was very dead indeed; even the Crooked Man could not keep him alive indefinitely. Eventually, Manius took his place in the room full of glass cases, and the Crooked Man would come to look at him sometimes, and smile as he remembered this most splendid of tricks.

There were many such stories in the Crooked Man's lair: a thousand rooms, and a thousand stories for every room. One chamber housed a collection of telepathic spiders: very old, very wise, and very, very large, each one more than four feet across, with fangs so poisonous that a single drop of their venom, placed in a well, had once killed an entire village. The Crooked Man often used them to hunt those who strayed into his tunnels, and when the trespassers were found, the spiders would wrap them in silk and carry them back to their cobwebbed room, and there they would die slowly as the spiders fed upon them, draining them drop by drop.

In one of the dressing-rooms a woman sat facing a blank wall, endlessly combing her long, silver hair. Sometimes, the Crooked Man would take those who had angered him to visit the woman, and when she turned to look at them they would see themselves reflected in her eyes, for her eyes were made of mirrored glass. And in those eyes they would be allowed to witness the moment of their deaths, so that they would know exactly when and how they would die. You might think that such knowledge would not be so terrible, and you would be wrong. We are not meant to know the time or the nature of our deaths (and all of us secretly hope that we may be immortal). Those who were given this knowledge found that they could not sleep or eat or enjoy any of the pleasures that life had to offer them, so tormented were they by what they had seen. Their lives became a kind of living death, devoid of joy, and all that was left to them was fear and sadness, so when at last the end came they were almost grateful for it.

A bedchamber contained a naked woman and a naked man, and the Crooked Man would bring children to them (not the special ones, the ones who gave him life, but the others, the ones he stole from villages, or those who strayed from the path and became lost in the forest) and the man and the woman would whisper things to them in the darkness of their chamber, telling them things that children should not know, dark tales of what adults did together in the depths of the night while their sons and daughters were sleeping. In this way, the children died inside. Forced into adulthood before they were ready, they had their innocence taken from them and their minds collapsed under the weight of poisonous thoughts. Many grew up to become evil men and women, and so the corruption was spread.

One small, bright room was decorated only with a mirror, plain and unadorned. The Crooked Man would steal husbands or wives from their marriage beds, leaving their spouses sleeping, and force the captives to sit before the mirror, and the mirror would reveal all of the bad secrets that their spouses kept hidden from them: all of the sins they had committed and all of the sins they wanted to commit; all of the betrayals already on their consciences and all of the betrayals that they might yet per-petrate. Then the captives would be returned to their beds, and when they awoke they would not remember the chamber, or the mirror, or their abduction by the Crooked Man. All they would recall was the knowledge that those whom they loved, and whom they thought loved them in return, were not as they had believed them to be, and in this way lives were ruined by suspicion and the fear of treachery.

There was a hall filled entirely with pools of what looked like clear water, and each pool showed a different part of the kingdom, so that little happened in the land beyond the castle that was not known to the Crooked Man. By diving into a pool, the Crooked Man could materialise in the place reflected in it. The air would ripple and shimmer, and suddenly an arm would appear, then a leg, and finally the face and hunched back of the Crooked Man, transported instantly from the depths beneath the castle to a room or a field far away. The Crooked Man's favourite torture was to take men or women, preferably those with large families, and hang them from chains in the room of pools. Then, while they watched, he would hunt down and kill their families before them, one by one. After each murder he would return to the room and listen to the pleas of his captives, but no matter how loudly they screamed and cried and begged for him to be merciful, he would not spare a single life. Finally, when all were dead, he would take the desolate men or women to his deepest, darkest dungeons, and there he would leave them to go mad with loneliness and grief.

Little evils, big evils, all were butter to the Crooked Man's bread. Through his network of tunnels and his room of pools, he knew more about this world than anyone else, and his knowledge gave him the power he required to rule the kingdom in secret. And all the time he haunted the shadows of another world, our world, and he made kings and queens of boys and girls and bound them to him by destroying their spirits and forcing them to betray children whom they should have protected. To the ones who threatened to rebel against him, he gave promises that, some day, he would release them and the child they had sacrificed to him from their bargains, claiming that he could restore the frail figures in the jars to life if he chose (for most, like Jonathan Tulvey, very quickly realised their mistake in striking a bargain with the Crooked Man).

But there were some things that were beyond the Crooked Man's control. Bringing outsiders into the land changed it. They carried their fears with them, their dreams and their nightmares, and the land made them real. That was how the Loups had come into being. They were Jonathan's worst fear: from his earliest childhood, he had hated stories of wolves and of beasts that walked and talked like men. When the Crooked Man finally lured Jonathan into the kingdom, that fear followed him, and the wolves began to transform. They alone did not fear the Crooked Man, as if some of Jonathan's secret hatred of the trickster had found form in them, and their numbers grew. Now they presented the greatest threat to the kingdom, although it was one of which the Crooked Man hoped he could yet make use.

The boy called David was different from the others whom the Crooked Man had tempted. He had helped to destroy the Beast, and the sorceress who dwelt in the Fortress of Thorns. David did not realise it, but in a way they were *his* fears, and he had brought aspects of them into being. What had surprised the Crooked Man was the way in which the boy had dealt with them. His anger and grief had enabled him to do what older men had not managed to achieve. The boy was strong, strong enough to conquer his fears. He was also beginning to master his hatreds and jealousies. Such a boy, if he could be controlled, would make a great king.

But time was running out for the Crooked Man. He needed another child's life to drain. If he ate Georgie's heart, the child's lifespan would become the Crooked Man's. If Georgie was destined to live to be one hundred years old, then the Crooked Man would be granted that time instead and Georgie's spirit would remain trapped in one of the Crooked Man's jars. All that was necessary was for David to say the child's name aloud, to indulge his hatred and thus to damn them both.

The Crooked Man had less than one day of life left in his hourglass. He needed David to betray his half-brother before midnight. Now, as he sat in his chamber of pools, he saw shapes appear on the hills around the castle, and for the first time in many decades he felt real fear, even as he put the finishing touches to his last, desperate plan.

For the wolves were gathering, and soon they would descend upon the castle.

While the Crooked Man was distracted by the approaching army, David, carrying Anna in her jar, made his way back through the warren of tunnels to the throne room. As they approached the door concealed by the tapestry, David could hear men shouting out orders, and the running of feet and the clanking of weapons and armour. He wondered if his disappearance was the reason for the activity, and tried to come up with the best way to explain his absence. He peered from behind the tapestry and saw Duncan standing nearby as he sent men to the battlements and told others to make sure all entrances to the castle were secure. While the Captain's back was turned, David slipped out and ran as quickly as he could to the stairs leading up to the gallery. If anyone saw him, they paid him no attention, and he knew then that he was not the cause of all this trouble. Once he was back in his bedroom, he closed the door and removed from his sack the jar containing Anna's ghost. Her light seemed to have grown dimmer in the short trip from the Crooked Man's lair to the castle itself, and she was slumped at the base of the glass, her face even paler than before.

'What's wrong?' David asked.

Anna held up her right hand, and David saw that it had faded to near-transparency.

'I feel weak,' said Anna. 'And I'm changing. I seem to be growing fainter.'

David did not know what to say to console her. He tried to find somewhere to hide her, and decided eventually upon a shadowy corner of an enormous wardrobe, populated only by the husks of dead insects trapped in an ancient web. But Anna called out to him as he was about to place the jar in his chosen hiding place.

'No,' she cried. 'Please, not there. I've been trapped alone in the darkness for so many years, and I don't think I'm going to be in this world for much longer. Put me on the windowsill, so that I may look out and see trees and people. I'll be quiet, and no one will think of searching for me there.'

So David opened one of the windows and saw that outside was a wrought-iron balcony. It was rusted in places, and rattled when he touched it, but it would safely support the weight of the jar. He placed it carefully in one corner, and Anna moved forward and leaned against the glass. For the first time since they had met, she smiled.

'Oh,' she said, 'it's wonderful. Look at the river, and the trees beyond, and the people. Thank you, David. This is all that I wanted to see.'

But David was listening to her no longer. Howls rose from the hills above, and he saw black, and white, and grey, shapes moving across the landscape, thousands upon thousands of them. There was a discipline and purpose about the wolves, almost like divisions of an army preparing for battle. Upon the highest point overlooking the castle, he glimpsed clothed figures standing on their hind legs while more wolves ran to and fro, carrying messages back and forth between the Loups and the animals on the front line.

'What's happening?' asked Anna.

'The wolves have come,' said David. 'They want to kill the king and take over his kingdom.'

'Kill Jonathan?' said Anna, and there was such horror in her voice that David looked away from the wolves and turned his attention back to the small, fading figure of the girl.

'Why are you so worried about him, after all that he's done to you?' he asked. 'He betrayed you and let the Crooked Man feed on you, then left you to rot in a jar in a dungeon. How can you feel anything but hatred for him?'

Anna shook her head and, for a moment, she seemed much older than before. She may have been a girl in form, but she had existed for far longer than her appearance suggested, and in that dark place she had learned wisdom and tolerance and forgiveness.

'He's my brother,' she stated. 'I love him, no matter what he has done to me. He was young and angry and foolish when he made his bargain, and if he could turn back the clock and undo all that has been done, then he would. I don't want to see him hurt. And what will happen to all those people below if the wolves succeed and their rule replaces that of men and women? They will tear apart every living thing within these walls, and what little that is good here will cease to be.'

As he listened to her, David wondered again how Jonathan could have betrayed this girl. He must have been so angry and so sad, and that anger and sadness had consumed him.

David watched the wolves assemble, all with the same purpose: to take the castle and kill the king and everyone who stood by him. But the walls were thick and strong, and the gates were firmly closed against them. There were guards at the stinking holes where the waste left the castle, and armed men stood on every roof and at every window. The wolves vastly outnumbered them, but they were outside and David could see no way for them to gain entry. As long as that situation continued, the wolves could howl all they wanted, and the Loups could send and receive as many messages as they chose. It would make no difference. The castle would remain impregnable.

XXX

Of the Crooked Man's Act of Betrayal

Deep below the ground, the Crooked Man watched the sands of his life trickle away, one by one. He was growing steadily weaker. His system was collapsing. His teeth were coming loose in his mouth, and there were weeping sores on his lips. Blood dripped from his twisted fingernails, and his eyes were yellow and rheumy. His skin was dry and flaking; long, deep cuts opened upon it when he scratched, revealing the muscles and tendons beneath. His joints ached, and his hair fell from his head in clumps. He was dying, yet he did not panic. There had been times in his long, dreadful life when he had been even closer than this to death, when it had seemed that he'd chosen the wrong child and there would be no betrayal and no new king or queen for him to manipulate like a puppet upon the throne. But, in the end, he had always found a way to corrupt them or, as he preferred to think of it, for them to corrupt themselves.

The Crooked Man believed that whatever evil lay in men was there from the moment of conception, and it was only a matter of discovering its specific nature in a child. The boy David had as much rage and hurt as any that the Crooked Man had yet encountered, but still he resisted his advances. It was time for one last gamble. For all he had achieved, and for all of the bravery that he had shown, the boy was still just a boy. He was far from home, separated from his father and the familiar things of his life. Somewhere inside, he was frightened and alone. If the Crooked Man could make that fear unbearable, then David would name the infant in his house and the Crooked Man would live on, and in time the search for David's replacement would commence. Fear was the key. The Crooked Man had learned that, when faced with death, most men would do anything to stay alive. They would weep, beg, kill, or betray another to save their own skins. If he could make David afraid for his life then he would give the Crooked Man what he desired.

So that strange, hunched being, old as the memory of men, left his lair of mirrored pools and hourglasses, of spiders and death-filled eyes, disappearing into the great network of tunnels that ran like a honeycomb beneath his realm. He passed below the castle buildings, under the walls, and into the countryside beyond.

And when he heard the howling of the wolves above him, he knew that he had reached his destination.

David had been reluctant to leave Anna, so weak did she seem. He was afraid that if he turned his back on her, she might disappear altogether. In turn, she, who had been alone in the dark for so long, was grateful for his company. She spoke to him of the long decades spent with the Crooked Man, of the awful things that he had done and the terrible tortures and punishments he had visited on those who had crossed him. David, in turn, told her of his dead mother, and of the house that he now shared with Rose and Georgie, the same house in which Anna had once briefly lived after her own parents died. The little girl's aura grew brighter at the mention of her former home, and she quizzed David about the house and the village nearby and the changes that had occurred since she had left it. He told her of the war and of the great army marching across Europe, crushing all in its path.

'So you left behind one war, only to find yourself in the midst of another,' she said.

David looked down on the columns of wolves moving purposefully across the valley and the hills. Their numbers seemed to swell with every passing minute, the ranks positioning themselves to surround the castle. Like Fletcher before him, David was most disturbed by their order and discipline. It was a fragile thing, he suspected: without the Loups the wolf packs would scatter, fighting and scavenging their way back to their own territories, but for now the Loups had corrupted the natures of the wolves, just as their own natures had been corrupted. They believed themselves to be greater and more advanced than their brothers and sisters who walked on four legs, but in reality they were much worse. They were impure; mutations that were neither human nor animal. David wondered what the minds of the Loups were like as the two sides of their being fought for supremacy. There had been a kind of madness in Leroi's eyes, of that much David was certain.

'Jonathan will not surrender to them,' said Anna. 'They cannot gain entry to the castle. They should simply disperse, but they won't. What are they waiting for?'

'An opportunity,' said David. 'Perhaps Leroi and his Loups have a plan, or maybe they're just hoping the king will make a mistake, but they can't turn back now. They will never assemble another army like this, and they won't be allowed to survive if they fail.'

The door of David's bedroom opened, and Duncan, the captain of the guard, entered. David closed the window immediately, just in case Duncan might spot Anna on the balcony.

'The king wishes to see you,' he said.

David nodded. Even though he was safe inside the castle walls, and surrounded by armed men, he first went to his bed and removed his sword and belt from where they hung on the bedpost, then cinched the belt around his waist. Doing this had become a routine with him and now he did not feel properly dressed without the sword. He was especially aware of his need for it after his foray into the lair of the Crooked Man. Down there, in the trickster's chambers of pain and torture, he had realised how vulnerable he was without a weapon. David also knew that the Crooked Man was bound to notice that Anna was missing and was sure to come looking for her when he did. It would not take him long to work out that David was somehow involved, and the boy did not want to face the Crooked Man's anger without the sword to hand.

The captain did not object to the sword. In fact, he told David to bring all of his belongings with him.

'You will not be returning to this room,' he said.

It was all that David could do not to glance at the window behind which Anna was hidden.

'Why?' he asked.

'That's for the king to tell you,' said Duncan. 'We came for you earlier but you were not to be found.'

'I went for a walk,' said David.

'You were told to remain where you were.'

'I heard the wolves and wanted to find out what was going on. But everybody seemed to be rushing around so I came back here.'

'You need not fear them,' said the captain. 'These walls have never been breached, and no pack of animals is going to do what an army of men could not. Come, now. The king is waiting.'

David packed his bag, added the clothing he had found in the Crooked Man's room, and followed Duncan down to the throne room, casting one last look back at the window. Through the glass, he thought he could still see Anna's light shining faintly.

In the woods behind the wolves' lines, a flurry of snow shot into the air, followed by clumps of dirt and grass. A hole appeared, and from it emerged the Crooked Man. He held his curved blade at the ready, for this was a dangerous business. There was no way that he could strike a bargain with the wolves. Their leaders, the Loups, were aware of the Crooked Man's power and trusted him just as little as he trusted them. He had also been responsible for the deaths of too many of their number for them to forgive him easily, or even to let him live long enough to plead for his life if one of the packs trapped him. Silently, he advanced, until he saw a line of figures before him, all of them dressed in army uniforms scavenged from the bodies of dead soldiers. Some were smoking pipes while they stood over a map of the castle that had been drawn in the snow before them, trying to work out some way to gain entry. Already scouts had been dispatched to get close to the walls in order to discover if there were any cracks or fissures, any unguarded holes or portals, that might be of use to them. The grey wolves had been used as decoys, and had died almost as soon as they came within reach of the defenders' arrows. The white wolves were harder to see, and although some of their number had also died, enough were able to approach close enough to the walls to conduct a minute examination, sniffing and digging in an effort to find a way through. Those that had survived to report back confirmed that the castle was as impregnable as it appeared to be.

The Crooked Man was close enough to hear the voices of the Loups and to smell the stink of their fur. Foolish, vain creatures, he thought. You may dress like men, and take on their manners and airs, but you will always stink like beasts and you will always be animals pretending to be what you are not. The Crooked Man hated them and hated Jonathan for conjuring them into being through the power of his imagination, creating his own version of the tale of the little girl in the red, hooded cloak in order to give birth to them. The Crooked Man had watched with alarm as the wolves began to transform: slowly at first, their growls and snarls sometimes forming what might have been words, their front paws lifting into the air as they tried to walk like men. In the beginning it had seemed almost amusing to him, but then their faces had begun to change, and their intelligence, already quick and alert, had grown sharper yet. He had tried to get Jonathan to order a cull of the wolves throughout the land, but the king had acted too late. The first party of soldiers that he sent out to kill them were themselves slaughtered, and the villagers were too afraid of this new threat to do more than build higher walls around their settlements and lock their doors and windows at night. Now it had come to this: an army of wolves, led by creatures who were half human, half beast, intent upon seizing the kingdom for themselves.

'Come then,' the Crooked Man whispered to himself. 'If you want the king, take him. I am done with him.'

The Crooked Man retreated, circling the generals, until he came to a she-wolf who was acting as a lookout. He made sure to stay downwind of her, judging his approach from the direction in which the lighter flakes of snow were blowing off the ground. He was almost upon her when she registered his presence, but by then her fate was sealed. The Crooked Man pounced, his blade already beginning its downward movement. As soon as he landed on the wolf, the knife sliced through her fur and deep into the flesh beneath, the Crooked Man's long fingers closing around her muzzle and snapping it tightly closed so that she could not cry out, not yet.

He could have killed her, of course, and taken her snout for his collection, but he did not. Instead, he cut her so deeply that she collapsed to the ground and the snow around her quickly grew red with her blood. He released his grip on her muzzle and the wolf began to yelp, alerting the rest of the pack to her distress. This was the dangerous part, the Crooked Man knew, riskier even than tackling the big she-wolf to begin with. He wanted them to see him, but not to get close enough to catch him. Suddenly, four massive greys appeared on the brow of a hill and howled a warning to the rest. Behind them came one of the despised Loups, dressed in all of the military finery he could muster: a bright red jacket with gold braid and buttons, and white trousers only partly stained by the blood of their previous owner. He wore a long sabre on a black leather belt, and he was already drawing it as he stood and looked down at the dying wolf and the being responsible for her pain.

It was Leroi, the beast who would be king, the most hated and feared of the Loups. The Crooked Man paused, tempted by the nearness of his greatest enemy. Although he was very ancient, and weakened by the dying of Anna's light and the slow slipping away of the grains of his life, the Crooked Man was still fast and strong. He felt certain that he could kill the four greys, leaving Leroi with only a sword with which to defend himself. If the Crooked Man killed Leroi, then the wolves would disperse, for he held their army together with the force of his will. Even the other Loups were not as advanced as he was and they could be hunted down by the forces of the new king.

The new king! The reminder of what he had come to do brought the Crooked Man to his senses, even as more wolves and Loups appeared behind Leroi, and a patrol of whites began to creep in from the south. For a moment, all was still as the wolves regarded their most despised foe standing over the dying she-wolf. Then, with a cry of triumph, the Crooked Man waved his bloody blade in the air and ran. Instantly, the wolves followed, pouring through the trees, their eyes bright with the thrill of the chase. One white wolf, sleeker and faster than the rest, separated itself from the pack, trying to cut off the Crooked Man's escape. The ground sloped down to where the Crooked Man was running, so that the wolf was about ten feet above him when its hind legs bent and it catapulted itself into the air, its fangs bared to tear out its quarry's throat. But the Crooked Man was too wily for it, and as it jumped he spun in a neat circle, his blade held high above his head, and sliced open the wolf from below. It fell dead at his feet, and the Crooked Man ran on. Thirty feet, now twenty, now ten. Ahead of him he could see the tunnel entrance, marked by earth and dirty snow. He was almost upon it when he saw a flash of red to his left, and heard the *swish* of a sword slicing through the air. He raised his own blade just in time to block Leroi's sabre, but the Loup was stronger than he had expected and the Crooked Man stumbled slightly, almost falling to the ground. Had he done so all would have ended quickly, because Leroi was already preparing to deliver the death blow. Instead, the blade cut through the Crooked Man's garments, barely missing the arm beneath, but the Crooked Man pretended that a grave injury had been inflicted. He dropped his blade and staggered backwards, his left hand clutched to the imaginary wound on his right arm. The wolves surrounded him now, watching the two combatants, howling their support for Leroi, willing him to finish the job. Leroi raised his head and snarled once, and all of the wolves fell quiet.

'You have made a fatal error,' said Leroi. 'You should have stayed behind the castle walls. We will breach them, in time, but you might have lived a little longer had you remained within their confines.'

The Crooked Man laughed in Leroi's face, which was now, except for unruly hairs and a slight snout, almost human in appearance.

'No, it is you who are mistaken,' he said. 'Look at you. You are neither man nor beast, but some pathetic creature who is less than both. You hate what you are and want to be what you cannot truly become. Your appearance may change, and you may wear all the fine clothes that you can steal from the bodies of your victims, but you will still be a wolf inside. Even then, what do you think will happen when your outer transformation is complete, when you start to resemble fully what once you hunted? You will look like a man and the pack will no longer recognise you as its own. What you most desire is the very thing that will doom you, for they will tear you apart and you will die in their jaws as others have died in yours. Until then, half-breed, I bid you . . . farewell!'

And with that, he disappeared feet first into the mouth of the tunnel, and was gone. It took Leroi a moment or two to realise what had happened. He opened his mouth to howl in rage, but the sound that emerged was a kind of strangled cough. It was as the Crooked Man had said: Leroi's transformation was almost complete, and his wolf voice was now being replaced by the voice of a man. To hide his surprise at the loss of his howl, Leroi gestured at two of his scouts, indicating that they should proceed towards the hole in the ground. They sniffed warily at the disturbed earth, then one swiftly poked its head inside, quickly pulling it back out in case the Crooked Man was waiting below. When nothing happened, it tried again, lingering longer. It sniffed the air in the tunnel. The Crooked Man's scent was present, but it was already growing fainter. He was running away from them.

Leroi got down on one knee and examined the entrance, then looked towards the hills behind which the castle lay. He considered his options. Despite his bluster, it was looking less and less likely that they would be able to find a way past the castle walls. If they did not attack soon, his wolf army would grow restless and hungrier than it already was. Rival packs would turn on one another. There would be fighting, and cannibalisation of the weak. In their rage, they would rebel against Leroi and his Loups. He needed to make a move, and make it quickly. If he could secure the castle, then his army could feed on its defenders while he and his Loups set about making plans for a new order. Perhaps the Crooked Man had simply overestimated his own abilities in using the tunnel to leave the castle and had taken an unnecessary risk in the hope of killing some wolves, or maybe even Leroi himself. Whatever the reason, Leroi had been given the chance he had almost despaired of receiving. The tunnel was narrow, wide enough for only one Loup or wolf at a time. Still, it would allow a small force to enter the castle, and if they could get to the castle gates and

open them from within, the defenders would quickly be overwhelmed.

Leroi turned to one of his lieutenants. 'Send skirmishers to
the castle to distract the troops on the walls,' he ordered. 'Begin
moving the main forces forward and bring my best greys to me.
Let the attack commence!'

XXXI

Of the Battle, and the Fate of Those Who Would Be King

The king was slumped on his throne, his chin upon his chest. He looked as though he was sleeping, but as David drew closer, he saw that the old man's eyes were open and staring blankly at the floor. The Book of Lost Things lay on his lap, the king's hand resting on its cover. Four guards surrounded him, one at each corner of the dais, and there were more at the doors and on the gallery. As the captain approached with David, the king peered up and the look on his face made David's stomach tighten. It was the face of a man who has been told that his one chance to avoid the executioner is to convince someone else to take his place, and in David the king seemed to see that very person. The captain stopped before the throne, bowed, and left them. The king ordered the guards to step away so that they could not hear what was being said, then tried to compose his features into an expression of kindness. His eyes gave him away, though: they were desperate, and hostile and cunning.

'I had hoped,' he began, 'to speak with you under better circumstances. We find ourselves surrounded, but there is no reason to be afraid. They are mere beasts and we will always be superior to them.'

He crooked his finger at David. 'Come nearer, boy.'

David ascended the steps that led to the throne. His face was now level with the king's. The king ran his fingers along the arms of the throne, pausing now and then to examine a particularly fine detail of its ornamentation, to caress lightly a ruby or an emerald.

'It is a wonderful throne, is it not?' he asked David.

'It's very nice,' said David, and the king glanced sharply at him as though unsure of whether or not he was being mocked by the boy. David's face gave nothing away, and the king decided to let his answer pass without rebuke.

'From the earliest of times, the kings and queens of the realm have sat upon this throne and ruled the land from it. Do you know what they all had in common? I will tell you: they all came from your world, not this one. Your world, and mine. As one ruler dies, another crosses the boundary between the two worlds and assumes the throne. It is the way of things here and it is a great honour to be chosen. That honour is now yours.'

David did not reply, so the king continued.

'I am aware that you have encountered the Crooked Man. You should not let his appearance put you off. He means well, although he has a way of, shall we say, *manipulating* the truth. He has been shadowing your path since you arrived here, and there were times when you were close to death and were saved only by his intervention. At first, I know he offered to take you back to your home, but that was a lie. It is not in his gift or his power to do so until you claim the throne. Once you have ascended to your rightful place, you may order him to do as you please. If you refuse the throne, he will kill you and seek another. That is how it has always been.

'You must accept what is being offered to you. If you do not like it, or find that it is not in you to rule, then you may order the Crooked Man to return you to your own land and the bargain will be concluded. You will be the king, after all, and he will be merely a subject. He asks only that your brother should come with you, that you might have company in this new world as you begin to rule. In time, the Crooked Man may even bring your father here, if you like, and imagine how proud he will be to see his first-born seated on a throne, the king of a great realm! Well, what do you say?'

By the time the king had finished speaking, any pity that David might have felt for him had disappeared. Everything the king had said was a lie. The king did not know that David had looked in the Book of Lost Things, that he had entered the Crooked Man's lair and had met Anna there. David knew of hearts being consumed in the darkness, and the essence of children being kept in jars to fuel the life of the Crooked Man. The king, crushed by guilt and sorrow, wanted to be released from his bargain with the Crooked Man, and he would say anything to get David to take his place.

'Is that the Book of Lost Things in your hands?' asked David. 'They say that it contains all kinds of knowledge, perhaps even magic. Is that true?'

The king's eyes glittered.

'Oh, very true, very true. I will give it to you when I abdicate and the crown becomes yours. It will be my coronation gift. With it, you can order the Crooked Man to do your will, and he will have to obey. Once you are king, I will have no more use for it.'

For a moment, the king looked almost regretful. Yet again, his fingers travelled across the cover of the book, smoothing down loose threads, exploring the places where the spine had begun to separate from the rest. It was like a living entity to him, as though his heart had also been removed from his body when he came to this land and had taken the form of a book.

'And what will happen to you once I am king?' asked David.

The king looked away before he replied.

'Oh, I will leave here and find some quiet place in which to enjoy my retirement,' he said. 'Perhaps I will even return to our world to see what has changed there since I left it.'

But his words sounded hollow, and his voice cracked beneath the weight of his guilt and lies.

'I know who you are,' said David softly.

The king leaned forward on his throne. 'What did you say?'

'I know who you are,' David repeated. 'You are Jonathan Tulvey. Your adopted sister's name was Anna. You were jealous of her when she was brought to your home, and that jealousy never went away. The Crooked Man came and showed you how a life without her could be, and you betrayed her. You tricked her into following you through the sunken garden and into this place. The Crooked Man killed her and ate her heart, then kept her spirit in a glass jar. That book on your lap contains no magic, and its only secrets are yours. You are a sad, evil old man, and you can keep your kingdom and your throne. I don't want it. I don't want any of it.'

A figure appeared from the shadows.

'Then you will die,' said the Crooked Man.

He appeared much older than when David had last seen him, and his skin looked torn and diseased. There were wounds and blisters upon his face and hands, and he stank of his own corruption.

'You have been busy, I see,' said the Crooked Man. 'You have been sticking your nose in places where you had no business. You have taken something that belongs to me. Where is she?'

'She does not belong to you,' said David. 'She does not belong to anyone.'

David drew his sword. It shook a little as his hand trembled, but not very much. The Crooked Man just laughed at him.

'No matter,' he said. 'She had reached the end of her usefulness. Be careful lest the same can be said of you. Death is coming for you, and no sword can keep it away. You think you're brave, but let's see how brave you are when there is hot wolf breath and spittle on your face and your throat is about to be ripped out. Then you will weep and wail. You will call for me, and perhaps I will answer. Perhaps . . .

'Tell me your brother's name and I will save you from any pain.

I promise that I will not harm him. The land needs a king. If you agree to assume the throne, then I will let your brother live when I bring him here. I will find another to take his place, for there are sands in my hourglass yet. You will both abide here together, and you will rule justly and fairly. All this will come to pass. I give you my word. Just tell me his name.'

The guards were watching David now, their own weapons unsheathed, ready to strike him down if he tried to hurt the king. But the king raised his hand to let them know that all was well, and they relaxed a little as they waited to see what would unfold.

'If you don't tell me his name, then I will cross back into your world and I will kill the infant in his bed,' said the Crooked Man. 'Even if it is the last thing that I do, I will leave his blood on the pillows and the sheets. Your choice is simple: the two of you may rule together, or you may each die apart. There is no other way.'

David shook his head.

'No,' he said. 'I will not allow you to do it.'

'Allow? *Allow?*'

The Crooked Man's face contorted as he forced the word out. His lips cracked and a little blood trickled from the splits, for he had only a little left to shed.

'Listen to me,' he said. 'Let me tell you the truth about the world to which you so desperately want to return. It is a place of pain and suffering and grief. When you left it, cities were being attacked. Women and children were being blasted to pieces or burned alive by bombs dropped from planes flown by men with wives and children of their own. People were being dragged from their homes and shot in the street. Your world is tearing itself apart, and the most amusing thing of all is that it was little better before the war started. War merely gives people an excuse to indulge themselves further, to murder with impunity. There were wars before this one, and there will be wars after it, and in between people will still fight one another and hurt one another and maim one another and betray one another, because that is what they have always done.

'And even if you avoid warfare and violent death, little boy, what else do you think life has in store for you? You have already seen what it is capable of doing. It took your mother from you, drained her of health and beauty and then cast her aside like the withered, rotten husk of a fruit. It will take others from you too, mark me. Those whom you care about – lovers, children – will fall by the wayside, and your love will not be enough to save them. Your health will fail. You will become old and sick. Your limbs will ache, your eyesight will fade, and your skin will grow lined and aged. There will be pains deep within that no doctor will be able to cure. Diseases will find a warm, moist place inside you and there they will breed, spreading through your system, corrupting it cell by cell until you will pray for the doctors to let you die, to put you out of your misery, but they will not. Instead you will linger on, with no one to hold your hand or soothe your brow, as Death comes and beckons you into his darkness. The life you left behind is no life at all. Here, you can be king, and I will allow you to age with dignity and without pain, and when the time comes for you to die, I will send you gently to sleep and you will awaken in the paradise of your choosing, for each man dreams his own heaven. All I ask in return is that you name the child in your house to me, so you may have company in this place. *Name him!* Name him now before it's too late.'

As he spoke, the tapestry behind the king shifted and billowed, and a grey shape materialised from behind it and pounced on the chest of the nearest guard. The wolf's head descended and twisted, and the guard's throat was torn open. The wolf let out a great howl, even as arrows shot down from the guards on the gallery and pierced its heart. More wolves poured through the doorway, so many that the ancient tapestry was wrenched from the wall and fell to the floor in a cloud of dust. The greys, the most loyal and ferocious of Leroi's troops, were invading the throne room. A horn sounded, and guards appeared from every doorway. A furious battle commenced, the guards slashing and spearing the wolves, trying to hold back their tide, while the wolves snapped and snarled, seeking any opening they could find in order to kill the men. They bit at legs and stomachs and arms, savaging bellies and opening throats. Soon the floor was awash with blood, channels of red flowing between the edges of the stones. The guards had formed a semicircle around the opening, but the sheer numbers of wolves were forcing them back.

The Crooked Man pointed at the teeming, fighting mass of men and animals.

'See!' he shouted at David. 'Your sword will not save you. Only *I* can do that. Tell me his name, and I will spirit you away from here in an instant. Speak, and save yourself!'

Now the greys had been joined by black wolves and white wolves. The wolf packs began working their way around the guards, invading rooms and hallways, killing everyone who stood against them. The king leaped from his throne and stared in horror at the wall of guards slowly being forced towards him by the pack.

The Captain of the Guard appeared at his right hand. 'Come, Your Majesty,' he said. 'We must get you to safety.'

But the king pushed him away and stared furiously at the Crooked Man. 'You betrayed us,' he said. 'You betrayed us all.'

The Crooked Man ignored him. His attention was focused only on David. 'The name,' he said again. '*Tell me his name*!'

Behind him, the wolves broke the wall of men. Now there were newcomers among them who walked on their hind legs and wore the uniforms of soldiers. The Loups slashed at the guards with their swords, forcing a path through to the doors leading from the throne room. Two immediately disappeared down a hallway, followed by six wolves. They were making for the castle gates.

Then Leroi emerged. He looked out upon the carnage before him, and he saw the throne, *his* throne, and he found within himself one last lupine howl to signal his triumph. The king trembled at the sound, even as Leroi's eyes found his and the Loup moved forward to kill him. Duncan was still trying to protect the king. He was keeping two greys at bay with his sword, but it was clear that he was tiring.

'Go, Your Majesty!' he shouted. 'Go now!'

But the words were stopped in his throat as an arrow struck his chest, fired by one of Leroi's Loups. The captain fell to the floor, and the wolves descended upon him. The king reached beneath the folds of his gown and withdrew a dagger, then advanced upon the Crooked Man.

'Foul thing,' he cried. 'After all that I did, after all that you made me do, you deceived me at the last.'

'I made you do nothing, Jonathan,' replied the Crooked Man. 'You did it because you wanted to. No one can make you do evil. You had evil inside you, and you indulged it. Men will always indulge it.'

He lashed out at the king with his own blade, and the old man tottered and almost fell. Quick as a flash, the Crooked Man turned to grab David, but the boy stepped out of his path and slashed at him with his sword, opening a wound across the Crooked Man's chest that stank but did not bleed.

'You are going to die!' cried the Crooked Man. 'Tell me his name, and you will live!'

He advanced on David, oblivious of his injury. David tried to stab at him again, but the Crooked Man avoided the blow and fought back, his nails tearing deep into David's arm. David felt as though he had been poisoned, for pain seeped into his limb, flowing through his veins and freezing his blood until it reached his hand and the sword fell from his numbed fingers.

He was against a wall now, surrounded by fighting men and snarling wolves. Over the Crooked Man's shoulder, he saw Leroi advancing upon the king. The king tried to stab him with his dagger, but Leroi swatted it away and it skidded across the stones.

'The name!' shrieked the Crooked Man. 'The name, or I will leave you to the wolves!'

Leroi picked up the king as if he were a doll, placing his hand beneath the old man's chin and tilting his head, exposing the king's neck. Leroi paused and looked at David. 'You're next,' he gloated, then opened his mouth wide, revealing his sharp white teeth. He bit into the king's throat, shaking him from side to side as he killed him. The Crooked Man's eyes opened wide in horror as the king's life drained away. A great patch of skin uncurled from the trickster's face like old wallpaper, exposing the grey, decaying flesh beneath.

'No!' he screamed. He lunged for David and held him by the throat. 'The name. You must tell me the name, or else we will both be lost.'

David was very frightened, and knew that he was about to die.

'His name is—' he began.

'Yes!' said the Crooked Man, 'Yes!', as the king's last breath bubbled in his throat and Leroi cast his dying body aside, wiping the blood from his mouth as he turned his attention to David.

'His name is—'

'Tell me!' shrieked the Crooked Man.

'His name is "brother",' said David.

The Crooked Man's body collapsed in despair 'No,' he moaned. 'No.'

Deep in the bowels of the castle, the last grains of sand trickled through the neck of the hourglass, and on a balcony far above, the ghost of a girl glowed brightly for a second before fading away entirely. Had anyone been present to see it happen, they would have heard her give a small sigh that was filled with joy and peace as her torment came to an end.

'No!' howled the Crooked Man, as his skin cracked and all of the foul gas began to burst forth from within. All was lost, all was lost. After time beyond measure and stories beyond telling, his life was at an end. And so furious was he that he dug his nails into his own scalp and began to tear it apart, ripping at skin and flesh. A deep cut appeared in his forehead, extending quickly down the bridge of his nose before bisecting his mouth. One half of his head was now in each of his hands, the eyes rolling wildly, yet still he tore, the great wound continuing through his throat and chest and belly until it reached his thighs, whereupon his body at last became two separate pieces and fell entirely apart. From the two halves of the Crooked Man crawled every nasty spineless thing that ever lived: bugs and beetles and centipedes, spiders and scorpions and pale white worms, all of them twisting and writhing and scurrying upon the floor until they, too, grew still, as the final grain of sand fell through the neck of the hourglass and the Crooked Man died.

Leroi looked down upon the mess, grinning. David had started to close his eyes, preparing to die, when Leroi suddenly shuddered. He opened his mouth to speak and his jaw fell away and landed on the stones at his feet. His skin and fur began to crumble and flake like old plaster. He tried to move, but his legs would no longer support him. Instead, they broke at the knees, so that he fell forward on the ground, cracks appearing across his face and the backs of his hands. He tried to scrape at the ground, but his fingers shattered like glass. Only his eyes remained as they had been, but they were now filled with confusion and pain.

David watched Leroi dying. He alone understood what was happening.

'You were the king's nightmare, not mine,' he said. 'When you killed him, you killed yourself.'

Leroi's eyes blinked uncomprehendingly, then ceased all movement. He became merely the broken statue of a beast, now without another's fear to animate it. Tiny fissures covered his entire body, and then he collapsed into a million pieces and was gone forever.

All around the throne room, the other Loups were crumbling to dust, and the common wolves, deprived of their leaders, began to retreat through the tunnel as more guards entered the throne room, their shields raised to form a wall of steel through which the tips of spears poked like the spines of a hedgehog. They ignored David as he picked up his sword and ran through the hallways of the castle, past frightened servants and bewildered courtiers, until he found himself in the open air. He climbed to the highest battlement and stared out over the landscape beyond. The wolf army had descended into confusion. Allies were turning on one another now, fighting, biting, the fast climbing over the slow in their urge to flee and return to their old territories. Already great columns of wolves were departing, fleeing for the hills. All that was left of the Loups were columns of dust that swirled for a moment before being scattered to the four winds.

David felt a hand upon his arm, and looked round to see a familiar face.

It was the Woodsman. There was wolf blood on his clothing and his skin. It dripped from the blade of his axe and pooled darkly on the stones.

David could not speak. He just dropped his sword and pack and hugged the Woodsman tightly. The Woodsman laid a hand on the boy's head and stroked his hair gently.

'I thought you were dead,' sighed David. 'I saw the wolves drag you away.'

'No wolf will take my life,' he said. 'I managed to fight my way to the horse breeder's cottage. I barricaded the door, then fell unconscious from my wounds. It was many days before I was well enough to follow your trail, and I could not get through the ranks of the wolves until now. But we must leave this place quickly. It will not stand for much longer.'

David felt the battlements shake beneath his feet. A gap opened in the wall. Others appeared in the main buildings, and bricks and mortar began to tumble down to the cobblestones below. The labyrinth of tunnels beneath the castle was collapsing, and the world of kings and crooked men was coming apart.

The Woodsman led David down into the courtyard, where a horse was waiting. The Woodsman told him to climb on, but David instead found Scylla in her barn. The horse, frightened by the sounds of battle and the howling of the wolves, whinnied with relief at the sight of the boy. David patted her forehead and whispered calming words to her, then mounted her and followed the Woodsman from the castle. Guards on horseback were harassing the rearguard of the wolf pack, forcing them further and further away from the scene of the battle. A steady flow of people was moving through the main gates, servants and courtiers loaded down with whatever food or riches they could carry as they abandoned the castle before it fell into ruins around their ears. David and the Woodsman took a route that led them away from the confusion, pausing only when they were safely distant from wolves and men. They stood on the brow of a hill overlooking the castle. From there, they watched as it collapsed upon itself until all that was left was a great hole in the ground marked by wood and brick and a cloud of filthy, choking dust. Then they turned their backs on it and rode together for many days until they came at last to the forest where David had first entered this world. Now there was only one tree marked with twine, for all of the Crooked Man's magic had been undone with his death.

The Woodsman and David dismounted before the great tree. 'It is time,' the Woodsman said. 'Now you must go home.'

David stood in the middle of the forest, staring at the length of twine and the hollow in the tree that had now revealed itself once more. One of the trees nearby had recently been scored by the claws of an animal and bloody sap dripped from the wound in its trunk, staining the snow beneath. A breeze stirred its neighbours so that their branches caressed its crown, calming and reassuring it, making it aware of their presence. The clouds above were beginning to part, and sunlight speared through the gaps. The world was changing, transformed by the end of the Crooked Man.

'Now that it is time to leave, I'm not sure I want to go,' said David. 'I feel that there's more to see. I don't want things to go back to the way they were.'

'There are people waiting for you on the other side,' said the Woodsman. 'You have to return to them. They love you, and without you their lives will be poorer. You have a father and a brother, and a woman who would be a mother to you, if you let her. You must go back, or else their lives will be blighted by your absence. In a way, you have already made your decision. You rejected the Crooked Man's bargain. You chose to live not here, but in your own world.'

David nodded. He knew that the Woodsman was right.

'There will be questions asked if you return as you are,' said the Woodsman. 'You must leave all that you are wearing behind, even your sword. You will have no need for it where you are going.'

David took from his saddle bag the package containing his tattered pyjamas and dressing-gown, and changed into them behind a bush. His old clothes felt strange upon him now. He had altered so much that they seemed as if they belonged to a different person, one who was vaguely familiar to him but younger and more foolish. They were the clothes of a child, and he was a child no longer.

'Tell me something, please,' said David.

'Whatever you wish to know,' said the Woodsman.

'You gave me clothing when I came here, the clothes of a boy. Did you ever have children?'

The Woodsman smiled.

'They were all my children,' he said. 'Every one that was lost, every one that was found, every one that lived, and every one that died: all, all were mine, in their way.'

'Did you know that the king was false when you began to lead me to him?' asked David. It was a question that had been troubling him ever since the Woodsman had reappeared. He could not believe this man would willingly lead him into danger.

'And what would you have done had I told you what I knew, or what I suspected, of the king and the trickster? When you came here, you were consumed by anger and grief. You would have given in to the blandishments of the Crooked Man and then all would have been lost. I had hoped to guide you to the king myself, and on the journey I would have tried to help you see the danger that you were in, but that was not to be. Instead, while others aided you along the way, it was your own strength and courage that brought you at last to an understanding of your place in this world and your own. You were a child when first I found you, but now you are becoming a man.'

He stretched out his hand to the boy. David shook it, then released it and hugged the Woodsman. After a moment, the Woodsman returned the gesture, and they stayed that way, garlanded with sunlight, until the boy stepped away.

Then David went to Scylla and kissed the horse's brow. 'I shall miss you,' he whispered to her, and the horse neighed softly and nuzzled at the boy's neck.

David walked to the old tree and looked back at the Woodsman. 'Can I ever come back here?' he asked, and the Woodsman said something very strange in reply.

'Most people come back here,' he said, 'in the end.'

He raised his hand in farewell, and David took a deep breath and stepped into the trunk of the tree.

At first, he could smell only musk and earth and the dry decay of old leaves. He touched the inside of the tree and felt the roughness of its bark against his fingers. Although the tree was huge, he could not go for more than a few steps before striking the interior. His arm still hurt from where the Crooked Man had pierced him with his nails. He felt claustrophobic. There appeared to be no way out, but the Woodsman would not have lied to him. No, there must have been some mistake. He decided to step outside again but when he turned round the entrance was gone. The tree had sealed itself up entirely, and now he was trapped inside. David began to shout for help and bang his fists against the wood, but his words simply echoed around him, bouncing back in his face, mocking him even as they faded.

But suddenly there was light. The tree was sealed, yet there was still illumination coming from above. David looked up and saw something sparkling like a star. As he watched, it grew and grew, descending towards where he stood. Or perhaps he was rising, ascending to meet it, for all of his senses were confused. He heard unfamiliar sounds – metal upon metal, the squeaking of wheels – and caught a sharp chemical smell from close by.

He was seeing things – the light, the grooves and fissures of the tree trunk – but gradually he became aware that his eyes were closed. If that was the case, then how much more could he see once his eyes were open?

David opened his eyes.

He was lying on a metal bed in an unfamiliar room. Two large windows looked out on an expanse of green lawn where children walked with nurses by their sides, or were wheeled in chairs by white-clad orderlies. There were flowers by his bedside. A needle was embedded in his right forearm, connected by a tube to a bottle on a steel frame. There was a tightness around his head. He reached up to touch it and felt bandages instead of hair. He turned slowly to the left. The movement caused his neck to ache and his head began to pound painfully. Beside him, asleep in a chair, was Rose. Her clothes were wrinkled and her hair was greasy and unwashed. A book lay on her lap, its pages marked by a length of red ribbon.

David tried to speak, but his throat was too dry. He tried again and emitted a hoarse croak. Rose woke slowly and stared at him in disbelief.

'David?' she said.

He still couldn't speak properly. Rose poured water from a jug into a glass and placed it against his lips, supporting his head so he could drink more easily. David saw that she was crying. Some of her tears dripped onto his face as she took the glass away and he tasted them as they fell into his mouth.

'Oh, David,' she whispered. 'We were so worried.'

She placed the palm of her hand against his cheek, stroking him gently. She couldn't stop crying but he could see that she was happy despite her tears.

'Rose,' said David.

She leaned forward.

'Yes, David, what is it?'

He took her hand in his.
'I'm sorry,' he said.
And then he fell back into a dreamless sleep.

XXXIII

Of All That Was Lost and All That Was Found

In the days that followed, David's father would often talk about how close David had come to being taken from them: of how they could find no trace of him in the aftermath of the crash; of how they'd become convinced that he had been burned alive in the wreckage; then, when no sign of him was discovered, fearful that he might have been abducted from them; how they had searched the house and gardens and forest, finally scouring the fields for him, assisted by friends, by the police, even by strangers troubled by their pain; how they had returned to his room in the hope that he might have left some hint as to where he was going; how they had at last found a hidden space behind the wall of the sunken garden, and there he was, lying in the dirt, having somehow crawled through a crack in the stonework and become trapped in the hollow by the falling rubble.

The doctors said that he had taken another of his fits, perhaps as a result of the trauma of the crash, and this one had caused him to lapse into a coma. David had stayed in a deep sleep for many days, until the morning when he awoke and spoke Rose's name. And even though there were aspects of his disappearance that could not be fully explained – what he had been doing out in the garden to begin with, and how he had come by some of the marks on his body – they were just glad to have him back, and no word of blame or anger was ever directed at him. Only much later, when he was out of danger and safely in his own room, did Rose and his father, when they were alone in their bed at night, remark upon how much the incident had changed David, making him both quieter and more considerate of others; more affectionate towards Rose, and more understanding of her own difficulties in trying to find a place for herself in the lives of these two men, David and his father; more responsive to sudden noises and potential dangers, yet also more protective of those who were weaker than he, and of Georgie, his half-brother, in particular.

The years went by, and David grew both too slowly and too quickly from a boy to a man: too slowly for him, but too quickly for his father and Rose. Georgie grew too, and he and David remained as close as siblings can be, even after Rose and their father went their separate ways, as grown-ups will sometimes do. They divorced amicably and neither of them ever married again. David went to university and his father found a little cottage by a stream where he could fish upon his retirement. Rose and Georgie lived together in the big old house, and David visited them as often as he could, either alone or with his father. If time permitted, he would step into his old bedroom and listen for the sound of the books whispering to one another, but they were always silent. If the weather was good, he would descend into the remains of the sunken garden, repaired somewhat since the crash of the plane but still not quite as it once was, and stare silently at the biggest crack in its wall, but he never tried to enter it again and no one else did either.

But as time progressed, David discovered that about one thing at least the Crooked Man had not lied: his life was filled with great grief as well as great happiness, with suffering and regret as well as triumphs and contentment. David lost his father when he was thirty-two, his father's heart failing as he sat by the stream with a fishing-rod in his hands, the sun shining upon his face so that when he was found by a passer-by hours after his death his skin was still warm. Georgie attended the funeral in his army uniform, for another war had commenced to the east and Georgie was anxious to do his duty. He travelled to a land far from this one and there he died alongside other young men whose dreams of honour and glory ended in a foreign field. His remains were shipped home and buried in a country churchyard beneath a small stone cross bearing his name, the dates of his birth and death, and the words 'Beloved Son and Brother.'

David married a woman with dark hair and green eyes. Her name was Alyson. They planned a family together, and the time came for Alyson to give birth to their child. But David was anxious for them both, for he could not forget the words of the Crooked Man: *'Those whom you care about – lovers, children – will fall by the wayside, and your love will not be enough to save them.'*

There were complications during the birth. The son, whom they named George in honour of his uncle, was not strong enough to live, and in giving brief life to him Alyson lost her own, and so the Crooked Man's prophecy came to pass. David did not marry again, and he never had another child, but he became a writer and he wrote a book. He called it *The Book of Lost Things*, and the book that you are holding in your hands is the book that he wrote. And when children would ask him if it was true, he would tell them that, yes, it was true, or as true as anything in this world can be, for that was how he remembered it.

And they all became his children, in their way.

As Rose grew older and weaker, David looked after her. When Rose died, she left her house to David. He could have sold it, because by then it was worth a great deal of money, but he did not. Instead, he moved in and set up his little office downstairs, and he lived there contentedly for many years, always answering his door to the children who called – sometimes with their parents, sometimes alone – for the house was famous, and a great many boys and girls wanted to see it. If they were very good, he would take them down to the sunken garden, although the cracks in the stonework had long been repaired, for David did not want children crawling in there and getting into trouble. Instead, he would talk to them of stories and books, and explain to them how stories wanted to be told and books wanted to be read, and how everything that they ever needed to know about life and the land of which he wrote, or about any land or realm that they could imagine, was contained in books.

And some of the children understood, and some did not.

In time, David himself grew frail and ill. He was no longer able to write, for his memory and eyesight were failing him, or even to walk very far to greet the children as once he had. (And this, too, the Crooked Man had told him, just as surely as if David had stared into the mirrored eyes of the lady in the dungeons.) There was nothing that the doctors could do for him except try to ease his pain. He hired a nurse to look after him and his friends came to spend time by his side. As the end drew near, he requested that a bed be made up for him in the great library downstairs, and each night he slept surrounded by the books he had loved as a boy and as a man. He also quietly asked his gardener to perform one simple task for him, and to tell no one else of it, and the gardener did as he requested, for he loved the old man very much.

And in the deepest, darkest hours of the night, David would lie awake and listen. The books had started whispering again, yet he felt no fear. They spoke softly, offering words of comfort and grace. Sometimes they told the stories that he had always loved, but now his own was among them.

One night, when his breathing had grown very shallow and the light in his eyes had begun to dim at last, David rose from his bed in the library and slowly made his way to the door, pausing only to pick up a book along the way. It was an old leather-bound album, and in it were photographs and letters, cards and trinkets, drawings and poems, locks of hair and a pair of wedding rings, all of the relics of a life long lived, except this time the life was his. The whispering of the books grew louder, the voices of the tomes rising in a great chorus of joy, for one story was about to end and a new story would soon be born. The old man caressed their spines in farewell as he passed from the room, then left the library and the house for the last time to walk through the damp summer grass to where the sunken garden lay.

In one corner, a hole had been opened by the gardener, big enough to accommodate a grown man. David got down on his hands and knees and crawled into the space until he found himself in the hollow behind the brickwork. Then he sat in the darkness and waited. At first nothing happened and he had to struggle to keep his eyes from closing, but after a time he saw a light growing, and felt a cool breeze on his face. He smelled tree bark and fresh grass and flowers in bloom. A hollow opened before him and he stepped through it and found himself in the heart of a great forest. The land had changed forever. There were no longer beasts like men or unformed nightmares that waited for their chance to trap the unwary. There was no more fear, no more endless twilight. Even the childlike flowers were gone, for the blood of children was no longer shed in shadowy places and their souls were at rest. The sun was setting, but it was a beautiful sight, lighting the sky with purple and red and orange as the long day came to its peaceful close.

A man was standing before David. He carried an axe in one hand and in the other a garland of flowers, gathered by him as he walked through the forest and bound together with lengths of long grass.

'I came back,' said David, and the Woodsman smiled.

'Most people do, in the end,' he replied, and David wondered at how like his father the Woodsman was, and how he had failed to notice it before.

'Come along,' said the Woodsman. 'We've been waiting for you.'

And David saw himself reflected in the Woodsman's eyes, and there he was no longer old but a young man, for a man is always his father's child no matter how old he is or how long they have been apart.

David followed the Woodsman down forest paths, through glades and over brooks, until they came at last to a cottage with smoke rising lazily from its chimney. A horse stood in a small field nearby, nibbling contentedly at the grass, and as David approached, it raised its head and neighed in delight, shaking its mane as it trotted across the field to greet him. David walked to the fence and bowed his head to Scylla's. Scylla closed her eyes as he kissed her brow, then shadowed his footsteps as he approached the house, sometimes nudging gently at his shoulder as though to remind him of her presence.

The door of the cottage opened, and a woman appeared. She had dark hair and green eyes. In her arms she held a baby boy, barely out of the womb, who clutched at her blouse as she walked, for a lifetime was but a moment in that place, and each man dreams his own heaven.

And in the darkness David closed his eyes, as all that was lost was found again.

AFTERWORD

Is it permissible to admit that I was afraid to return to *The Book of Lost Things* after all this time? Never mind, there it is. I have not looked at these pages since the novel was published, and I was very reluctant to do so now, a decade after it first appeared. Not because I'm ashamed of it – quite the opposite, in fact: I suspect it may be the best thing I've written, and maybe, for all its flaws, the best thing I'll ever write – but because I was worried that I'd feel the urge to alter it, to tinker.

Writers should never be allowed to return to their earlier books. Time passes, and writers change. They hope that they're getting better at what they do, but this may not be true. It may simply be something they tell themselves because it's reassuring, and the truth of their decline is too hard to face. So I was concerned that I'd open this book after ten years, and see only loose threads at which I wanted to pull. Once that starts to happen, the whole tapestry is in danger of unravelling.

Actually, even composing this afterword is difficult. I have little memory of the writing of *The Book of Lost Things*, or how it came into being. It is as if I wrote it in a kind of dream, and so the process of its creation remains the oddest of my life as an author. I started only with its first line – 'Once upon a time – for that is how all stories should begin – there was a boy who lost his mother.' – and a vague notion of exploring myths and folk tales, and grief and loss, and the nature of books and stories and their effect on those who read them (and vice versa, because books are not fixed objects, and as readers we bring our own life experiences to bear on whatever we read, and thus shape our books according to our own imaginings).

I can only conclude that what happened next was similar to what befalls David in the book: I opened a door, and all kinds of strangeness poured through the gap. Some of it came from my own childhood, and my recollections of mortality and bereavement, but most of it came from an older, deeper place, the atavistic corner of human memory from which so many of the fables referenced in the book first emerged. We carry with us these stories and the creatures that inhabit them, passing them down from generation to generation. We may ascribe different names to them according to our cultures or our times, but the nature of them remains the same and, if offered the opportunity, they will seize their chance to emerge again.

For example, I never set out to include slightly altered versions of those old stories, such as the tale of Red Riding Hood told by the Woodsman to David, or the variant on Beauty and the Beast that appears later in the book. I would simply be writing, and a character would begin to recount a fable that was both familiar yet unfamiliar, and I would follow the path of this tale to its end. It was an odd feeling, and not entirely a comfortable one. So perhaps now you can see why I was so reluctant to return to *The Book of Lost Things*. One can't recreate such moments, and there's a danger that, in trying to do so, one may damage what is already present. It's why I've never written a sequel to this book, because the experience wouldn't be the same. Perhaps I'm not even sure that I could, even if I wanted to.

When it came to publishing this tenth anniversary edition of *The Book of Lost Things*, all involved were agreed on two things. The first was that it should include the woodcut illustrations created by the artist Anne Anderson for a very limited edition of the novel published by Edel Torr in 2007. Edel Torr is the publishing company set up by David Torrans and Claudia Edelmann of No Alibis Bookstore in Belfast, and those two lovely individuals were among the earliest champions of the book. It was they who approached Anne Anderson with a view to creating a visual component to accompany the text and, fortunately, she found that she shared their affection for the story. Only 125 copies of the limited edition were created, and I always felt it was a shame that more readers did not get to see Anne's beautiful work. This version of *The Book of Lost Things* rectifies that situation.

The second matter on which we concurred was that the cover should remain the same. The old adage suggests that one should never judge a book by its cover, but this is true of most things except books. As readers, we are frequently drawn to take a book from a shelf precisely because the cover has attracted our attention. I suspect that Rob Ryan's magical illustration for the front of *The Book of Lost Things*, painstakingly cut from paper, was the main reason why many readers picked up the novel to begin with. It was simply the perfect complement to the story, and I remain indebted to Rob for putting his genius and imagination to the service of my little book.

The Book of Lost Things found its readership by word of mouth, through the love and enthusiasm of readers, and booksellers, and librarians. It's a book about the love of books, and I like to think that those who love books saw a reflection of themselves in its pages. The deep fondness that readers have expressed for it, and the generosity of their comments about it, remain the happiest experiences of my writing life.

In a way, though, it's not really my novel any more. Maybe it ceased to be my novel as soon readers began to read it. If so, that's true of all novels. The writer's intentions largely come to naught as soon as the reader begins to read, for the reader will make of the book what he or she will. That's the beauty of a novel: as I mentioned earlier, it is not immutable, but takes on the character of its reader. It is as much mirror as glass.

So I stepped very gently as I looked again at this book. I changed words here and there, but only because the occasional repetition jarred, or because I spotted some small error which would be better corrected than left untouched. But I did go in with the intention of changing one word in particular, and it goes to the heart of what I have been trying to say in these lines about the relationship between books and their readers, and to the heart of *The Book of Lost Things* itself.

Some years ago, I was speaking at a bookstore in Michigan. The store had organized a group reading of *The Book of Lost Things*, and it had been arranged that I should chat informally with those readers before my signing. One young woman arrived with her father and spoke of how much the book meant to her, particularly while she was coming to terms with her sexuality as a teenager. She was referring in particular to Roland and the object of his quest: the young man named Raphael, who Roland knows in his heart to be dead, and, this being so, beside whom he wishes to lie for eternity. The novel makes no explicit comment about the nature of their relationship. Like so much else in the book, it is left up to the reader to decide on his or her own interpretation.

What the young woman said was interesting. She had a problem with only one word in the book. At a crucial moment, Raphael is referred to as Roland's 'friend'. This, said the young woman, was not the right description. It wasn't sufficient to encompass the love that they felt for each other. It was the wrong word.

And she was correct. In my desire to allow for the reader's freedom of interpretation, and for the ambiguity that I felt was necessary for the novel to work, I had accidentally chosen a word without weight. The right word, she told me, was 'companion'. In my defence, 'companion' had been used at various points throughout the story to describe Roland's connection to Raphael, but at a crucial moment I had stumbled. I agreed with her: 'companion' it should have been, and 'companion' it now is. After all, a book is given life by the combined efforts of writer and reader. If it is not locked into a single form for one, why should it be for the other?

Some years ago, just as I was starting out on my path as a novelist, I wrote a review of a book for a newspaper. It was a review that I subsequently regretted writing. It was glib and unkind. The fact that it had made it to print caused me only shame. Finally, I could live with my guilt no longer. I wrote to the author in question – with whom I had been in touch over the years, without any mention of the review passing between us – to confess, and to apologise for the piece. In return, I received the most gracious and generous of notes, absolving me of my sin and noting that the book in question was not the one with which its author would want to be buried. I thought it was a lovely way of expressing a writer's relationship to his work, and so I will borrow it here. *The Book of Lost Things* is a book with which I would not feel ashamed to be buried – although, frankly, I think I'd prefer to be buried with a book that I hadn't written, or even read.

Preferably a long one.

Just in case.

John Connolly, Dublin, June 2016

TWO TALES FROM THE UNIVERSE OF
THE BOOK OF LOST THINGS

AUTHOR'S NOTE

The first of these tales, 'Cinderella (A Version)', was written as a thank you for Graham Glusman, the son of my American editor. Graham was one of the first readers of this book to write to me about it, and the lighthearted little story was a way of showing my appreciation. 'The Rat King', meanwhile, is a much darker piece, and was written specially for this edition.

CINDERELLA (A VERSION)

Once upon a time there was a beautiful girl named Cinderella. She lived with her father, for her mother was dead, and the old man doted on her and spoiled her something rotten. No one ever dared to tell Cinderella that she was not the most wonderful, the most perfect, the most darling girl ever to set foot on earth, and so she came to believe this was the case. She was, not to put too fine a point on it, rather awful.

Then it came to pass that her father met a woman, whom he married, and this woman had two daughters, and they all came to live with Cinderella and her father in their big house on the hill above the town. Now, the two daughters were not as beautiful or as perfect as Cinderella. To be honest, they were distinctly plain, and one of them had a left eye that was not quite level with her right, which made her look as though she were standing on a slight slope. The other sister was a little overweight, and too fond of bread and jam for her own good, but she was a kind-hearted soul nonetheless, as was her sister.

Cinderella hated both of them. She was jealous of how they took up her father's time, time that had once been devoted entirely to her, and disliked having to share his affections, even though he had love enough for all. Cinderella decided to call them her ugly stepsisters, on the grounds that, if they were not quite ugly, then they were at least uglier than she was, and these things are all relative. Cinderella never tired of criticizing these two unfortunate girls who were not wonderful and perfect and darling, and would never be, or of belittling her wicked step-mother – who was not wicked in the slightest, but simply felt that Cinderella was a spoiled brat, and treated her as such when she misbehaved.

A year went by, during which Cinderella did no housework at all, and instead spent her days regaling anyone who would listen (including the butcher, the baker, and the candlestick maker, who worked in the same building as her father and felt that it was only a matter of time before someone wrote a nursery rhyme about them) with details of how terrible her life was.

Eventually, a vote was taken in the house, and Cinderella was presented with a choice by her family. Actually, it wasn't much of a choice at all: Cinderella would have to make up for all the housework that she had not done, which was calculated as at least a week's worth of cleaning, and cooking, and tidying. She was told that she could do a little more than her daily share every day for six months, or she could take on the burden of all the cooking and cleaning in the house for one week, after which her debt would be paid. She would also be forced to miss the prince's ball as punishment for her laziness and nastiness, a fact that caused Cinderella to stamp her feet and cry, and generally behave like quite the little madam.

In the end, Cinderella decided to complete everything in one week, because she was that kind of girl and didn't like to think that she might have to do something useful every day for a long time. Actually, though, she didn't do very much at all, but just sat in the kitchen and moaned about her cruel treatment at the hands of her awful family. After six days had gone by, during which her family did their best to ignore her, and watched dust and dirt pile up while they subsisted on pies from the baker, a passing fairy godmother heard Cinderella's cries and appeared before her in the kitchen.

'What ails you, child?' the fairy asked.

'My mother has died, and my father has remarried,' Cinderella replied, 'and now his new family has forced me to spend my days alone in this kitchen' – all of which was true, in one way, but untrue in another.

'Why, that is terrible,' said the fairy godmother, who was a trusting soul and not terribly bright.

'What's worse,' continued Cinderella, 'is that tonight there is to be a ball at the prince's castle, and they will not let me attend. My stepsisters are jealous of me. They are afraid that the prince will see me and fall in love, and free me from their tyranny at last.'

Even the good fairy thought that this was a bit vain of Cinderella. Admittedly, Cinderella was a good-looking girl, but princes were known to have very high standards about these things, and it wasn't entirely proper for a young woman to believe that she could capture a prince's heart so easily. Nevertheless, the fairy godmother gave Cinderella the benefit of the doubt on the grounds that she might be somewhat traumatised by her circumstances.

'You shall go to the ball, Cinderella,' said the fairy godmother.

'But how?' asked Cinderella. 'I have only this tattered dress to wear.'

Her dress was shabby, but that was because she had picked the oldest dress in her wardrobe to wear in the kitchen, even if she had no intention of actually doing any work there. So the fairy godmother waved her wand and provided Cinderella with a beautiful gown, and changed a couple of shocked mice into coach horses, and transformed a pumpkin into a coach that smelled distinctly – but hardly surprisingly – of pumpkin, and was quite a virulent shade of orange. She also gave Cinderella a pair of glass slippers to wear. The slippers weren't very comfortable, but Cinderella decided that perhaps it might be wise to keep quiet about this fact, as she didn't want the fairy godmother to think she wasn't a deserving cause. Neither did she complain about the midnight curfew imposed by the fairy godmother, as she knew that nice girls didn't stay out beyond midnight, and she wanted to be thought of as a nice girl, even if she wasn't one.

That night, Cinderella danced and danced, and caught the attention of the handsome prince. He spent the evening waltzing with no one but Cinderella. He fell in love with the mysterious young woman, but before he could ask her name, the clock began to strike midnight and she fled, leaving behind a glass slipper with a vicious heel that had painfully bruised the prince's toes once or twice as he danced with the unknown beauty.

A search commenced the next day. The prince and his men went from village to village, and house to house, trying the slipper on the foot of every young woman that they found, but none had a foot that fitted. After three days, they came to the house of Cinderella, and discovered her in the cellar, not doing very much. The prince placed the slipper on Cinderella's foot, and it fitted perfectly. Great celebrations ensued, and even the stepsisters joined in, so pleased were they that they would soon be rid of Cinderella forever.

The prince and Cinderella were married, and they lived happily ever after.

Except they didn't. They lived happily for about a week, until the prince discovered that Cinderella was a cow, whereupon he returned to her father's house with the unpleasant young woman in tow.

The prince knocked on the front door. Cinderella's father answered. He took in the prince and his daughter and understood immediately what had happened. He briefly considered closing the door again and refusing to come out until they went away, but he suspected that the prince would order someone to kick the door in and he liked his door as it was. Still, he pretended to be surprised, if only for form's sake, even if he wasn't very surprised at all.

'Well . . .' said the prince.

He now realized that the situation was a bit awkward. It was one thing returning a dodgy pot, or a cart with a buckled wheel, but quite another to start trying to hand back an actual person, especially one whom you'd recently married. Nevertheless, he persevered, because he was a prince, and also because he really wanted to see the back of Cinderella.

'I'm afraid that I don't like this one,' said the prince. 'She's nasty, and lazy, and whiffs of pumpkin. I wonder if I might swap her for one of the others?'

And so the prince divorced Cinderella and married the sister whose eyes were not quite level, and they did, in fact, live happily ever after, even if the prince sometimes got a headache from trying to stare into both of his wife's eyes at the same time.

As for Cinderella, she used her father's money to open a store specializing in glass slippers.

It went broke.

THE RAT KING

Once upon a time, so long ago now that I cannot quite tell what was imagined and what was real – but that is the curse of those who dwell in darkness – there came upon our town a dreadful plague.

It began slowly, because where there are humans, so too will there be rats. As a consequence, it took some time before the people noticed an increase in the rat population, or that these were rodents of unusual savagery. When faced by dogs, the rats attacked rather than fled, and while they would inevitably be overcome, dreadful injuries were inflicted on their tormentors before they succumbed. Cats, meanwhile, had no chance against them, and it gradually became a matter of routine to find some seasoned ratter torn to pieces, its eyes nibbled from its head, its teeth bared in its final agonies.

And that was only when confronted by two rats, or even one. As the pack increased in size and ferocity, the dogs themselves grew to fear them, and soon the hunters became the hunted. It seemed that the rats moved with a certain agency, as though controlled by a governing intelligence, and that intelligence came at last to reveal himself.

It was a single giant rodent, the size of a big man's arm – and that was without the tail, which itself resembled a thick, grey snake – with a spur of bone upon his head like a crown.

The Rat King took as his throne room an old grain store in the centre of the town, and surrounded himself with so many of his fellows that even to approach his lair was to risk injury, or death. Fire was suggested, with the aim of incinerating the rats and their king with the building, but the weather added to the town's misfortunes – that, or the rats had the elements at their command. As soon as a flame was lit, the wind would rise, so that to set the grain store ablaze would have been to risk putting the entire town to the torch.

And still the rats grew in number, and the Rat King watched over all.

In the third week of the plague, the Mayor's baby son, barely a month old, was found in his cradle, his face half-eaten and his eyes gone from his head. As a final horror, the rats had placed one of their own in the child's mouth: a dead infant, pink and hairless, like a second tongue. It had helped to smother the baby's cries.

And as the Mayor's wife wept, and her husband – ineffectual, but good-hearted – wondered how his life and town had come to this pass, the Corporation met in the Guildhall, the Mayor sitting silently at the head of the table, lost in his grief. From the streets below came the sounds of scuffles and cries as men and women chased rats from their doors before skewering them with pikes, beating them with cudgels and hacking at them with blades – for all the good it did, since each rat that was dispatched appeared to spawn two more in its place.

'What shall we do?' said the Apothecary. 'I have made all the poisons I know, and the rats consume them without injury.'

'What shall we do?' said the Armourer and Brassier. 'I have armed every man, woman and child in the town, and put them on notice to kill any rat they can trap, but still the creatures come, and still they breed.'

'What shall we do?' said the Currier and the Cutler, the Plumber and the Poulter, the Saddler and the Salter, as each told of what action had been taken on his part, and each despaired of its effect.

In the end, it was decided to send an emissary to the king in the hope that some solution might be found by the great minds assembled in his court, although it appeared likely to the populace that they would be forced to abandon their town long before any help could arrive from the palace – that, or die like the Mayor's son, for the rats were growing more brazen in their assaults. Two more people had been killed in the days since, and few now dared to walk the streets alone or without a weapon, and never at night.

Just as the Corporation was about to rise, there came a knocking at the door. When it was opened, they saw before them a most peculiar figure: a man tall and thin, clad in a surcoat formed of patches containing every colour known to the eye, but so cunningly crafted that it was impossible to tell where one piece of material ended and the next began, so gently did each blend into the other. He was handsome, in his way, but it was the thin, pinched beauty of one who was fading away of hunger. From his neck hung a carved pipe.

The sight of him was so strange that it roused even the Mayor from his sorrows.

'What manner of man are you?' he asked.

The stranger spoke, and there was a kind of melody to his speech, so that he seemed to be singing rather than speaking the answer, but in time to a music only he could hear.

'I am a minstrel, of sorts,' said the stranger. 'It has been given to me to charm the beasts of air and earth and sea, although my gift works best with those creatures which are most cursed – snakes and spiders, toads and newts, bats, gnats and . . . '

'What about rats?' asked the Apothecary.

The stranger thought upon the question for a moment, as though it had never before crossed his mind to consider binding a rat with his spell.

336

'Why, yes,' he replied at last. 'Rats, too.'

'And what do they call you?' asked the Mayor.

'They call me the Pied Piper,' the stranger responded, and as he did so, his fingers danced above – but did not touch – the pale, graven pipe hanging from his neck. The Armourer and Brassier thought that he discerned in it the form of a weapon, although he could not have explained why.

'So you claim that you can rid our town of these rats?' said the Mayor.

'I do not claim it. I promise it.'

'And their king too?'

'If they have a king, I will make him my subject.'

'And what will you charge us for your services?'

'I don't know,' said the Pied Piper. 'It's hardly for me to say.'

'Anything!' said the Mayor, who was thinking only of his dead infant, and the rat corpse left in its mouth. 'Ask anything at all!'

'A thousand gold marks?' the Piper suggested, almost doubt-fully.

'A thousand?' said the Mayor. 'To lift this curse from us, we would pay you ten thousand. Fifty thousand!'

'Steady,' whispered the Chandler, a notoriously thrifty man.

The Piper lowered his head, hiding his face from their gaze.

'I would not ask so much,' he said. 'If you gentlemen are agreeable, I will write my price on a piece of parchment and seal it with wax. In the event that I am unsuccessful – unlikely, I admit, but one must be open to every possibility – I will pay you a thousand gold marks from my own purse to atone for my failure. But if I succeed, you must promise to meet my price.'

And – oh! – these guildsmen who prided themselves on their acumen, these sage elders, the best and brightest for miles around, perceiving a bargain they believed they could not lose, assented to the Piper's terms without further discussion.

Into the street the Piper stepped, the Mayor and the Corporation at his heels. (And was that ivory from which the

Piper's instrument was made, the Armourer wondered to himself, for it certainly had the look of ivory to it: ivory, or bone.) The Piper paused, the instrument almost touching his lips, and spoke.

'I must give you one warning. The spell cast by my notes is delicate, and can easily be broken. I know you are angry, and fearful of these creatures, but you must not interfere with them, or attempt to injure even one as they are drawn out. If you do so, the charm will be ruined, and will not work again.'

So word was passed through the town that the rats were not to be harmed. Dogs and cats were led away to safety, and men, women and children gathered at the Guildhall, so that the Piper might be left to perform his magic unhindered by rash acts.

The Piper's eyes – orbs of blue-green, like stones from the ocean depths – flickered with an odd, cold light as he put his lips to the pipe and blew three shrill blasts from it. I have to confess that the sound was pretty, and I felt my feet move in response to it, as though summoned to a dance. But it had an unpleasant undertone as well, like a knife being sharpened on a whetstone, or a butcher's saw cutting through cartilage.

All the townsfolk were silent until the last note faded away. As it did so, its place was taken by a deep murmur, and a pattering and rustling as of many animal bodies jolted into activity. The ground shook beneath our feet. Dust and straw fell from the roofs of houses. And from every open door and window, every crack in a wall or hole in the ground, rats emerged: great and small, lean and brawny, brown and black, grey and tawny. They formed a stream of fur and flesh that flowed down the streets, and leading them all was the Rat King himself, with his spur of bone upon his head. By now the Piper had begun to play in earnest, a tune both new yet familiar, like some mother's song remembered from infancy, and he danced his way to the gates of the town in time to the music, the rats following at his heels. When they arrived at the river, the rats plunged into its depths, and all were drowned save for the Rat King himself, who made it to the far bank and scrambled over reeds and rushes until he found himself on dry land. For a moment the dreadful animal stared back at the town, as though to fix it in his memory, then continued on his way until, at last, he was lost from sight, and the Piper's tune came to an end.

The bells of the town rang out in celebration. The Mayor gave orders to dig up the rats' nests and fill every hole so that no such plague should ever befall the population again.

But the Piper raised his hand.

'Before you proceed,' he said, 'there is the matter of my payment.'

The Mayor, who was a fair man, retrieved the parchment from the folds of his coat. He opened it, and stared at the words that the Piper had written. His eyes grew wide. His mouth hung slack. He could barely bring himself to speak, but somehow he found the words.

'This is impossible,' he said. 'You cannot seriously expect us to pay such a price.'

'You agreed, and so you must pay.'

'But we thought that you wanted only gold.'

'I never claimed gold was my desire. That was your assumption.'

Now others had begun to crowd around the Mayor to read what was written, and those who were not themselves lettered asked the more educated to discover the contents, and soon the whole town knew of the Piper's demand.

Ten children: five boys and five girls. This was the Piper's price.

'Why?' asked the Armourer and Brassier. 'What could you want with children?'

'Perhaps I have none of my own, and wish to train them in my magic,' replied the Piper. 'It would be a shame if my skills were to die with me. In any case, it's no concern of yours why I might want them. You agreed, and so you must pay.'

The Mayor stepped forward.

'We will not meet such a price,' he said, 'and by demanding it you have revealed yourself to be more monstrous than those beasts whose corpses now pollute our river. Begone from here!'

'No,' said the Piper, 'I will not depart until you have paid me as agreed.'

'Then we will make you leave.'

Armed men, led by the Armourer and Brassier, now appeared behind the Mayor, and many of the townsfolk grabbed whatever weapons they could find: sticks, and pitchforks, and kitchen knives. Faced with a wall of angry people bristling with blades and spikes, the Piper was forced to retreat, until he found himself once again outside the walls of the city, by a river clogged with the bodies of drowned rats. The gates were closed in his face, and from behind them came the voice of the Mayor, warning the Piper that if he had not decamped by nightfall, it would be the death of him.

And indeed, when night fell the Piper was gone.

And now, a confession: I did not witness anything of what I have described to you. Oh, I was there, make no mistake about that. Rats crawled over my bare feet while I slept in my bed, and one even had the temerity to nibble at my toes. I heard the Piper's tune and wanted to dance to it. But I am blind, and have been since birth: of the Piper's appearance and the extraordinary colours of his coat, of the yellow-boned hue of his pipe and the dead-star light that flashed in his eyes before he cast his spell, I have only the word of others.

I had always cursed my blindness, until the Piper came. Now I know it was only my blindness that saved me when he returned.

He arrived in the dead of night. I woke to the sound of his music, as did every other child in the town. In truth, there were two melodies, each a counterpoint to the other, and his charmed instrument played both at the same time, so that one kept the adults in a deep, dreamless sleep while the other roused the children from their beds. The notes placed visions in my mind of a joyous land where water gushed and fruit trees grew, and honey-bees had lost their stings, and horses were born with eagles' wings. And though I had never set eyes on any of these wonders, yet they were revealed to me as I rose from my bed, and my feet moved in time to the Piper's song, and an unseen sprite in my room whispered to me that in the Piper's realm none was blind or deaf, that every child saw and heard, and every youth danced and sang.

But the notes alone were not sufficient to separate children from their families, for a child's love for its parents is stronger even than the spell of a Piper, and so each boy and girl woke to a flickering before them, a wash of hues like a rainbow in human form, as though the Piper had sent some manifestation of himself into every home. It was this that finally drew them from their beds and led them through the streets to the walls of the town, where the strongest among them opened the gates so that all might join the Piper. And this they did, dancing to his tune while the Piper's ghosts frolicked around them, as a wondrous portal opened wide in the mountain above the town, and into this they vanished and were never seen again.

I know this because Jacob, the miller's son, as deaf since birth as I was blind, held my hand as we stood at the gate and spoke to me in his distorted voice of what he was witnessing. He stopped my dancing feet from following in the steps of the others, and I saved his sight from being bewitched, and so we were the only ones able to tell of what had occurred once the portal closed behind the Piper, and the sound of his music was cut off entirely.

The mountain was searched, every foot and inch of it. Miners tapped and dug, but to no avail. The king dispatched troops to scour the land, and the Mayor and the Corporation sent word north, south, east and west, promising the Piper all the profits of the town for generations to come, if only he would return its children. But no reply ever came, and the Piper was never again glimpsed in our land. In time the people raised a monument at the foot of the mountain to all who were lost, and on it was carved the name of every abducted child: one hundred and thirty in total, a generation stolen away in a single night.

But I lived, and Jacob the miller's son lived, and we two married, but we never had children of our own. It was not our intention to die childless, and we rarely spoke of it, but we both understood, I think, that our bodies had somehow made the decision for us. Deep in the core of our beings was the knowledge that we had managed to thwart the Piper, and the Piper did not care to be thwarted. If we had been blessed with a family, then some night, while we slept a deep, dreamless sleep, the Piper might have come and made our children dance for him.

Jacob died many years ago. He lived to a good age, but that is no consolation to me, I who have lived to a bad one, and I miss him every day. No matter: I can hear the last grains of sand slipping through the neck of the hourglass, and soon I will be reunited with him. I have lived longer than anyone in this land. I am 138 years old.

I am too old.

But perhaps I have been kept alive for a purpose, as this story is not quite done. Some days ago, a man came to me from the kingdom across the water. A state of simmering conflict had long existed between our two kings, but then the old kings died and the new kings found common cause against another enemy, and trade and communication recommenced between us. This man, a merchant, had travelled over the Empty Sea to find me out, and sit by my fire, and tell me a tale.

Some months earlier, the merchant was passing through the mountains above a remote village at the northern edge of his country, and there he glimpsed a strange figure: a blighted being like a gargoyle, dressed in a surcoat of many colours, seated upon a rock. As he sat, this creature's hands worked on a length of bone, carving holes in it to complete an instrument: a pipe. The bone was small, but recognizably human, and the merchant thought that it might have come from a child's arm. While the merchant watched, almost spellbound, the figure cut and carved, chiselled and cored, until finally he raised the pipe to his lips and tested it. A discordant note emerged, and its creator, dissatisfied, returned to its work.

This figure was humpbacked, the merchant said, with twisted limbs and the nose of a carrion bird: a crooked man.

No, *the* Crooked Man.

On a stone beside him stood a huge rat with a spur of bone on his head that he wore like a crown.

The Crooked Man spoke to the rat as he worked.

'A new pipe,' he said, 'for a new town.'

The rat licked at his paws in anticipation of what was to come, just as the Crooked Man tested the pipe again, this time finding its music more to his liking. He got to his feet and removed a bottle from his pocket. Something moved inside it, and even from a distance the merchant could see that it was the glowing miniature of a boy, and he knew it to be the spirit of the child – his soul – trapped behind glass. A red stain marked the front of the boy's shirt, just above his heart, as though that organ had been wrenched from his chest, killing the child but leaving his spirit behind.

The Crooked Man uncorked the bottle, and the merchant heard the boy begin to wail in terror, but the sound was quickly lost as the Crooked Man put the bottle to his lips and sucked the spirit of the child down.

Instantly, the Crooked Man was transformed. He grew tall. His back became straight, his limbs adjusting their proportions to match his frame. His nose shortened, and the light of malice in his eyes was dimmed, although it was not extinguished entirely.

The merchant had seen enough, but he was not done with

horrors for that day. He heard and felt a rumbling from the ground beneath his feet. A portal opened in the rock face and from it poured forth an army of rats, which gathered itself around the Crooked Man and the Rat King on the stone, waiting.

At the sight of them, the merchant turned to flee, but in doing so he lost his footing and tumbled down the mountainside, injuring himself grievously. He lay unconscious for a day and a night, and when he returned to his senses he discovered that one of his legs was broken. He crawled for another day, dragging his wounded limb behind him, and so great was the pain that he lost consciousness again, and might well have died had he not been discovered by riders from the village.

They were searching for its lost children.

This time, the Piper had done his work in days, not weeks.

I was eight years old when the Piper first came to our town. Now, one hundred and thirty years later, he had emerged once again from his lair. One hundred and thirty years, one hundred and thirty children: it cannot be a coincidence. He was feeding on children, and now his store had run dry.

I do not believe that he could simply steal them away, though. A bargain, however maliciously intended and weighted in favour of one side, had to be struck, then broken. Once that was accomplished, he could take the children he desired, feeding on their spirits while the Rat King gnawed on their bones, then bred new subjects which slept until they were required to plague another town.

The merchant left. He will spread the word, just as I have tried to do in my small way. He will wander from town to town, from country to country, and he will warn all to beware of the Rat King, although the rat is no true king. Not every ruler wears a crown, and the real power often lurks behind the throne.

Watch for the Piper, he will tell them. Listen for his tune.

Because he is coming.

344